SHROUDED

IN

THOUGHT

ଔଈ໖

Also by N. S. Wikarski

The Evangeline LeClair Mystery Series:
The Fall Of White City

SHROUDED

IN

THOUGHT

by

N. S. Wikarski

Northgate Press

NORTHGATE PRESS LLC
P. O. Box 377
Waukegan, IL 60085
www.northgatepress.com

Shrouded In Thought
2nd in the Evangeline LeClair Mystery Series

First Edition: May 2005

Cover Design by A. M. Scott

Art: Photograph courtesy University of Illinois at Urbana
Champaign Archives, Lorado Taft Papers, Record series
26/20/16.

Library of Congress Control Number: 2004099508
ISBN: 0-9720335-1-3

Table Of Contents

Epigraph

cs❀ℛ❀so

The mere wish to sin entails the penalty,
for he who meditates a crime within his breast has
all the guilt of the deed.

Juvenal
Satire xiii - line 208

Prologue

ෆ⚜ඌ

Desmond Bayne woke from a fitful sleep--the only kind possible when he was huddled in a frayed overcoat, in the filthy corner of a concrete loading dock on a dank and windy spring night. His eyelids fluttered open briefly and resettled themselves.

"Please don't!"

There it was again. He thought he'd heard voices. Voices coming from below by the edge of the river. Indistinctly, he heard the low rumbling of a man's voice. He couldn't catch the words. The wind carried them in the other direction but the tone was coaxing, seductive.

The girl's voice, more shrill, carried farther. "No, I said stop! Heights make me dizzy!"

Desmond edged out of his corner, but all he could see was a hulking shadow that leaned against a wooden guard rail fastened to the retaining wall of the river. The next sound he heard was the crack of dry timber and the girl's scream. Desmond leaned even farther forward in time to see the shadow split in half. One part tumbled into the churning, oily water. The other part stood above, looking down.

The shrill voice cried, "Help me! For God's sake! You know I can't swim!"

The demi-shadow standing above seemed to be craning its neck in the darkness, trying to focus on the hapless creature struggling to keep afloat.

The waves frothed around her as she tried to tread water. "Why...won't you...do something!"

The garbled cries became less and less distinct over the rush of the current. Desmond could hear the desperate pitch of her voice rise in volume as her body sank.

"Why...wh...why...won't... Please...help..."

The demi-shadow turned and, without an appearance of undue haste, walked away from the last ripple disturbing the surface. The river resumed its serene course. Desmond waited long enough to make sure it had and then, with all due speed, he followed the sound of retreating footsteps.

CHAPTER 1
Current Events

൫ℋ൯

Frederick Ulysses Simpson had never seen a freshly drowned corpse before. As a junior reporter sent to cover an important story, he felt a thrill of joy that transcended mere verbal expression. There she lay, on the cobblestone carriageway between the loading dock of a factory and the retaining wall of the river. A girl in her early twenties with damp brown hair curling around a pale, bluish face. A fragile puff of pearl-gray silk surrounded by a ring of men dressed in blue and brass with bullet-shaped helmets bearing the insignia of the Chicago Police department.

Freddie Simpson allowed himself to savor a sense of exultation for several more seconds before his innate decency asserted itself. He sternly reminding himself what a cad he was. Still, he said to himself, he wasn't the only one. He paused a moment to drink in the sounds around him. The relentless clop-scrape of horses' hooves pulling delivery wagons over the North Avenue bridge. The clang of the trolley motorman's bell warning pedestrians to get out of the way. The booming whistles of the barges churning up and down the river making their appointed deliveries the same as any other day. Even the cooing of the pigeons foraging for food did not diminish respectfully as they scavenged ever closer to the corpse. Freddie brushed a flake of soot from his coat sleeve and looked up absently at the bleak sky. The air was thicker with it than usual. Every factory smokestack in the city seemed to be conspiring to blot out even the wan light that a cloudy April morning could provide. Still life went on. It went on even in the face of an event that defied reason. A girl barely out of her teens, dead and gone for no reason that he could fathom.

Clearing his throat self-consciously, he took a notebook from his pocket and stepped up to one of the policemen standing guard over the body. "Do you mind if I ask you a few questions?"

The officer thus addressed swung toward him with a face that would have done a bulldog credit. "Who might you be, boyo, to be asking questions around here?"

Freddie stepped back a few paces, eyeing the policeman's billy club nervously. "I...I'm a reporter for the *Gazette*. The City Desk sent me down to cover the murder."

Freddie's explanation did nothing to diminish the cop's belligerence. "You look more of a dandy than any newshound I ever saw!" he barked. "And who told the City Desk it was a murder in the first place? We don't know that for sure yet!"

Freddie tried to sound inoffensive. "Well, it does seem kind of odd that a girl would go diving into the Chicago River for a swim at midnight, fully clothed, with the temperature barely above freezing."

The cop twirled his billy club strap around his thumb contemplatively while he pondered the matter.

Freddie retreated a few steps farther. He was mentally debating the wisdom of abandoning his short-lived search for truth when another policeman intervened.

"Sean, lay off the kid. I'll take care of it." The officer who stepped forward had a face somewhat less canine than his colleague's. He motioned with his head that Freddie should follow him toward the loading dock to talk more privately.

"Thank you, officer." Freddie's gratitude was tinged with no small measure of relief.

The policeman chuckled. "Sean's all right but he's a deal happier when he's protecting the public than when he's speaking to it."

"More like barking at it," Freddie murmured *sotto voce* as

he held out his hand in greeting. "Simpson's the name. Freddie Simpson. I'm a reporter for the *Gazette*."

Freddie was over six feet tall and big-boned, yet the policeman who shook his hand managed to cover it with a paw that was twice as wide as his own.

"My name's O'Rourke. I'm in charge of the investigation. I'll tell you what I can, but that's not much."

With no need for further encouragement, Freddie flipped open his notebook and drew a pencil out of his vest pocket. "Well, for starters, who is she and what happened?"

The cop smiled. "Isn't it always the way of things that the better part of a copper's job is answering just those two little questions." He scratched his head as a spur to recollection. "The people here" --again he motioned with his head to a knot of onlookers several feet away-- "tell us her name is Nora Johnson and that she worked as a secretary in the factory we're standing in front of. Her roommate from the boardinghouse reported her missing early this morning. Said she didn't come home last night. Well, we'd already gotten a call from the factory this morning. Seems one of their fellows had walked out onto the pier to look for the coal barge when he noticed something pale bobbing up and down across the way. It looks like the current carried her down a ways from the pier until her coat snagged on a piling on the other side. It's a good thing she washed up near enough to where somebody knew who she was, otherwise she might have floated down past Goose Island and then we would have had a time of it. As it was, we had to call for a police boat from the Rush Street dock to fish her out. Then we hoisted the body up this side for identification."

"Any idea where she drowned?"

The sergeant nodded. "Right on the factory grounds is where it must have happened. You see that guard rail?" O'Rourke pointed to a broken piece of wood hanging suspended from the top of the retaining wall overlooking the river some ten feet below.

Freddie looked up briefly, barely taking his eyes off the page where he was furiously scribbling notes.

"Well, it looks like she went over the railing right there and drowned."

"Was she pushed?"

O'Rourke shrugged matter-of-factly. "Hard to imagine her crashing through that rail any other way but we can't rule out that it might've been an accident."

Freddie frowned in concentration, wanting to make sure he left no questions unanswered. "What about suicide?"

O'Rourke gave a half-smile. "It seems to me there's easier ways to kill yourself than running full-tilt through a guard rail. That's a thick piece of timber, that is. As small as she was I'm not even sure that at full-tilt she could've managed it. If I was her and wanted to end it all, I'd just walk a few yards farther to the company pier, close my eyes and jump in."

"Yes, I suppose that makes sense," Freddie murmured, half to himself, as he continued writing. "What's the next step? Will there be a murder investigation?"

O'Rourke scratched his chin. "We don't have enough evidence to make a case for murder. The coroner will probably rule cause of death as accidental drowning and it's all the same to me if he does. We've got plenty to do with a city full of drunken idiots shooting each other at point-blank range on a Saturday night and fifty witnesses standing by to point the finger. Why go chasing our tails after something like this when nobody was around nor heard nor saw anything to help us find a killer, if there's one to find at all."

"Really?" Freddie registered surprise. "No one saw anything?"

O'Rourke scanned the faces clustered along the brick wall of the building. "No, lad, but you might try talking to the factory guard. He's up there in the blue uniform with all that extra-fancy gold braid. We've already got the short version but you may as well have a crack at him before we get round to him again for an official statement." He pointed to an arthritic-looking septuagenarian who was seated on the loading dock sunning himself in the fitful rays afforded by the cloudy, sooty sky.

Freddie, his attention momentarily drawn to the watchman, turned back to realize O'Rourke had walked away to rejoin the company of policemen trying to keep spectators and a few other reporters away from the body.

"Thank you, sergeant." Freddie doubted that O'Rourke heard him. He then turned to walk up the stairs to the loading dock platform. The old man hadn't moved. His eyes were closed.

"Uh, excuse me?" Freddie began his interrogation feeling all the swagger and self-assurance that a novice reporter usually possesses.

"Hmmm? What's that?" The old man jolted himself to attention, his hand instinctively going for the gun in his holster.

Freddie leaped back. "Hold on there, mister, I just want to ask you a few questions. I'm a reporter."

The old man relaxed his newly awakened vigilance and his grip on the holster. "Oh, oh, I see." He lapsed into a vacant stare, looking out over the choppy current of the river.

Since no other information was forthcoming, Freddie unceremoniously sat himself down on the cold platform beside the old man. "My name's Simpson with the *Gazette* and you're..." He waited for a response.

After a few seconds the watchman roused himself again. "Thaddeus Sparrow. I'm the night watchman here."

Freddie quickly scanned the notes his editor had given him earlier. "This would be the Hyperion Electroplate Company?"

Sparrow nodded. "Sorry to be so slow, Mr. Simpson. I'm the night watchman, you see. It's a good deal past my usual bedtime."

The young man let down his guard. Sparrow's odd behavior seemed less attributable to senility than to fatigue. "The police asked you to stay around for awhile?"

The watchman nodded again.

"Did you hear or see anything suspicious last night?"

The old man sighed. "Like I told the coppers, not a thing. They all think because she'd been in the water awhile when they found her, that she probably drowned sometime around midnight. Well, I didn't see or hear anything around then. Just made my usual rounds--every hour just like always. Mr. Allworthy, that's the owner of the factory, he left at around half past nine or so. He was the last to go. Miss Nora, she must have left at the regular time with everybody else, six o'clock. I didn't see anyone else about except for Mr. Allworthy when I made my first rounds at nine."

"Is he here now?" Freddie glanced around at the faces

nearby.

"Was here but got called away. The coppers already talked to him. He didn't see anything either." The old man looked down self-consciously at his hands. "She was a nice girl, Miss Nora. Always sweet to everybody. I wish I could've done something, that's all. I just wish I could of..." He hesitated, looking out over the river again.

Freddie, not knowing what to say by way of comfort, merely said, "Thank you", stood up and dusted himself off to go.

At that moment, his attention was caught by a young woman with a ridiculous amount of red hair piled precariously on the crown of her head and covered by a small waffle of a hat. She was walking straight up to the police and after a brief interchange, they let her through their line to view the body. Freddie was far enough away that he couldn't hear what transpired, but he witnessed a pantomime of grief and agitation that ended with O'Rourke escorting the young woman across the carriageway and seating her on the loading dock near where Freddie stood.

She pressed a handkerchief to her face and began sobbing violently. "There, there, miss." O'Rourke patted her shoulder awkwardly. "I know this must be hard for you. I'll have one of the lads fetch you some water."

The girl shook her head vehemently, rejecting the offer. "I'll b...be all r...right," she quavered. "It's j...just the shock of seeing her that way." The image triggered another bout of tears.

"Well, if you need anything..." O'Rourke trailed off lamely and glanced at Freddie for sympathy.

Sensing a potential for some additional information, Freddie sat back down and gallantly offered to keep an eye on the young lady.

"Thanks." O'Rourke appeared happy to divest himself of his charge. "Her name's Sophie Simms. She was the drowned girl's roommate."

"Oh!" Freddie exclaimed. "Don't worry. I won't let her out of my sight."

O'Rourke turned away with a half-smile. "No, I was fair certain you wouldn't, Mr. Simpson."

Freddie shuffled the pages in his notebook. "Is there

anything I can get you?"

The only response he got was a shake of the girl's head. Her face remained buried in an increasingly sodden handkerchief.

Freddie sat in silence as the sobs turned to sniffles and the sniffles subsided by degrees. Finally, with a coquettish glance in his direction, Miss Simms began to dab delicately at the corners of her eyes to indicate the bout of weeping was over.

"I'm very sorry." Freddie decided to try a new tack. "I understand you shared a room with her? At a boarding house?"

She mouthed the word "yes" in a barely audible, but altogether tragic, whisper.

"You reported her missing to the police?"

The girl nodded, her waffle hat flapping in agreement, infirm on its shifting pillar of hair. She finally spoke. "Yes. It wasn't like her. She was gone all night. In the morning I panicked. Instead of going to work, I went to the police. And they..." Her lower lip began to tremble, signaling a new eruption of grief. "And they..." She tried and failed again.

"There now, miss." Freddie patted her hand soothingly. "You don't have to talk about it if you don't want to." He secretly prayed she would contradict him.

"No, it's all right," she sobbed. "Maybe it will help to talk." Wiping her eyes, she took a deep breath and began again. "The police said they'd try to find her. They said I should run along. I was already very late for work. I work as a sales girl at Campion's Department Store, you know." Her voice carried a tinge of pride at announcing her occupation. Belatedly catching herself, she continued. "Anyway, that's neither here nor there. So I went to work and about an hour after I got there the floor manager called me aside and told me the police wanted me to come here to..." She wavered. "To..." Her lip was trembling again.

"To identify the body," Freddie offered.

She nodded. Her hat flapped by way of confirmation. "Y...y...yes!" she wailed as a new torrent of emotion swept over her.

Freddie, convinced that the display of lamentation was at least partly the result of a desire for attention, busied himself with doodling in his notebook until it subsided. Punctiliously, he asked, "You're sure there's nothing I can do?"

She shook her head and sniffled.

He sighed and waited awhile longer.

"Today was her birthday. It was so sad she never saw them."

"Never saw what?" Freddie became instantly alert.

Sophie took another deep breath and seemed finally to have gotten a grip on her emotions. "The flowers. She never saw the lovely bouquet she received this morning."

"Who were they from?" Freddie wasn't sure whether the information was relevant but was unwilling to leave any avenue unexplored.

"I never knew. From time to time she got flowers from someone. She was very close-mouthed about him, but I think it was somebody she worked with here at the factory. The notes were always the same so I knew they were always from the same gentleman. They always read, 'From your greatest admirer.' And I'd tease her when they came and say, 'Tell me, Nora. Who's it from?' She'd always just smile and tuck the note away. She kept a little cedar box just for the notes and saved them all. But the note today was different." Sophie fumbled in the depths of her reticule to find a fresh handkerchief.

"Different, how?"

"Today it read, 'Happy Birthday from your greatest admirer!'" She began to wail. "Only it was to be her last birthday! Oh, what will he do when he hears the news! Poor man! Poor, poor man! And poor Nora!"

Freddie had taken some notes about the flowers. When he looked up again, he saw O'Rourke making his way back toward them. The policeman held out his hand to Sophie. "Miss Simms, we have a few more questions for you if you're ready to speak to us now."

With one final sniffle, she smiled sadly at Freddie and gave the officer her hand. He led her back down to the guard rail. Freddie watched them go, at a loss for any further source of information. While pondering his next move, he idly began to listen to the murmured conversations going on behind him.

"Well, even if she was just goin' in for a swim, the acid would've probably killed her anyhow."

He turned around to see a dark-skinned boy lounging with a few of his friends in the doorway that led from the loading dock into the factory. He wore a spattered apron over his clothes, causing Freddie to assume he was one of the Hyperion employees.

Without ceremony, Freddie turned on the group. "What do you mean?"

Taken aback, the boy shuffled his feet. "Nothin', nothin' at all, mister."

Freddie got up and walked over to where the trio stood. "What acid?"

The boy shrugged. "It was just a joke. A stupid joke, that's all. I shouldn't of said it. Nora was a nice girl an' it was a rotten thing to poke fun at somebody who's dead."

Freddie waited in silence.

With an exasperated sigh, the boy continued. "Well, if you're not gonna let it go." He shifted the topic abruptly. "How much d'you know about the electroplating business?"

"What?"

"Electroplating. It's not somethin' you'd be likely to stain your lily-white hands over."

Freddie looked at the boy's fingers, which seemed to bear traces of burn marks, and then down at his own brown kidskin gloves.

"Well, to make all those bright, shiny copper an' brass fittings that you rich people like puttin' on your carriages, we gotta use poison an' acid."

"Acid?" Freddie echoed uncomprehendingly.

"That's right. In the 'lectroplate tanks. We use cyanide. Sulfuric acid for some things. Why else d'you think we wear these?" The boy pointed ruefully to his spattered apron. On closer examination, Freddie realized there were holes in the apron where the acid had eaten through the fabric. "Oughtta wear gloves too, but the company's too cheap to give 'em to us."

"But I still don't understand what that has to do with the drowning."

The boy sighed at Freddie's simplicity. "Every once in awhile, the tanks gotta be drained out, see. We mix up a fresh solution an' dump the old stuff in the river."

"Right here?" Freddie was incredulous.

"Right down by the railin' there. Sometimes from the pier." The boy shrugged. "Where else we gonna take it, mister? There's no law against it. Nobody fishes the river around here anyhow. Like I said, it was just a bad joke an' I shouldn't of said it. Besides, we didn't drain any of the tanks lately so it couldn't of been that. Forget I said it, all right?"

The boy, clearly unwilling to continue the conversation, turned on his heel and walked back into the factory. He was trailed by his companions who seemed afraid that they might become the target of Freddie's inquisition if they remained outside.

Gradually, the crowd down by the police line had thinned out. Freddie watched to see who was left. Sophie had already been escorted to a hansom by one of the cops. A few workmen still loitered on the dock for a final smoke before going back inside. Freddie's attention was drawn to a scruffy-looking man in a frayed overcoat who was standing on the fringe of what remained of the crowd. He wasn't wearing work clothes but a ragged approximation of a gentleman's dress--a derby hat badly in need of brushing, a stained fawn-colored vest and satin cravat. His complexion was dark. Everything about him seemed dark--a black beard and eyes the color of obsidian. Unlike everyone else standing around the police line, craning their necks for a look at the body, he seemed to have a purpose of some sort. He was working his way methodically from one end of the crowd to the other, leaning in as if to grasp whatever bits of information he could snatch from the conversations going on around him.

On impulse, Freddie moved back toward the watchman, who by this time was dozing again. Freddie crouched down beside him. "Mr. Sparrow?" He shook him gently by the shoulder.

"Wha...who?" The man roused himself and snorted a few times before recognizing where he was and who was addressing him.

"I'm sorry to startle you, but I wondered if you recognize that man down there?"

"What's that you say, young man?" Sparrow adjusted his spectacles.

Freddie patiently pointed out the shabby character standing to one side of the broken guard rail.

Sparrow squinted hard for several seconds. "I can't say that I've ever seen him around here before."

"He doesn't work at the factory?"

"No, he surely doesn't. Looks like a bum to me." Sparrow resettled himself decisively to resume his nap.

Freddie decided to venture closer. As he was walking back down to the crime scene, he heard the dog-faced policeman shout at the ragamuffin. "Hey, you there! Didn't I tell you to clear out? You've got no business here so be off with you!" He shook his billy club in the man's face. "If you don't, I'll run you in on vagrancy charges or worse!"

The man gave one more furtive look toward the body and took to his heels, his shabby overcoat flapping behind him in the breeze like the wings of some huge bird of prey.

Freddie would have puzzled over the matter a good deal longer but just then he heard O'Rourke shouting orders to his men. "Right lads. The patrol wagon's here. Time to get her to the morgue."

Freddie watched as the boxy, top-heavy conveyance, drawn by a pair of tired-looking grays, pulled around the corner of the building and two men loaded the body into the back.

"Well, I guess that's all there is to know." Freddie tucked his notebook into his pocket as he briskly hiked back to the office to write up the story.

CHAPTER 2
A Noted Family

ೞ ❀ ೞ

Later that same afternoon after turning in his article, Freddie felt unusually pleased with himself. Unable to resist the temptation to brag, he caught the early commuter train from the loop to the northern suburbs that bordered Lake Michigan where his friend Evangeline LeClair resided when she wasn't staying at her townhouse in Chicago. Freddie had grown up in the wealthy suburb of Shore Cliff and had known Evangeline since he was a child, forming romantic designs toward her at the tender age of nine. The lady had always and, no doubt, would always regard him as a younger brother who could be bullied and teased and occasionally coddled. She was too rich, too well-educated, too attractive, and too damnably independent to seriously consider the prospect of matrimony. Freddie preferred not to contemplate the folly of his attachment. He was still too young to allow himself to be defeated by reality.

He arrived in Shore Cliff at about four o'clock, hoping that his timing might garner him an invitation to tea. The sun was casting a warm slant of light against his back and gilding the treetops of the hundred-year-old oaks that arched over the boulevard as far east as the lakefront. He passed a variety of architectural confections along the way--some colonial, some

Georgian, some Italian. Just ahead of him he saw a toddler in
a sailor suit break free of his nanny and frolic into the empty
street. With a furtive look toward Freddie, the nanny chased
after her charge, bundling him into her arms and scolding
him for running away. Freddie smiled to himself. There was
so little to fear in this village. So little danger. That was why
his parents had come here. Evangeline's parents, too, for that
matter. Their wealth had built this fortress of serenity and
created an illusion of permanence. Nothing could touch this
place. Nothing would ever change here. It was a pleasant
enough fantasy for those who could trick their minds into
believing it.

As he strolled down Center Street to the three-story brick
mansion Evangeline liked to call her "little house by the
lake," he quickly formed a strategy to circumvent what he
anticipated to be an ugly confrontation. He knew Delphine,
the housekeeper, kept a vigilant watch over the welfare of
her mistress. For some reason she had long ago consigned
Freddie to seventh circle of hell and did not consider him fit
company for her "*chère mademoiselle.*"

Rather than be given the boot by the housekeeper, Freddie
turned down a side street one block before he reached
Evangeline's door. He approached the house from the south,
hoping he could blindside Delphine if she happened to be
performing sentry duty in the foyer. He walked past the
coach house and through the side yard until he came to the
servant's entrance at the back. He was tall enough just to be
able to peek through the kitchen window to see if anyone
was about. He caught the eye of Marie, Evangeline's cook, and
motioned her to keep quiet by putting a finger to his lips. He
let himself noiselessly through the door next to the kitchen.
Luckily, Marie was a neutral observer in the epic struggle
between Freddie and Delphine. She merely chuckled and
went back to kneading her bread dough.

Freddie knew the layout of the house by heart and also
knew where to find Evangeline at this time of the afternoon.
He prayed she wasn't out making a round of calls as he
pressed his back against the wall of the long hallway that led
from the kitchen to the foyer and thence to the front parlor.
Delphine was nowhere about. On tiptoe he skirted the edge
of the front hall and noiselessly twisted the handle of the

parlor door. Only after rounding the door and closing it behind him did he draw a free breath.

"Sanctuary at last!" He exhaled dramatically.

Light streamed through the western windows and spread over the polished tabletops, glinted off the silver candelabra, and formed an incandescent glow around the lady herself who was sitting in a wing chair, dangling a piece of string for Monsieur Beauvoir, her orange tabby. The cat, weighing at least twenty pounds and the size of a spaniel, was enraptured by the game--all four feet in the air, swatting furiously at the string. Evangeline, equally entranced by the sport, was giggling at his antics. Freddie had never known her to giggle, at least not in the presence of humans.

She looked up toward her visitor without surprise, despite an interval of two months since their last meeting. "Oh, it's only you, Freddie."

The young man briefly indulged himself in looking at her-- the perfect form and features of an exquisite china doll clad in burgundy silk. He belatedly reminded himself that the eyes of china dolls were generally blue, not brown, and usually conveyed an expression of vacuity rather than archness. The contrast was enough to snap him out of his romantic fancy and remind him to take offense at her last comment.

"Engie, if you had any notion what I went through to get here, you might be more gracious in your welcome."

The lady mollified him with a demi-smile. Rising to her statuesque height of five feet and one-half inch, she crossed the room with both hands extended in greeting.

"You must tell me all your tribulations. Indeed you must. Your face is wearing a most beleaguered expression." She even laughed archly. "It's not at all attractive. I wish you'd change it this instant."

"Only if you let me stay for tea." He secretly applauded his own smoothness.

Evangeline paused for what seemed like a decade to consider the matter before grudgingly acquiescing. "Well, I suppose you must stay, now that you're here." She led him to the sofa next to the tea table and rang the servant's bell, then scowled as a new thought struck her. "How did you get in?"

"Snuck in through the back door." Freddie felt particularly

proud of that navigational feat.

"Well, you'd better not tell Delphine or she'll start locking that one, too!"

As if the mention of her name had conjured the woman herself, Delphine opened the parlor door. Taking one look at Freddie, she muttered, "*Mon Dieu! Qu'est-ce que c'est! Quelle horreur!*"

"Horror though he may be, it makes no difference, Delphine." Evangeline forestalled any further objection. "We are presented with a *fait accompli.* Since he's here, we must make the best of it." The look she now cast in Freddie's direction was beyond arch.

"I'm most obliged to you, Engie, for coming so strongly to my defense." The young man relaxed, knowing that however lackadaisical the protection, at least he wasn't about to be given the boot.

"It seems we are required to have him stay for tea, Delphine." Evangeline sighed. "Please see to it."

While Freddie imagined he saw flames shooting from the housekeeper's eyes, she held her tongue and returned to the kitchen to fetch the tea tray.

After she left, Freddie allowed himself a brief moment of self-pity. "I have no idea what I've ever done to that woman to make her hate me so!"

"She's never forgiven you for what happened to Jonathan." Evangeline alluded to one of her former suitors who happened to be Delphine's favorite. The housekeeper, like Freddie, preferred to deceive herself as to Evangeline's views on matrimony.

"As if his behavior was my fault!"

"I didn't say it was a plausible reason." Evangeline smoothed the wrinkles out of her gown. "Just a reason." She paused to stare fixedly at her visitor. "What are you doing here, anyway? Since you moved into your bachelor flat in the city you've made yourself scarce in these parts."

"I hardly thought you'd notice." The faintest note of the martyr crept into his voice.

"Of course, I've noticed. It's been very dull with no one here to tease!"

She idly walked across the room to retrieve the cat's piece of string. The tabby had been waiting for just such an opportunity and sprang out from under a chair to grapple once more with his adversary. Evangeline affectionately contemplated the flailing mound of striped orange fur.

Freddie broke into her reverie. "Besides, what do you need me for when you've got him?"

She appeared to ponder the matter. "I'll agree he's far better company than you, and generally more rational in his conversation--"

Freddie snorted in disbelief.

She looked back at her companion, the vaguest twinkle in her eye. "But you have your uses, too."

"Such as?" Freddie held his breath, hoping against hope for a compliment.

"Well, you can be quite amusing whenever you give yourself the trouble to be. And" --she smiled more broadly-- "you did help me solve a murder last fall."

"Speaking of murder." Freddie had been looking for an opening to brag. "That's what I came here to tell you."

"Whatever the reason for this intrusion, I'll be glad when telephone service is installed all the way up the north shore instead of just in the city. That will eliminate these unexpected visits."

"Be that as it may," Freddie persisted, "I finally got my first murder assignment."

"Really?" Evangeline dropped the string, clearly impressed. Monsieur Beau continued the game on his own as she returned to her chair opposite Freddie. "You mean to tell me this is the first since..." She trailed off, apparently thinking of the murder story that had gotten Freddie his job with the *Gazette* in the first place. The murder that he and Evangeline had solved together during the World's Fair.

"The very first," Freddie confirmed proudly. "They weren't ready to trust me with anything too important. The closest I got was an arson story in Streeterville last month. But this!"

"Tell me all!" Evangeline sat forward.

Their *tete-a-tete* was interrupted by the return of Delphine bearing the tea tray. She thumped it down on the table next to Freddie's sofa and drew herself up to an oratory stance. Addressing her employer, she began, "You know, *cherie*, it is not for me to say who you will see and who you will not."

"That is correct," Evangeline assented mildly.

Delphine continued. "But when you consort with...with..."
She searched her memory for the English equivalent of
"*canaille*" and spat out, "this riff-raff! *Mon Dieu*, what will
people say? *On doit penser à la réputation!*"

Freddie understood very little French but he understood
the last word. "Delphine, if she cared at all about her
reputation, she never would have started wearing those God-
help-us bloomers when she rode her bicycle in Lincoln Park
last fall."

"That's enough from both of you!" Evangeline settled the
matter. "Delphine, if I need anything more, I'll ring. You may
go."

The housekeeper nodded and, casting one more daggered
look at Freddie, retired.

"As for you!" Evangeline turned her attention to her
visitor while she dispensed refreshments. "You will
peacefully drink your tea and refrain from mentioning
bloomers for the balance of this conversation."

"My word as a gentleman." Freddie wolfed down a
cucumber sandwich as if it had been a gumdrop.

Evangeline settled herself and resumed more pleasantly.
"Now, we were speaking of murder."

That was all the encouragement Freddie needed to regale
his attentive companion with the events of the morning.

After he had finished his narration, Evangeline reproached
him. "But you misled me. It's not a murder after all, is it?"

"Ye gods, Engie! What else could it be? Do you seriously
believe it was an accident?"

"It isn't beyond the realm of possibility."

"Maybe not, but it certainly pushes the boundaries of
probability. Besides, I saw something suspicious when I was
interviewing people this morning."

"What was that?" The lady poured him another cup of tea
and helped herself to a biscuit.

"There was a fellow skulking about."

"I should think any crime scene would draw its share of
skulkers."

"Idlers, curiosity-seekers, maybe, but this was different.
This fellow had a purpose."

"What do you mean?" Evangeline sounded intrigued.

"He seemed to be working the crowd. I watched while he

paced back and forth along the police line, listening to everything that was said. I saw him examine the broken railing very carefully. I saw him look at the dead girl's face as if he wanted to memorize every feature."

"Maybe he worked at the factory and knew her." Evangeline inspected the remaining sandwiches on the tray for anything interesting.

"That's just it!" Freddie exclaimed triumphantly. "He didn't. I checked with the night watchman. This fellow was a vagrant. The police drove him away. Mark my words, he's the murderer!"

"Well, well. Are you saying that you're about to launch a new murder investigation, Mr. Simpson?"

"With your help, if you're interested," he offered hopefully.

The lady demurred. "Under other circumstances, the idea might be appealing, but right now Mast House is taking all my attention." Evangeline referred to the settlement house in Chicago where she taught English classes to the immigrants who lived in the area. The settlement was also a focal point for the city's charities.

"Oh, I thought maybe..." Freddie trailed off in a small, disappointed voice.

Evangeline regarded her visitor gravely for a few moments before speaking. "Have you forgotten why Mast House so urgently needs my help now? Not six months since, I sat in this very parlor and declaimed the waste and expense of the World's Fair. I said the money might have been better spent on wage increases." She sighed heavily. "I was more right than I knew. The Fair created an artificial boom for the city last year. The rest of the nation was in a depression but not Chicago. Jobs were plentiful..." she paused, "until the Fair closed and winter came."

Freddie looked down at the floor, unable to meet her gaze.

"I'm sure you remember last winter. It was the winter when jobless men were sleeping in police lock-ups just to stay warm. When the soup kitchens ran out of supplies to feed the hungry and all the temporary lodging the Central Relief Association could find was filled to capacity. It was the winter when all of us at Mast House, once again, were charged with the task of cleaning up the mess that the captains of industry created. Despite our best efforts, the mess remains."

A pall settled over the room. Freddie felt duly chastened for his thoughtlessness. He was about to excuse himself and slink away but Evangeline seemed to read his thoughts and take pity on him.

"Cheer up, my lad," she said softly. "For what it's worth, I may be able to give you a good start on your investigation. I know the family."

"Family? What family?" Freddie brightened.

"You said the Hyperion Electroplate Company, did you not? The one on North Avenue by the river."

"The very same. What's that got to do with it?"

"I know the family. The company is owned by the Allworthy family."

"Oh, that family! How do you know them?"

"They own a brownstone in the city on Schiller and Dearborn, a few blocks away from mine on Astor. We travel in the same social circles, attend the same functions, that sort of thing. And here's another surprise--"

"Wait just a minute." Freddie reached into his coat pocket for his notebook. "Do you mind if I take notes on this?"

"Note away." Evangeline smiled at a secret joke. "You know, the one affectation you've adopted since trading a career as a failed junior lawyer for that of a journalist is that you always carry that silly notebook wherever you go. I expect your pajamas must have a pocket to accommodate it."

Freddie glowered at her by way of reply.

Unfazed by the silent rebuke, she laughed. "Are you ready now?"

"Go ahead. You were saying there was another surprise."

"Yes, quite. The Allworthy family is building a country villa here in Shore Cliff."

"Really, where?" Freddie knew the area and couldn't recall any new construction.

"I'm surprised you didn't see it. But then again, you have been skulking in the city of late. You should take a walk down Aurora Avenue sometime."

Evangeline was alluding to the prestigious street that fronted Lake Michigan and commanded a spectacular view of the lake from the bluff for which the village was named. Many a well-to-do resident of Chicago had paid a premium for land to build a summer palace that would afford a sunrise from that vantage point.

"They're building a block off of Center Street. The lot must have cost a fortune. Construction began last month. It promises to be another rococo horror with far too much Italian marble for my taste."

"When will it be finished?"

"By the middle of the summer."

"Hmmm, that's interesting." Freddie scratched out some more notes and helped himself to a third cup of tea. "What else do you know about them?"

Evangeline looked off toward the windows, searching her memory for relevant facts. "Well, the factory technically belongs to the wife, Euphemia Allworthy née Dalrymple. She controls the family fortune. I believe it was a condition of their marriage contract, but she allows Martin, that's the husband, to manage their holdings."

"Didn't he have any money of his own?"

"Apparently not. He came from a blue-blooded family out east whose wealth no longer matched its social pretensions. As far as I can tell, his only distinguishing characteristics are a good pedigree and a spotless reputation."

"There's that word again." Freddie laughed, recalling their earlier conversation with Delphine.

"Yes, and knowing how little I care about other people's opinions of mine, you can imagine how little I sympathize with Martin Allworthy's sense of values."

"He's like Caesar's wife?"

"Quite so. Above reproach and, therefore, far beneath my notice."

"The night watchman said Allworthy left the factory before I got there, so I never saw him. What does he look like?"

"Well, he's in his late forties, with blond hair and a goatee, though both are going gray so it's hard to tell what color they are anymore. Blue eyes. He's developing a bit of a paunch which seems to be *de rigueur* for a captain of industry these days. His temperament is relatively self-effacing."

"What about the wife?"

"She's a bit older. Probably around fifty. A tall woman of formidable weight and temperament. Her hair has already decided its color--steel gray." Evangeline considered a moment. "On the whole, I rather like her."

"Really?" Freddie looked up from his notes. "She sounds like an absolute terror."

"But she stands for something."

Freddie stared at her blankly until she elaborated.

"Euphemia knows who she is, and if it ever came down to a choice of doing what was right or what other people thought was appropriate, she would do what was right."

"And?" Freddie prompted.

"And I'm sorry I can't say the same for her husband."

Freddie pondered her comment as he watched her rise and walk to the writing desk at the opposite end of the parlor.

"And then there's this." Returning to her chair, Evangeline held out a card for Freddie to read.

"On May 12th, the honor of your presence is requested-"

Evangeline cut him short. "It's an invitation to a dinner party at their house in the city a few weeks from now. Would you like to escort me?"

"Would I!" the young man exclaimed eagerly.

"Yes, I thought you might." Evangeline rang for Delphine to clear the tea things as she walked Freddie to the door. The one at the front of the house. The one that Delphine double-bolted immediately after his departure.

CHAPTER 3
A Respectable Trade

ര‰ജ

Martin Allworthy glanced nervously at the clock on the breakfast room wall. 7:42 AM. His coddled eggs and toast should have arrived at 7:41 precisely. He prided himself on punctuality. Euphemia had gone to Shore Cliff early that morning to oversee the construction of the country villa, but as soon as she returned, he most assuredly would speak to her about the kitchen staff. The servants had never shown him the proper respect. They never came to attention when he entered a room the way they did for Euphemia. And now, his breakfast delayed the minute she left the house. It was a deliberate attempt to flout his authority. Of that he was convinced. A deliberate attempt. He would certainly speak to her about it. At the first opportunity.

Martin's plans for retribution were interrupted when the butler, Garrison, entered at 7:43 AM carrying his breakfast tray. After glaring at the butler and looking significantly at the clock on the wall, Martin grudgingly took the napkin from the proffered tray and folded it precisely into a triangle before placing it on his lap. He then took the morning copy of the *Gazette* which Garrison handed him. He folded the paper in half and then again in quarters and began to read.

His breakfast proceeded without incident until he reached

page three. Martin abruptly stopped chewing his toast when he came to an article entitled "TERRIBLE TRAGEDY AT NORTHSIDE FACTORY." Yes, it had been a tragedy. How could something like this have happened--at his company of all places? He had worked night and day to build the reputation of the business, though Euphemia never gave him credit for even half of what he'd done. And now this! He anxiously scanned the two-column story, then breathed a sigh of relief. At least the coroner had found the cause of death to be accidental drowning. He could scarcely bear to contemplate the scandal if the police had believed Nora's death had been murder. Good Lord, the lurid publicity--the infamous notoriety that would attach to his business, to his reputation. It was too painful to even consider. But, thankfully, the crisis had passed and things could return to normal.

Just at that moment, the door opened and Garrison entered again. This was quite irregular. "Yes?" Martin asked pointedly.

"I'm sorry to interrupt your breakfast, sir, but there's a...ahem...a gentleman who wishes to speak to you."

"Now?" Martin was appalled at the thought. "It's not even eight o'clock in the morning. Tell him to meet me at the factory during normal business hours."

Garrison lowered his head apologetically. "I did just that, sir. The...ahem...gentleman wished me to convey a message to you. He said the matter is of the utmost importance and it can't wait."

"Well, who is he?" Martin demanded.

"He did not offer me his name, sir. He merely said his business was with you, and there would be serious consequences if you refused to speak to him."

"Well, this is going to cause me to be late for work!"

"Yes, sir," Garrison agreed in a mild tone, clearly insensitive to the enormity of the offense.

Realizing that he had no alternative but to see the fellow, Martin conceded. "Show him in, if you must."

"At once, sir." Garrison bowed out the door only to return a few moments later. "The...ahem...gentleman wishes me to announce him." Garrison stepped aside to let the visitor enter. "Mr. Desmond Bayne to see you, sir." The butler discreetly closed the breakfast room door behind him and retired out of earshot.

Martin had gulped down the remainder of his breakfast and coffee in the interval. He made no move to rise and greet his visitor. He merely sat and stared at him across the table.

Bayne spoke first. "Now that's what I call a proper introduction! Sure and it was the prettiest thing I ever heard."

"You're...you're...Irish!" Martin stammered out the nationality with the same inflection he might have reserved to pronounce the word "leper."

Bayne raised an amused eyebrow. "Faith, Mr. Allworthy. You'll not be telling me you've never encountered a son of Erin before? All the Irish and Germans and Poles living in this great city today outnumber them that's left in Dublin and Berlin and Warsaw taken together!"

Martin made no reply. Instead, to his horror, he had fixated on the liberal amount of dirt under Bayne's fingernails. He proceeded to scrutinize the stained waistcoat and tie, and the even more stained yellow teeth. He became vaguely aware of the odor of alcohol among several other even more offensive odors permeating the air in the room ever since Bayne had entered it.

"You'll not be minding if I take a seat, will you now, Mr. Allworthy?"

Martin's horror reached its apex at the thought of Bayne's filthy overcoat coming into contact with the brocade upholstery of his breakfast room chairs. "I...uh..." He tried to stammer an objection but Bayne, in one quick motion, pulled a chair away from the table, swept the tails of his coat out of the way and sat.

"Ah, that's better now. It seems I've been standing on me feet for days. I'm much obliged to you, sir, for the respite."

"Please state your business, Mr. Bayne." Martin kept his voice cold.

Bayne took off his hat to reveal greasy black locks in need of a trim and scratched his head, as if in a quandary about how to begin. "Well, to put it plainly, sir, I've come to discuss the murder of the late Miss Nora Johnson."

"Murder!" Martin exhaled the word in shock. "Who said it was a murder? I hold in my hand a copy of a newspaper article that clearly calls her death an unfortunate accident!"

He shook the *Gazette* in front of the Irishman's face for emphasis.

Unflustered by Martin's reaction, Bayne took the paper and examined it briefly. "Well, well. Does it now. Surely, Mr. Allworthy, you're not such a babe in the woods that you'd believe everything you read in the newspapers." He handed the paper back. Martin placed it next to his breakfast plate, his hand trembling slightly in the process.

Bayne continued speaking, more to himself than to his host. "Accident they're calling it? Murder is what I call it. I saw the place where it happened with me own eyes. Went there after the police dragged little Miss Nora, God rest her soul, out of the river. Saw the guard rail broken clean in half, it was. Snapped like a twig. And I've been asking meself ever since, 'Desmond,' I says, 'Desmond, why would a wee thing like that run full-tilt against a wood rail?' Who knows if the poor girl had enough strength to break it at all, even if she tried. That is, unless she had a bit o' help."

"Well, that's something no one will ever know for sure, is it." Martin bridled at the implication. "Sheer speculation on your part!"

"Ah, but there's more." Bayne paused for effect.

Martin raised an eyebrow and waited.

The visitor leaned in closer to Martin's chair and put a finger to his lips as a sign for secrecy. "I saw it happen," he whispered.

Martin felt himself blanch at these words. "You, you what?" he whispered back, nearly deprived of the power of speech.

"Aye, that I did. Saw it all from a corner of your loading dock. Saw the wee thing go into the river and a man standing over her all the while. Heard her, too. I did. I can still hear her piteous little voice crying out clear as a bell." In an exaggerated falsetto, he mimicked, "'Help me! Why won't you help me? You know I can't swim!'"

Martin felt his forehead break out in a cold sweat. He began to dab at his face with the triangulated napkin. "This is unbelievable!" he gasped. "How could this have happened?"

"Is it now, Mr. Allworthy? Is it so unbelievable as all that? I'm wondering why, seeing as how you were there all the while. You were the one who shoved her in!"

Martin jumped up at the accusation, his chair falling backward. He hastily righted it and began to pace around the room. "Are you mad? What are you suggesting?"

"Oh, I didn't see a face clear that night, but I'm guessing it was you all the same. Aren't you asking yourself how I come to know that fact? How I come to be here with you at all?"

Martin, still pacing, spat back, "That's easy! You could have asked anyone the name of the man who owned the factory. You could have asked anyone where I lived."

"Aye, that I could have, but that wasn't the way of it," Bayne replied with great aplomb. "I found my way to your door by following a man that night. The man who pushed Miss Nora into the river came straight to this house. I saw him go in the back door and never come out again that night. You can be sure I waited to see."

"The servant's entrance?" Martin shot back in disbelief. "You saw a man go in through the servant's entrance? I am the master of this house! I have no reason to use that door!"

"Maybe you did that night, though."

"This is utterly ridiculous. I can see right through your little game. You found out the factory was owned by a wealthy man and you decided to capitalize on this unfortunate event by concocting this ridiculous story!" Martin could feel his face turning an unhealthy shade of fuschia.

Bayne maintained his serenity despite the attack. "Maybe the police won't think the story is so ridiculous."

"Look at you! You're a common vagrant! I'm a respectable businessman. It's my word against yours. Who do you think they'll believe?"

"Oh, aye. There's that. I don't cut as dashing a figure as you, to be sure. Not yet anyway. But 'tisn't just my word against yours. It's my word, your word, and this." With a quick motion of his hand, Bayne dug into his coat pocket and threw a small metal object on the table.

Martin took one look at it and sat back down heavily in his chair. He held his head in his hands to steady himself. "Good God! Where did you get this?"

"'Twas the fellow I shadowed that night. The fellow without a face. Before he got all the way back here, he stopped long enough to take something out of his pocket and throw it into a pile of trash in an alley. It's a weakness of my character that I'm the sentimental type. I like to collect mementos and this one's a beauty. Don't you think so, Mr. Allworthy?"

Martin reached across the table to touch the object, but Bayne snatched it up and put it back in his pocket. "Tut, tut, sir. None of that, now. Finder's keepers, as the saying goes."

"You say you saw a man let himself into this house through the servant's entrance that night?" Martin asked pointedly.

"Aye, that I did."

"But you never saw his face?"

"That I did not."

Martin was silent for several moments, pondering what to do. The good name of his family, of his factory had to be preserved at all costs. The alternative was unthinkable. Still unable to comprehend the turn his life had just taken, he asked simply, "What do you want?"

Bayne broke into a broad smile, displaying the full extent of his dental deformities. "Ah, that's better now. I'm rejoicing to see you're a reasonable man." He patted Martin on the back. Allworthy winced at the contact.

"And you'll be finding me a reasonable man, too. Of that you can be sure," Bayne continued. "I'm not asking for much. I've got a mind to be respectable. I want to learn a trade."

"A trade?" Martin echoed in disbelief.

"Aye, a trade. The honorable trade of electroplating is what I'm thinking I should know."

"You want a job at my factory?" The words still refused to make sense.

"Oh, not just any job, Mr. Allworthy. I've got a powerful longing for a grand title. Maybe something like 'Vice President.'"

Martin was aghast. "In charge of what?"

"In charge of clock-watching mainly." He patted Allworthy again reassuringly. "You're a resourceful man, sir. I can see that right enough. You'll think of something. I leave it entirely to you. I know you'll not be disappointing me."

Martin felt sick to his stomach at the thought of this foul creature in such close proximity to him. "What else?" he asked tersely.

"Oh, a little retainer to tide me over until payday. I'll be needing a bath and a new suit of clothes before you introduce me around to your society friends, and I'll be needing cash to pay for both." He held out his hand impishly.

Martin wordlessly took out his wallet and handed Bayne a hundred dollar bill.

The Irishman wafted the green piece of paper beneath his nose several times and then exhaled with great satisfaction, his eyes glowing. "Sure and there's nothing like the smell of money. The air in your house is sweet with it, but this is my own personal bit of sachet to carry away with me." He folded the bill and put it tenderly into his breast coat pocket, patting it for reassurance after it was safely tucked away.

"Anything else?" Martin prayed that this ordeal of humiliation would end soon.

"Just one more thing and I'm thinking it's something we'll both be needing."

"Yes?" Martin's patience was wearing thin.

"An alibi for the night of Miss Nora's unfortunate demise."

"I don't need an alibi!" Martin shot back. "After I left work, I went out for a long walk."

"Here now, you needn't take that uppity tone with me, Mr. Allworthy. I'm the best friend you've got in the world at this moment." There was a hint of warning in Bayne's last statement and a glint of danger in his eyes. "I'd hate to think what might happen to you if you lost your best friend. A man needs friends, sir. Indeed he does. He always needs to keep the loyalty of his friends!"

Martin backed off. "What do you propose?"

"Well, seeing as how you say you were out walking." Bayne held up his hand to forestall any objection. "And I'll say I believe you for the sake of argument. If nobody else saw you that night, then you'll still be needing an alibi, won't you, Mr. Allworthy?"

Martin merely nodded, beaten for the moment.

"Then I'd propose that we stick together in this. Let's just say you were out walking and you ran into an old pal of yours from bygone days, namely me. Let's just say the two of us decides to go to a saloon and renew an old acquaintance. What do you think of that, now?" Bayne looked at Martin for approval.

"I suppose it's as good a lie as any," Martin agreed sullenly.

"Ah, you'll be finding, if you practice a lie often enough, and sincerely enough, it starts to have the ring of truth to it in your own heart. That's good advice from one who knows. You must sincerely believe in your own lies, Mr. Allworthy. Come what may. That's the secret."

Martin was at a loss for a reply.

Bayne resumed his story. "And then in the course of the evening, let's just say you learn that your old friend Desmond has fallen on hard times. There now, that'll ease your conscience because that's the gospel truth of things. Let's just say that in years gone by your old friend Desmond saved your life. In a manner of speaking, that's not far from the truth either. So being the good soul you are, you offer your friend a job at your very own factory, sort of to pay him back for the kindness he showed you long, long ago. What could be finer than that?" Bayne slapped Allworthy on the back for emphasis. "Lord love you, Mr. Allworthy, and the world will know what a good friend you've been to old Desmond. I'll sing your praises until the angels come to carry me away, and that's a fact!"

"Angels?" Martin echoed in wonder.

"Well, 'tis just a figure of speech. Pay it no mind." Bayne concluded by extending his hand. "Let's shake on the deal, then, and call it done and done."

Martin felt himself trapped in a nightmare from which he desperately wished to awaken. This could not possibly be happening. He saw a horrifying vision of his family name-- that spotless field of new-fallen snow that had maintained its purity for generations--now marred without warning by the filthy, bloody footprints of this insinuating scoundrel. There was no help for it. He seemed to be observing his own actions from a great distance. He watched in numb horror as he shook hands with the devil.

"Since we're now such fast friends, I'm thinking we should be on a first-name basis. You can call me Desmond."

CHAPTER 4
Questionable Characters

ଔଞ୍ଚଓ

Freddie knocked at the door of Evangeline's townhouse on the evening of May 12th with far less trepidation than if he had been presenting himself at the house in the country. The door swung wide to reveal a man as thick as the trunk of an oak tree and seemingly rooted just as firmly in the earth. Upon seeing the visitor he flashed a broad smile revealing a gold front tooth.

"Evening, Mister Freddie," the oak tree said.

"Evening, Jack. How have you been?"

"Can't complain." The oak tree ushered the young man in. "It's been quiet around here with Miss Engie spending so much time up in the country. Just me and the maid and the cook rambling around until she decides to come to town and then everything springs to life again."

Freddie glanced nervously around the front hall. "She didn't bring Delphine with her this time, did she?"

Jack grinned. "No, not this time. Can't understand why she won't take to you. Delphine's a right old gal most of the time."

"To everyone in the world except me, Jack."

"There now, Mister Freddie, don't take it to heart," Jack offered comfortingly. "She'll come round some time or other if you let her be. You just go on into the drawing room, and I'll pour you a brandy to make you forget your cares. Then I'll let Miss Engie know you're here."

"Thank you, Jack, you're a good man."

Freddie settled himself into one of the leather chairs by the fireplace to wait. The young man had always been glad of Jack's presence in the LeClair *ménage*. It made him worry less about Evangeline's reckless independence knowing Jack was around to keep an eye on her. Like Delphine, Jack's association with the LeClair family went back into the dim recesses of memory. He had been the foreman of a work crew on one of Armand LeClair's early railroad ventures. Evangeline's father, valuing Jack's dependability and loyalty, had made him the caretaker of the family's city residence. Evangeline shared her father's respect for Jack, and since her parents' death, he had functioned not only as the major domo of the townhouse, but as part-time coachman and, if need be, bodyguard. Freddie remembered how handy his presence had been when Evangeline decided to bait a trap to catch a murderer the previous autumn.

Freddie was roused from his musing when Jack wordlessly handed him a glass and went off in search of the lady of the house. The young man sipped his brandy, a drowsy warmth spreading through his limbs and relaxing him. He had nearly drifted off on a cozy cloud of sleep when he was jolted by a voice from the doorway.

"Freddie, what are you doing lounging around in there? Not napping, I hope! Hurry up, or we won't just be fashionably late, we'll be unforgivably late, and I really don't care to face a reprimand from Euphemia!"

The soporific effects of alcohol were no match for this unnerving assault on his eardrums. "I'm coming, I'm coming." He rolled his eyes and downed the rest of his drink in one gulp.

Walking back into the front hall, he was greeted by a visual image far more pleasing than the voice that preceded it. Evangeline, as always, was dressed elegantly. This time it was an indigo satin evening gown embroidered with roses. Around her neck she wore a diamond choker and diamond teardrop earrings. One of the maids helped her on with her cape while Jack went out to bring the carriage around to the *porte cochère.*

Even though the Allworthy townhouse was scarcely two blocks away, the prospect of walking the short distance to a formal dinner party was unthinkable. It was simply never done. Despite Evangeline's general defiance of convention, she picked her fights carefully. She was skillful in engineering her own social survival. She had always managed to stay on the right side of the line that separated an eccentric from an adventuress, thus insuring that her name remained on the approved side of the guest list--even in the best society.

Mild eccentricity displayed over a long period of time had conditioned her friends to measure her behavior by a different set of standards than their own. They merely shrugged their shoulders, raised their eyes heavenward and said, "Oh, well, it's Engie's way. What can one do? I'm sure she means no harm." This degree of social latitude even allowed her to appear at a dinner party in the company of a young man who was neither fiancé nor relative without anyone questioning the nature of the relationship or drawing any negative conclusions as to its propriety.

Freddie helped Evangeline into the carriage and the two traveled in silence until the vehicle turned into the driveway of the Allworthy residence. Every window in the house radiated a glow of gaslight that suggested a banquet for a hundred had been prepared instead of a modest dinner for twelve.

Before Evangeline took Freddie's hand to alight, she stood on the top step of the carriage and whispered her instructions to Jack. "You may as well come back around eleven. If things take an unusually boring turn I may affect a sick headache and ring you earlier."

The major domo *qua* coachman nodded and touched the brim of his hat before turning the horse around and back into the street.

Evangeline linked her arm through Freddie's as they walked up to the front door. "Do they know I'm coming?" he asked with some trepidation.

"Of course. They'll even welcome you with open arms. I told Euphemia you were the scion of a prominent Shore Cliff family. Since she's eager to know the local set, I'm sure she'll grill you thoroughly on your bloodline."

"Oh God!" Freddie sighed.

"I did, however, neglect to mention your sordid affiliation with the *Gazette.*"

The young man looked at his companion in surprise since Evangeline had been instrumental in helping him get the newspaper job in the first place.

"Well, if you want to get any tidbits on that drowning business, I thought everyone might talk more freely in front of you if they didn't know. Just don't take out that blasted notebook of yours, or we'll both be tossed out into the street."

Freddie patted her hand reassuringly. "I won't and, by the way, thanks for looking out for my interests, old girl."

"It's all right. I'll think of some way for you to pay me back."

Freddie gulped at the prospect.

While the butler took their wraps, the couple was greeted by their hostess. She threw both arms wide in an expansive gesture. "Welcome, welcome dear friends!"

As Evangeline had said, Euphemia Allworthy was a formidable presence. She would have dominated any room by size alone, having passed the weight of fashionable embonpoint some fifty pounds before. She towered over Evangeline. Freddie guessed her to be about five feet ten inches, and she had augmented her height by attaching a supercilious plume from some unfortunate fowl to the top of her already elevated pompadour. It touched the door frame as she swept through.

Taking Freddie's hands in both her own she looked at him quite fixedly, all the while rambling on to Evangeline.

"So this is the young man you were telling me about? Quite pleasant-looking, isn't he? You say he's one of the Shore Cliff elite? Oh, how I long for good society once the country villa is finished. How fortunate it was for us, Engie, that we knew you and that you could be our neighbor in both localities. And now we shall know this young man's family as well. How lovely. What's your Christian name, Mr. Simpson?"

Freddie snapped to attention. He hadn't anticipated a direct question, so his gaze had begun to wander around the room.

"Speak, Freddie." Evangeline's prompt sounded suspiciously like a canine command.

"F...F...Freddie...ahem, that is, Frederick. Frederick Ulysses as a matter of fact."

"Oh, lovely." Euphemia squeezed his hands for emphasis before finally relinquishing them. "In honor of our great war hero, I expect."

Taking Evangeline's hand this time, the hostess led the couple forward into the drawing room. "There are a few people here you may not know, Engie, and I'm sure we'll need introductions all around for Mr. Simpson. Everyone!" Euphemia clapped her hands for attention and abruptly all conversation in the drawing room ceased. "Everyone, this is Miss Evangeline LeClair, a dear friend and neighbor, and with her a young man whose family will, I hope, prove to be good neighbors once the country villa is complete. May I present Mr. Frederick Simpson, whose family is quite prominent in Shore Cliff."

Everyone in the room nodded by way of acknowledgment and Euphemia began singling them out for introductions. "I don't believe either of you are acquainted with Mr. Horatio Waxman and his wife Maisie." Euphemia indicated an elderly couple seated on the sofa together. "Mr. Waxman is a friend of my husband's and quite the real estate tycoon, I'm told."

Waxman brushed the compliment aside. "Oh, nothing like that, Mrs. Allworthy. A fellow owns a few prime lots on State Street, and the next thing you know people are calling him a tycoon." The businessman chuckled to himself, apparently pleased by the accolade despite his self-deprecation. His wife timidly glanced at her husband for confirmation before smiling at the newcomers.

"And here next to the Waxmans are my cousin, Bessie, and her daughter Minerva."

"I don't believe we've met." Evangeline stepped forward to shake hands.

Cousin Bessie showed a strong resemblance to Euphemia. Her daughter showed a strong resemblance to a stork. She seemed all beak and bones. The girl retained a fair degree of awkwardness, causing Freddie to conclude that she was barely out of her teens. Incredibly, she must have already made her debut. What a sad affair that must have been for all concerned.

Euphemia continued her introductions. "Engie, you already know Martin. Mr. Simpson, may I present my husband."

Freddie shifted his attention to the man in the far corner who had been in the process of pouring a drink when they entered. As the man turned to face him, Freddie was struck by the accuracy of Evangeline's earlier description. A slightly portly, altogether nondescript middle-aged man.

Martin stood up straighter. "I'm pleased to make your acquaintance, Mr. Simpson." He enunciated his words in precise, clipped syllables. "Engie, always a pleasure, I'm sure." The lack of warmth in the inflection belied the sentiment the words expressed.

"And over here by the fireplace is Martin's nephew, Roland." Euphemia paused. "You've met Roland before, haven't you, Engie?"

"Yes, indeed I have." A certain edge in Evangeline's voice alerted Freddie to some veiled dislike. He studied the youth--blond hair that flopped over one eyebrow, probably in his early twenties, some six or eight years Freddie's junior. The fellow seemed to be propped against the fireplace for the sole purpose of holding up the wall. He didn't bother to change his relaxed stance during the introduction, nor did he speak. He merely grinned and went back to swirling the liquor in his glass.

Euphemia turned her attention to another guest. "Oh, yes, and I mustn't forget Theophilus."

The person thus introduced stepped forward. He had been standing to the left of the door, out of Freddie's range of vision. Freddie gave a start as Theophilus glided up beside him without seeming to have used his legs at all to get there. He was a small, egg-shaped oddity with a set of prodigiously waxed and twirled moustachios. Freddie's face must have registered surprise, if not shock, because the egg-shaped man seemed to be suppressing a smile as he bowed to acknowledge the introduction.

"I'm so sorry, Theophilus. I almost overlooked you. You have such a talent for blending into the wallpaper." Euphemia waved her arm airily. "Sometimes, I think he manifests and disappears at will, like some free-floating bit of ectoplasm. Ha, ha, ha!" She laughed broadly at her own humor. "It's all I can do to keep track of you at all."

Theophilus exhibited flawless aplomb in the face of Euphemia's heavy-handed wit. "Don't trouble yourself as to my whereabouts, Euphemia. I am near at hand whenever the need arises." He extended a hand to Freddie. "I'm very pleased to meet you, Mr. Simpson. The name is Theophilus Creech."

Since Evangeline hadn't been introduced, Freddie assumed she already had some information on the man. He wanted to ask her, but held his curiosity in check as a new subject diverted his attention.

Garrison, the butler, entered the drawing room with an announcement. "Miss Serafina has arrived, madame."

At these words Euphemia clapped her hands together in ecstasy. "Oh, our guest of honor. How I've looked forward to this! Garrison, show her in immediately." In a conspiratorial tone, she whispered to the others, "I've been dying to have her as a house guest. She made quite a stir at the last meeting of the Chicago Metaphysical Society."

Freddie raised an eyebrow and looked at Evangeline for clarification. She put a finger to her lips and mouthed the word "later."

Euphemia bustled to the door of the drawing room as her newest visitor was entering. "Oh, my dear!" The hostess seemed in a transport of delight. "I am so pleased you were able to attend this little *soirée* of mine. Everyone, this is Serafina. She is a most gifted spiritualist and medium. Quite the most gifted in the world, I'm told, if Theophilus is to be believed." Creech bowed. Seemingly inexhaustible in the performance of her duties as hostess, Euphemia launched into another round of introductions.

In the interval, Freddie studied the newcomer. She was of medium height and dark coloring--obviously foreign, although Freddie could not be certain what nationality. Her vocal inflections and her olive complexion suggested that she might be Spanish or Italian. While her hair was a brown dark enough to be mistaken for black, her eyes were light-colored--if they could be said to have a color at all. They were a shade of gray that seemed almost transparent. They reminded Freddie of a misted windowpane on a rainy day. Freddie noticed the moonstone brooch she wore fastened to her gown. A luminous reflection that, like her eyes, seemed to capture its light from another source.

"I'm sorry, I didn't hear your last name," he apologized when the introductions got around to him.

She had the voice of a child and gave her reply in a sing-song whisper. "Only Serafina, that is all."

Euphemia had begun murmuring to herself in the background. "Let's see. One, two, three. Are we all here?"

"Not quite." Martin's voice was barely perceptible.

Euphemia shook her head impatiently at her own absent-mindedness. "Oh, yes of course. I quite forgot about that friend of yours."

Garrison walked in again to announce another arrival. "Mr. Desmond Bayne, madame."

Euphemia looked perplexed. She turned to her husband. "Martin, perhaps you'd better do the honors."

"Yes, I suppose I must." Martin clipped his syllables even more precisely than usual. He walked toward the center of the room just as Bayne entered.

At the sight of the new arrival, Freddie's mouth began to open and close like that of a fish just pulled from the water. He looked urgently at Evangeline, but all that emerged from his throat were gurgling noises. She glared back at her friend as if he'd lost his mind and muttered a warning under her breath. "Can't I take you anywhere without some new fit of lunacy emerging? Whatever it is, it will have to wait."

At that moment, Martin walked up to the couple. "May I present a...uh..."

Bayne cut in. "An old friend from long, long ago. Pleased to make your acquaintance." He kissed Evangeline's hand and then shook Freddie's. The young man could barely stammer, "P...pleased to meet you," before the pair moved on and Martin continued the introductions.

Bayne's fortunes had apparently improved immensely since Freddie had seen him last. He was attired conservatively in a black tail coat and trousers, with a white silk vest and tie. Bathed, shaved, and shined, he almost looked as if he belonged there. Almost. There was something about the way his eyes traveled around the room, calculating the probable value of every object and every person there, that caused Freddie to wonder. And then there was the accent. It was bogtrotter Irish--straight off the boat. A man like Martin Allworthy seemed acutely aware of class distinctions, and befriending a fellow like this defied reason. Even Euphemia was staring at the man every time he opened his mouth, but in an attempt to perform her duty as a well-bred hostess, she tried to hide her concern and make him feel welcome.

Garrison walked up to whisper in her ear. She nodded, in what appeared to be relief, and clapped her hands for attention. "My dear friends, let us all go into the dining room. Dinner is served."

CHAPTER 5
Course Manners

Euphemia seemed to forget her concern about Desmond Bayne as she busied herself assigning guests to their proper seats around the table. "As you can see from your placecards, Mr. and Mrs. Waxman, you're opposite one another at the end next to Martin. Bessie, you're on Mr. Waxman's left and uh...Mr. uh...Bayne, was it? Yes, well, you're opposite my cousin Bessie."

Desmond smiled waggishly. "Sure and it's a lovely view I'll be having with me soup this evening." Bessie pursed her lips and nodded at the compliment. Her eyes were not smiling.

"Let's see now. Roland, you're next to Bessie with Minerva across from you."

"Why, thank you, auntie." Roland leered at the awkward young woman across from him. This had an alarming effect on Minerva, who was clearly unused to that sort of attention from a gentleman. She'd been nervously toying with an earring, which now dropped to the floor. She escalated the awkwardness of the moment by managing to bump heads with Garrison as he dove down to retrieve it for her. Maintaining his dignity, the butler gravely stood and held forward the missing object. "Your earring, miss."

Evangeline looked on with an expression of pity as

Minerva sheepishly reattached the bauble to her person.

"Now, where were we," Euphemia continued. "Oh yes. Engie, you're next to Roland with Mr. Simpson across from you. Serafina, you'll be next to me on one side with Theophilus on the other. There now, I think that accounts for everyone."

Desmond had already seated himself, apparently oblivious to the fact that the rest of the guests were awaiting their hostess' signal. He had lifted a saucer and was studying the gold stamp on its underside. Euphemia glanced nervously at Desmond--a mild approximation of the look her husband was shooting in Bayne's direction.

Choosing not to make a point of his behavior, she smiled graciously. "Please, everyone be seated."

The gentlemen present, with the exception of Desmond, helped the ladies to take their seats. Minerva had to shift for herself which seemed less painful than being visited with the attentions of the gentleman to her left. The butler rushed to her aid once more as her mother looked on helplessly.

Euphemia waited until everyone was settled before giving Garrison the command to begin.

The butler nodded and officiated as several other servants bustled around the table filling glasses and presenting serving dishes.

Through the first few courses of the meal little occurred of any note other than Freddie's frequent attempts to gain Evangeline's attention by staring at her and then rolling his eyes significantly in Bayne's direction. He was met each time by a frosty glance from his friend. Finally he gave up and decided to wait for a more opportune moment.

Meanwhile, Desmond seemed perplexed by the array of cutlery next to his plate. He picked up a shrimp fork and examined it as if it were a surgical instrument before deciding to use it to skewer his salad. Martin made no attempt to correct him, but Freddie noted the number of times the host ran his index finger irritably underneath his collar.

The talk at Euphemia's end of the table centered on Serafina's visit. "I am so thrilled to have you here, my dear!" she exclaimed again.

"Serafina has several speaking engagements in the

midwest." Theophilus offered an explanation for the benefit of Freddie and Evangeline. "She made such a stir at the last meeting of the Metaphysical Society..."

Euphemia touched his arm conspiratorially. "Of which Theophilus just happens to be the president."

He smiled and forged ahead. "...that several of our members have begged her to attend private assemblies in their homes."

"Do you give lectures at such occasions, as well?" Evangeline sounded intrigued.

Serafina's wispy voice could barely be heard above the rattle of conversation and cutlery. "Sometimes. And sometimes I am asked to perform readings."

"Readings?" Freddie was bemused. "From what books?"

His friend elucidated. "Not those kinds of readings, Freddie. Spiritual readings."

"From the Bible?"

Evangeline was all ice and patience in her explanation. "No, clairvoyant readings."

Serafina nodded. "Yes, and sometimes I will perform what you call a séance if my guides are with me."

"Why, if you need a guide to find your way around the city, I'd be happy to offer my services."

By this time Evangeline was sending a volley of killing glances in the young man's direction. "I would assume she means spiritual guides, Freddie."

Serafina laughed--the sound of tiny bells. "I sometimes forget that these words they can mean so many things. This is especially so to people not acquainted with the unseen world."

"Yes, I would appear to be learning a whole new vocabulary." Freddie smiled ruefully. "And I thought I already knew how to speak English."

"There are those who would debate the point," Evangeline muttered under her breath.

Her enthusiasm unbroken by the undertow, Euphemia jumped in. "I'm hoping that Serafina's schedule will allow her to spend some time as our guest and perhaps even give us a glimpse into the realm beyond."

Serafina inclined her head modestly. "Mrs. Allworthy, you are too kind. I have been pressed by many gracious invitations from the ladies in your city. I have many times over rearranged my speaking tour to accommodate them. I must soon leave for engagements in San Francisco and will not return this way until the end of June. I cannot stay with you now but after that perhaps. I will see what I can do."

"Oh, that would be lovely if you could!" Euphemia exclaimed. "The end of June would be only too perfect. By then the country villa will be complete. Engie, you must come, and so must Mr. Simpson. We could arrange a séance one evening. What a delightful experience it would be."

"I'll admit the idea does intrigue me," Evangeline said.

Freddie looked at her face to see if she was joking. She wasn't.

Roland chose that moment to rise to his feet, glass in hand. "A toast, ladies and gentleman." Everyone turned to look at him expectantly. "To the lovely Miss Minerva."

The lovely Miss Minerva appeared to be mortified by the attention and was hiding behind her fan. Her mother intervened. "Really, Roland, that isn't necessary."

"Oh, reason not the need!" he declaimed grandly. "It is entirely right and fitting that a young lady should be toasted by her greatest admirer."

The words stirred a faint memory in Freddie's consciousness.

Bessie threw up her hands in dismay and allowed her daughter to be toasted as a celebrated beauty. The guests all managed to get through the ritual with solemn faces, except for Roland, who appeared to be ogling Miss Minerva over the rim of his wine glass.

In an attempt to salvage the moment, Martin rose and somewhat less grandly offered a salute of his own. "And I would like to propose a toast to my good friend, Otto Waxman."

The old man beamed with pleasure.

Martin continued. "About a month ago he did me the kindness of hiring my nephew here in order to teach him the real estate business." The words were met with a sincere round of applause. Desmond pounded his hand repeatedly on the tabletop with great gusto. In a somewhat softer voice, Martin added, "It seems the electroplate industry didn't suit Roland's temperament."

The nephew, undisturbed by the veiled reprimand, raised his glass again. "To a most successful business venture!"

"Success!" his listeners affirmed as they drank a round.

Freddie, who had been watching Desmond all evening from the corner of his eye, noticed that Garrison was having some difficulty keeping Bayne's wine glass filled as frequently as the fellow seemed to require it.

Not to be outdone by the others, Desmond now rose, albeit unsteadily. "Sure and it's my turn to let all you good people know..." He paused, apparently having lost his train of thought. "Oh yes, there it is. To let all you good people know that you're sitting in the presence of a saint, and that's a fact."

The guests eyed one another suspiciously, none of them having the least illusion of the sanctity of anyone present.

"It's him at the head of the table, I'm referring to." Desmond pointed dramatically toward Martin, spilling wine from his glass, which Garrison hastened to refill. "Yes, a living breathing saint if ever there was one. Ladies and gentlemen, the saying goes 'a friend in need is a friend indeed,' and truer words were never spoken."

Martin had begun to tap nervously on the table, apparently wondering when the testimonial would end.

"And this man, this saint of a man," --again Desmond pointed at Martin-- "saw that his old friend Desmond was down on his luck and offered him a job at his very own company. There's not many would do such a thing. Lord love you, Martin." He raised his glass. "I say again, ladies and gentlemen, a toast to Mr. Martin Allworthy. The nearest friend that ever I had in all the world and am likely ever to have."

"To Martin," the party all murmured uncertainly.

Having said his piece, Desmond sat down without further ceremony and gave his undivided attention to the cutlet on his plate. The lapse in conversation that his odd behavior had caused was soon covered by eddies and ripples of small talk from various directions. Thankfully, no further outbursts of bonhomie from either Desmond or Roland were forthcoming.

As the last course was being cleared, Freddie began to grow restive. No one had yet mentioned the one topic he longed to hear about. He was too far from the head of the table to ask Martin directly. Calculating the social damage of offending his hostess, he tried to frame the question as innocently as possible. "Quite an unfortunate accident at your husband's factory last week, Mrs. Allworthy."

Euphemia sighed. "Yes, quite unfortunate. The poor child."

"The coroner has determined it was an accident?" Freddie maintained a tone of casual interest.

"So it would seem."

Despite the intervening distance, Martin had caught the gist of his wife's conversation and jumped in. "What is that you were speaking of, my dear?"

"Oh, Mr. Simpson was inquiring about the drowning at the factory."

All other conversation at table immediately ceased as rampant curiosity took hold. Everyone waited for the host's next words.

Martin darted a swift look at Desmond. "Yes, it was quite unfortunate. A needless accident. But the workers are sometimes just like children. They require someone to look out for them every second."

"Oh?" Evangeline raised an eyebrow skeptically.

"Yes, I've seen fellows burn their hands time and again in the acid baths out of pure carelessness."

"There's no possibility their working conditions were unsafe?"

Freddie had begun to sense danger. He fidgeted with his napkin, knowing that once Evangeline had decided to engage in battle, there was little that would distract or deter her.

Martin looked at Evangeline in surprise, as if the thought had never occurred to him. "Unsafe? Why, if you give a man a knife to work with and he cuts himself with it, whose fault is that?"

Evangeline shrugged. "It would depend on the circumstance."

Without appearing to be rude, Martin's demeanor had turned a shade chillier. "I don't wish to contradict a lady but, under the circumstances, I think my judgment of the case is to be trusted. Workers are like sheep. They frequently do foolish and careless things. They need a strong hand to guide them."

"You and George Pullman seem to agree that you both know what's best for everybody else." Evangeline calmly took a sip of wine.

There was an audible gasp heard from around the table. The strike at the Pullman Palace Car Works was the talk of the town. After repeated attempts to gain a hearing from management, the laborers had finally walked out of the Pullman shops only the day before. The foundation of the model town which George Pullman had built to house his workers was crumbling. There was wild speculation as to what direction the strike might take. Ever since the Haymarket Riot of 1886, Chicago's captains of industry had slept uneasily, with dreams of anarchists dancing in their heads threatening a full-scale working-class revolt.

Martin's response was icy. "George Pullman has a right to determine conditions in his factory. He owns the company."

"Even when he insists on cutting wages in half without decreasing rents? The past year has been hard on everyone but especially hard on the workers at Pullman. I've heard some of the men went home after working a sixty-hour week with nothing more to show than a two-cent paycheck. And when they complained, Pullman refused to hear them."

"No employer wants to be held hostage by his workers."

"There's quite a difference between being held hostage by them and granting them simple justice!"

Martin changed his tactic. He adopted the stance of a father trying to reason with a temperamental child. "No doubt your affiliation with Mast House and its radical element has unduly affected your judgment. I can hardly believe you would betray your own class for any other reason than misplaced sympathy. Your father was, after all, a railroad man himself."

Freddie noticed an unpleasant flush creeping into Evangeline's cheeks. He wanted to nudge her under the table to keep her temper, but his foot didn't extend that far.

She charged forward. "My father was wise enough to realize that the success of his company depended on the loyalty of his men. He paid them a fair wage."

"I wouldn't expect a lady to understand this," Mr. Waxman chimed in softly from Martin's right, "but we all know labor is cheap."

"You might just as well say life is cheap," Evangeline shot back. "The going rate seems to be two cents a week!"

During this entire confrontation, Desmond had avoided any comment. Freddie assumed his silence was partially the result of how much wine he had imbibed. Bayne seemed content to beam happily at all present through an alcoholic haze.

"Freddie!"

The young man jumped to attention as Evangeline addressed him directly. He dreaded her anticipated question.

"Do you remember that interesting comment that was being passed around the newsroom? The one a Pullman worker made just before the strike."

Knowing the comment Evangeline was referring to, but refusing to be drawn into the fray, Freddie demurred. "No, I'm afraid I don't recall it offhand."

Evangeline smiled knowingly. "How fortunate for you that my memory is better than yours. The worker is reputed to have said, 'We are born in a Pullman house, fed from the Pullman shop, taught in the Pullman school, catechized in the Pullman church, and when we die we shall be buried in the Pullman cemetery and go to the Pullman hell.'"

The silence in the room reverberated from wall to wall, broken only by a sharp intake of breath from Garrison standing at the sideboard. Martin stared at Evangeline coldly, refusing to make any further comment. She returned his stare. Freddie had dropped his napkin and was prepared to dive to the floor and spend the remainder of the evening retrieving it if need be, when Euphemia stood decisively and intervened.

Smoothly and without any appearance of urgency, she ended the battle. "Well, I think it's time we leave the gentlemen to their brandy and cigars while the ladies retire to the drawing room for coffee."

Having made her point, Evangeline inclined her head as a gesture of deference to her hostess and left the room with the others. Freddie gave a deep sigh of relief and forgot about retrieving his napkin when Garrison began pouring brandy and proffering the cigar box.

ॐॐ

In the drawing room, the ladies settled into agreeable small talk, studiously avoiding any further mention of unions, strikers, and the Pullman Palace Car Works. Euphemia enthused by turns over the plans for the new house and Serafina's proposed visit. The lovely Miss Minerva, who apparently still had not recovered from the attentions of Roland, sat staring at a wall for the remainder of the evening despite her mother's attempts to revive her. Serafina proved an intriguing conversationalist, regaling the others with stories of her travels throughout Europe and the Far East. Evangeline was surprised that Freddie did not immediately follow the ladies as he usually did when confronted by companions not to his liking, but this time he remained with the men.

A half hour later, they finally trailed into the drawing room, reeking of cigar smoke.

After allowing Freddie to reanimate himself with a cup of coffee, Evangeline rose to take her leave. Euphemia would not be dissuaded from her idea for a séance and, as the couple was walking out the door, she exacted a promise from Evangeline and Freddie that they would attend.

When the two were safely back in their carriage Freddie could contain himself no longer. "That was him!" he burst out.

"That was who?" Evangeline scarcely heard him. She was still mentally revisiting her battle with Martin and already tired from an evening of chatter.

"That Desmond fellow! He was the one I saw by the factory, the day after the murder."

"Really?" Evangeline stifled a yawn.

"Well, don't you think it's suspicious?"

"What is?"

"That he shows up at Allworthy's house looking like he just won the lottery?"

"In a manner of speaking, I suppose he did." Evangeline still was not caught up in Freddie's excitement. "Didn't he admit it himself at dinner? He was down on his luck and Martin offered him a job."

"But that's no excuse." Freddie's enthusiasm was temporarily dampened by logic.

Evangeline stared at her friend with a long-suffering demeanor.

"Well, why was he at the factory, looking like a vagrant, right after a murder had been committed? Answer me that!"

Evangeline shrugged. "He was probably trying to work up the courage to contact Martin and stumbled across that unfortunate accident."

Freddie threw up his hands in disgust. "Accident? Accident, my foot! What's happened to you? After Elsa died you were relentless until you found out who was responsible!"

Evangeline smiled sadly at the memory of her dead friend. "That was different. I had good reason to become involved. A murder had been committed, and the wrong person was charged with the crime. Right now, I have my hands full with Mast House and the new crisis at Pullman. I would need something better than your hunch to drop all that and go running off on another detecting adventure. Besides, no one even knows if it was a murder at all. At present, all you have is a theory. To me, Miss Johnson's drowning is just a story in a newspaper."

"Well, it isn't to me!" Freddie exclaimed heatedly. "I saw the body. I saw the place where it happened, and I saw Bayne skulking around there. He's involved somehow, and I mean to find out how."

"Suit yourself." Evangeline yawned again. "The only cause about which I am personally impassioned is a crusade to demonstrate to the world that Martin Allworthy is a consummate ass." Choosing to drop both the matter of Martin's character and Freddie's intended manhunt, she steered the topic in another direction. "What did you think of Young Squire Addlepate?"

"Who?"

"Roland, of course."

"What a piece of work that one is!"

"Apparently his family sent him to live with Martin and Euphemia several months ago to see if he could be gainfully employed. I think they just wanted to rid the house of him. I've heard he made a complete mess of his job at the electroplate factory. Judging from what happened this evening, it would seem Martin has been able to foist him off on poor Mr. Waxman. We'll see how long that lasts. And his behavior toward Minerva was rather odd!"

"Oh, I don't know about that. I thought he was sweet on her."

"Roland fancies himself to be quite the lady-killer. I think he was just using Minerva for target practice."

"It's a good thing she didn't hear him carrying on after you all left the room. Bayne started singing a song about a three-legged dog, and Roland wanted to learn the words. I thought the two of them were going to break into a jig to 'There Once Was a Girl From Nantucket.'"

"Yes, I'm sure the air was tinged a shade of blue after we left," Evangeline observed.

"It probably still is! The way those two were carousing, you'd think they were the ones who had been lifelong friends instead of Bayne and Allworthy."

"Didn't Martin try to tone things down?" Evangeline registered surprise.

"Several times, but it didn't make any difference. The looks he was shooting at Bayne were anything but friendly. That's why I still suspect"--

"Yes, yes, you've already articulated your suspicions." She paused for thought. "On the whole, I rather hope you succeed in pinning the girl's death on him."

By this time they had arrived back at Evangeline's townhouse and Freddie was handing her out of the carriage. "I'm glad you still care about seeing justice done, Engie. I was beginning to worry."

His friend contradicted him. "No, that's not the reason. I just don't look forward to the prospect of sitting at table with that fellow again. By all means, prove he's a murderer. That will solve the problem. I even hope you can implicate Martin in it somehow!"

She winked at Freddie playfully before calling up to her coachman, "Jack, you'd better drive him home. We don't know what other mischief he may find along the way if we allow him to walk."

CHAPTER 6
The Pullman Hell

03 ❀ 80

"Things have certainly reached a pretty pass, haven't they?" It was less a question than a comment. Evangeline slid a worried look at her companion. The tall woman in the pristine white shirtwaist and brown skirt was none other than Jane Eaves--the founder of Mast House and Chicago's foremost humanitarian. Jane smiled cryptically by way of reply.

The two ladies emerged from the Illinois Central train station which had just disgorged passengers twelve miles south of the city at a village on the shores of Lake Calumet. The district carried the imprint of its founder and a visitor would have been hard-pressed to find anything there that didn't bear his name from the Pullman Palace Car Works directly ahead of them to the model town of Pullman stretching on either side. As with the uniformity of the name, there was an architectural conformity to the town and factory. Every building was red brick and every horizon was Pullman.

"Jane, your reputation as a champion of the downtrodden has pulled Mast House into many a municipal fray, but this is, without a doubt, the strangest. You ask me to accompany you on a fact-finding expedition to Pullman without telling me anything about why we're here."

Jane raised a parasol against the afternoon sun. The day was surprisingly muggy for late May. "I have said little because I didn't want to compromise your objectivity. You'll find out soon enough."

Evangeline's scowl prompted Jane to elaborate. "The Civic Federation has asked us to look into things."

"Things," Evangeline echoed, laughing. "What a unique turn of phrase. To which specific things were they referring? The chintz curtains at the hotel or the revolt of the lower orders at the factory?"

Jane's reply was unruffled. "Pay attention to the little things and the big things will take care of themselves."

Evangeline fanned herself with a train schedule. "Then it's to be the curtains, is it?"

"No, dear," Jane countered gently. "It's to be the houses. But before we examine anything, we're supposed to meet Mr. Bracecote. I wonder where he could be?"

In answer to her question, a little man in a black suit, sweating profusely in the heat, came scurrying in their direction at top speed.

"Miss Eaves?" He came to a dead stop before them, out of breath. "You are...Miss Eaves...aren't you? And you're Miss...LeClair from Mast House?"

"Right on both counts," Evangeline confirmed as she shook hands.

"I'm Henry Bracecote, Chairman of the Central Strike Committee. So very glad to make your acquaintance." The little man shook Evangeline's hand again for emphasis before dabbing his forehead with a handkerchief.

"Miss Eaves has been unusually reticent regarding the purpose of our visit, so I must apply to you for more information, Mr. Bracecote." Evangeline smiled engagingly. "What is it you wish us to look into?"

Assuming a more official persona, Bracecote straightened up and cleared his throat. "Well, ladies, ahem, in short, I wish you to look into the town of Pullman: the houses, how we live, and what we pay for the privilege of living here. We believe you are in a better position to judge whether or not we have a legitimate cause for complaint--that our wages have been slashed without a corresponding reduction in our rents. You can carry our story to the wider world." Bracecote stopped abruptly and cast his eyes toward Jane for confirmation.

The lady nodded. "The Civic Federation is of the same opinion, Mr. Bracecote. Since neither I nor Miss LeClair are affiliated with your strikers or Mr. Pullman, we may be able to provide an outside assessment of the situation. We will inspect the housing arrangement here and will endeavor to determine if you are paying more than you might if you lived elsewhere in the area."

"That's all we ask, madam." Bracecote nodded his head vigorously. "Let the Civic Federation know, let the newspapers know, that we aren't wild-eyed anarchists. We are simply men who have been ground down to a state of desperation. And no one will listen."

"We will," Evangeline affirmed. "Lead on, Mr. Bracecote. We follow."

The chairman seemed relieved and relaxed his stance a bit. He replaced the hat which he had removed when greeting the ladies and swept his arm forward. "This way, if you please."

With the train tracks behind them, the trio headed east along One Hundred Eleventh Street at a leisurely pace. Bracecote pointed out various landmarks as they passed.

"Ladies, I would ask you to take particular note of the factory which you see on your left. This is where we make all the Pullman railway carriages."

Evangeline's eyes went first to a clock tower rising several stories above what she took to be the main administration building. With its steeply pitched roof and various outcroppings, it looked more like a cathedral than a factory. It was flanked on either side by long, low sheds of brick and glass. No smoke rose from the factory chimneys. All was quiet. Too quiet.

"Mr. Bracecote, I confess I'm surprised. You are, after all, on strike. I expected to see picket lines but there is nobody about."

Bracecote stopped to contemplate the scene. "When the strike began, Miss LeClair, we gave our word there would be no demonstration. Management's response was to lock the gates so the factory is completely shut down until further notice. A few security guards have been posted around the property but there is no need. This is a peaceful protest."

"I admire your restraint, Mr. Bracecote," Evangeline teased. "Were I in your shoes I would at least be tempted to hurl an occasional rock."

Bracecote grinned as Evangeline. "I admit a secret urge to do the same, Miss LeClair, but I must remember the men whom I represent. I must set an example."

"Engie, you shouldn't tempt Mr. Bracecote to forget his duty." Jane's eyes twinkled.

"Of course not. Let us be guided by the voice of reason." Evangeline nudged Jane. "That's you, in case there was any doubt."

"If you would be so kind?" Jane hinted for their guide to resume the tour.

Bracecote shook himself out of a dejected contemplation of the factory and started forward. "Yes, quite so. To your right you will see the Arcade Building. It houses our post office, a theater, the library, and the bank."

"Is that the bank where your rents are paid?" Jane asked.

"Yes," Bracecote replied quietly, "or where we are driven into debt because we cannot pay."

"But surely the bank that doles out your wages knows you haven't any money left for rent," Evangeline protested.

Bracecote shrugged. "They tell us we must pay what we can each month. When we cannot, we are treated with scorn. Rude comments are made that we are cheating the company."

"A sad choice," Jane observed. "To keep a roof over your heads, you must deny your children bread."

"This past winter was the worst. The depression that swept the nation finally came to Chicago. Our wages were cut almost in half but our rents remained the same. Some of the children didn't have shoes or warm clothes and couldn't leave their homes to attend school. But they were luckier than the ones whose parents couldn't afford the heating bill. The little ones had to stay in bed, huddled in blankets all day just to keep warm."

"This is an outrage!" Evangeline exclaimed, but a warning frown from Jane silenced further comment.

The trio continued to stroll down One Hundred Eleventh Street. To their left, the factory loomed. To their right stood several ornate houses. From the perspective of a common laborer, they might have appeared as mansions.

"I take it the workers don't live in these?" Evangeline asked dryly.

"No, these are reserved for the company managers. The front windows face toward the factory."

"To what purpose?"

"To watch." Bracecote replied simply.

"To watch what?" Evangeline persisted.

"To watch everything." Bracecote sighed. "To watch everything and everybody. Everything that goes on in the factory and everything that goes on in the town. Mr. Pullman has spies everywhere."

"Spies!" Both women cried in unison.

"The company wishes to know at all times whether its employees are loyal. It is said there are spies in every parlor. A man who says something unfavorable about the company at Sunday dinner may find himself dismissed from work on Monday morning."

"My word, this is too much!" Evangeline was incensed. "Who could live under conditions like these? Why not move to the city where you wouldn't be watched day and night?"

Bracecote appeared crestfallen. "It wouldn't help. The common belief is that preference is given to those who live at Pullman. When jobs are available, they are given first to residents."

"Is that actually the case?" Jane sounded doubtful.

"Perhaps not, but it is the perception and so we remain. Last winter when work was scarce everywhere, the men chose to remain here in case something opened up. Even if it meant going into debt to pay the rent."

The little group paused again before an ornately landscaped park to their right. Just ahead of them was a building of some four stories. Its size and elaborate Queen Anne architecture suggested it was something other than a residence.

"This must be the Hotel Florence," Jane said.

"How odd that it shouldn't be named after Mr. Pullman. Everything else is," Evangeline added.

Bracecote cleared his throat uncomfortably. "In a way it is. It is named for Mr. Pullman's favorite daughter."

"Of course. Why not." Evangeline rolled her eyes.

Their attention was caught by a group of well-dressed men lounging on the hotel's wraparound verandah and smoking cigars. This was the first sign of human activity they had seen since stepping off the train.

Evangeline scrutinized the idlers for a few moments. "Do those men work at the factory?"

Bracecote shook his head. "The hotel was built for business associates, management, and clients of the company. Mr. Pullman also maintains a suite there overlooking the car works. None of the laborers are allowed inside." Their guide laughed deprecatingly. "It is the only place in Pullman that serves liquor."

Even Jane's mild features registered surprised at this statement. "Mr. Pullman is afraid his workers might imbibe?"

"The workers imbibe at the thirty-odd saloons in Kensington. It's a well-worn path." Bracecote lowered his voice. "Although Mr. Pullman is a temperance advocate, that isn't the real reason for keeping the workers away. You see, when the town was first constructed, it was something of an attraction. A factory town built along principles of thrift, hard work, cleanliness, and sobriety. People came from all over the world to see it."

"And they stayed at the hotel?" Evangeline inferred.

"Yes. Tours were arranged for them to view the factory and the town. Many visitors to the Columbian Exposition last year also came here."

"So, you all became curiosities in Mr. Pullman's zoological garden but no one was allowed to feed the animals!"

At her words, Bracecote turned pale.

"Engie!" A warning tone crept into Jane's voice. "We are only here to observe."

"I suspect the one thing that the town of Pullman has had in abundance is observation," Evangeline muttered.

Jane quickly changed the subject. "I notice that those gentlemen on the verandah all wear miniature American flags in their lapels while you wear a white ribbon. What is the significance of this?"

Bracecote shifted his stance backward as if dreading the question. "That has become a sore spot for the strikers. We have taken to wearing white ribbons in a show of unity. Anyone who is in sympathy with the workers does the same. The company managers and their friends have adopted the American flag instead to show their support for Mr. Pullman."

"Suggesting that the strikers are less patriotic than everybody else?" Evangeline asked.

"Exactly," Bracecote concurred.

"No rational person would believe that."

One of the men seated on the verandah railing caught Evangeline's eye. He flicked some cigar ash into the flower bed below his perch and tipped his hat to her. A languid smile that bore a close resemblance to a sneer hovered on his lips. Evangeline pointedly turned her face away.

The strike chairman ushered his little group past the hotel without acknowledging the contemptuous comments of the group on the porch. They walked along for another block before turning down a side street where they were confronted by red brick row houses on their right and what appeared to be block houses, or tenements, on their left.

"Not all the workers' homes are in the same style," Evangeline noted.

"A variety of accommodations have been provided depending on a man's circumstances," Bracecote explained. "For example, the tenements are the cheapest. They have the smallest rooms and shared conveniences. It is usually the bachelors and the immigrants who move in there. The workers' cottages are more spacious. Some have five rooms, and some more."

"And all of them have running water?" Jane asked.

"From that standpoint, the town of Pullman is a model city. All the buildings have indoor plumbing, gas heat, and the company provides a sewage system and daily garbage pickup. All the streets are paved with macadam and there are wooden sidewalks as well. In addition, the company maintains the flower gardens in the front yards of the cottages."

The tree-lined street stretching before them with its spring blooms seemed neat and well-tended.

"It is very clean," Evangeline admitted grudgingly. She paused in mid-stride to study the row of houses to her right. Her two companions regarded her quizzically.

"They're all connected," she murmured.

"What, Engie?"

"Each individual unit is built right next to the one beside it. There's no way to get from the front of the house to the back without walking around the block and going through the alley."

"That is correct," assented Bracecote. "Though the alleys are paved and kept sanitary."

"Well, I suppose that's a relief." Evangeline glanced at Jane. "After your battle with city hall last year to get the garbage removed from the alleys around Mast House, this must be quite appealing to you."

Jane raised an amused eyebrow.

Evangeline continued. "I'm impressed less by the cleanliness of the alleys than by the monotony of the design. Some attempt has been made to vary the units but still...It's less like a neighborhood than an army barracks. Or worse."

"Worse?" Jane asked calmly.

"I'm reminded of something Martin Allworthy said a few weeks ago at a dinner party. Jane, you remember Allworthy, don't you? Pompous sort. His wife donates generously to Mast House. He said that workers are like sheep."

"Sheep!" Bracecote echoed in disbelief.

"Yes, sheep who presumably need to be confined to keep them from running off in all directions. These row houses must make excellent sheep pens."

Evangeline marched forward, leaving her shocked companions to catch up. At the end of the block, the row houses gave way to a small square. At the center stood an imposing building.

"This is Market Square," Bracecote announced. "It contains a grocery, a butcher, and sundry other shops."

"And the residents of Pullman are allowed to set foot here?" Evangeline strove to keep an edge out of her voice. She did, however, fan herself vigorously with her now wilted train schedule.

"Yes, this was where the families shopped. That is, until they could no longer afford to buy food..." Bracecote trailed off glumly.

"Isn't there a Relief Committee providing for the strikers now?" Jane offered.

"Yes. A Relief Store has been set up south of here and donations have been generous from around the country. We have gotten everything from flour to chewing tobacco. No luxuries, you understand, but all the basic necessities in abundance."

"It's good to know the sympathies of the people are with you," Evangeline remarked.

"I don't know how we would manage to hold out without their support. This may prove to be a long siege."

Bracecote steered the ladies down a side street to the right. They walked a bit further and came to a small church of an unusual color.

"What a charming little building!" Evangeline exclaimed.

"It's called the Greenstone Church but no one uses it much."

"No one has any inclination to pray in Pullman?" Evangeline laughed.

Bracecote smiled nervously. Evangeline's direct observations had apparently unsettled him. "It's because the rent Mr. Pullman charges for the church is so high that no denomination can afford it."

"Even religion must pay its way," Evangeline mused. "What an admirable capitalist sentiment."

Jane steered the topic in another direction. "I was hoping we might see the interior of some of these buildings."

"Quite right, Miss Eaves. That's our next destination." Bracecote led them down another street and then stopped before a row house in the middle of the block. "I'll take my leave of you here and place you in the care of three lovely girls who can give you a different point of view about life in Pullman."

Bracecote walked up the stairs and rapped on the door. It was immediately opened by a blond girl of about twenty. She must have been waiting for the visitors. Bobbing a quick curtsy, she gestured for the party to enter.

"Come in, come in. You're very welcome here, ladies. We've been looking out for you all afternoon."

Bracecote tipped his hat to the girl and shook hands solemnly with the visitors before departing.

Once inside the foyer, Jane and Evangeline were assailed by three young women all talking excitedly at once. Hands were shaken and reshaken and the visitors were ushered into a parlor at the front of the house.

The spokesgirl for the group stepped forward. "My name is Flora, and this is Olivia, and Tess." The other two bobbed a few more curtsies and giggled. Olivia was plump, short, and wore her hair in ringlets. Tess was angular with quick, darting eyes.

Flora continued. "Please excuse us, but we've never entertained anybody important before." More giggling.

"Oh, I don't think we're all that important," Evangeline winked and took a seat on the sofa by the front window.

The parlor seemed narrow and incommodious by Evangeline's standards though the newly whitewashed walls helped to brighten it.

"Do all of you live here together?" Jane asked.

"Oh no, this is where Flora lives with her two brothers and mother," Tess volunteered. "Olivia and me live down the block but all three of us work in the sewing shop at the factory. We got voted as kind of a delegation by the other women strikers--to give you our point of view. Everybody said we talk the most so we should do the most talking." The other two chortled appreciatively.

Even Jane smiled at their exuberance. "Perhaps I might respectfully ask the delegation to give us a full tour of this house?"

All three girls popped out of their chairs simultaneously as if the furniture had been set on fire. They raced to open the parlor door together, nearly colliding until Flora took command of the situation.

She glared at her companions. "Settle down now! A fine opinion the ladies will have of us. Dashing around like headless chickens!" She placed her hands on her hips. "Now we're going to do this in an orderly fashion. Olivia, you get those papers we put together on prices in the shop. Tess, you can set the kettle on for tea." Flora's scowl evaporated when she turned her attention back to the visitors. "If you ladies will follow me, we can start with the first floor."

It required little time for the party to tour five rooms. The downstairs consisted of a parlor which took up the front of the house, and a combination dining room and kitchen which took up the entire back. The upstairs arrangement mirrored the floor plan below--a large bedroom at the front of the house and two smaller ones behind. The toilet was installed in a small closet off the upstairs hall. The rooms on the second floor were particularly stifling on this muggy afternoon because the only ventilation came either from the front of the house or the back. The two side walls adjoined neighboring units. A little additional ventilation was afforded by the skylight suspended over the hallway but it wasn't enough to dispel the oppressive humidity.

"By the standards of Polk Street, this is quite nice," Jane acknowledged.

"At twice the price, no doubt," Evangeline retorted under her breath.

The tour continued into the back yard. Each cottage had a green space allotted to it, along with a wood shed and a path leading into the paved alley. Flora and her mother had planted a small vegetable garden though, as Flora explained, "Nothing is coming in yet but we'll have fresh tomatoes and peas soon enough."

She then led them into the basement to see the storage space. It was blessedly cool compared to the close air above stairs. When the ladies had recovered from the heat, Flora returned them to the parlor. Olivia greeted them with a nervous smile and, as they seated themselves on the sofa, thrust a sheaf of papers into Evangeline's hands.

She studied the cryptic columns of words and numbers as Jane read over her shoulder. "1893, a one window drapery, one dollar. 1894, a one window drapery, forty five cents." The list went on for pages.

Evangeline regarded Olivia quizzically. "How does this all add up?"

Unnerved to be the focus of attention, Olivia began to stutter. "Well...it's just that I...I..." She took a deep breath to collect her thoughts. "I just put the list together. Let Flora explain." She flounced down in an armchair, overcome.

Tess backed through the parlor door carrying a tea tray. She set the tray down when she noticed Olivia's face. "What's the matter with you?"

"You and Flora explain it." Olivia stared at her friend accusingly. "I just wrote what you told me."

The other two girls traded long-suffering looks. Flora and Tess seated themselves on either side of the visitors to explain the significance of the list.

As they started going through the numbers, Olivia jumped up to dispense tea with bread and butter sandwiches. She was about to hand around the plates when Jane stopped her.

"Forgive us but we really can't accept your hospitality."

"Why not? What did we do?" Tess asked bluntly.

Evangeline picked up the thread from Jane. "We know you're out on strike and you must be hard-pressed for food. You shouldn't waste your necessities on us."

"No need to worry about that, Miss LeClair," Flora chimed in. "The strike committee knew you were coming so they voted us extra shares from the Relief Store. Eat hearty." She nodded to Olivia, who emphatically shoved a plate at Jane.

"Take it, please. We'd feel awful if you didn't stay to have tea with us." Olivia's lower lip was quivering with distress. "Everybody would think we didn't know how to act around society ladies and that we drove you away with our bad manners."

Jane accepted without further protest.

Flora, after darting a quick look of exasperation in Olivia's direction, returned to the matter at hand. She pointed to various items on the paper. "You can see what we made last year compared to this."

"I see the prices for items but what is your daily wage?" Evangeline asked, bewildered.

"Oh, that's easy," Tess offered. "We get paid by the piece mostly. For sewing. Everything in a Pullman Palace railway carriage has some sewing to it. The carpets, the drapes, the upholstery. Even the tablecloths and napkins in the dining car."

"So these prices for one enclosed section curtain would have been thirty five cents in 1893"--

"And fifteen cents in 1894!" Flora cut in.

"Less than half," Evangeline murmured.

"Less than half!" Tess echoed angrily.

"It isn't only the price cuts. We couldn't make up the hours either." Olivia finally regained her buoyancy and contributed to the conversation. "Sometimes the company would only let us work half the hours we used to because their orders were down and they had nothing for us to do."

"Half the hours at half your previous rate?" Jane asked.

"That's right," Flora affirmed. "In 1893, I could make $2.25 a day which was very good wages for a girl. This year, before the strike I was lucky to make eighty cents a day."

"Oh, but that's not the worst of it." Olivia's tone had become confidential now. "We don't dare talk about this out in public but our forewoman is a tyrant."

"An absolute tartar," Tess agreed solemnly.

"She has her favorites." Flora nodded.

"And she gives all the best jobs to them so they can earn the most!" Olivia's lip was quivering again. "And the rest of us, she grinds us down to nothing. She could be so mean that some girls quit who would still be at the company today if she hadn't hounded them. If she could make you do a piece of work for twenty five cents less than the going price, she would do it every time."

Evangeline's attention traveled from one girl to the next. She noted how heated the conversation had become.

"I've seen her cut down prices herself, even below what the supervisors wanted." Flora had jumped up and was pacing now.

"That's right." Tess backed her. "She did it because she thought it would make her stand in better with the company. She was earning her regular $2.25 a day so what did she care if we had enough to live on or not? Just so long as she could save the company a few dollars."

"At your expense," Jane offered quietly.

Olivia had started to cry. "That's right. It all came back on us." She fumbled in her skirt pocket for a handkerchief. "And some of us that complained got let go so we learned not to complain because nobody in the company would listen."

Flora walked over to put her arm around Olivia's shoulder. She gazed earnestly at the visitors. "You understand now why we struck, don't you? Nobody believed us and there was nothing left for us to do."

The two ladies exchanged glances of wordless agreement.

"I can't speak for the multitude," Jane said, "but you've impressed upon us the misery of your situation. In our small way, we'll try to do what we can."

Evangeline took a sip of tea before adding thoughtfully, "I do believe George Pullman will live to regret his inability to hear any voice but his own."

CHAPTER 7
A Striking Coincidence

 C3 ℋ 80

Freddie continued to nurse his suspicions regarding Desmond Bayne but he found little time to prove that his hunch was more than mere fancy. The crisis at Pullman had now entered its sixth week, consuming all of Evangeline's attention and much of his own as he had been assigned to report on the strike's progress. He despaired of ever advancing his own investigation when fate intervened. A new labor problem had erupted on the north side of the city and Freddie was sent to cover it. The location was the Hyperion Electroplate Company.

As Freddie stepped off the North Avenue streetcar in front of the factory, he had the distinct impression of reliving the past. For the second time in as many months he was confronted by a line of men in blue and brass. Instead of forming a protective circle around a dead girl, they had formed a solid line protecting the front entrance to the factory. Before them stood a second line of men--factory workers in threadbare woolen pants and shoes lined, no doubt, with wads of paper to cover the cracks in their soles. These men carried hand-lettered signs. One proclaimed, "Hyperion steals the bread from our children's mouths!" Another read, "The workman is worthy of his hire!"

The workers marched back and forth in front of the entrance, careful not to step off the sidewalk, careful not to make eye contact with the police. Freddie scanned the faces of the men in blue. No one looked familiar, but every face held the same grim expression. He looked at the faces of the picketers--more angry than grim. He recognized a few. In particular, he noticed the dark-skinned boy with the acid-burned hands. The boy wasn't wearing an apron today to protect his already patched clothing. Freddie walked up to him and offered a casual "Good morning."

The boy eyed Freddie's silk cravat contemptuously before replying. "Maybe to you it's a good morning." He spat in the gutter for emphasis.

"I heard there was a strike here." Freddie held himself ready to flip open his notebook if anything interesting emerged.

"What's it to you if there is? You got fine clothes an' no reason to worry where your next meal's gonna come from."

Undeterred, Freddie held out his hand in greeting. "I'm Freddie Simpson with the *Gazette*. I came to cover the story. I'd like to hear your side."

The boy refused to return the greeting. "I seen how the papers tol' the story at Pullman. You wanna hear my side so's the papers can say we're a bunch of anarchists trying to destroy free enterprise, instead of a bunch of poor gutter rats trying to keep ourselves an' our families from starving to death."

Freddie was insistent. "As I said, I'd like to hear your side."

The boy relented slightly. In a mildly suspicious voice, he said, "My name's Orlando."

"Orlando what?" Freddie took out his notebook and began writing.

"Just Orlando. That's enough for you to know."

"Well then, Orlando, what's this all about?"

"It's about going from eight bucks to five on payday, that's what."

Freddie raised his eyebrows in surprise. "That would be somewhere around a forty percent wage cut."

Orlando laughed scornfully. "That'd be the difference between shivering in a alley somewhere an' eating garbage or keeping a roof over your family's head."

Freddie looked around to see if Martin Allworthy was anywhere in sight. "What reason did the owner give for cutting wages?"

Orlando glowered with suppressed anger. "They said orders was down. They wasn't down that far! We was all still working from dawn to dusk an' here comes this new cock o' the walk strutting around telling us all to work harder yet!"

"Who do you mean?" Freddie already guessed the answer.

"Why, him that's talking to that copper over there." Orlando jerked his head to the side, indicating a well-dressed man whispering to a policeman at the end of the line.

Freddie gave a start when he realized that the man was Desmond Bayne. To the young man's amazement, Bayne didn't acknowledge his presence, even though he was staring in the reporter's direction the whole time he was conversing with the policeman. Freddie concluded that Bayne must have been three sheets to the wind when they were introduced at the Allworthy's dinner party and probably didn't recall anyone he met that night.

"Mr. High an' Mighty, that one thinks he is! Treating us all like we was his slaves. Even the girls in the packing room. Like it was his own pers'nal candy store!" Orlando was becoming angrier with every word.

Freddie refocused his attention on the striker standing in front of him. "What do you mean?"

Orlando kicked angrily at a scrubby patch of grass attempting to cling to life at the edge of the sidewalk. "You know what I mean all right, mister! He kept after 'em. Saying he'd be extra nice to them if they was extra nice to him. My sister works there an' she told me. When he wouldn't keep his hands off her an' she slapped him, he said he'd have her job for it." Orlando spat out the words. "If that bastard tries anything again with her, I'll kill him!"

Freddie had stopped taking notes. This wasn't something that his editor would allow him to print. "When did all the trouble start?" Again he guessed the answer.

"Right after that swaggering so-an'-so started at the beginning of May. 'Mr. Bayne, sir' we're supposed to call him. Mr. Allworthy introduces him around an' tells us we should treat him with all due respect--that he's the new vice president. Christ Almighty! How many overseers are we gonna get in this shop? We already got a foreman an' a general manager sweating the blood out of us. And now we got this Bayne blustering up an' down the livelong day, telling us what a poor excuse we are for workmen. If that's not bad enough, a month after he starts, we get rounded up an' told there's to be pay cuts because orders is down. That was the limit! After three weeks of it, we had enough. We're through talking. The whole shop struck."

"Have you given a formal list of grievances to Mr. Allworthy?"

Orlando shrugged. "If you wanna know about all that, you should talk to Tibbs." The worker motioned to a mild-looking man at the opposite end of the picket line. "We put him in charge of talking. Me, I don't wanna talk no more. I just wanna go back to work an' get paid what I used to get paid!"

Abruptly, Orlando turned his back on Freddie and rejoined the picket line.

Blinking once in surprise at the young worker's unceremonious departure, Freddie sauntered over to start up a conversation with the *vox populi*. "Mr. Tibbs?" he began hesitantly.

Unlike Orlando, Tibbs didn't exhibit any violent emotion. He turned calm eyes toward Freddie. "Yes?"

"Frederick Simpson with the *Gazette*. I'm here to cover the strike and one of your co-workers told me you are their leader."

Tibbs laughed deprecatingly. "Eustace Tibbs, at your service, though I'd hardly call myself their leader, Mr. Simpson." He lifted his hat to wipe his forehead with a handkerchief. Freddie noted he was quite bald for a man of about thirty. "We're not a union shop. Just a rabble in need of a voice. I appear to have been chosen."

"You don't sound like a factory worker."

"That's because I'm not." Tibbs smiled. "I'm the company bookkeeper. I'm responsible for Mr. Allworthy's financial records. But as far as pay cuts go, I'm affected to the same degree as the rest of these men."

"You mean Allworthy cut your wages, too?" Freddie was appalled.

Tibbs nodded. "Everyone was cut except, of course, Mr.

Allworthy, Mr. Bayne and the managers."

"Ah, yes, speaking of Mr. Bayne..." Freddie launched into his favorite topic with relish, casting a furtive glance to see if Desmond was anywhere nearby. The rogue was still deep in conversation with the police and hadn't noticed Freddie. "Speaking of Mr. Bayne, I've been told that the trouble all started shortly after his arrival."

"That would be correct." Tibbs sighed. "Mr. Allworthy always ran a tight ship. The men were usually a little discontented, but Mr. Bayne's arrival seems to have pushed them over the edge." The bookkeeper shook his head in wonderment. "He seems almost to have appeared out of thin air, like some evil genie."

Freddie's ears perked up at the statement. "Just between you and me, I've been conducting a private investigation into Mr. Bayne's background. I haven't been able to turn up anything about him. It's as you say. He seems to have appeared out of thin air."

Tibbs took Freddie by the elbow and steered him away from the picket line. "Since we appear to be sharing confidences, Mr. Simpson, I'll tell you a few things that are to remain strictly off the record."

They walked about a half block west of the factory before Tibbs stopped and began speaking again. "The compensation Mr. Bayne is receiving is the direct reason for this strike."

"What?" Freddie gasped.

"If I told the men that, I believe they'd form a lynch mob, so I haven't said anything. I was hoping Mr. Allworthy would come to his senses. He's usually a rational man, if a bit pompous." Tibbs hesitated. "I don't know what's happened to him over the course of the past six weeks. He seems blind to reason."

"What indeed," Freddie murmured darkly.

Tibbs continued. "The day Mr. Bayne started, I was instructed to pay him an annual salary of one hundred thousand dollars."

Freddie was thunderstruck. "How much?"

"That's what I would have said if I'd been at liberty." The bookkeeper smiled sympathetically. "As it was, I just marked that one with all the zeros following it in my ledger book. But it represented a problem for the company."

"I'll say!"

"No, I don't mean about Mr. Bayne personally." Tibbs shook his head. "That's an entirely different story. I mean that our orders had been down for a few months."

Freddie looked at him quizzically.

"In accounting terms, we weren't bringing in enough income to offset our expenses. After adding in Mr. Bayne's salary, our books would have shown a loss. I pointed that fact out to Mr. Allworthy, and he said he would ponder the matter. Well, he pondered the matter for a month. Two weeks ago he reached a decision. I was instructed to decrease wages by forty percent across the board. That is, except for management."

"Didn't you tell him that the men might strike?"

"Yes, I did point that out. Mr. Allworthy got rather upset and said he was the master in his own place of business and that he would make the rules. Personally, I think he was more afraid of what Mrs. Allworthy would say if profits were down."

"Ah, yes, I've met Mrs. Allworthy." Freddie thought back to Euphemia's breadth and girth. "I understand she owns the company. Didn't you tell her about this?"

Tibbs looked down at the ground self-consciously. "If I'd had the nerve, I would have. As it was, Mr. Allworthy always said we shouldn't trouble his wife with the day-to-day operating details of the company. It was enough if we showed a clear profit each quarter."

"Still, she's bound to find out after this." Freddie motioned to the strike scene behind them.

"I imagine Mr. Allworthy will say we are a pack of insubordinate ruffians and should be replaced by a more tractable work force."

"A work force willing to slave for what he's willing to pay."

"Yes," Tibbs assented quietly.

"Then why are you doing this?" Freddie was at a loss. "Of all of them, surely you can see you're fighting a losing battle."

The bookkeeper sighed. "It isn't about winning or losing. It's about justice. Simple justice, that's all." He smiled ruefully. "Workers aren't cattle, Mr. Simpson. Someone has to show the owners that. Someone has to make them see. Enough workers, in enough shops. They'll have no choice but to see." Tibbs turned to gaze out over the line of pickets--the line of men in blue.

"What about Bayne?" Freddie broke into his thoughts. "I've heard it wasn't just his salary everyone's upset about."

"Yes, he's indulged in some odd behavior since he started. I'm not sure what his duties are meant to be, but he's taken it upon himself to nose around in every corner of the business. He asked me to turn the books over to him one night so he could study them."

"And did you?"

"What could I say? He is supposedly Mr. Allworthy's right-hand man. I allowed him free access to the company's records."

"I'm surprised the fellow can read." Freddie scribbled a few more notes about Bayne.

Tibbs regarded the notebook with an expression of mild annoyance. "I said this was to be off the record, Mr. Simpson."

"And so it is," Freddie hastened to reassure him. "I'm keeping a separate set of notes on Bayne for my personal reading."

"Ah, I see."

Freddie shifted his attention to more printable fare. "For the record, what do you expect will happen next?"

"I imagine Mr. Allworthy will try to replace us with strikebreakers and reopen the shop."

"When?"

Tibbs shrugged. "It could happen any time now. I hope the fellows can keep their tempers when it does."

The two men stood for some time contemplating the parallel human chains before them. The air was thick with tension but no violence had erupted yet.

Freddie broke the silence. "I'm reminded of an observation recently made by a friend of mine."

Tibbs looked at him with curiosity.

"She commented that it's only when a man feels he has nothing left to lose that he becomes truly dangerous."

"Perhaps your friend should share her views with Mr. Allworthy." Tibbs kept his eyes on the picketers.

"She has," Freddie responded, "but he seems to have a hearing problem."

Tibbs chuckled. "Well, I'm not surprised." He mopped his forehead once more and turned resolutely back in the direction of Hyperion. "I suppose I should be getting back to my place in line."

The two strolled back to the front of the factory. The bookkeeper retrieved his placard and rejoined his fellow workers.

Freddie was about to leave when he noticed something odd. Out of the corner of his eye, he thought he saw Bayne slip a folded bill into the hand of the cop he'd been conversing with. The cop dropped the bill into his pocket.

Just at that moment, a canvas-covered delivery wagon drawn by a team of draft horses crossed the bridge over the river and made its way to the factory entrance. Another wagon followed. Freddie watched as the men in the picket line began to grow restless, whispering to each other and pointing to the wagons.

Ten men stepped out of the back of the first dray. Another ten stepped out of the second. Some of the police moved forward as a shield between the newcomers and the picketers. A few of the strikers picked up stones and hefted them for weight.

"Remember, all of you, this is a peaceful demonstration!" Tibbs tried to make himself heard above the rising tide of angry voices.

The men unloaded from the wagons meekly followed the police through the door of the factory.

Freddie saw the cop who had been in conversation with Bayne walk up to Orlando. The young man was already seething with rage. It wouldn't take much to push him over the line.

"You, Orlando?" the cop asked in an insolent tone.

"That's right." The boy glared at him.

Freddie was reminded of a picture he'd once seen of David and Goliath.

"Gettin' into trouble must run in the family." The cop paused to ruminate a moment over his chewing tobacco. He spat casually on the ground in front of Orlando, narrowing missing the boy's boot. "I think it was yer sister I ran in last night."

"What?" Orlando challenged in disbelief.

"Yeah, sure it was her. She was out walking Clark Street around midnight, looking for business. I ran her in for prostitution."

"You lying son of a--"

Before Orlando could leap at the cop, two of his co-workers pinned his arms.

The cop grinned. "But maybe I made a mistake."

Orlando relaxed slightly and the two strikers loosened their grip on him.

The cop rubbed the back of his neck, seemingly deep in thought. "Yeah, that's right. I did make a mistake. Now that I think about it. It wasn't yer sister."

Orlando looked at him skeptically.

"It was yer mother that was the whore!"

Before his friends could stop him, the young man had leaped for the cop's throat, attempting to throttle him. The patrolman was quicker. He raised his club and brought it down squarely on Orlando's skull. Freddie winced as he heard the dull crack of wood against bone.

At the sight of the attack, the other picketers broke their line and began pelting the police with rocks, broken glass, bricks, and anything else they could lay hands on. The cops retaliated by striking back with clubs. A few shots were fired, and Freddie saw a picketer drop to the ground and roll around on the sidewalk, grabbing at a shattered, bloody ankle.

One of the cops blew his whistle, summoning reinforcements. Almost instantly, three patrol wagons came charging around the corner.

The police subdued the strikers by kicking them, clubbing them, and finally shooting into the crowd. The men were rounded up at gunpoint and loaded into the patrol wagons. Freddie saw Tibbs smile crookedly at him through a cut lip before being shoved into the back of the last wagon.

Freddie noticed Bayne standing on the top step of the factory entrance languidly smoking a cigar. In a second-story window directly above the doorway, Freddie caught a glimpse of Martin Allworthy anxiously watching the scene below. Freddie shook his head in disgust as he turned to go. Simple justice for the strikers would be a long time coming. In the meanwhile, Hyperion had reopened for business.

CHAPTER 8
The Presence Of Spirits

 CR⌘ℬ

By the third week of June, both Evangeline and Freddie were feeling the strain of Chicago's labor unrest. Evangeline had volunteered to work at the Pullman Relief Store and Freddie was being sent all over town to cover strike stories. Exhausted, the pair had mutually agreed that one night of frivolity would do them good. It was the evening of the much anticipated séance at the Allworthy villa and Freddie had come to the country house to collect his friend.

"How goes your murder investigation?" Evangeline slipped on her gloves and took one last approving glance at herself in the foyer mirror.

Looking suspiciously around him, Freddie ignored her question and asked one of his own. "Where's Delphine this evening?"

"When she found out who my escort was to be, she developed a fit of the sulks and retired to her room for the nonce." Evangeline held out her hand as a prompt for Freddie to offer his arm. "Shall we?"

Belatedly recovering his manners, he complied. One of the maids let them out.

Evangeline paused on the front steps, momentarily diverted by the contentious chirping of birds on a long summer evening. The sun was just beginning to dip to the horizon, and a pleasant breeze was blowing in from the south, bearing the scent of roses.

"No carriage?" Freddie sounded surprised.

"I believe we'll walk." Evangeline had chosen to ignore the rules of decorum regarding their mode of conveyance since they were now in the country, and none of the etiquette books with which she was acquainted addressed the topic of appropriate transportation to and from a séance. The evening being a delightfully cool one, the Allworthy villa a mere four blocks away, and the lady in need of exercise, they walked.

As the couple turned down Center Street, Evangeline persisted in her line of inquiry. "I repeat the question. How goes your investigation?"

Freddie hung his head in discouragement. "Deuced badly, I'm afraid. You heard about the strike this past Monday, of course?"

"Yes. A deplorable business that confirms my already dismal opinion of Martin Allworthy's judgment. What can the man have been thinking! With Pullman refusing to arbitrate, the mood of Chicago's working class toward factory owners in general is becoming increasingly angry. He's just given them one more reason to resort to desperate measures."

"Once they got out of jail, all the Hyperion men lost their jobs. Replaced by strikebreakers."

"At a steep wage reduction, no doubt?"

Freddie nodded sadly. "I tried to ask around to find places for a few of the fellows, but everyone I know is afraid to hire anarchists."

"It's a sorry state of affairs when a man who will not quietly consent to starve to death is labeled an anarchist." Evangeline sighed despondently. "And what about the malevolent Mr. Bayne? Any new facts to feed your fancies regarding him?"

Freddie's expression changed from gloom to exasperation. "The scoundrel must be Old Nick himself. He appears in a puff of black smoke with no past and no acquaintances in the city to speak of. I've managed to discover where he lives, and it's a pretty high-toned neighborhood, but he's never there. I've even stayed up nights, propping myself against a lamp post across the street from his flat, in hopes of seeing him engage in something nefarious, but to no avail."

"You'd better have a care, my friend. The police are likely to take you for a suspicious character, not him, and run you in for questioning."

Freddie laughed ruefully. "That would be just the perfect irony, wouldn't it? Is he supposed to be attending this hocus-pocus tonight?"

"The correct term is séance, not hocus-pocus, and I don't believe so."

The couple had by this time ambled along Center Street all the way to the lake and turned down Aurora Avenue. Spread out to their left in all its restless blue expanse was Lake Michigan. To their right stood an edifice which might suitably have been named Versailles on the Lake.

"Well, here we are," Evangeline announced. "*Un peut de trop, n'est-ce pas?*"

"What?"

"Excessive, isn't it."

"In ways too numerous to mention." Freddie stood gaping at the front of the building. "Now I know why you were surprised that I could have overlooked it."

The house possessed no coherent architectural style but rather seemed content to borrow from a variety of sources. The façade consisted of a hodge podge of multi-colored stone surmounted by a flurry of turrets and dormers and gables. If Euphemia Allworthy had hoped to be noticed by the local set, she would certainly get her wish.

Garrison opened the door to their knock and silently took their wraps. Although the two braced themselves for a torrent of welcome from Euphemia, she greeted the couple in a subdued manner in keeping with the solemnity of the occasion.

"This evening is meant to be a *soirée intime*, my dears. Too many people clattering about will frighten the spirits. At least that's what Serafina says."

Evangeline noted with relief that Euphemia's hair was dressed without its characteristic aigrette, and the lady of the castle had opted for a simple gown that did not silently reproach Evangeline's choice of a teal silk walking suit.

While Evangeline cared little for the opinion of others

regarding her eccentricities of manner, she had no intention of displaying her eccentricities while badly dressed. Freddie, bless his heart, had been oblivious to the intricate fashion dilemma before him and had failed to change into formal evening clothes for the occasion. Attired in a plain business suit, he had, therefore, stumbled onto the appropriate costume for the event.

~•„

Euphemia led her visitors into the drawing room whose elaborately gilded and frescoed ceiling aspired to be mistaken for that of the Sistine Chapel.

Bracing himself for an onslaught of introductions, Freddie was almost disappointed when Euphemia said simply, "I believe you already know everyone present."

Freddie's eyes swept around the room. He saw Serafina seated in an oversized armchair that seemed to dwarf her delicate frame. Theophilus Creech was hovering attentively nearby. Martin nodded curtly in greeting. As Freddie turned to look toward the opposite wall he noticed a familiar prop holding up the fireplace mantel--Roland.

Following the direction of his gaze, Euphemia whispered a confidence in his ear. "Roland wasn't supposed to be here. He invited himself."

Unfortunately, Euphemia's idea of a whisper was more oratorical than most, prompting Roland to defend himself. "Oh auntie, I didn't mean to be a burden. Really, I didn't. It's just that the city is so dull this time of year."

"Didn't you have matters of business to attend to?" Martin asked tersely.

Roland waived his hand dismissively. "Mr. Waxman said he could do without me."

"Indeed." His uncle allowed the single word to hang reproachfully in the air.

Before the conversation took an unpleasant turn, Euphemia diverted their attention. "Shall we go into the dining room, my friends? I've planned a light supper. Nothing elaborate, you understand. Serafina tells me this is best. Wouldn't want anyone nodding off after a heavy meal and offending the inhabitants of the astral plane, now would we?"

"Do ghosts care what we eat for dinner?" Freddie murmured in Evangeline's ear. She trod on his foot by way of comment.

☜☞

The party was well into the final dish of a simple ten-course dinner when a loud pounding was heard coming from the outer door. Given the cavernous dimensions of the Allworthy villa, it was no small feat of strength for a knock to make itself heard all the way to the dining room over the chatter of the guests and the bustle of the servants. Garrison rushed to see who was causing the racket. Small talk in the dining room was suspended as everyone speculated on the meaning of the intrusion.

Their silence was broken by the echo of boisterous voices coming from the foyer, reverberating off the wainscoting in the hall and bouncing through the door of the dining room.

"See here, fellow!" a raucous voice boomed. "You'll be showing me in to see my friend straightway, or I'll be showing you the head of me cane about your scrawny neck."

A strident female laugh accompanied the booming voice.

Martin hastily rose from the table. He seemed to recognize the voice but dreaded to acknowledge it. "I'll just go and see who it is."

Before he could reach the door and avert disaster, in walked Desmond, or rather, in staggered Desmond with a blowsy, berouged female draped over his arm. She was dressed resplendently in a fur-trimmed mantelet which the balmy summer evening did not require, white satin opera gloves, and diamond bracelets on both wrists. Despite her regal accoutrements, she seemed to have as much difficulty in standing upright as her companion. The two managed to remain somewhat vertical only by the process of leaning against each other.

At the sight of Martin, Desmond's face beamed with joy. "Ah, there's a sight for me eyes, Maggie. Didn't I tell you, and you not believing a word I said. Didn't I tell you I'd take you round and introduce you to my friends in society."

"That you did, Desmond. That you did." She thumped her

companion repeatedly on the chest for emphasis. "And I'm a sorry bitch for not believing you."

Euphemia gasped. Even Evangeline, who was used to the seamier side of life on the streets around Mast House, appeared to be at a loss for words. Freddie felt his eyes growing round as saucers. It was only with the greatest act of self-restraint that he kept himself from diving into his coat pocket for his notebook to add to his secret file on Desmond Bayne.

Martin made a superhuman effort to maintain his dignity. "We weren't expecting the pleasure of your company this evening, Desmond. Nor that of your, uh...lady."

Desmond howled with glee at Martin's words. "It was supposed to be a surprise! I says to Maggie, Maggie my girl, I'll take you round to the country house of my friend, Mr. Allworthy. We'll hire a carriage and pack some refreshments and take ourselves a pleasant drive. We'll surprise him at home. And a right old surprise it was too, I'll be bound. The look on yer face is priceless, that it is!" Standing up as straight as his inebriated condition would allow, Desmond attempted to make introductions. "Ladies and gentlemen, I'd like you to meet a particular friend of mine. This is Miss Maggie Darling."

Miss Maggie, in what she took to be the proper behavior of a lady on such occasions, squatted into a deep curtsy. "Most honorable and pleasured to be sure."

To the horror of everyone present, her tipsy condition had affected her balance. She dipped to the side and tried to steady herself by grabbing at the first object she could reach. This proved to the scarf on the sideboard, which went down with her as she sank, along with a vast number of silver chafing dishes and their contents.

Desmond gulped in dismay and bent down to assist his gravy-spattered light o'love.

"Oh Desmond, help me!" she wailed, attempting to wipe off a gobbet of chicken grease from her mantelet. "I've disgraced meself in front of all yer fine friends. God damn me for a clumsy slut if ever there was one!" She clutched at Desmond's tie which had the dual effect of constricting his windpipe and dragging him down on top of her.

Freddie glanced at his host. Martin appeared too stunned

to move. Garrison straightened his waistcoat with a deep sigh and dove into the fray. With the help of two other servants, he managed at last to raise Desmond and Maggie to their unsteady feet. Evidently he determined it was his responsibility to take the appropriate course of action while his master was incapacitated by shock. The butler nudged Desmond and his companion toward the hall. "Let me show you to the door, sir."

Nonplussed by the turn his surprise had taken, Desmond didn't dispute the matter. "Aye, aye. That'll be fine, me lad. Show us the way." He sheepishly pushed Maggie out of the dining room door ahead of him, pausing only long enough to tip his hat to the assembled guests. "A good evening to you all, ladies and gentleman." He then wove his way precariously down the hall and out the door.

Because of the dead silence that prevailed in the dining room, the sound of voices outside the front door carried a good while after the pair departed. The wailing and hissing reminded Freddie of a catfight of epic proportions. Only after the screaming match subsided and the feral couple apparently weaved off to nurse their grievances elsewhere, did anyone at the table feel at liberty to speak.

Evangeline tried to pass the entire matter off lightly. "Really, Martin, I am much obliged to you for hiring the entertainment. I was prepared for a séance, but the Punch and Judy show was an unexpected diversion."

Martin smiled thinly as nervous laughter erupted around the table. Euphemia's face had gone white with rage. Freddie could guess that the subject of Desmond's behavior would be discussed at great length by the Allworthys into the wee hours of the morning.

In a tiny voice, Serafina suggested an alternate amusement. "Perhaps it is time for us to begin."

Rousing herself from the contemplation of murder, Euphemia attempted a smile. "Yes, you're perfectly correct, my dear. It's growing quite late, isn't it." She rose. "If you'll all just follow me into the parlor, I believe we have a table large enough to accommodate the party. Garrison?" She looked inquisitively at the butler.

"At once, madame." He bowed and went off to retrieve the requisite furniture.

While the servants were setting up the apparatus of the séance, the guests sipped coffee and made small talk. Even Roland, normally oblivious to matters of tact and decorum, made no allusion to the strange visit that had just transpired. Instead, he engaged Freddie in a harmless discussion of pheasant hunting.

When everything was ready, Serafina took charge. She instructed Garrison to extinguish all the lights in the room, leaving only a candelabrum in the center of the table.

She motioned to the guests. "If you will all please to be seated, we may begin."

They silently complied with her request. The only servant remaining in the room was Garrison, who stood by the parlor door, presumably in the unlikely event that a spirit required admittance through a conventional portal.

Theophilus attempted to join hands with Serafina on his left and Euphemia on his right but the medium stopped him. "No, not yet, Theophilus, I feel I must do impressions first."

"Impressions?" Freddie asked cautiously.

Apparently knowing the variety of interpretations his satiric mind could make of that small word, Evangeline cut in. "I believe she wishes to tell us about ourselves. Isn't that so?"

Serafina nodded. "Yes, it is for my benefit also. It helps me to know the energy that surrounds me. A séance can be full of surprises if you are not prepared." She laughed lightly.

Euphemia beamed indulgently, for the moment forgetting the outrage of the previous hour in her pleasure at having netted the social catch of the season. "That would be most amusing for all of us, I'm sure." She patted her husband's hand. "Wouldn't it, Martin?"

Martin mumbled some form of assent, obviously not convinced that the show about to begin would be any less humiliating than the one that had so recently ended.

Serafina nodded, took a deep breath and closed her eyes. Freddie watched as her eyelids fluttered like tiny birds. She opened them again and swept her gaze across the table. "You..." She looked directly at Freddie.

Taken aback by her unexpected approach, the young man squeaked, "Me?"

"Mr. Simpson, calm yourself." The medium laughed. "I

mean you no harm. I have just formed an impression of you first, that is all."

"Oh." Freddie felt a certain amount of trepidation nonetheless.

"I see many pieces of paper around you. They are whirling around in the air. They seem to come from a big machine. A machine that looks like a furnace. And when it opens its mouth, these many pieces of paper come flying out. You understand this image?"

"Yes." Freddie's reply was terse. He didn't want to give her any extra information since he was far from a believer when it came to matters of the occult.

Evangeline raised an amused eyebrow, accurately inferring the amount of surprise the young man was feeling.

Serafina continued. "These papers. I think they are newspapers. You work for a newspaper, Mr. Simpson?"

"Yes." His response was barely a whisper.

Euphemia drew in a sharp breath. She evidently now understood the reason for Freddie's interest in the Allworthy family.

Switching to another subject, Serafina turned toward Evangeline. "This young man thinks much of you."

Evangeline laughed. "He's underfoot constantly and has been since he was still in knee pants."

Serafina smiled at Freddie's inability to conceal a pained expression. She must have realized that she had exposed his feelings. "Do not trouble yourself, Mr. Simpson. The lady has a great regard for you as well. More than she will say."

Freddie felt a warm glow. Though he was willing to discredit every other word Serafina spoke as pure hokum, he clung to that one statement as gospel truth. He snuck a quick glance at Evangeline to see how she had taken the disclosure. In the flickering candlelight, he noticed the right corner of her mouth lifted in a secret smile of amusement.

Serafina focused her attention more fixedly on Evangeline. "I see you with many people surrounding you. People of different ages, of different countries, all in a room together with you. How can this be? You live in this city, do you not?"

"That is true." Evangeline was far more forthcoming than Freddie. "I am a teacher."

"Ah, I see." The medium nodded. "But this is a different

school. People come from everywhere. It is open to all who wish to go."

"Also true." Evangeline appeared to be impressed. "I teach at the Mast House settlement. The immigrants come there to learn English, to learn crafts, many different things."

"But that is not all you do," Serafina corrected. "You are...you are... What is the English word for this?" She paused a moment. "Ah yes, you are what they call a detective."

Freddie laughed out loud.

"No, I am not," Evangeline retorted gently.

In an even softer voice, Serafina insisted, "You think you are not, but you are, or will be soon. That is your destiny. You are a detective."

"I'll call the Pinkertons for you in the morning, shall I?" Freddie's comment was only half-derisive since he was well aware of his friend's abilities in that line of endeavor.

"I see around you a statue of justice. With a sword in one hand and the scales in the other. But she is not as in the statues we always see."

Evangeline raised an eyebrow quizzically.

"She has not the blindfold. She sees the truth. You are like her. You see things as they are. You are one of us."

"One of you?" Evangeline repeated, uncomprehending.

"Like me, a sensitive. You have the same gift. But you use your thinking too much. You must learn to listen to your heart--your inner voice--more often. It will not lead you in the wrong path. You have considered this matter often."

Freddie was amazed when he looked at his friend's expression. He expected her to make some witty reply and laugh off the advice. Instead, her face bore a look of serious concentration. "Yes, you are right," she said.

Serafina turned her attention to her next subject. "You come from an illustrious family."

Martin sat straighter in his chair and acknowledged the truth of her observation with a nod.

"They go back this way for many generations. Row upon row of distinguished ones preceding you."

In the dim light, Freddie fancied he saw Martin almost smile.

Serafina continued. "I see each one clasping hands. Like links in a chain. A strong chain, but it is a chain that binds you."

"What?"

"Yes, it is so. A strong chain but a heavy one. I see you carry the weight of it all. You stumble. I see you falling because the weight is too heavy."

Martin waved his hand, dismissing her words. "Absurd. I don't know what you mean!"

Serafina gave a small shrug. "Sometimes, I do not know what these pictures mean either. You must forgive me if I have offended."

"Of course you haven't offended, my dear." Euphemia glared at her husband. "Please continue. We are all attention."

"Now you, my kind hostess," the medium forged on. She closed her eyes for a moment and her brows knit in concentration. "This I do not understand." She opened her eyes. "I see you are a good woman. A woman of strong character. You are much distressed by something that has happened in the past few days, but you will set things to rights."

"Most assuredly," Euphemia interjected with determination.

"But that is not all. I see you holding a glass. But the glass falls from your hand and it shatters. I have a bad feeling. You must be careful in the weeks to come. Be very, very careful." Serafina's voice had taken on an urgent tone.

Euphemia seemed disturbed by the medium's prediction but tried to hide it. "Oh, perhaps a household accident and nothing more."

"Perhaps," Serafina echoed uncertainly.

Euphemia attempted to distract her guest from distressing thoughts. "You must give us your impressions of Roland next."

"Yes, yes, I will try." Serafina sighed and closed her eyes. She breathed deeply a few times, apparently trying to clear away the dark image she had just seen. A smile formed on her lips as she opened her eyes to gaze at the youth across the table from her. "You have many interests in life, and it is hard for you to settle on any one thing. You have an eye for the ladies, do you not?"

Roland laughed without a trace of self-consciousness. "You've caught me there, Miss Serafina. And may I say you're quite a pleasing prospect to contemplate."

Serafina ignored the comment. "Yes, yes, it is romance that you live for. The thrill of the chase. The conquest, and then always you begin again. It is what makes the sun rise and set for you." She fixed her attention on some invisible object behind Roland's left shoulder. Freddie followed her gaze, peering off into the shadows beyond the range of the candlelight. He could see nothing.

"There is a figure. A young woman, I think, standing behind you."

"What?" Roland turned in disbelief.

"Yes, she is there, but you will not see her with your eyes. It is with the second sight that I see her. She is flitting back and forth behind you."

Serafina squinted a moment in the half-light, trying to make out some detail of the apparition. "But this is strange. Her hair is wet. So are her clothes."

Freddie felt the hair on the back of his neck stand on end.

Roland evidently felt no such reaction. He merely exclaimed, "Really! How odd."

At that moment, Freddie noticed that Martin had begun to tap his fingers nervously on the tabletop.

The reporter jumped in to ask a question. The urgency of his tone must have surprised everyone. "Her hair, what color is it?"

Serafina replied without hesitation. "It is dark brown. There are damp curls all around her face. Her lips are blue from the cold. She is so very, very cold."

"And her gown. What color is that?"

Serafina squinted again. She hesitated. "I think it is gray. A very light gray. Not white. Maybe the gown is silk."

Freddie became distracted by Martin. The host had taken out a handkerchief and was dabbing at his forehead, even though the room was a trifle drafty. His breathing had become rapid and shallow.

Roland was exhibiting no signs of concern, only curiosity. "How odd. I'm sorry to say I can't place this bathing beauty you describe. Is she pretty? I'd like to meet her if she is!"

Serafina raised her hand to silence him. "Wait," she commanded tensely. "She is saying something and I cannot hear her." The medium began to silently mouth the words. "I cannot...I cannot...sw...swi..."

"It's suffocating in here. The air is too close!" Martin sprang from his chair. He tore impatiently at his collar. "Garrison, the lights. I must have light!"

The butler hastened to turn up the gas jets.

"I...I'm sorry. The room is too stuffy. Cursed dizziness. I must go outside for a breath of air." With that, Allworthy hastily departed the room, leaving the other guests stunned and disoriented.

Serafina looked dazed, her concentration broken.

Euphemia flew to her side. "Are you all right, my dear? Garrison, a glass of water!"

"No, please do not concern yourself, madame. When I am concentrating, it is like a trance, and to have it broken so abruptly..."

"You must forgive my husband." The hostess appeared mortified.

"Of course, it was not his fault. Please do not worry."

Garrison rushed forward with a glass of brandy instead of water. Serafina drank it without protest.

Euphemia hovered solicitously. "Do you feel well enough to continue?"

The medium gave a helpless little shrug. "I am afraid I cannot. She is gone. I do not think she will return tonight. I am so sorry, Mrs. Allworthy. I do not believe I can do any more this evening. I am very tired now."

"My dear, you must not fret. I understand that such matters cannot be regulated like winding a clock. You must go to your room and get some rest."

Serafina patted the older woman's hand comfortingly. "We will speak again tomorrow."

❧❦

Martin was pacing back and forth under the porch light. He took in huge gulps of air, but his lungs never seemed to stretch enough despite his efforts to fill them.

"How could that young ass sit there without blinking! 'I'm sorry but I don't recall this particular bathing beauty.' The witless fool!"

Martin shakily tried to light a cigar. The smoke didn't

calm him. It made him cough and further irritated his shortness of breath. It was too impossible to believe. He leaned his head against one of the columns on the front porch. The stone felt cool to the touch. Soothing. His heart was still hammering away, and it took several more moments before he could regulate its pounding by a sheer act of will.

"This can't be. Someone must have told her. The alternative is unthinkable!" Martin began to grow anxious about what the others would say. He was about to re-enter the house when the door opened and Evangeline and Freddie emerged.

"What, are the festivities over so soon?" His hands were still shaking.

Evangeline gave him a searching look. "Yes, I'm afraid so. Serafina seems rather done in for the evening."

"Well, another time perhaps."

"Yes, another time," Evangeline said evenly. "Thank you for a most interesting evening."

"Most interesting." Freddie took Evangeline's arm to help her down the front stairs. The street lamps were no more than feeble pinpoints of light that afforded little assistance under the cloudy night sky.

Martin watched the couple recede into the shadows beyond the reach of the porch lamps. Taking his first full breath, he straightened his tie, ground out his cigar and re-entered the house.

☞◈

"Well, that was a unique experience," Freddie said wryly once they were out of earshot of the villa.

"I thought Serafina was quite gifted."

"Oh, rubbish, Engie! How can you believe such nonsense?"

"She was accurate, wasn't she?"

"Accurate!" Freddie cried in disbelief. "Everything she said could have been information fed to her beforehand. I've no doubt her friend Creech is a confidence trickster as well. My profession, Allworthy's background, even your dabbling as a detective are all facts that are common knowledge to any of our acquaintances!"

"Why do you find it so difficult to credit an honest

medium?" Evangeline sounded nettled.

"Because it's a contradiction in terms. There is no such thing as an honest medium. All this mumbo jumbo can't be proven. It's all smoke and mirrors. The idea of ghosts is utterly absurd!"

"Freddie, are you a Christian?"

"What?" The young man was taken aback by the abrupt change in topic. He stopped dead in his tracks and peered down at his companion in the shadowy glow of a street lamp.

"I asked if you are a Christian or not."

"Of course I am! What's that got to do with anything?"

"Then you believe in the existence of God?"

Beginning to sense a philosophical trap, the young man answered cautiously. "That is the most basic principle of the Christian faith. Yes, of course I do."

"How do you know He, if indeed He is a He, exists?"

Freddie groaned in exasperation. "I have it upon the good authority of generations of holy men that He does. Some of them have even testified that they saw Him."

"Indeed. And I have it upon the good authority of generations of witnesses who testify that they have seen ghosts. Why is your belief more worthy than mine?"

"Because yours is ridiculous, that's why! Disembodied forms floating around in the air frightening people into having fits!"

Evangeline maintained her composure. "As a Christian, you believe that a virgin gave birth to a man who walked on water and rose from the dead, do you not?"

Freddie refused to admit that her reductive description made this fundamental religious tenet sound as ridiculous as his own portrayal of ghosts. Instead, he chose to take the moral high ground. "Have a care, Engie. You're implying heresy to say you don't believe in it, too."

His companion laughed at his pompous defensive strategy. "I'm not spouting heresy, Freddie. You'd be surprised how conventional some of my beliefs are, but I merely wish to point out an inconsistency in your thought process."

Freddie calculated the further verbal humiliation he faced if he opposed her. Rather than argue the point, he sighed and asked, "What might that be?"

"Since the existence of God or the existence of ghosts are matters that ultimately come down to a question of belief, I hardly think you can prove anything one way or another. What is it your Saint Paul says? 'We walk by faith and not by sight.'"

The young man crossed his arms truculently. "Hmmph!" He made a great show of offended dignity.

"Furthermore, the belief in one type of disembodied form, namely God, opens the door to the belief in another type of disembodied form, namely ghosts. Logic demands it. If you are willing to countenance the one, you must countenance the other." She paused for effect. "Unless, of course, you'd rather be thought irrational--just like all those silly people who believe in ghosts."

Freddie made one last attempt. "But what about all the charlatans out there who practice spiritualism to line their own pockets, capitalizing on credulousness as their stock in trade? Can you deny they exist?"

Evangeline shook her head gravely. "I do not deny they exist. And may I remind you that priests sold false relics during the Middle Ages. The Christian church has had its share of charlatans, too. I'm merely saying that each practitioner must be judged on his or her own merits. I am equally as opposed to blind credulity as I am to blind skepticism."

"What is the lesson I am to infer from all this?" the young man inquired stiffly.

Evangeline shrugged. "Nothing more than the need to keep an open mind. All that we know is not all there is to know. To think otherwise is the grossest kind of intellectual arrogance."

Freddie escorted her the rest of the way to her front door in silence, still not wishing to admit defeat in the face of her relentless logic. He secretly cursed Evangeline's advanced education and harbored a suspicion that a Jesuit lurked somewhere in her academic background.

Just as she turned to enter, she offered one parting salvo.

"Oh, Freddie, by the way..."

"Yes?"

"Did any of the newspapers provide a physical description of that girl who drowned at Hyperion? Her hair color or the dress she was wearing?"

"No, not that I know of."

"But you saw her, didn't you?"

"Yes." The young man sighed. Knowing the inevitable question to follow, he braced himself.

"Just out of curiosity. What was her hair color?"

"Brown. Dark brown."

"And her dress?"

"It was a light gray silk." He could barely force the words out through tightly clenched teeth.

In the shadowy light, Freddie could see Evangeline's triumphant smile as she turned to enter the house.

"Good night, dear boy. I trust you will draw the appropriate conclusion."

CHAPTER 9
Fired With Conviction

ରଃଇଚ

By midnight, tranquility reigned once more over the Allworthy villa. Serafina had been escorted to her room, attended by Mrs. Allworthy's personal maid, as well as her own, to see to her comfort. Theophilus had been pressed to remain as a house guest until the following morning, at which time he would take the train back to the city. On somewhat less cordial terms, Roland was suffered to stay the night on the understanding that he, too, would return to the city in the morning and thereafter apply himself to business.

After she had seen to the accommodation of her guests, Euphemia retired to her bedroom and sighed with relief as one of the maids unlaced her corset. Donning a dressing gown, she sat down at her vanity table. By the time the maid finished brushing out her hair, she felt herself slipping into a comfortable state of relaxation

Her restful mood was abruptly snapped when she chanced to look into her vanity mirror and caught the reflection of Martin quietly closing the door between their adjoining bedrooms. She had purposely left it open.

She attempted to keep the tone of her voice calm for the sake of the servant. "Martin, a word, if you please."

She could imagine that Martin was silently damning

himself for not escaping her notice before he had bolted the door.

In an equally civil voice, he assented. "Of course, my dear. Of course. I am at your disposal. I'll just tell my man to go and be right with you." Martin stuck his head back into his own bedroom and waved his valet to retire.

Euphemia dismissed her maid. Still seated at the vanity table, she turned to stare at her husband. "Shut the door, please." She knew that the tone of her voice was a signal to him of rough weather ahead.

Martin swallowed hard and did as she instructed. He returned, albeit unwillingly, to the middle of the room and stood before her. A single boudoir lamp burned on the vanity, throwing his shadow against the opposite wall. The shadow dominated the room--something the man who cast it could hardly be said to do.

Folding her hands in her lap, Euphemia didn't mince words. "Martin, ever since that ugly business at the factory, I've been in a quandary about what to do. Tonight has settled the matter for me."

Her husband laughed nervously. "Why, whatever do you mean, my dear? The matter is already settled. The men have been replaced. Order has been restored. There's no need for you to concern yourself further about it. Do you mind if I smoke?" Martin drew a gold cigarette case out of his pocket.

His wife inclined her head and waited while he struck a match. She knew he only smoked cigarettes when he was excessively nervous.

"Martin, I have always trusted your judgment to run my concerns in a profitable manner."

"Of course." Martin exhaled a puff of smoke in what he must have hoped was a casual manner.

"I'm sorry to say, the time has come when I seriously question your judgment."

"Please explain what I have done to lose your confidence." Euphemia could tell from the expression on his face that he dreaded the answer.

"I do not agree with the wage cuts you ordered nor with the way you subsequently dealt with your workers."

Using the approach of an indulgent parent speaking to a slow-witted child, Martin knelt before Euphemia's vanity bench and took her hands in his. "My darling, as I've already explained to you, our orders were down. What other course of action could I take? You didn't want to see your profits destroyed, did you?"

Euphemia coldly withdrew her hands from her husband's grasp. "Of course I don't wish to see profits destroyed, but I have reason to doubt your explanation of events. I have reason to doubt the wage cuts were precipitated by a steep decline in orders."

"Really?" Martin stood back up. He turned his back on his wife and strode to the opposite end of the room. She assumed this was in order to conceal the nervous tic in his right eye, which had begun to jump ever so slightly. He extinguished his half-smoked cigarette and absent-mindedly lit up another.

"Mr. Tibbs paid me a visit last week."

Martin turned to face his wife with an expression of disbelief. "The bookkeeper? He was fired along with the other strikers. In fact, he was their leader!"

"Quite," Euphemia replied simply. "He told me he no longer had anything left to lose. He showed me a copy of the company books and related some interesting anecdotes about Mr. Bayne, his exorbitant salary, and the manner in which he conducts himself at my factory."

"Malice!" Martin protested. "Pure spite! What would you expect him to say? He was fired and wanted to lash out at me by spreading lies!"

Euphemia turned back to face her mirror. Slowly removing her rings, she spoke to Martin's reflection. "That thought had crossed my mind, and so I kept silent until I could weigh the facts. Mr. Bayne's performance this evening leaves me in no doubt as to the veracity of Mr. Tibbs."

Martin gulped down a prodigious amount of smoke. He furtively cast a glance at his wife's reflection, staring back at him in her mirror.

"Why are you protecting this man, Martin?" Her voice was dead calm.

The master of the house turned away from her again and began to pace. He shrugged, his back to his wife. "I told you. I owed him a favor. A rather large favor."

"What favor? What could be of such consequence that you

would jeopardize a thriving concern to shield him in this manner?"

"It...it's a matter between gentleman. I...I...cannot speak of it."

"Gentlemen?" His wife was incredulous. "You have the audacity to call that man a gentleman after his behavior tonight?"

Martin cut in frantically. "No matter what his behavior is or was, I am still a gentleman and must bear my obligations as one! You must understand, it's a matter of honor that I fulfill my part of the bargain. A matter of family honor! You must trust me in this. I will say no more about it!" Martin's voice had risen in pitch. Something akin to desperation had crept into his tone.

Euphemia rose and turned to face her husband. He stopped in mid-stride as she stared him down.

"You have spoken of your honor, but I am a practical woman. I suggest you think less about your pride and more about running an efficient operation. What you have done makes for bad business. It is bad business to cut the wages of honest workingmen in order to pay the salary of a parasite. It is worse business to let a hundred experienced workers go and replace them with novices in order to protect the salary of this same parasite. It was bad enough when Roland joined the company. This is ten times worse. Bad business all around.

'Not only that. Your timing leaves a great deal to be desired. Because of the Pullman strike, Chicago is teetering on the brink of a worker's revolt yet all you can do is add fuel to the fire. I want the original workers brought back and their wages reinstated. Above all, I want Mr. Bayne removed."

Euphemia watched her husband pace around the room like a caged animal. He seemed panicked, scarcely rational. "I need time! You must understand, it is paramount that I not offend him in this! Do not ask me why, for I am not at liberty to explain myself further. Perhaps I can find him another place. Perhaps I can work out some other arrangement that will be satisfactory to him."

"How much time?" Euphemia asked coldly. "I hope you understand that you are in no position to bargain here."

Martin hesitated a moment. "Two weeks. Give me two

weeks to settle matters for him."

Euphemia continued to stare. "And at the end of two weeks, then what?"

Martin never stopped pacing. "As I said, I want to remain on cordial terms with him, so I'll invite him out here on a Saturday afternoon. I'll explain matters to him. I'll offer him better terms elsewhere and...that will be that."

Euphemia nodded. "Very well. I accept your provisos with respect to Mr. Bayne."

Martin appeared ready to slip through the door to the safety of his own room, but his wife stopped him.

"Wait!" she commanded. "I'm not finished yet. While we're on the subject of questionable behavior, I also have something to say about Roland."

Her husband stood suspended in mid-flight. "Yes?" he asked mildly.

Euphemia considered her words carefully. "The vision Serafina saw behind him at the séance has started me thinking in an entirely new direction about Roland. It aroused a suspicion that he may have had something to do with the death of that poor drowned girl. I can't think of any other reason for the apparition."

"Euphemia, my dear, you can scarcely condemn him because of that."

Euphemia held her hand up for silence. "I intend to make inquiries into his behavior while he worked at my factory. Perhaps Mr. Tibbs would like to perform that little service for me."

Martin opened his mouth to protest but Euphemia's cold stare silenced him.

"So help me, Martin, if anything comes to light that connects your nephew with that girl's death, being cut off without a penny will be the least of his worries. For the time being, just tell him to keep his distance from me and this house. Is that clear?"

Martin nodded silently.

"Very well then. I leave it to you to take the necessary steps regarding Roland and Mr. Bayne without any further intervention from me."

She resumed her seat before the vanity and dismissed him offhandedly as she faced the mirror. "You may retire now,

Martin." Euphemia watched as his reflection bobbed his head and made hastily for the door.

"And Martin..."

"Yes?" He paused with his hand suspended over the doorknob.

She continued to address his reflection. "After your final *tete-a-tete* with Mr. Bayne two weeks from now, I never want to see that man in my house again. Is that also understood?"

"Yes, my dear," Martin nodded vigorously. "Perfectly." Before she could offer any additional comment he scurried into his own room and closed the door swiftly behind him.

৵৹৵

Only when he was alone did Martin give way to his silent rage.

His valet was gone, so he had to undress himself. He threw off his coat and kicked it into a heap in the corner. Tugging angrily at his collar, he sent buttons snapping and flying in every direction. For a moment he contemplated smashing a lamp, a mirror, anything that would make a satisfying crashing sound. He breathed deeply several times to clear his head, to regain control. Finally, walking over to his dresser, he propped his elbows on it, running his fingers through his thinning hair, trying desperately to think of a way out.

He stared at himself in the mirror--not seeing his own reflection--seeing instead the image of a ghost with damp brown hair.

"This won't do," he muttered to himself. "This cannot continue as it has. I must take steps. I must put an end to this once and for all!"

He felt the weight of the invisible chain of his family honor grow heavier and tighter around his neck.

CHAPTER 10
Trained Troops

ය ж ৪০

Much to his chagrin, Freddie was forced to halt his desultory investigation into the death of Nora Johnson for awhile. Chicago had become the focus of national attention and every reporter in town was kept hopping. It was now the beginning of July and the Pullman strike had reached a critical stage. Despite the efforts of the Civic Federation to urge arbitration, George Pullman had remained adamant. "There is nothing to arbitrate," was his only comment. After closing his shop for the summer, he had retreated to his island castle down east.

His workers, left stranded, appealed to the American Railway Union for assistance. Because Pullman owned a few small railway lines to transport his cars, his workers were qualified to join the ARU. And join they had. On June twenty sixth, the ARU, led by its fiery president, Eugene Debs, voted to boycott Pullman cars. This meant that any train which carried a Pullman Palace sleeping car would not be manned by an engineer, fireman, conductor, or switchman who happened to be an ARU member.

As Debs repeatedly emphasized, the boycott was intended to be peaceful. Any train that uncoupled its Pullman cars was free to travel. However, the men who managed the railroads took a dim view of this arrangement. They insisted they had a contract with Pullman to carry his cars and carry his cars they would. They weren't about to let "Dictator Debs" tell them how to do business. Debs ordered his men to quietly walk off the job. If the railroads hired replacements, they were entitled to do so. The ARU would not resort to violence. Unfortunately for Debs, the ARU, the Pullman strikers, and the citizens of Chicago, things didn't work out as planned.

Unbeknownst to the major players in the drama, the starvation winter of 1894 had curiously affected the mood of Chicago's poor. Hungry, homeless, and angry, they were looking for a target for their rage. They found it in George Pullman and the railroads. Pullman had let his workers starve while he continued to pay a six percent dividend to his shareholders and maintained a multi-million dollar capital surplus in his company. Railroad expansion was the main reason for the great depression of 1893 and the railroads were carrying Pullman cars. That was all about to change.

The ARU boycott ignited a firestorm on Chicago's south side as roving mobs sought to bring the railroad industry to its knees. Switches were spiked, trains derailed, engineers dragged from their compartments and beaten. Thousands gathered to tip over boxcars and set them on fire. The tracks that hadn't been ripped up were rendered impassable because of the twisted masses of smoking metal lying across them.

An injunction was issued to force the ARU strikers back to work. Even if Debs had obeyed, it would have made little difference. The wild fires in the freight yards were spreading too fast. There was rioting as far away as Sacramento and at many points in between. Finally, when the railroads complained that the delivery of mail was being impeded, the White House intervened. The army was sent to restore order to Chicago and get the trains moving again.

On the fourth of July, 1894, the Fifteenth U.S. Infantry, two companies of the Seventh Cavalry, and a battery of the First Artillery arrived by train from Fort Sheridan. They were quickly deployed to the terminals on the south side which had been hardest hit by the mobs--the Union Stockyards, Blue Island, and Grand Crossing. As the troops struggled to curtail vandalism in the freight yards, the passenger lines serving the embattled neighborhoods shut down, making the simple act of moving around the city increasingly difficult.

Freddie was painfully aware of the rigors of travel as he glanced down at the pedals of his bicycle. It had been years since he had attempted to ride a wheel and his balance was a bit shaky. When his editor gave him the assignment to cover troop movements at the stockyards, his first task was to improvise a means of getting there. Since traveling forty blocks on foot was hardly efficient, he pleaded with one of the boys in the print room to lend him his wheel. The price of renting the contraption was exorbitant but Freddie was in dire straits. He paid the lad three dollars and mumbled something about buying one for less as he wobbled off down Dearborn Street in search of a story.

It was ironic, he thought. The government always knew how to make a bad situation worse. While the rioting had been alarming, the mayor and governor were on the point of getting matters under control. It was only when the federal troops marched in that all hell broke loose. To arrive on the fourth of July, of all days. Freddie laughed bitterly to himself. Whose independence were they protecting? Not the ARU's, nor that of the workers at Pullman.

He turned down Van Buren Street and headed toward the lake. In the one day since the troops arrived, reports of violence had doubled. Granted, none of it had touched the Loop, but even at this distance Freddie could smell the smoke.

When he reached Michigan Avenue, an unusual sight awaited him. Directly ahead, on the green field known as Lake Park, he could see white tents. The infantry had set up camp there. They certainly had a good view, overlooking the Illinois Central tracks and Lake Michigan, with Chicago's grandest hotels at their back. It seemed like a parade ground. Gentlemen and ladies with parasols were strolling along Michigan Avenue to review the troops. Some of them waved and called out encouragement to the boys in camp.

Freddie pedaled on southward. He was finally getting a feel for the machine and his sense of balance was returning. When he reached Sixteenth Street, he decided to swing over to millionaires' row on Prairie Avenue. He was curious to see how the *hoi poloi* were dealing with this affront to their sensibilities.

The street was quiet. He supposed many of the residents had fled to their country houses until order was restored. A deathlike stillness hung over the Pullman mansion in particular. Freddie could see no movement. All the curtains were drawn. Though the lawn was trimmed, there was no sign of a caretaker either. He speculated that when George Pullman left town, no one remained behind to tell tales to the press.

Freddie became increasingly aware of the afternoon sun as it scorched his back. He was wearing a dark wool suit, not the sort of thing one ought to wear in July while cycling. He could feel sweat dampening his hat band and streaming down his temples, but he reminded himself that it would be ten times hotter when he reached his destination.

At Thirty Ninth Street, he veered west toward Halsted Street and the sprawling expanse of the stockyards. Reports had been coming into the press room all morning of various locations where mobs had formed and dispersed, so Freddie decided to head directly for the train tracks at the north end of the yards. Sooner or later, the troops would try to move a train through that point and, sooner or later, they would be met by something ugly.

When Freddie finally slowed his wheel and dismounted to survey the situation, none of the descriptions he had read prepared him for what he saw. He caught his breath in shock. Boxcars had been reduced to piles of molten metal. Several were lying on their sides, their burning remains strewn across the tracks as if tossed there by some careless giant. An engine had jackknifed where it had been derailed by a spiked switch, still coupled to the cars behind it. Its humped back gave the appearance of a beached whale.

And then Freddie saw an even more chilling sight. The face of the mob. There were thousands of men, women, and children but they all wore the same enraged expression. Many were screaming curses: at the sky, at the trains, at the troops who were bringing an engine up the one track that was still open. The men were hatless and coatless, their sleeves rolled up. Some carried ropes to topple the few cars that remained upright. Others carried half-empty whiskey bottles and staggered as they searched for the next object of their wrath.

The women were more frightening than the men: wild-eyed furies, their hair streaming in all directions, shrieking at the engine as it came into view. They reminded Freddie of pictures he had seen of the Parisian women who stormed the Bastille a hundred years earlier.

Most frightening of all were the children, their faces pinched and hardened by hate. Some, no more than toddlers, were screaming obscenities along with their elders. He glimpsed a gang of boys, about nine years old or younger, lighting fires beneath empty boxcars. Their parents must have taught them how and set them the task because the police wouldn't shoot children.

Bombarded by the violent images directly ahead of him, Freddie stepped back a few paces, almost tripping over his bicycle. He retreated to a safe distance on the other side of the street where he saw a few onlookers gathered. They were men who wore business suits and derby hats. Respectable citizens who had come to gaze at the curiosity of humanity gone mad.

Freddie smiled nervously at a short, rotund man to his left. The man sported an enormous gold watch dangling from his vest. "Hello," he offered tentatively.

"Quite a sight," the short man commented jovially. "Something to tell the grandchildren."

"Assuming we live to have any." Freddie gulped.

His companion chuckled. "It isn't us they're after. They hate the roads and the men who built them. If any of the railroad managers was to show his face in the yards, there would be a lynching for sure." He held out his hand. "Silas Mayhew, pleased to make your acquaintance."

The young man returned the greeting. "Freddie Simpson. I'm a reporter for the *Gazette*."

Mayhew nodded. "All the papers have come to the yards looking for stories lately."

"There must be several thousand people gathered here!" Freddie was awestruck.

"They come and go. I've been watching them for a few days now. They swarm around anything that's moving. They tear it up or burn it down and then go off looking for something new, somewhere else."

"Is that what's drawn them here?" Freddie pointed to an engine that was backing up to join two freight cars standing behind it. The freight cars were being guarded by about twenty soldiers carrying rifles, bayonets pointed toward the encircling crowd.

"The soldiers are trying to move the beef."

"I don't see any cattle." Freddie squinted to get a better view.

"Not the live ones, son. They come in from the west on the hoof and go out to the east as dead meat. Those two cars are packed with dressed beef on ice. Bound for New York if the troopers can manage to get 'er moving before all the ice melts."

Freddie remembered an article in the *Courier* from the day before. "Meat famine threatened in New York." He had thought the headline was absurd. Nobody was in any danger of starving to death for lack of sirloin--especially not the customers at Delmonico's, who would have to make do with lobster until their filet mignon arrived.

He realized with a start that his loquacious companion was still talking. "...and that's how it stood until this morning."

"I'm sorry, I didn't catch that."

"Why the meat cars, son, the meat cars. They've been sitting here for two days and the mob didn't want to let the ice men come through. 'Let it all rot!' they said. But that wasn't the best of it. Some idiot from one of the packing houses tried to reason with 'em."

"How?"

"He climbed up on a boxcar and started reading them the injunction." Mayhew shook with laughter until tears came to his eyes. "What a sight that was."

Freddie was shocked. "They must have tried to kill him!"

"Nope. Even they knew he had to be crazy as a bedbug to do a thing like that. One of the mob just climbed up next to him and tore that piece of paper right out of his hands. Kicked him off his soapbox, too, and that was the end of it. Just about that time, the troops came in. Uncle Sam's boys have been trying to get an engine down here ever since. Looks like they finally did it."

Mayhew nodded toward the tracks where Freddie could see that the engine had been successfully coupled to the freight cars. He could also see an officer standing on the stairs next to the engineer's compartment, his saber drawn and pointing toward the sky. "On my order! Forward, double-time, march!"

The train sprang into motion. Two dozen soldiers flanked it, bayonets still pointing at the crowd. Additional guards were posted on top of the freight cars, ready to shoot any of the mob who attempted to climb aboard. The sullen crowd drew back when the train gained speed. Its guardians broke into a run to keep up. As the engine pulled out of view, the soldiers clambered aboard to escort the train the rest of the way into the city.

After its departure, only a dozen police and deputy marshals remained behind to keep order, but there seemed to be no need. The mob had lost a locus for its anger. It began to scatter. Knots of people wandered off in different directions.

Freddie was about to mount his bicycle and go in search of an interview at the military encampment at Dexter Park when he noticed the mob gathering again. People were pointing excitedly in the opposite direction from the departed meat train. With a growing sense of horror, Freddie realized what they were pointing at. A milk train was moving slowly up the track toward them. The rear two cars of the train contained passengers. From where Freddie stood, he could see their faces pressed anxiously against the glass. They were mainly women and children. He noticed some of the rioters looking around for rocks. "Oh, my God! They wouldn't!"

Mayhew's face was grim. "Afraid they would, son. Better hope the coppers can stop 'em."

The police and marshals saw the source of the mob's interest. They rushed to reach the engine but couldn't move fast enough. Missiles were flying through the air--stones, slag, coupling pins, chunks of cinder, and even broken bits of wood. The air was torn by the sound of shattering glass, the voices of women screaming, and children crying. The engine compartment windows burst. A stone clipped the engineer on the temple, and he slid to the floor of the cab. Every window in the passenger cars was smashed as the occupants crouched down to shield themselves from flying slivers of glass.

The police began firing randomly into the mob. Several rioters slipped in pools of their own blood. A deputy marshal climbed onto the stairway of the engine compartment to defend the train. The engineer staggered to his feet in a superhuman effort to keep the train moving.

"Stay back or I'll shoot!" the marshal shouted.

A youth jumped onto the bottom stair of the engine compartment. Freddie felt a chill go up his spine when he recognized the rioter. It was Orlando from the Hyperion factory--the dark-skinned boy with acid-burned hands. Orlando's eyes held a crazed look. His clothing was torn and smeared with soot. He clutched an empty gin bottle in his left hand.

"Shoot, you coward, why don't you shoot me!" the boy screamed.

The marshal hesitated.

Orlando smashed the bottle and waved the jagged end in front of the marshal's face. "You're all cowards. You hide behind your badges and your guns and your money. Your time is coming! We're gonna kill you all!"

Orlando climbed another step, still waving the smashed bottle at the marshal. The deputy hesitated only a second longer. Then he shot the boy point-blank in the chest.

"No!" Freddie screamed and tried to run forward but Mayhew locked onto his arm and held him back. "Let it go, son. You can't help him. Nobody can."

Orlando toppled backward into the arms of the stunned rioters. They set him down on the ground. One of them checked for a pulse. "He's dead! You killed him!"

A roar rose from the mob. They crawled over the engine like ants until police at the back of the crowd started shooting again. The marshal ducked and ran. Instead of running toward the police line, he became disoriented and ran in the opposite direction. About a hundred rioters followed close on his heels.

"Oh, no," Freddie gasped.

They chased the marshal into a vacant lot where they cornered him. He waved his pistol but the mob had picked up rocks and started stoning him before he could fire another shot. The marshal went down as the crowd lunged in, kicking and beating him.

By this time, the police had caught up from the rear. They fired into what remained of the mob. This time it scattered for good, leaving the injured strewn about the field of battle to fend for themselves or be hauled into custody.

Freddie abandoned his position and ran up to where the marshal had fallen. The reporter realized with a shock that the man was gray-haired, about sixty. "Is he...?" He looked questioningly at a woman who was kneeling beside the man, attempting to wipe the blood off his face.

She shook her head. "No, he's beat up pretty bad though." She turned to the nearest cop. "You better get him to a hospital fast."

Several men raced over to carry the deputy marshal into a waiting cart. They sped off.

The train had continued its flight into the city, but Freddie ran over to where it had been, hoping to find Orlando. The boy's body was gone. The reporter sank to his knees at the spot where the youth had fallen, disoriented by the sudden silence, too stunned to move.

He knelt there for what seemed like hours before he heard a noise behind him. Thinking it was a fresh wave of rioters, he jumped to his feet. It was only Mayhew.

"Here, son. Here's your wheel." The portly man handed the bicycle over to Freddie. "Nothing else to see here. They've moved on."

Mayhew studied Freddie's face, apparently noting his stricken expression. "You knew that boy, didn't you?"

"Yes, I met him a few months ago. He lost his job during a strike at his factory. I guess his life was all he had left to lose."

"I'm sorry to hear it." Mayhew patted Freddie comfortingly on the back. "I think a lot of them that you saw here today were in the same boat as your friend. They don't figure they have anything left to lose. Might as well get some of their own back while they can. Makes 'em feel like for once in their lives, they're calling the tune." He held out a hand. "You take care now."

Freddie watched Mayhew amble away before he mounted his bicycle to head north. He knew the mob had wandered in the opposite direction to make trouble but he had no heart to chase any more stories or witness any more savagery. He had seen enough to last a good long time.

Meanwhile, as Chicago burned, George Pullman stood in the turret of his summer castle at Thousand Islands waiting for the winds to change.

CHAPTER 11
A Fair To Remember

രജ്ജ

The fires kindled during the afternoon of July fifth raged on into the evening, fed by the rioters' insatiable appetite for destruction, but the biggest disaster was yet to come. Evangeline was teaching an evening literature course when the news reached Mast House. The White City was ablaze! She immediately dismissed her class and, trailed by some of her more adventurous students, headed toward Hyde Park.

The Columbian Exposition, or White City, as it was commonly known, had been a national attraction during the summer of 1893. It outshone even the Paris Exposition of 1878 for grandeur as twenty seven million people came to Chicago to witness the eighth wonder of the modern world.

Because the exposition buildings were wooden skeletons covered with a plaster-burlap mixture called staff, they were never intended to be permanent. There had been much speculation in the press regarding the fate of the White City. The winter of 1894 weakened the abandoned structures, making them a hazard to the scores of homeless who took shelter and kindled fires there for warmth. Although the city fathers finally sold the buildings to a salvage company, no demolition had yet begun. If rumor held true about what was

transpiring eight miles south of the city, the wrecking ball
would not be required.

Since the Illinois Central had limited its passenger service
during the ARU boycott, the city elevated train was the
quickest means of making the journey. As was to be
expected, the El was jammed with standing passengers.
Evangeline could scarcely turn her head in the crush. She had
become separated from her students who had squeezed into
available spots in other cars.

"So, the White City has found a way to reclaim center
stage," she thought morosely. Her feelings about the fair had
always been mixed. While she admired the ingenuity that
went into its design, she deplored the reason for its
construction--a form of self-congratulation by the captains of
industry who financed it. These same captains of industry
with their high-handed labor practices were to blame for
Chicago's, and the nation's, current economic woes.

"Does anyone know how it started?" asked a woman's
voice behind her.

Evangeline was pinned between two taller passengers and
couldn't turn to see the speaker. Answers floated in from all
directions.

"I heard it started in the Terminal Station."

"That's right. Some little boys were playing and they came
across a fire in a corner of the building. Tried to stamp it out
but they couldn't, so they ran for help."

"Didn't do much good though. The whole building went
up in a matter of minutes. Now it's spreading."

The first woman's voice rose again. "When did it start?"

"They say around six o'clock."

Evangeline had begun teaching her class at six o'clock. She
couldn't maneuver into a position to consult the watch
pinned to her shirtwaist, but it had to be nearly seven by
now.

"Hope we get there in time for the rest of the show."
Appreciative laughter followed the comment.

Although speculation continued for the rest of the trip, no
other salient facts emerged. Evangeline would have to see for
herself.

Passengers first began to disembark at Fifty Sixth Street
and Stoney Island Avenue--the northernmost entrance to the

fairgrounds. Each succeeding cross street disgorged more spectators allowing Evangeline to breathe and turn around at last. She couldn't locate any of her students and finally gave up on the idea of reassembling her group. Instead, she would have to strike off on her own. Since the blaze had begun in the Terminal Station which was at the south end of the fairgrounds, she reasoned she would get a better view by exiting the train at Sixty Fourth Street. When she passed through the entrance gates, she realized that the view was a bit too close for comfort. She was walking right toward the heart of the blaze.

Ahead of her and to the right, she could see that the Terminal Station had completely collapsed. A strong breeze was blowing from the southwest and sparks from the original fire had been carried to adjoining structures. The Administration Building to the east of the station, which many considered the architectural jewel of the fair, was incinerated--its central dome and stately columns reduced to rubble.

The fire then jumped to the two buildings directly north-- Electricity and Mining. Since only a narrow walkway separated the two, it was inevitable that the fire would spread from one to the other simultaneously. Firemen were battling the blaze from the path between the buildings as Evangeline approached. Their hoses drew water from the lagoon and the Grand Basin--a purpose the fair's planners had never anticipated. Evangeline could hear shouts among the firemen warning each other to relinquish their efforts and come out from between the buildings. She was sickened to see one of their horses collapse and expire from smoke inhalation. The firemen had to abandon it and run for their lives before the buildings caved in around them.

Just to the west of the main blaze, other firemen were attempting to save the Transportation Building. They trained their hoses on the roof to good effect. Although part of the cornice was damaged, they kept the flames from taking the building.

"Nice evening for a stroll."

Evangeline turned with a start. "Why, Bill Mason, what on earth are you doing here?"

A rumpled, middle-aged man with a cigar dangling from his lips stepped up beside her. "You know I'm a newshound, Miss LeClair. This is big news."

Mason, a veteran reporter, had been instrumental in getting Freddie a job at the *Gazette*. He was a walking contradiction. A man of slovenly personal habits and razor keen powers of observation. Evangeline found him highly entertaining.

She eyed his cigar disapprovingly for a second. Mason's taste in cigars ran toward the cheap and acrid. After some deliberation, Evangeline decided that it hardly made a difference in the charred atmosphere that surrounded them. "Of course, I should have known. Is Freddie here with you?"

"Nope, last I heard, Junior was sent down to the stockyards to cover the rioting this afternoon. Haven't seen him since."

"I hope he's all right." Evangeline's voice held a note of concern.

"He'll be fine. Had his wheel in case things got dicey."

Evangeline stared at Mason in disbelief. "You mean to tell me that he rode into the fray on a bicycle?"

"That he did." Mason rocked back on his heels, his hands in his pockets. "Though I have to say, for once, the boy's idea made sense. With the streetcars and trains snarled up, it's the fastest way to move around the city. As a matter of fact, this area right where we're standing looked like a bicycle rally about an hour ago."

"Really?"

"Must have been a thousand people on their wheels. I suppose they'd all been out in the parks for an evening ride and they saw smoke coming from the Terminal Station." Mason puffed on his cigar speculatively. "It looks like they've moved farther north to follow the course of the fire." He offered his arm to Evangeline. "That's what we should be doing too, Miss LeClair. I'd like to be an eyewitness that lives to tell the tale."

Evangeline smiled. "Quite right, Mr. Mason. Where do you propose we go?"

He pointed to a green space past the inferno. "People have been moving to the wooded isle. I don't think any sparks will carry that far, and it's a good piece of high ground for viewing the show."

The two beat a hasty retreat from a shower of falling cinders.

As they walked toward their destination, Evangeline quizzed the reporter for details. "Rumor has it that the blaze started in the Terminal Building."

Mason nodded. "Everybody is in agreement about that, but nobody knows who's responsible."

"No chance of it being an accident?"

Mason smiled waggishly. "What do you think, Miss LeClair?"

Evangeline pursed her lips. "I think that on a day when angry mobs all over the south side are destroying railroad property, a fire kindled in the one building at the fairgrounds associated with the railroads can hardly be a coincidence."

Mason paused to grind out his cigar with the toe of his boot. "Madam, you are as perspicacious as you are beauteous."

"And you, sir, are a shameless flirt." Evangeline laughed. "Have you been here all evening?"

They resumed their stroll.

"I got here about half past six, just as the first firemen were called in. You should have seen the Administration Building go up. That was a sight. First, smoke belching out of the dome. Next, a column of fire shooting straight up in the air and then the whole thing collapsed. Not too many people had gotten here yet. Just the cyclists mostly. Funny thing though. You remember those gewgaws around the building?"

Evangeline stared at him with a puzzled expression. "The allegorical statuary?"

"That's it. You've hit it. High falutin' beaux-art nonsense. 'Water Uncontrolled' and so on. Well, what do you think but the last one standing, the one that resisted the longest before it went the way of the others, was the sculpture called 'Fire Uncontrolled.'"

"You have a sharp eye for poetic irony, Mr. Mason."

By now, they had reached their destination, crossing over the little bridge that spanned the lagoon and led to the wooded isle. The pair made for the rose garden on the

southeast tip of the island since it faced directly on the
blazing buildings.

Evangeline noticed clusters of people had taken up
different vantage points on the grass. Some sat, others
reclined, all were clearly entranced by the spectacle.

"Here's another bit of irony, for you," she offered.

Mason cocked an eyebrow, waiting.

"A year ago, crowds gathered on this very spot to witness
the evening fireworks at the fair."

Mason rubbed his chin speculatively. "After the show
tonight, I'd say those other people didn't get their money's
worth."

Evangeline found herself laughing in spite of her best
efforts to remain suitably grave.

Sounds of "ohhh" and "aaah" could be heard rising from
the crowd around them--the same reaction one usually heard
at a fireworks display.

By this time, the Mines and Electricity buildings had been
reduced to ruin and the fire had jumped to Manufacturing
and Liberal Arts. The immense structure stood directly east
of the spectators' vantage point and the flames were blasting
through it with the speed of an express train.

Evangeline could see fireman dousing the roof of the
Government Building, which stood next in line to the north,
in the hopes it might be saved. She turned to look over her
shoulder. The sky was still light enough that she was able to
observe how large the crowd had grown. People covered the
island and then lined its perimeter on the opposite shore.
Beyond them, other crowds filled the gap back to the
Horticulture Building and then formed a ring as far east as
the lakefront. Women, men, and children of every conceivable size, shape, and station in life.

"Why, there must be a hundred thousand people here!"
she exclaimed.

Mason followed her gaze. "I believe you're right. Quite a
turnout. Too bad nobody thought to charge admission for
this. Might have netted a few more pennies for the gray
wolves on the city council."

They moved along the island to track the progress of the
fire from the south end of the Manufacturing and Liberal
Arts building to the north. It consumed roofing, cornices and

pillars as it went. With a mighty crash, the roof of Machinery Hall collapsed to the south at the same moment as the last columns of the Liberal Arts structure toppled.

A small, disappointed voice rose out of the crowd. "Oh, it's all over."

A stillness settled over the island for a few moments. Then, here and there, people roused themselves for the journey home. Comments could be heard from every quarter as the multitude surged toward the exits to await the next northbound El.

"Wasn't it grand?"

"What a glorious sight!"

"A magnificent spectacle!"

"A noble end."

"Better this than the wrecking ball."

Mason offered his arm once more. "Can I escort you back to the city? I have to go to the office and write this up for tomorrow's edition."

"What a fickle town Chicago is." Evangeline sighed as she took the reporter's arm. "Two years ago, everybody was in a lather to see the buildings erected. Now they're even more excited to see them destroyed."

Mason paused to light another cigar but said nothing.

"Where do you suppose it will end?" Evangeline asked as they resumed their journey.

The newsman chuckled. "I don't guess you mean the fires."

"No, the ARU boycott and the Pullman strike."

He shrugged. "I expect it will end the way every strike has. The big money men will get their way and that'll be that."

Evangeline frowned. "I suppose you're right. In the near term, the boycott will be crushed by the federal troops which will mean the end for the Pullman strike as well. But if one takes a longer view of things, order cannot be permanently maintained through tyranny. I fear these fires signal a war that's yet to come."

"Now, there's a grim thought." Mason flicked soot off the shoulder of his coat.

"Stop a moment, please." They had reached the entrance gates. Evangeline glanced back at the smoke rising from the

demolished buildings. "Something momentous has transpired here tonight."

Bill took a long draw on his cigar. "I suppose it's not every
day you see a city, even a fake city, go up in flames."

"No, that isn't what I meant." Evangeline's voice was
pensive. "The White City was a riddle wrapped in papier
mache. The captains of industry meant for it to ask the
question of where America is heading after four hundred
years of progress."

Bill tilted his head quizzically.

"Tonight, I believe we've witnessed labor's answer."

Off in the distance at the end of the Great Basin, the
Statue of the Republic raised her soot-blackened arms in
benediction over a pile of charred rubble.

CHAPTER 12
The Solution To The Problem

છ𝕏ૡ

It was now the seventh of July. The fires continued on the south side, but everyone knew the ARU boycott was on its last legs and the Pullman strikers would soon be brought to heel. Martin Allworthy barely noticed. He had other matters to consider. This was the day he was to meet with Desmond Bayne and settle things once and for all. He stood at the sideboard in the dining room, lost in thought. Two cordial glasses and a sherry decanter stood before him. He carefully removed the stopper from the decanter and filled one of the glasses almost to the brim. Heaving a sigh, he morosely meditated on the ordeal that awaited him and the lengths to which one must go to preserve family honor. He really needed to steady his nerves. His hand trembled as he set down the decanter.

It wasn't as if this were something he would choose to do in the ordinary course of events! He had been forced to this point. Backed into a corner. It hadn't been his decision at all. Not his fault really. There was simply no other way.

He took a deep breath. Odd that the room should seem so warm. Odd that he should feel so weak at the moment when his difficulties were so nearly over. The turmoil of the past weeks, the constant terror of scandal, all soon to come to an end, once and for all.

Martin picked up the sherry and examined its clarity in the afternoon light. He swirled the glass contemplatively a few times, then, feeling dizzy, set it down again. He placed both hands on the sideboard to steady himself but could not turn his eyes away from the glass. He told himself that it was only his imagination, but the sherry continued to swirl long after he set it down. He felt almost as if he were being dragged into the vortex that came to rest at the bottom of the glass. He looked up to break his concentration, but the patterned ribbons on the wallpaper seemed to be moving as well. Live snakes intent on coiling their way unevenly up the wall. He shook his head but the vision remained. A wave of panic washed over him. Hastily, he left the room and made for the front door, where he collided with one of the maids.

"Oh, I'm sorry, sir." The girl took it upon herself to apologize for his awkwardness.

"Quite all right, Ingrid. I...I...uh...I'm going out for a breath of air." He rubbed his forehead distractedly.

"Sir, are you feeling well?" The girl advanced to touch his arm.

Allworthy recoiled. "Quite all right, I assure you." He brushed off his coat sleeve and continued toward the door.

He barely heard her as she protested, "But sir, isn't Mr. Bayne expected shortly? What are we supposed to..." The door closed behind him.

❧❦

A few minutes before four, Euphemia descended the grand staircase. Noticing the butler passing below her in the front hall, she called out, "Oh, Garrison, have you seen Mr. Allworthy?"

The butler thought a moment. "I believe I saw him last as he was entering the dining room, madame. That must have been half an hour ago."

"No matter," the lady of the house said airily. "I'll just poke my head in to see if he's there. You do know he's expecting that Mr. Bayne sometime this afternoon, don't you?"

"Yes, madame." The butler winced ever so slightly at the

mention of the name, but betrayed no further evidence of his negative opinion of Mr. Allworthy's friend.

Euphemia noticed the subtle grimace and smiled when she reached the bottom of the stairs. "I believe this is the last visit we are to expect from that gentleman."

As she passed on toward the dining room she almost imagined a jubilant tone in the butler's, "Very good, madame!"

"Martin?" she called tentatively as she opened the dining room door. Her husband was nowhere to be seen. "That's odd." With a shrug of her shoulders, she turned toward the parlor, where Serafina and tea awaited.

❧❦

Promptly at four o'clock the doorbell rang. Garrison steeled himself for what he hoped would be his final encounter with the Irish gentleman. Much to his surprise, the figure on the doorstep was not Desmond Bayne.

"Why, Mr. Roland, sir, we weren't expecting you!" He opened the door wider to admit his employer's nephew.

Roland put a cautionary finger to his lips. "It's a surprise, Garrison. I didn't tell auntie or uncle I was on my way up for the weekend."

The butler hastened to take Roland's proffered hat and coat.

"Where are they? I ought to pay my respects."

"I last saw Mr. Allworthy in the dining room, sir, and Mrs. Allworthy is in the parlor having tea with Miss Serafina."

Roland held out his overnight bag. "If you'll be good enough to take this up to my room, Garrison, I'll go say hello to uncle."

"At once, sir." The butler headed toward the stairs with Roland's valise while the young man made for the dining room.

"Uncle?" he asked uncertainly as he entered. He found no trace of his relative but he did find a decanter on a tray with two glasses. One was already filled. "Well, what have we here?" He decided to seize the opportunity that presented itself.

❧❦

Euphemia and Serafina were just getting settled when there was a light knock on the parlor door.

"Enter," Euphemia called out.

The two ladies were greeted by the sight of Roland bearing the sherry tray and its contents.

"A good day to both you lovely ladies." The young man bowed with a flourish.

Euphemia's demeanor hardly exuded a sense of welcome. "Roland, what are you doing here?"

"I came to make amends, auntie. Uncle said you were cross with me, and I came to apologize for whatever it is I did to upset you. You mustn't scowl at me so." He smiled as he set the tray down on the table. "You see, I've even brought you a peace offering." He knelt down next to his aunt's chair. "Do say you forgive me, auntie. I couldn't bear for you to be angry at me, not even for a moment."

Serafina was amused at the young man's charming audacity.

For the moment, Euphemia chose to ignore his apology. "Where did you get that sherry? Martin keeps it under lock and key."

The young man grinned. "Well, he left it out in plain view in the dining room and finder's keepers has always been my motto!"

"Oh, Roland, do get up." Euphemia seemed slightly less menacing, presumably because she didn't wish to display the full extent of her displeasure with her nephew before Serafina.

Mistaking his aunt's prudence for pardon, the young man leaped back to his feet. "Ah, I can tell you've forgiven me!" he declared ecstatically. "Here, let me finish pouring this and then I'll leave you ladies to your gossip. I know the conversation at a tea table is sacred and gentlemen aren't allowed." He placed the sherry glasses on the table.

While Roland was filling the second glass, Ingrid entered carrying a tray of cakes and tea. She bustled about setting the refreshments on the table but looked at Mrs. Allworthy in surprise when she noticed the decanter and glasses.

Euphemia apparently guessed the direction of the maid's thoughts and offered an explanation to Serafina. "You know, my dear, it's not my usual habit to serve strong drink during tea time, but since Roland has been so importunate and it's probably the only way we'll get rid of him, I believe we shall have to drink his peace offering."

Roland placed his hand over his heart. "I'm honored by your condescension, auntie."

"Yes, yes, be off with you." She waved him away impatiently. Undaunted by her peevish humor, he kissed her lightly on the cheek and left the room. "You may go as well, Ingrid," she instructed the maid. "I believe we have everything we need for the moment."

"Yes, madame." The girl dipped a curtsy and scurried back to the kitchen.

Euphemia's mood improved the minute her nephew departed. She raised her sherry glass. "Let us drink a toast, my dear. That you may continue to be the talk of the town."

"I think I am not that, surely!" Serafina protested in surprise.

"I meant it only in the most positive sense," Euphemia insisted. "You've created quite a sensation among my friends, and my wish is that your reputation may continue to expand among all my acquaintance." Euphemia smiled and touched Serafina's glass. Her guest laughed and returned the salute.

"As you wish, Mrs. Allworthy! To my reputation."

Just as the two women were about to sip their cordials, Garrison entered the room. Euphemia set her glass down. "Yes?"

"Madame, it's a quarter past four."

Euphemia consulted the Regulator clock on the wall. "Why, so it is." She lifted an eyebrow inquisitively toward the butler.

"I believe Mr. Bayne is expected at any moment, madame."

Euphemia's eyebrow did not move.

The butler continued. "Well, ahem, madame, it's just that I cannot find Mr. Allworthy anywhere, and I don't know how to dispose of the, um, gentleman, when he arrives. Will you receive him, madame?"

The expression on her face hardened to stone. "No, Garrison, I will not. You may show him into the library to wait until Mr. Allworthy reappears from wherever he has gone."

"Very good, madame." The butler bowed himself out of

the room. His parting expression suggested that he had little relish for another encounter with the dubious Mr. Bayne.

"Now, where were we?" Euphemia raised her glass again to complete the toast. "Your reputation?"

Serafina smiled and raised her glass in response. Again as they were about to sip the contents, a knock was heard at the parlor door.

"Good Lord, what is it now!" Euphemia set her glass down a second time. "Enter!"

Ingrid came into the room timidly. "Excuse me, madame, but I heard you were looking for Mr. Allworthy."

"Yes, Ingrid, and apparently so is Garrison." Euphemia sighed in exasperation.

The girl bobbed a curtsy. "I'm sorry, madame. I should have told you sooner. Mr. Allworthy went out for a walk."

"He did what!"

The sharpness in Euphemia's voice made Ingrid nearly jump out of her skin. "Madame, please forgive me, madame, for not telling you sooner, but it happened all of a sudden. He looked awful bad, madame."

"What on earth do you mean? He's expecting a visitor at any moment."

"That's what I told him, madame. But he left just the same. Said he needed to take a walk to clear his head. It's not my place to say, madame, but he looked kind of pale and sick when he walked out."

"How perverse of him. Still, I suppose, given the nature of the meeting…"

"Madame?" Ingrid waited for further instruction.

"Well, there's nothing to be done until he returns. I've already given Garrison instructions for how to deal with Mr. Bayne. Go fetch us another pot of tea, Ingrid. This one will be cold by now." Euphemia motioned her out of the room.

The girl nodded and ran for cover.

Shaking her head in irritation, Euphemia returned her attention to her houseguest. "I do apologize for all these intrusions, my dear. Shall we try just once more?" She lifted her glass.

Serafina did likewise. "We were speaking of my reputation, which you hoped would become notorious."

"That's not exactly what I meant, dear. I said I hoped you

would be the talk of the town."

"Si, is it not the same thing?" Serafina looked puzzled.

"Let's just toast to your illustrious future. I may not have the gift of second sight, my dear, but I can predict exciting times ahead for you."

The two ladies raised the glasses to their lips, this time without interruption. Euphemia swallowed half the contents of hers. Serafina was just about to do the same but set her glass down when she noticed a strange expression on her hostess's face. The odd expression was soon followed by an event even more unaccountable. Euphemia fell to the floor clutching at her throat, gasping for breath.

"Oh, my dear lady, what is this?" Serafina rose and rushed over to the other side of the table. Her hostess's eyes were shut and her limbs began to twitch and contract in violent spasms. She appeared to be suffering from some sort of seizure.

"*Mio Dio!* What can be the matter!" Serafina immediately ran to the kitchen to find help. She returned with Ingrid and Garrison, who were greeted by the sight of their mistress rolling around on the floor in convulsions, frothing at the mouth.

"Good Lord!" was Garrison's only exclamation as he rushed from the house to fetch a doctor. His efforts were to prove in vain, for when he returned fifteen minutes later with Doctor Fowler, Mrs. Allworthy was quite dead.

❧❦

Martin had taken what he hoped would appear to be a casual stroll along Aurora Avenue. His heart was racing, his head was dizzy, and when passersby greeted him, he could barely murmur a furtive hello in return. He must have been gone the better part of a half hour before the world ceased to spin before his eyes. He had walked all the way to the train station by the time he belatedly remembered that Bayne was expected any moment and that he had better return and settle matters with him. Bracing himself, he turned back and retraced his steps.

As he rounded the corner from Pleasantview to Aurora, he glimpsed a female figure strolling directly toward him. When he neared the gravel walk to his own front door, he was confronted by the not altogether welcome sight of Evangeline LeClair making for the same destination.

"Why, Martin, what a surprise." Her voice held the degree of enthusiasm one would expect from a lady who had just discovered a spider crawling up her parasol.

"I might say the same." Martin's tone was equally enthusiastic. "Calling on my wife, are you?"

Evangeline nodded curtly. "Yes, I thought I might drop by to belatedly thank her for the dinner party you gave a few weeks ago. I haven't been able to tear myself away from obligations in the city until now. I do hope she's not engaged."

Martin opened the door and gestured for her to precede him.

Neither was prepared for the spectacle that the open door revealed.

Servants were running to and fro to no apparent purpose. Roland stood back against the wall, looking vaguely off into space, his hands in his pockets. Serafina sat in the hallway, slumped forward in her chair. Doctor Fowler hovered next to her, vainly attempting to check her pulse.

Garrison scurried forward with a cold compress for the medium's head, while two other servants were carrying a heavy object covered by a sheet through the front hall.

"What in God's name is going on here!" Martin exclaimed in shock.

"What indeed!" Evangeline echoed.

The two servants nervously dropped the object on the floor with a loud thud when they heard the tone of their master's voice.

Doctor Fowler looked up from his ministrations long enough to recognize who was addressing him. He relinquished Serafina's hand and took Martin aside.

"I'm afraid I have some unhappy news for you, Mr. Allworthy. I believe your wife has been poisoned to death."

CHAPTER 13
Suspect Behavior

౧ℋ౭

Desmond Bayne wove his way unsteadily up the stairs to his apartment building. He had achieved a mellow state of intoxication in which the world looked much more pleasing as it grew more out of focus. He looked up briefly at the foggy corona surrounding the streetlight outside his door. It afforded him little assistance as he conducted a thorough search of his person, endeavoring to locate his latchkey. Once having found it, he made a fierce attempt to focus his eyes as he held the object up to the light, striving to establish which end was up. His scowl deepened into a look of fixed attention as he then tried to fit the key into the lock--an operation far trickier than it might seem to a teetotaler by the sober light of day.

Hunched over the lock, deep in concentration, he did not see the shadow glide up next to him and put a stealthy hand on his shoulder.

"Saints preserve us!" he yelped, dropping the key in the process.

"Keep your voice down!" The shadow placed a warning finger over Bayne's lips. "I've been waiting for you for hours!"

Bayne squinted in the gloom, trying to identify the man who had accosted him. After several seconds his feeling of terror was replaced by one of mawkish pleasure. "Faith, if it isn't Marty himself! Marty, what're ye doing here? Come to pay old Desmond a visit in the wee hours of the morning?"

Allworthy ignored the greeting. "Where were you this afternoon?"

"This afternoon. This afternoon?" Bayne repeated thickly. "Let's see, what day is it now?" He began to count on his fingers. "Monday, Tuesday..."

"It's Saturday! This afternoon you were to come to my house in the country. Where were you?"

Desmond took off his derby and scratched his head. The fog was parting, albeit slowly. "Was it today I was to come to the country? Faith, was it really today?" He sat down heavily on the front stoop to ponder the matter further.

"Yessss!"

"How did the day get away from me?" Desmond asked in wonderment.

Allworthy, clearly not in a mood to reply to rhetorical questions, plucked Bayne impatiently by the elbow and attempted to raise him. "We don't have time for this now! I need to talk to you. Something has happened!"

Bayne made a superhuman effort to follow the movement of Allworthy's lips as they mouthed the words. "Talk?" he echoed hazily. "Why, Marty, I'm all ears. Whatever you have to say to me"--

Allworthy cut in. "Not here. I don't want to discuss this in the middle of the street. Besides, I need a drink. Are there any saloons in the neighborhood still open at this time of night?"

Desmond laughed and slapped his knee in delight. "Now, that's the spirit. I can name two or three right off the top of me head. Just help me up, and I'll be showing you the way."

అ~ఆ

Allworthy refused to answer any of Bayne's incoherent questions until they had found shelter in a dark corner of one of Desmond's favored establishments--the Green Mill. At two in the morning, there were few other patrons left and those few were too deep in their cups to bother to look up as the pair slid through the door. Before Bayne could saunter up to the bar and resume his drinking bout, Martin led him straight to a booth in the back corner.

As the two settled themselves, Bayne asked magnanimously, "What'll ye have? Say the word and I'll fetch it. Nothing's too good for me old friend Marty!"

Allworthy looked furtively around the dim, smoky den. He squirmed in his seat trying to find a comfortable position, but the plank booth was unyielding. It creaked and groaned at each move but offered no relief. The sole of his shoe had come into contact with something sticky on the floor, but he had no desire to inspect the area beneath the table for fear of what he might find. He sighed in resignation. "You may bring me a bottle of whiskey and a glass. Get yourself a cup of coffee."

"Paugh!" Bayne spat. "Vile witches' brew, that is!"

"Nevertheless, you'll drink it this evening. I need you to be sober for what I have to tell you."

Martin could see that Bayne's intoxication had subsided to the extent that he could smell an opportunity in whatever Allworthy was about to disclose. An opportunity that he might be able to translate into cash. Without further objection, he retrieved the order from the bartender.

Allworthy waited until Bayne had grimaced his way through three cups of coffee and begun to show signs of returning mental activity. He also waited for the two shots of whiskey he himself had drunk to have their effect in calming his own rapid heartbeat.

Eventually, it appeared as if Bayne's vision had lost its ability to multiply copies of every object it perceived. His head no longer bobbed and weaved like a cross-eyed cobra. As his ability to focus improved, he was evidently struck by the expression on Allworthy's face. "By all the saints, Marty! You look pale as a sheet, that you do. Something terrible must have happened. What is it, boyo? Tell old Desmond and we'll set it to rights."

Lowering his voice to a barely audible whisper, Martin began. "My wife is dead."

"Wha...what's that you say?" Bayne must have thought his ears, as well as his eyes, were playing tricks on him.

"My wife is dead and I am suspected of killing her."

Any vestiges of inebriation that remained prior to Martin's

last statement were effectively banished. Bayne stared at Martin with a look of cool appraisal. "And did you do it, lad?" Allworthy grew flustered. He stared down at the table. "Well...I...uh...I..."

"Which is it then? Yes or no. Tisn't the sort of question that can be answered by a maybe."

Allworthy looked askance at Bayne. He took a deep breath and tried again. "It's terribly complicated and I really can't' explain."

"Oh, ho!" Bayne laughed. "So that's how it is. Say no more, Marty, say no more. Ye needn't tell me aye or nay. I can guess right enough. Let's us just talk in hypotheticals for now. Tell old Desmond what may have happened."

Allworthy nodded. "Suffice it to say that it was an accident. An unfortunate accident. I was in the process of pouring a glass of sherry in the dining room, but I felt a bit dizzy and set it down. I needed a breath of fresh air and so I left the house. To clear my head, you see. Just to clear my head. After I left, someone served the sherry to Euphemia with poison in it. When I got back to the house, she was dead and the doctor was already there, and he suspected foul play and ordered an autopsy, and that insufferable LeClair woman showed up to witness it all." Martin's voice had taken on a panicky note.

Desmond seemed mystified. "But how did the doctor come to be there so quick, and how did he know it was poison?"

Allworthy rubbed his face distractedly. "Because of a wretched chain of events that shouldn't have occurred, that's how. Euphemia had gone to see this Doctor Fowler in Shore Cliff only a few days ago. For her nerves. I knew nothing about it. She told this doctor she was upset about business matters at the factory, and she needed something to calm her. He recommended laudanum, but he also examined her and pronounced her to be physically healthy as a horse. So when he arrived and found her in convulsions, he knew she had no physical condition that would cause such symptoms."

"But the poison, man, the poison? How could he know of it?"

Allworthy squirmed about uncomfortably once more in the rigid wooden booth. "Because there were witnesses who saw her fall into a fit immediately after she drank from the cordial glass. And because there is a particular type of poison, cyanide, that gives off a faint odor of bitter almonds. As fate would have it, the doctor detected it." Martin hastily gulped down another shot of whiskey. "Before I knew what was happening, the doctor had already given orders to take the remaining contents of the sherry glasses and decanter for analysis. My sherry glasses! My decanter! From my liquor cabinet which is kept under lock and key! It's bound to look bad for me."

"But nothing's proved, man! You were out of the house when it happened. You didn't hand her the glass. That's the one to pin it on."

Martin equivocated. "An argument could be made that I left the sherry in plain sight intending that she should drink it, or that I intended to serve it to her but was interrupted on the way. Besides, none of the people milling about in the house had any reason to kill her."

Bayne scratched his head in perplexity. "But neither had you, boyo. You'd no reason to go killing your own wife now."

Allworthy's face took on a pinched expression. "In the normal course of events, one might assume that to be true. But there were certain aspects of our marriage agreement that were rather unconventional and might be construed as a motive."

"Construed? Who'd be construing them?"

"Ah, that's the worst part of it. Let me finish and you'll see who."

Bayne put a cautionary finger to his own lips. "Aye, aye, I'll shut pan. Go on and tell me the rest of it, Marty."

"As I was saying, by the time I got back to the house, the doctor had already called the sheriff. He arrived shortly and began asking everyone questions. And Evangeline LeClair was still hovering around."

"LeClair?" Desmond repeated the name. "Is it somebody I know?"

Martin regarded Bayne with a feeling of cold disgust. "Yes, you've seen her on at least two occasions, though I think you were too intoxicated to notice either time. She's a beady-eyed spinster who makes a habit of sticking her nose into other people's business and lecturing them on how they ought to conduct their affairs."

"Oh." Desmond stared off at the back of the booth behind Martin's head, obviously still trying to match a face to the name as Allworthy continued.

"Well, I attempted to point out to the sheriff that she really wasn't involved and had just arrived at the same time I did, but he would have none of it. Insisted on taking statements from everyone. Garrison, Ingrid the maid, Doctor Fowler, that medium Serafina, LeClair, and myself."

Desmond, presented with this new barrage of names, began to mumble to himself and count on his fingers-- presumably in the hope that enumerating the number of witnesses would help him remember who some of them were.

"Ahhh!" Martin waved his hand in disgust and fumbled in his coat pocket for his cigarette case. After he had soothed his nerves by drawing in as much smoke as his lungs would hold, he continued. "I kept watching her out of the corner of my eye--"

"Who's that, Marty?" Desmond's brain evidently had trouble containing the number of characters introduced into the narrative.

"Why that pestilential LeClair woman, of course! Every time the sheriff let one of the others come out of the parlor, she'd pounce and start whispering her own questions. Insinuating things that never happened, you can be sure. Jogging their memories to fancy all kinds of suspicious behavior in me. Mark my words, she won't be content until she sees me swinging from the gallows!"

"Marty, Marty, me boy!" Desmond adopted a conciliatory tone in an effort to reassure him. He eyed the whiskey bottle enviously.

Martin scarcely registered the direction of Bayne's interest. "Do you know what she did next?"

"Indeed, I don't." Bayne's hand crept across the table toward the object of his desire. "But I'm hangin' on every word, that I am. Here, let me fill yer glass again."

Too caught up in the outrage perpetrated against his good name, Martin hardly noticed as Desmond decanted the whiskey into the shot glass and then his own coffee cup.

"After the sheriff announced that he wanted everyone to

remain available for more questioning, she piped up and said it was unsuitable to allow an unmarried woman to remain as a house guest in the Allworthy villa now that the lady of the house was deceased."

"Who'd she mean?"

"Why, that Serafina woman, of course! That charlatan of a medium! She was our house guest. She was having tea with Euphemia when the whole thing happened!"

"Serafina?" Desmond rubbed his forehead. "Do I know her?"

Martin steadied his nerves, not having the strength to remind Bayne of the circumstances of their prior meeting. "No!" he said flatly. "I know what she's up to. She doesn't give a tinker's dam about propriety. It's just a ruse."

"Who doesn't give a tinker's dam?" Desmond appeared to be completely muddled by Martin's dexterity with pronouns.

"Evangeline LeClair, of course! How often must I repeat myself?" Allworthy sighed and tried to elucidate matters more plainly to the simpleton seated across from him. "She just wanted to get Serafina out of the house so she could siphon out every detail of what happened and turn the facts against me. That's all."

"Oh..." Desmond trailed off, his concentration broken, no doubt, by the aroma of whiskey emanating from his coffee cup.

"Well, she succeeded. The sheriff ordered Serafina's maid to pack an overnight bag for her, and LeClair whisked her off for safekeeping to her own house."

"Hmmm." Desmond attempted to sound ponderously intelligent when in fact he had lost the thread of the story yet once more."...but she couldn't resist one parting shot. The final nail in my coffin."

"Eh, what's that Marty, I didn't catch that last bit."

Martin ground out his half-smoked cigarette and lit another. "LeClair. Perdition take her! She turned to leave, but just before she went, she wheeled around as if she'd forgotten something. Forgot, my foot! She had it planned. Innocently, almost casually, she turns to me in the presence of the sheriff and says, 'Oh Martin, I understand that the family fortune was held by Euphemia in her own right. Now that she's gone, who stands to inherit?' You could have heard a pin drop in that room. Everyone was standing there looking at me. I decided to put a bold face on things. 'I do,' I said. She looked like the cat who swallowed the canary. 'I see,' she said. 'Is that a fact,' the sheriff said. You could tell from the way he was looking at me that she'd done a proper job of making me the prime suspect! It's the same as if she had just stood up and announced 'Martin Allworthy is the only person in this house who had a motive to kill Euphemia!'"

Martin's hands were shaking as he tried to hold the cigarette to his lips.

"Marty, lad, ye mustn't carry on so. She's only a wee little woman."

"Only a woman, you say? Let me tell you, I fear that wee little woman, as you call her, more than I fear the devil himself! She's as clever as Old Nick and twice as tenacious. I heard she solved a murder once. The last thing I need is a female detective dogging my every move and unearthing facts that are nobody's business but mine. I won't have a moment's peace unless I can get rid of her insinuations once and for all."

"Here, have another sip. It'll do you no harm." Desmond plied them both with another round. Martin no longer cared that Desmond's cup was filled to the brim with something other than coffee. Allworthy was preoccupied in rubbing the back of his neck. His shirt collar chafed as if it were made of sandpaper.

Bayne continued affably. "And tell me now, how do you plan to get rid of those, how do ye call 'em, insinuations of hers?"

Martin leaned forward over the table. "That's where you come in. I need you to take care of a few things for me."

"Aha! Now the mist begins to part and I see daylight, sure enough! Marty, boy, you've hit upon me true calling in life. I have a natural gift for setting things to rights." Desmond lowered his voice to a whisper. "Though I must say with the trail o' corpses you're leavin' behind, you might do better to hire a man in a white uniform with a push broom to follow you round town."

"I'm sure you'll do well enough." Allworthy drew himself up, the picture of offended dignity.

Desmond's eyes showed a hint of calculation as he

regarded his companion. "You do know I'll be needin' to drive the price up a bit. Silence is a dear commodity these days."

Allworthy laughed bitterly. "Yes, I'd anticipated a price increase. I'm prepared to pay the going rate for services rendered."

"And what might those services be, lad. What's in yer mind?"

Martin looked quickly around the bar to make sure no one was within earshot.

"I want you to give Miss LeClair something besides me to be concerned about. This is what you'll need to do..."

CHAPTER 14
Four Tolled

❧ ❀ ☙

Evangeline heard the grandfather clock from the staircase landing as it chimed the hour. Four o'clock in the morning. She had heard its predictable reproach at fifteen minute intervals ever since midnight. Still she sat motionless, wide awake in the small parlor, staring out into nothingness. Monsieur Beauvoir, utterly untroubled by insomnia in others, lay curled in her lap asleep. Evangeline noted with mild irritation that he was the only cat she had ever encountered whose sonorous breathing could rival a human snore. The steady drone seemed to rebuke her own lack of composure.

She had extinguished all the lights in the room and, as the evening was mild, had opened the windows. The full moon cast a phosphorescent glow across the lawn, dimmed now and again by clouds scudding across its face. Trees sent encroaching shadows into the room and across the parlor rug—dark shapes that shook and quivered in the wind and sometimes disappeared altogether as each new cloud obscured the moon. Lace curtains billowed in a strong western breeze, undulating on the air currents like indecisive spectral visitors. The wind carried a hint of dampness, of rain falling somewhere far off in the distance.

"A strange night," Evangeline mused to herself,

"succeeding a day of even stranger events." She thought of the incidents that had transpired no more than twelve hours before. She thought of an innocent social call that had quickly escalated into a full-blown murder investigation. She thought of Euphemia Allworthy--an amusing and vital woman—-transformed into an inert mound of flesh under a white sheet on the floor of her own foyer while a bizarre procession of strangers traipsed through her home. She thought of Euphemia's servants--Ingrid twisting her apron in a knot of helpless regret, Garrison clearing his throat and trying to maintain his *sang froid* in the face of disaster. She thought of Roland, vague and staring off into space unless someone asked him a direct question. Most of all, she thought of Martin--nervous, shocked, outraged by the intrusion of chaos into his well-ordered life. Of all the many emotions she had watched Martin display that afternoon, why could she recollect no expression of grief among them? It was made conspicuous by its absence. Odd. Very odd indeed.

Evangeline's ruminations were cut short by the creaking sound of the parlor door opening. Monsieur Beau, immediately vigilant to the sound of an intruder, lifted his head, ears perked forward. Evangeline turned her face languidly toward the door, expecting Delphine to approach and scold her for being up so late. Instead, she saw a slighter shape bearing a night light.

"Excuse me. Have I disturbed your quietness?" a sing-song voice asked.

"No, Serafina." Evangeline smiled wearily. "Please come in and sit down if you like. I couldn't sleep."

The medium, who was barefoot and dressed in a nightgown and cotton shawl, came to sit in the armchair opposite Evangeline. She placed the lamp carefully on the table between them, dimming it so that the shadows in the corners of the room, which had been briefly held at bay since her entrance, re-emerged. The feeble light flickered uncertainly and reflected off the pallid faces of the two women who now sat regarding one another.

"It's been quite an eventful day, hasn't it?" Evangeline offered.

"Yes, that is so." The medium seemed on the verge of

saying more but thought better of it.

Monsieur Beau chose that moment to announce his presence to the visitor. He jumped down from his place on Evangeline's lap and perched himself on the arm of Serafina's chair. He looked at her curiously, head tilted to one side-- purring.

Evangeline raised her eyebrows in mild surprise. "Well, that's out of character for him. He's usually reserved around strangers."

The medium solemnly stroked the cat's head. "Our little protectors," she murmured.

The mistress of the house smiled at her pet's unabashed flirtation with the visitor. "Why do you say that? Since I don't fear mice, I seriously doubt he could protect me from much of anything."

"No, I do not mean the body. God made them to protect us from lies--the cats, the dogs, and all such animal friends-- because they are honest."

Evangeline laughed ruefully. "I believe you're right. They don't seem to have the gift for emotional deception that humans are blessed with in such abundance. Whether they love you or hate you, they don't lie about it. Insincerity is a peculiarly human trait."

By now Beau had hopped into Serafina's lap, eyes glazing over in bliss while she rubbed his ears. "They do not fool us, and they do not fool themselves about us. They always know the good people from the bad."

Evangeline contemplated the idea. "It certainly makes them ideal companions. I can't imagine a heaven without animals in it, can you? As for our little friend's ability to ferret out dishonesty, maybe I should just put him on a leash and let him find Euphemia's murderer for me. Or better yet" - -she brightened in the gloom-- "I suppose I could just ask you. After all, you're gifted with the second sight. The truth should be child's play for you while I have to dig and dig for clues."

Serafina looked over the wavering light at Evangeline. Her face was troubled. "If only I could help. Once it would have been easy. But something has happened."

"What do you mean?"

"My guides, they have abandoned me. They will not come

into the presence of such great distress."

The lantern flame hesitated and retreated still further from the drafty air currents, throwing vague shadows across Serafina's face.

"Whose distress?" Evangeline asked.

"My own." Serafina's voice was heavy with dejection. "I cannot help it. It was because..." She winced, recalling the moment. "Because I was there to watch Madame Euphemia when she--"

Evangeline intercepted the memory. "Yes, it must have been awful to witness that."

"*Si*, you understand," the medium agreed readily. "When people ask me to tell them the future, I close my eyes and I can see..."

"What?"

"Pictures of their days ahead but now when I close my eyes, all I can see...all I can see is a picture from the past. Madame Euphemia and her face as it looked in her last moments. It was like...like...what is the English word for this monstrous thing? I can remember when I was little, I saw one crouching on the roof of a church, and it frightened me so. With wings like a bat and a terrible, evil smile. Like a devil made of stone...like...oh, what is the word?" She shook her head, trying desperately to remember.

"Like a gargoyle," her companion offered quietly. The mental picture was unnerving enough to Evangeline even though she had not been present to see Euphemia's convulsions. She could only imagine the effect it might have on a sensitive nature like Serafina's.

"I have too much feeling here." The medium put her hand over her heart. "And the feeling is all bad." She ran her fingers through her hair distractedly. "All bad. Even in my nightmares I never saw such a thing as terrible as this. And my guides will not return until I am peaceful again." The medium paused. "I very much liked Madame Euphemia. She had a most generous spirit."

"Indeed she had," Evangeline agreed sadly.

"And I am more sorry still that I could not stop this thing from happening. I have taken this matter much to my conscience." Serafina sighed heavily. "Even at the séance, I could not understand the picture that I saw." She raised her hands helplessly.

Evangeline jumped in. "Ah yes, I recall. You saw a glass falling from her hand and shattering on the floor."

"But I did not see the true meaning of that vision. It was not the glass that fell and shattered, it was she who fell. I did not know how to warn her, and now it is too late."

Evangeline sat forward. "Serafina, it wasn't your fault. You mustn't think that!"

The medium looked down at the floor. "I have been given this gift of second sight for a purpose. It is to help people so they can avoid harm. But I could not help her and I am sorry for it."

"Well, if it's any comfort, I don't think the murderer will be at liberty for long. Even if you can't help confirm my suspicions, I'm fairly certain I've narrowed the field to two possible culprits."

Serafina looked at Evangeline in surprise.

"Well, it's either Roland or Martin."

"You are so sure?"

Evangeline shrugged matter-of-factly. "Who else had a motive? I've sat here all night remembering every detail of what I saw today. Though of the two, Martin's behavior was certainly more suspicious. Especially after I watched how he carried on this afternoon. He and I walked into the house together and both were confronted with the sad news at the same moment. He didn't act like a grief-stricken husband. He acted like an outraged landowner who sees too many strangers traipsing through his property after he's posted a 'No Trespassing' sign."

"Perhaps that is just his way."

"I doubt it. He used every means at his disposal to obstruct the investigation from the start. Didn't you notice how he argued that the doctor had no right to order an autopsy? He objected even more strenuously when he was informed that Sheriff Weston was on his way over. He wanted to send Roland packing the minute the sheriff was through questioning him. He didn't want the servants questioned at all, and above all, he didn't want me there to see any of it."

"Why would this be?" The medium sounded puzzled.

Evangeline explained. "Perhaps you don't remember what you told me at the séance. You said being a detective was my destiny in life."

Serafina nodded her agreement.

"Unfortunately, under these sad circumstances, it now appears that prediction is coming true. My friend Freddie and I solved a murder awhile back. We pointed the finger at some former friends who live hereabouts. I'm sure Martin must have heard rumors about our last investigation and he's afraid I may discover something."

"Did you see anything that the others did not notice?"

"I think I may have done. Martin and I walked into the parlor together. I remember I looked at his face. The first place his eyes went was to the table. He saw the cordial glasses and decanter sitting there on a tray. I was struck by his expression of sheer horror. His face turned a ghastly pale. He appeared about to move toward the table when the doctor came up behind us and said nothing in the room was to be touched until the sheriff arrived."

"But perhaps he was only upset to see the place where his wife had died. Perhaps it was grief."

"Perhaps it was guilt," Evangeline countered. She paused, thinking aloud. "And yet, he wasn't in the house when the poison was administered. Perhaps he's covering for Roland. Why else would he want his nephew out of the house so quickly? Roland was the one who actually served Euphemia the sherry. I'm sure he had a motive too. Since you told me he brought the cordials in as a peace offering, he'd probably had a rift with his aunt. Maybe she'd threatened to cut off his inheritance. Maybe she suspected he was somehow involved in the drowning at Hyperion. You did, after all, see that poor girl's ghost hovering behind his chair at the séance. If I was able to put two and two together, I'm sure Euphemia did as well." Her voice held a note of anxious appeal. "Can you help me understand this? Can you sense anything at all about which one of them did it?"

Serafina squeezed her eyes shut tight for a moment. She seemed to be engaged in a mental battle with herself to overcome the image that was ever-present to her, to try to see beyond the horror of Euphemia's last moments. When she reopened her eyes, they held an expression of despair. "It is no use. She is still with me. I can only see a little beyond. Flashes of things here and there. Jumbled pictures that make no sense. Of the young Roland, I can see nothing at all. Of Mr. Allworthy, all I see is fear. He is haunted by something even worse than what I feel. As before, I see him with a heavy weight of chains around his neck, around his back. But this time I see him in water."

"A pool?" Evangeline prompted.

"No, deep water. Like a river or lake or maybe even an ocean. His feet do not touch the bottom. He is terrified of something. He can swim but the weight of these chains is very heavy and that is what pulls him down. I do not see what surrounds him, but I feel that he will pull down whoever is near him to keep his own head above the water."

"Interesting." Evangeline looked up as a strong gust of wind stirred the curtains to life. They billowed like sails. "I'm sure he'll do something to cover his tracks, or Roland's for that matter."

"Maybe that is an explanation for my dream."

"Your dream?"

"Yes, that is why I came looking for you." Serafina's voice became urgent. "I wished to find you, to tell you. It is the only clear image I have had of anything since this terrible tragedy happened. It was so clear it woke me up, and sometimes when a dream is strong the feeling of it will stay with me for many hours after I wake. You have felt like this, perhaps?"

"Yes, that's one reason why I prefer not to remember my dreams if I can help it."

"This dream, you were in it as well."

"Really?" Evangeline sat forward on the couch, intrigued.

"It was night. Very late, as it is now. You and I, we were standing in a small field, and the field was surrounded by water."

"An island in the middle of a river?"

Serafina frowned in deep concentration, trying to recall the image. "It was not exactly so. The water ran around and around the land. Where it started, it also ended."

"More like a moat around a castle," Evangeline offered helpfully.

"Yes, it was like that. A ring of water around a field, and we stood in the middle of this field."

"Just like the bull's-eye of an archery target."

"Unfortunately, that is like what it was. For the arrow tries to find the bull's-eye of a target, does it not?"

"Yes," Evangeline confirmed guardedly. "I don't particularly like the analogy. Are we the target?"

"I fear something like this. Though it is not an arrow. This place that I was speaking of. We are standing in the middle of it in high grass. And all around I hear sounds that are like...like..." she paused, casting about for the right word. "Like a hissing and slithering."

"You mean snakes in the grass?"

"Yes, yes!" Serafina agreed intensely. "That is the picture. There are snakes crawling everywhere around us, but it is dark and the grass is high, and it is very hard to see where they are hiding."

"Are we in any danger?" Evangeline was disturbed by the image.

"I fear so, for these snakes all have poison in their fangs. Wherever we walk, if we tread on them, they will strike."

"Well, that's disconcerting. What happened next?"

"In my dream, you took me by the hand and said, 'Look, Serafina, there is a path here. We can go this way. You see, there is a boat down by the water if we can only get to it. I will show you.'"

"And then?" Evangeline urged.

"And then I woke up," the medium finished weakly. "I heard the clock strike and...and...that is all."

"How very disappointing." Evangeline had gone from being enthralled to mystified. "What do you make of it?"

"That is what I came to tell you. I think there is danger coming to us. To you and to me in the days ahead. But my dream is saying you will find a path for us to get away from this deadly place. You will know what to do."

"I suppose that's meant to be comforting, but I have no idea how your premonition will unfold or what I'm meant to do when the time comes."

"It is enough for me to know that you will pick out a path for us. You will find a way for us to get to safety."

"Let's hope so, though I'm not sure your confidence in my ability as a scout is justified." Evangeline shivered as the breeze gusted the curtains once more. She rubbed her arms to keep warm and rose to leave. "I think I'll try to sleep for a few hours. I doubt anything I meet in my dreams will be as disturbing as what I've just heard. Are you coming?"

"No, I believe I will stay here for some while longer with our little friend. He is so calm, perhaps I will catch the sleepiness, too."

Monsieur Beau had begun his sonorous breathing again, a signal that he was now slumbering in the medium's lap. Serafina stroked the cat's neck. He stretched briefly in his sleep.

"He is smiling. Do you know that cats can smile?" she asked.

"Yes, I've often observed it. Whenever I mention that fact to other people, they look at me as if I've taken leave of my senses."

"They have eyes but they do not see." Serafina quoted Scripture, evidently thinking once again of her own obscured vision.

"Still, I suppose that in order to see something you have to be looking for it in the first place."

"Perhaps that is what the Christ was saying, too."

Evangeline laughed. "Yes, but I doubt the subject under discussion at the time was smiling cats." She paused and looked at her guest fixedly for a moment. "Will you be all right?"

Serafina nodded. "*Si*, it will take time, but all will be well."

Evangeline relaxed her concern slightly. "Good night, then." She walked toward the door. "You needn't wish me pleasant dreams. I've had enough waking nightmares to last me quite awhile."

CHAPTER 15
Portrait Of A Lady Suitable
For Framing

ﻌﺠﻌ

Even though Evangeline had slept to the unheard-of hour of ten o'clock in the morning, sleep had done little to dispel the fatigue and foreboding that had pursued her since the previous evening. Her dissipated state was at least partially due to the manner in which Delphine startled her into consciousness by sweeping peremptorily into the bedroom, raising the shades to a glaring burst of sunlight, and huffing several times about the deleterious effects to the complexion of sleeping late. To this Evangeline retorted that she was in more immediate danger of the deleterious effects of a heart attack after being shocked awake in such a rude manner. Delphine, having created as much distress as she possibly could to ensure that her mistress was completely alert, left the room highly satisfied.

When the lady of the house finally could bring herself to stumble over to her dressing room mirror, she scarcely believed anyone would take notice of her sallow complexion since the shadows beneath her eyes dominated every other feature. She sighed, rose to the occasion and made a supreme, though futile, effort to repair the damage with several layers of face powder. After this she went downstairs to see if her house guest had breakfasted.

When she inquired of Delphine as to Serafina's whereabouts, the housekeeper sniffed that Mademoiselle Serafina and her maid had gone to mass, as all good Catholics ought to have done on Sunday. Since this was an old bone of contention between the housekeeper and her employer, the latter wisely decided not to rise to the bait. She simply wasn't up to the challenge on an empty stomach. Ignoring the comment, and with as much dignity as she could muster, she asked Delphine if her own breakfast had been arranged or if she was to suffer the pangs of hunger along with fatigue for the rest of the morning.

Delphine, somewhat mollified by the sight of her lady's ravaged appearance, hinted that she might find something to her liking in the breakfast room. "*Tu vois, cherie*, it is just as I have said. You see what comes of staying up all night and sleeping *jusqu'apres-midi*. You see how you suffer for it, but I say no more."

With Delphine's eloquent silence reverberating in her ears, Evangeline went to restore her still-frayed nerves by partaking of some croissants and café au lait.

అ•ఈ

Serafina returned shortly before noon to find her hostess in the conservatory, inspecting a pot of lilies which had just begun to bloom. Several vats of coffee had artificially restored her characteristic esprit, and Evangeline was humming to herself as she tended the flowers.

"You do not go to church?" the medium asked in surprise.

Evangeline smiled ruefully. "Not since I was at school. Traditional religion and I don't get on well. I confess I'm somewhat surprised that you attend, given the nature of your occupation. The church doesn't exactly smile on such endeavors."

The medium shrugged. "What the good priests think is not so important as what God thinks. I do not tell them what they do not need to know. On this day above all, I thought it would be a good day for praying."

"To which I say a hearty 'Amen.' I would also add that today is a good day for a drive in the country. I guarantee it will banish that solemn look from your face." Evangeline's eyes held a twinkle. "I can have Jack bring the carriage round if you like. A drive through green fields might help clear the cobwebs out of both our heads."

Serafina smiled broadly. It was the first sign of cheerfulness Evangeline had noticed since the tragedy the day before. Taking the smile as a sign of assent, the lady of the house decided the matter. "Yes, I think that would be just the thing." She rang for the carriage, instructing Jack to put the top down on the barouche as the weather had continued fine.

ॐॐ

Late that afternoon, in a more rested and sanguine frame of mind, the ladies returned from their outing. No sooner had Evangeline descended from the carriage than her brief good humor was extinguished by a most unexpected sight. A lanky, gray-haired man with a drooping mustache and a crumpled slouch hat stood on the sidewalk in front of her home. He appeared to be on his way to her front door, but when he saw the carriage round the corner, he stopped and waited for the occupants to alight.

"Afternoon, ladies." The lanky man ambled over in their direction, hat in hand. His voice contained the faintest remnant of a southern drawl.

Evangeline watched nervously as Jack handed Serafina out of the carriage. The medium remained poised uncertainly on the bottom step.

"Why, Sheriff Weston, what brings you here? Any further news regarding the unfortunate events of yesterday?"

The sheriff scraped the toe of his boot self-consciously in the dirt of the driveway. "Uh, yes, ma'am. It so happens that's why I've come."

There was something in the sheriff's manner that put Evangeline on her guard. "Would you like to come inside? May I offer you some refreshment while you give us your news?"

"That won't be necessary, ma'am. Thank you all the same." The man paused, clearly ill at ease. His lack of composure did nothing to alleviate Evangeline's concern.

"What is it?" she asked tensely.

"I don't rightly know how to say this, ma'am. Don't rightly know how to go about it, either. This never has happened before." Sheriff Weston sighed and looked up at the trees briefly for inspiration. "As you must know, Miss Evangeline, I'm new in these parts. I was a career military man. A cavalry officer out west. I know how to fight Indians and such."

Evangeline looked skeptically at the sheriff, not quite sure what obscure line of reasoning he was following.

"But a man gets tired. He gets old and all he wants is some peace and quiet." Sheriff Weston's face held a woebegone expression. "So when the time came for me to quit that life, I was happy to collect my pension and bring the missus back east. Took this job in this quiet little town of Shore Cliff where nothing ever happens. Just to keep my hand in. Just to remind me I'm still alive, but..." He twirled his hat around contemplatively in his hands. "...nothing was ever supposed to happen here. I surely never wanted anything to happen, you see."

"Ah, yes." Evangeline sensed that he was leading up to an ominous disclosure.

"So it grieves me something fierce to have to tell you this, ma'am, but...but I've come to take somebody in for questioning."

"Sheriff, what are you talking about?"

Jack edged forward protectively.

The sheriff glanced at him briefly, appraisingly. He shook his head. "Take it easy, friend, it's not like that. It's not Miss Evangeline I'm here for. I've come for the other lady."

"What!" Evangeline gasped.

"It's Miss Serafina there." The sheriff motioned toward the medium, who was still standing on the lower step of the carriage. She appeared to be listing to one side, and Evangeline feared she might faint.

"Jack, help her down!" she commanded urgently. "What on earth can you mean by this, sheriff?"

The sheriff twirled his hat a few more times before continuing. "Well, Doctor Fowler finished his examination of Miz Allworthy, and it looks for certain that she was poisoned."

"That's hardly a surprise, sheriff, but what has that to do

with Serafina?"

The rumpled gray man gazed stoically off in the direction of the town hall and jail. "Maybe Miss Serafina and I should talk about it down the street."

"Would you have any objection to my tagging along?"

The sheriff hardly seemed the sort to stand on either ceremony or procedure. He casually shrugged his shoulders. "Whatever suits you. I don't know what-all is the proper form in such matters, so we'll just make it up as we go." Sweeping his arm in the general direction of the municipal building, he said, "After you, ladies."

The coachman seemed inclined to follow along, but Evangeline stopped him. "No, Jack. You stay here. I'm sure we can clear this matter up quickly but if not..." she paused a moment, "tell Serafina's maid to pack an overnight bag for her mistress."

Jack nodded grudgingly and headed toward the back door of the house. Evangeline, Serafina and Sheriff Weston made for the village jail.

The incongruity of their destination on a fair summer afternoon struck Evangeline full force. She smiled encouragement at Serafina while the sheriff remained stolidly uncommunicative until they had entered his small office. It looked like any other municipal bureau--wooden floor, wooden desk, wooden chairs, but the bulletin board displayed wanted posters, not memoranda. Evangeline noted to herself with a smile that none of those desperados would be likely to visit Shore Cliff at any time in their dark criminal careers, but the smile left her face when she happened to glance toward the back room. Instead of a door, it was separated from the front by iron bars.

"Things've reached a pretty pass now, ma'am." The sheriff grimaced. "The mayor's afraid of a crime wave and he's forcing me to hire a deputy."

"A deputy?" Evangeline repeated skeptically. "To do what?"

The sheriff indicated that the two ladies should be seated in front of his desk while he retreated behind it. "To guard dangerous criminals, I guess." It was clear from his tone of voice that the sheriff did not share the mayor's concern.

"About the only crime wave I've seen around here is when

the college boys go over to the Reilly Club of an evening and get a brick in their hats. Most of the time I just round 'em up to sleep it off here in the back room. That is, the ones that aren't out tipping cows or trying to dive off the bluff for a late night swim." The sheriff chuckled briefly at the thought of his usual ne'er-do-wells. "That's about the limit of wrongdoing hereabouts, until now." He cleared his throat self-consciously and looked at Serafina.

The medium, who had been quiet up to that point, broke her silence with a startling observation. "Someone has said that I have killed Madame Euphemia, is that not so?"

Evangeline rose to her feet in outrage. "What!"

"Take it easy, Miss Evangeline. Take it easy. If it comes to that, it'll be for a court to decide." He gestured for her to return to her chair.

"What basis do you have to suspect this lady?" Evangeline persisted, still standing.

The sheriff sighed and rummaged around on his desk to locate a specific piece of stained and crumpled paper on which he had taken some obscure notes. He pawed around in his desk drawer trying to find his reading spectacles. When he had perched these on his nose, adjusted them properly, and perused the unimpressive document before him, he began. "Well, certain evidence has been brought against her, and it's my job to sort out what's what." He looked up mildly over his glasses. "Miss Evangeline, I'd be much obliged if you'd sit down, ma'am. You do give a body the jitters standing there looking like you're fit to wake snakes."

Evangeline allowed herself a momentary smile at the mental image. "Very well, sheriff. I shall conduct myself in a more seemly manner." She reclaimed her seat. "Now what's this all about?"

Scanning the paper before him once more, the sheriff continued. "Well, it's like we thought. Doctor Fowler finished his autopsy and found cyanide poisoning to be the cause of Miz Allworthy's death."

"At least now we know the nature of the poison."

"He did some tests on the liquor that was left, too. Seems the poison was only in the one glass. Not the one by Miss Serafina's plate and not in the flagon either."

"Well, that tips the scales a bit in Roland's direction.

Martin couldn't have known who would drink"-- Evangeline caught herself in mid-sentence.

"What was that, ma'am?" The sheriff looked up briefly from his paper.

"Oh, nothing, nothing. Just rambling. Please continue."

"Well, there's that, and then there's the information I got from Mr. Allworthy this morning."

Evangeline hesitated to breathe. "And what did he have to say?"

The sheriff took off his glasses and looked at the two women. "He said a few things that are kind of worrysome to figure out." He paused and, with great deliberation, opened his desk drawer again and drew out two letters. Weston pushed the two pieces of paper forward on the desk.

"I'm not asking you ladies to read any of this, but does it look like these two letters were written by the same hand?"

Warily, Evangeline and Serafina scrutinized the documents together. The stationery was scented and of good quality bond paper. The handwriting was neat with a few embellishments here and there that suggested a feminine author.

"They would appear to be," Evangeline said cautiously. "The same color ink, the same scent, same paper. The shape of the characters appears similar."

"That's what troubles me, ma'am," sighed the sheriff. "One is a note from Miz Allworthy to her husband. The other is supposed to be from Miz Allworthy to that whadda-ye-call-it metaphorical society."

"You mean the Chicago Metaphysical Society?"

"Yup, that's the one. The letter hints that Miss Serafina here is a fraud." The sheriff uttered these words very softly.

"Let me see that again." Evangeline whisked the paper off the desk and looked it over carefully. "This is unbelievable!" she gasped.

Serafina took the letter and studied the wording as well. "It is from Madame Euphemia to my friend Theophilus. She says my powers are not what she expected. She is disappointed and thinks I could be a confidence trickster. She warns him not to recommend me to any of her friends. She says if she could find proof she would expose me as a fraud. It is dated the morning of the day she died. This is...is...impossible!" She let the letter slip nervelessly through her fingers, and it fluttered back down onto the desk.

The sheriff had been studying her face as she read. His own expression was unreadable.

"Surely you don't believe this, sheriff," Evangeline exclaimed. "It must be a forgery! And this supposed evidence coming from Martin, of all people!"

"I wish I could go along with you on that, ma'am. But there's other things as well. You see, I went back to the house and I searched Miss Serafina's room."

"She hasn't been back there since the murder was committed."

"Yes, I know that, ma'am. All the more reason to check and see if there was anything left behind."

Dreading the response to her next question, Evangeline asked, "And was there?"

The sheriff continued to stare intently at Serafina. "Tucked under the mattress, I found a packet of powder. Do you use medicinal powders, Miss Serafina?"

The medium looked confused. "No, I do not. I have no packets of headache powders. No powders of any kind except for face powder, and that I keep in a little china box. I do not know what this could be."

"Well, ma'am, I sent it on to Doctor Fowler to see if he could maybe help me figure out what it might be. But if I was to hazard a guess..."

Evangeline completed his thought. "You'd guess that the packet contains cyanide powder. Wouldn't you, sheriff?"

"Yes, ma'am, that'd be the most likely answer."

Evangeline sat very still, too much in shock to be outraged.

Serafina observed softly, "It is as I said, sheriff. I am suspected of killing Madame Euphemia."

"Well, the facts surely don't go in your favor, I'm sorry to say. If you knew about this letter that Miz Allworthy was going to send, then there's your motive. If the packet does contain poison, why that's the means, and you were the only one in the room with Miz Allworthy when she died. That's the opportunity."

Evangeline broke in. "But, sheriff, is it at all likely that Mrs. Allworthy would have been calmly sipping tea with a woman she considered a charlatan?"

Weston, unruffled by the distress his words had caused, merely rubbed his chin. "It's like Miz Allworthy said in the letter. She just had her suspicions. Didn't have any proof so maybe she just wanted to part company with Miss Serafina on good terms. To get her out of the house before blowing the whole thing sky high."

"It's a plausible theory, but I fear not a just one." Evangeline's tone was bitter.

"I'm not saying I'm convinced of anything one way or another, Miss Evangeline. I just wanted you to see how things stand with all this new evidence Mr. Allworthy so kindly brought to my attention."

Evangeline shot a quick glance in the sheriff's direction to see if she could detect in his expression a trace of the sarcasm his words suggested. His face was still a mild-mannered mask.

"He's done a proper job of it, hasn't he," Evangeline muttered under her breath.

"Who's that, ma'am?"

"Never mind, sheriff. I was just thinking out loud again."

Weston gave her a long, appraising look with eyes that were remarkably keen in a face so tired. "So you see how it is, ma'am."

"Yes, sheriff, I do indeed see how it is."

"I'm afraid Miss Serafina will have to bide here for a bit until we find out what was in the packet."

Evangeline looked in dismay at the back room with its iron bars. "But, sheriff, this is no place for a lady. The lack of privacy..."

The sheriff stood up and smiled reassuringly. "Don't you worry, Miss Evangeline. I've asked Miz Weston to help me out with this...uh...situation. She'll be coming by soon. We'll hang a curtain in front of the cell and she'll be here to keep Miss Serafina company. For common decency's sake."

"Thank you, sheriff. That was most thoughtful of you."

Rummaging through his desk drawer once more, the sheriff reached in and found a large rusty key which he used to unlock the cell and deposit his unfortunate guest inside.

Serafina walked meekly behind the metal grille, a wan birdlike creature dwarfed by her surroundings. She looked around plaintively. "Such heavy walls and big iron bars. All to keep little me inside."

Evangeline reached through the grate and touched her hand. "I'll send your maid Fannie round with more clothes for you. This could take awhile to sort out. Do you have a lawyer?"

Serafina appeared puzzled. "Why should I need a lawyer? I have done nothing."

"My dear, innocence is the poorest shield of all under circumstances such as these. I'm sure I can get Freddie's uncle to help. And in the meantime, I'll move heaven and earth to get you out of here."

"You see, it is as I told you in my dream." Serafina smiled weakly. "You will find a way out."

Evangeline looked askance at the medium. "I hope your confidence in me isn't misplaced."

The sheriff put a friendly hand on Evangeline's arm to escort her out. "I truly wish you luck, ma'am. A body doesn't live as many years as I've done without learning a few things about human nature along the way." He let Evangeline infer what his own suspicions were in the silence that followed as they walked out the door.

The sheriff stood outside with her for a few moments, looking speculatively off in the direction of the lakefront. "Don't know what I'll do with the boys from the Reilly Club if they decide to cut up rough tonight. Probably have to handcuff 'em to a lamp post and let 'em sleep it off under the stars."

"I'm sure the night air will exert a most salubrious effect in awakening their moral character." Evangeline turned to walk off down the darkening street. "Good night to you, sheriff. And thank you," she added softly.

૭ન્જી

Upon returning home, she went directly in search of Jack. She found him in the coach house polishing the brass carriage lanterns.

"Everything all right, Miss Engie?" His question sounded almost too casual.

"No, Jack. Far from it. I'll have to curtail my duties at Mast

House and Pullman for awhile. A more pressing matter requires my immediate attention. I'd like you to take the early train back to the city tomorrow."

The caretaker looked up in surprise.

"I want you to get things in order at the townhouse. I'll be staying there for the next week or two."

Jack said nothing for a moment, continuing to polish industriously. When he finally spoke, his observation sounded almost nonchalant. "You're going to hunt down Mrs. Allworthy's killer, aren't you, Miss Engie?"

"Yes, Jack, I am." The lady folded her arms decisively.

The coachman grinned in amusement, his gold tooth flashing briefly in the lantern light. "Then I'd say the guilty party's chances of surviving are about as good as a snowball's in hell. You'll pardon the expression, miss."

Turning toward the door, Evangeline said over her shoulder, "Yes, I'd agree with your assessment, Jack. Get some rest. Tomorrow will be a very busy day."

CHAPTER 16
Pressed Into Service

❧❦❧

Once she had decided on a course of action, Evangeline wasted no time in executing her plan. Jack left shortly after dawn on the first morning train to the city. She followed him on the next. Instead of going to the townhouse, she went straight to the offices of the *Gazette*, Chicago's most widely-read newspaper. The *Gazette* took up a four-story building on the corner of Dearborn and Madison in the heart of the downtown business district. Evangeline went there, at least in part, to perform an errand which was occasionally required but which she found highly distasteful nonetheless-- admitting to Freddie that he had been right about something.

She had visited him a few times at his office since he made the transition from jurisprudence to journalism, so she had a vague idea of which cramped corner of the bullpen on the third floor he occupied. She braced herself for the usual zoolike sounds of hyena laughter, bird whistles, and cat calls, all of which passed for communication in some odd reporter language she had never quite grasped. Freddie had lately become proficient in the pig grunt variation of that language- -a fact which distressed Evangeline greatly.

She recalled her last foray into this den of masculine iniquity. One particularly impudent youth had leered at her and asked, "Hey Sis, what's your name?" to which she replied, "My friends call me Miss LeClair, but you can call me Ma'am!" The impudent youth thereupon being rendered speechless, Evangeline was left in possession of the field. She had no desire to draw blood today. She had come on a peaceful errand, but if the challenge was given, she wasn't one to run from battle.

Thus steeled for the fray, she was quite surprised that, upon opening the door, no one seemed to take the slightest notice of her. There were at least twenty desks heaped with a mad array of copy and waste paper, typewriters, and men hunched over them hammering furiously at the keys. The sight of a woman in that bastion of adolescent good fellowship wasn't greeted with as much stupefaction as a few months before. She found this change remarkable until she happened to glance toward the window where she saw a crisp little woman in a white shirtwaist and ascot tie hammering away at a typewriter keyboard along with the rest. It would seem the management of the *Gazette* had finally bitten the bullet. Since the *Daily Courier* and the *Trans-Ocean* had both hired female reporters, another sacred bull was in its death throes.

Evangeline jumped when a telephone rang on the desk near where she stood. As if in sympathy, three others began to jangle all at the same time from different points around the room while men scurried one way and another to silence the peevish summons.

Thankful for the diversion, she wove her way unnoticed between the desks until she came to the corner at the opposite end of the room where, she recalled, Freddie lurked. The poor underling's desk appeared about the size of the student desks Evangeline saw in all the classrooms at Mast House. She fully expected that his chair would be bolted to the floor, but it moved backward when she pushed it away from the desk.

He wasn't there. She was in the process of writing him a note to call her at her townhouse when her nostrils became irritated by the reek of cigar smoke. Very cheap cigar smoke. Without even looking up to establish the source of the offensive aroma, she guessed the name of the perpetrator.

Keeping her eyes on the note she was writing, she asked,

"Mr. Bill Mason, I presume?"

"Gad, Miss LeClair! Your powers of deduction are truly amazing!" The veteran newsman beamed at her. He had apparently been standing next to Freddie's desk for several moments unannounced.

Evangeline finally looked up and greeted her friend's unkempt and aromatic mentor with a rueful smile. "You needn't praise my powers of deduction too highly, Mr. Mason. I fear your presence would be self-evident to anyone possessed of a normal olfactory sense."

Mason blushed in embarrassment. "Oh, uh, truly sorry, ma'am. I do beg your pardon." He ground out the cigar on a typewritten sheet of copy on Freddie's desk. "Hmmm." He viewed the charred streaks he had left on the page. "Well, it wasn't too good anyhow. The boy's going to have to rewrite that one for sure."

He slipped the extinguished cigar back into his coat pocket. "No sense in wasting a perfectly good stogie."

Evangeline decided to let her opinion of the quality of the stogie pass unarticulated. "Have you seen Junior?" She gestured toward Freddie's vacant chair.

"I think I just saw him skedaddle into the editor's office. He's sure he's onto a hot story about that society dame who just got poisoned up your way the day before yesterday. The way he's been carrying on, you'd think it was the crime of the century. You wouldn't happen to know what he's babbling about, would you?"

Evangeline kept her response guarded. "I think I have a fairly good idea where his thoughts are tending."

Mason's journalistic instincts had become alerted. "Care to share any of it?"

"Not quite yet, Mr. Mason."

The reporter laughed, an appreciative gleam in his eye. "Uh-oh. Whenever it's just Freddie who's off on a wild goose chase, I pay it no mind. Two weeks ago, he was sure he'd heard a rumor that Bathhouse Johnny Conklin was going to quit politics and enter the theater as a ventriloquist. Freddie cooked up this scheme to start going through Conklin's trash to see if he could find any wood shavings. You know, from the dummy. I didn't want to hurt his feelings by telling him who I thought the dummy was. He couldn't get me or anybody else to bite on that worm. But this is different. When you get involved, I kind of start to take things seriously. I can't help remembering what happened the last time..."

Evangeline gave her best impression of demure propriety. "I'd hardly think that catching a killer once should create a pattern of expectation, Mr. Mason."

The reporter shook his head. "As I recall, I lost the credit for a perfectly good story because I made you a promise, and I wouldn't like to lose another opportunity because I was caught napping."

"Your vigilance does you credit, sir. As does the fact that I can rely on you to keep your word. You are indeed a man of integrity, Mr. Mason."

"By holding that opinion, Miss LeClair, you're in the distinct minority. Ah, here comes the young rapscallion now." Bill gestured toward the editor's office door, from which Freddie had just emerged. "How now, Hal, what time of day is it, lad?" Bill had a penchant for quoting Shakespeare at the most irrelevant moments.

"Hal?" Freddie echoed in bewilderment.

"You've got a visitor, my boy. Not polite to keep a lady waiting." Temporarily forgetting his own need to be polite, Mason had just fished the cigar of dubious quality out of his pocket and caught himself in the act of relighting it. "Oh nuts!" he cursed mildly and allowed said unlit cigar to remain perched on his lower lip. "Sorry, Miss LeClair. Can't seem to help myself."

Freddie threaded his way across the room to his own desk.

He seemed surprised to see his friend. "Engie, what are you doing here?"

Bill stood back silently, evidently hoping for some crumb of information to drop unheeded.

"Just an innocent social call, Freddie, that's all." Evangeline had no intention of alerting Mason's reporter instincts further.

Freddie looked at his friend as if she'd lost her mind. He was well aware that she never pursued any course of action without a purpose.

She grabbed his arm to forestall any more questions. "Can we go somewhere for a stroll? The air is so stuffy in here."

"But, Engie, I've got mountains of work to do." He picked up a sheet of paper from his desk. Unfortunately, he chose Bill's makeshift ashtray to illustrate his point. "Hey, who did this?"

"Well, have to be going." Mason backed away from the desk as if it were a bomb about to explode. "Always a pleasure, Miss LeClair." He bent to kiss her hand.

Evangeline smiled, guessing the unasked question that remained. "Mr. Mason, I assure you when there's anything to tell you'll be the first to know."

"What?" Freddie, even more perplexed, allowed Evangeline to steer him through the maze of desks and out the press-room door.

"We need to talk!" she told him. "But somewhere where the walls don't have ears or cigars."

"But...but..." Freddie objected weakly.

"This way!" Evangeline forged on toward the stairwell.

"Wait a minute, old girl. Wait a minute. I know the perfect spot."

Freddie led Evangeline down to the ground floor and through the double doors to the print room. The roar of the presses rattled the walls, the floor, and the teeth of the room's occupants. "How's this?" He beamed proudly, waiting for her approbation.

"What?" she howled over the hammering of the nearest machine.

"I...said...isn't this...better?"

Evangeline read Freddie's lips because she couldn't hear him. "No!" she thundered.

Sighing in exasperation, he took her by the arm and led her to the corner of the room nearest the windows and farthest away from the infernal din.

Her ears still ringing, she scowled at him as she tried to readjust her hat. The vibration from the machines had knocked it askew.

"Just trying to be of help." He rolled his eyes heavenward in persecuted martyrdom.

She relented slightly. "Well, I suppose this will do. Is there anyone who could overhear us?"

"You mean hear us, don't you? There's nobody else around except for a few typesetters, and they're over at the other end."

"Good." Evangeline launched into her story. "You've heard about Euphemia Allworthy, I suppose."

"No thanks to you!" Freddie was off and running. "Why didn't you try to send me word? I had to find out when the news was telephoned in from one of the suburban papers."

"I rather had my hands full, having strolled onto the scene of the murder about fifteen minutes after it happened."

"But that's wonderful, Engie!" Freddie went instantly from accusatory to exuberant as he flipped open his ever-present notebook. "You can give me an eyewitness account of everything that happened!"

Evangeline shot a grim look at her friend before filling him in on the interrogation scene at the Allworthy villa. When she came to the end of her narration, she paused. "But then something even worse happened yesterday that kept me from contacting you."

"Worse?" Freddie looked bemused. "What could be worse than a murder?"

"An innocent person framed for committing it, that's what." Evangeline then regaled her friend with an account of Serafina's arrest.

"The swine," Freddie said between clenched teeth. "Setting her up to take the fall for him or for Roland!"

"Well, we're in agreement on that point. Now all we have to figure out is how to make one of them confess and clear Serafina."

"I'd bet anything that Bayne is involved in this somehow."

"Yes, Freddie, I'd agree with you on that point as well." Evangeline spoke in a whisper that would have been barely audible in a quiet room. Her words were fairly drowned in the echo of the presses.

"What was that, Engie? I didn't hear you." Freddie had become proficient at lip-reading above the racket, but apparently he just wanted to hear her say it again.

"You were right." She enunciated for his benefit in clipped and very loud syllables. "There! Are you happy now? I freely admit it. Your instincts about the nefarious Mr. Bayne proved to be correct."

"Engie, don't speak. I beg you. Don't say another word! I just want to savor this moment." Freddie sighed and closed his eyes in deep satisfaction.

The lady allowed him all of twenty seconds to revel in his victory. "Are you through?"

"No, but you may continue." A smirk still lingered on his face.

Ignoring his irritating expression, Evangeline forged ahead. "I kept trying to find a motive for Martin's behavior. After all, he's not in any financial difficulties. He had free access to Euphemia's fortune before. So inheritance, in and of itself, wouldn't be reason enough to want to kill her. And then I started thinking about the mysterious Mr. Bayne."

"Who shows up shortly after Nora Johnson is murdered." Freddie looked at his friend impishly. "And, oh, by the way, is there anything you'd care to contradict in my last statement?"

She returned a baleful glare. "Really, I'd think a person would be content with one concession per day."

"Engie, come on," he wheedled.

"Very well! I see there'll be no living with you after this!" She sighed and took a deep breath. "Yes, all right, I agree that Nora Johnson was murdered. Once again, your theory was correct. Can we proceed now?"

"Of course." He waved her magnanimously to continue.

"As I was saying, the mysterious Mr. Bayne makes his appearance shortly after Nora Johnson's murder and claims to be a long-lost friend of Martin's. Martin gives him a job in his company with a big title and a paycheck to match. The obvious conclusion is that Bayne is blackmailing Martin because he possesses some evidence implicating Martin in Nora's death."

"Implicating him!" Freddie cried in disbelief. "He's the one who killed her!"

"On that point, we do not agree. What was his motive? He's far too proper to get involved in a secret affair. Roland seems the more likely culprit."

"Roland?" The thought evidently had never occurred to Freddie before.

"Yes, Roland is the lady's man in the family and he might very well have been seeing Nora on the sly. Given his general lack of self-discipline, I could easily envision a lover's quarrel turning into something more ugly if he couldn't control his temper. Remember that Serafina saw Nora's ghost standing behind Roland's chair, not Martin's."

"Serafina!" Freddie snorted. "So now we're relying on spectral evidence to prove a case?"

"No, Freddie, we're relying on common sense. Martin is rich. Roland is not. Of the two, Martin is the obvious target for a blackmailer. Both men bear the Allworthy surname, and I think Martin would do anything to protect his family honor, no matter what he might think privately of his nephew's character."

Freddie nodded in assent. "I guess you're right about that."

Evangeline continued in her line of reasoning. "Whatever the case may be, one fact of which we can be sure is that Bayne was there to see something, in fact has some material evidence, that he's using to blackmail Martin."

"Do you suppose Martin killed Euphemia because she wanted him to get rid of Bayne?"

"I don't think so." Evangeline shook her head. "It seems logical to conclude that whoever killed Nora also killed Euphemia to cover up the first crime. It's only the first murder that's hard. It seems to get easier after that, or so I've heard. If we're assuming Roland was vicious enough to kill Nora, he wouldn't stick at killing his aunt either. I discovered that Roland was not in his aunt's good graces just prior to her death. Maybe he feared she had uncovered something about Nora's accident that pointed to him as the murderer. Remember, he's also the one who served her the poisoned wine and there was no way Martin could have known ahead of time which glass Euphemia would drink from since he was out of the house when it happened. No, it's too far-fetched to think Martin did this, but he does seem to be implicated as well. I can't be sure if he actually knows that Roland killed his wife or only suspects he did. But he seems to be moving heaven and earth to cover it up and--"

"And pin the crime on Serafina with false evidence." Freddie completed her thought. "It doesn't look good for her."

Evangeline tapped her chin, deep in thought. "Freddie, do you have any time to spare for detective work?"

"Now that you're finally willing to help, I'll make the time!

With the strike winding down, I ought to be able to slip away to do some investigating."

"You know where the mysterious Mr. Bayne lives, don't you?"

"I should say!" The young man laughed ruefully. "I spent so many nights leaning against a lamp post across from his flat that it probably still has the imprint of my shoulder on it."

The lady sighed with all the appearance of profound regret. "Well, for the third time today, Frederick Ulysses Simpson, I am forced to acknowledge that you are right."

"How's that?" Freddie sounded suspicious.

"Yes, yes, even now I see the brilliance of your plan. We get possession of whatever Bayne is using to blackmail Martin with. It may give us evidence to prove that Nora was actually murdered, and with that we can establish a motive for Euphemia's death as well."

"Why, uh, yes." Freddie puffed out his chest importantly. "That's what I meant all along."

"Then I certainly wish you the best of luck and look forward to an account of your daring exploit with the greatest anticipation!"

"Exploit?" Freddie found it difficult to maintain the pretense that he had any idea what she was talking about.

"Yes, of course. I could scarcely call it anything less when you intend to break into his flat tomorrow and search for evidence."

"I'm going to do what?"

Evangeline laughed demurely. "Oh, Freddie, you needn't turn modest all of a sudden and fail to own up to such an ingenious idea. And you're right, of course. It's the only way we'll ever get possession of the evidence we need. Well done!" She had begun to edge in the direction of the print-room doors.

Freddie trailed, bleating, "But...but...how...when...?"

They stood in the corridor near the front doors of the *Gazette* building. Evangeline flashed a disarming smile as she consulted her watch. "Oh my goodness! Is it that late already? Must be going. Best of luck." She whisked through the front door, leaving Freddie to ponder the notion that being acknowledged right wasn't all it was cracked up to be.

CHAPTER 17
A Break In The Case

ଔ 𝓗 ଓ

Once Freddie got over his pique at having walked into yet another one of Evangeline's verbal snares, he decided that her strategy might have some merit. After all, he felt a personal desire to get even with Bayne. Not just with Bayne, but with his whole cursed apartment building.

During all those nights of fruitless vigilance, Freddie had felt that the structure itself was mocking him. There it stood, solid and black against the night sky--yielding no light, revealing no clues, and thwarting Freddie's every attempt to pry out its secrets. Well, he would find out something incriminating even if he had to break in to do it! Breaking in. Ah, there was the rub. He had no idea how to go about it.

He recalled all the penny dreadfuls he'd read as a feckless youth about daring thieves who never got pinched[1] and sent to the cooler[2] for so much as forking a super.[3] But none of their clever plans quite applied to his situation. With his luck, he'd get pulled by a leatherhead[4] and black-gowned[5] in five

---

[1] Apprehended by the police.
[2] Jail.
[3] Stealing a pocket watch.
[4] Arrested by a policeman.

minutes flat. A master cracksman[6] he was not, though knowing one at this particular juncture might have come in handy.

He had a sneaking suspicion that Bill Mason might have been able to point him in the direction of someone who could supply him with a set of skeleton keys. He even suspected that Bill owned a set outright, but he was afraid to ask him. Afraid to ask anybody in the newsroom for fear of arousing suspicion. Alas! No skeleton key, no bar-key[7], not even a lowly widdy[8] to aid him in his endeavors! He had to think of another alternative.

Tuesday afternoon, no nearer a viable strategy, he took the Dearborn streetcar north and got off a block away from Bayne's residence. The shady rascal had rented a flat in one of the posh tree-lined side streets that intersected the busy thoroughfare. Freddie whistled casually as he walked up Bayne's block. He wished to appear as an idle fellow out for an afternoon stroll. The last thing he wanted anyone to notice was that he had a purpose and a destination in mind. He tipped his hat gallantly to two young ladies coming toward him from the opposite direction. After they passed, he snuck a furtive glance to either side of the street to ensure that no one else was about.

With his heart hammering, he stopped before Bayne's apartment building. It was a three-flat graystone, though the city soot had stained the façade to a charcoal-black. Curved stone bays looked out over the street. Each floor was identical from the exterior, and presumably each was a separate apartment. He knew Bayne lived on the second floor because he had once seen him enter the building after dark and had then seen his face illuminated inside a second-story window after the fellow had turned up the gas jets.

Now, as he stood looking up at the darkened window, Freddie realized with a start that someone might be standing just out of sight, looking down at him. He hoped not!

---

[5] Sentenced by a judge.
[6] Burglar.
[7] The shaft of a simple key with a slot for attaching bits of variable sizes to fit different types of locks.
[8] A small piece of bent wire with a string attached. This bow-shaped object is slipped into a keyhole to trip a lock.

Evangeline told him Bayne had gone to the country house to stay with Martin in his time of need. Time of need certainly described it! The two blackguards needed to present a united front in case the sheriff came back to ask more questions.

Freddie took a deep breath and ascended the front stairs to the main entrance. He was presented with a thick oak door with a beveled glass panel in the middle. When he tried the doorknob, he realized the sturdy wooden portal was protected by an even sturdier metal deadbolt lock. It was his worst fear. "Rats!" he cursed under his breath, looking over his shoulder to see if anyone happened to notice him jiggling the doorknob. The street was still quiet, though he feared that someone might be watching him from one of the windows across the street. "Oh knock it off!" he told himself sternly. "This is no time to worry about getting bagged!"[9]

Whistling nonchalantly, hands in his pockets, he strolled back down the stairs and toward the opposite end of the block--trying to buy himself some time while he thought of a plan. The locked outer door was certainly to be expected, but Freddie had been hoping that someone might have forgotten to secure it. He'd had visions of the door opening to his touch as the Red Sea parted before Moses. Alas, the days of miracles were long since past! He'd have to work for his victory.

He thought about cutting a hole in the glass and tripping the lock from inside. For this he would need a glass cutter which fell into the same category as a widdy--unquestionably desirable but momentarily unobtainable. He then contemplated finding a locksmith somewhere in the neighborhood. Perhaps he could concoct some heart rending story that he lived in the flat and had been unfortunate enough to have his keys stolen. Unfortunately, the locksmith might actually ask him for proof that he lived there. Another brilliant plan gone by the wayside!

By this time, Freddie had turned the corner and stood before the alley that ran behind Bayne's block. On an impulse he decided to see whether the back door presented quite as much of a dilemma as the front. He threaded his way through heaps of garbage piled up along the sides of the

---

[9] Jailed.

alley, disturbing swarms of flies as he went. From the size of the hills of trash, he judged that garbage day was tomorrow. A grayish-brown rat the size of a small rabbit scurried over the top of a mound of rotting potato peelings but, seeing Freddie, it slipped out of sight. The young man ruefully looked at his recently polished boots and did his best to step fastidiously around the horse dung scattered down the center of his path.

He picked his way through the rubble for another half block until he judged himself to be directly behind Bayne's building. He stealthily opened the wooden gate that separated the small patch of yard from the alley. A narrow concrete walk led from the gate to the rear of the house. He studied the exterior for a moment. Each back door opened onto a wooden porch that ran the width of the building. These porches were criss-crossed by flights of stairs that led from the ground up to the third story. There were no gates to prevent someone from climbing from one apartment level to the next.

Glancing hastily around him to ensure he still hadn't been noticed, Freddie crossed the gangway and ascended to the second floor porch. He didn't observe any activity coming from the apartment on the first floor, so he hoped no one was home. A few of the stairs creaked under his weight, cautioning him to move on tip-toe after that. Before he reached the top of the stairs on Bayne's landing, he paused to listen for signs of activity within the apartment. He heard nothing but the distant clang of the trolley and the monotonous clop of horses' hooves coming from Dearborn Street. So far, so good.

The back entrance was covered by a screen door. Freddie cautiously pulled the handle and the door swung open. Elated, he tried turning the knob of the back door itself. The knob turned but the door refused to budge. It was locked.

"Double rats!" Freddie swore to himself. He was quickly running out of ideas and didn't know how long his skulking would remain unnoticed. He looked up and down the porch for any other means of entry.

Next to the door was a window looking into the kitchen. Freddie tried to peer inside through the lace curtains but could see little except for the prominent latch in the middle of the window frame, which appeared to be fastened securely. Sighing, he moved a little farther down the porch until he came to a much narrower window. He presumed this might lead into the pantry. With awe and wonderment, he saw that the window lock had been left open.

Pressing the tips of his fingers against the top of the frame, he raised it enough to slip his hands under the bottom of the window and hoist it up. Once again, he looked over his shoulder, at the houses across the alley, at the houses on either side. No signs of movement yet. He tried to squeeze noiselessly through the window, but a six-foot-tall body wriggling through an aperture no more than two feet wide is a mathematical absurdity. Such a feat cannot be accomplished gracefully without great personal cost. He landed on his ear with a thud, banging the window with his foot as he fell through. His hat rolled across the pantry floor. "Owww!" he moaned and sat up, rubbing his ear, then his shoulder, and finally his ankle.

After the momentary pain subsided, he realized he'd done it! He'd actually done it! He was inside. He stood up and slid the window closed behind him so nothing should look different from the outside. He paused and listened again. Still quiet. No vibrations from the floor below to suggest that someone had heard him and become suspicious of what was going on upstairs.

Stealthily, he moved into the kitchen. The curtains were drawn and the room was in shadow. The first sensation that hit him was the smell of stale tobacco and unwashed linen. He wondered how long the windows had been shut but he was afraid to open them for fear of attracting attention. The kitchen was equipped with plates and cutlery and cooking utensils, although none of them seemed to have been used. Freddie looked through all the cupboards. The icebox had no ice in it, and no food either. Bayne must be taking his meals elsewhere. He didn't seem like the sort of fellow who would have had the presence of mind to fit out a kitchen, so Freddie inferred the apartment had been rented furnished.

He moved on into the dining room. A lace table cloth graced the mahogany table, but given the room's current state, Freddie didn't think Bayne would be likely to entertain. Crumpled laundry was strewn about helter-skelter--shirts, undergarments, collars, cuffs, and socks, seemingly abandoned in the spot where Bayne had removed them.

Other than the abundance of discarded clothing, Freddie could find nothing personal or unique. No newspapers, no scribbled notes, no mementos or trinkets to indicate the character of the man who lived there. The only fact I can glean from this, Freddie thought, is that he doesn't know the whereabouts of the nearest laundry!

The young detective looked into the bedroom next. The bed was unmade, though how recently its occupant had departed would have been impossible to determine, since the bed was probably always left unmade. Freddie opened the cedar closet. Here he found new suits displaying the label of one of the city's most expensive tailors. A few bureau drawers contained new linen; the others were empty.

"Stranger and stranger," Freddie murmured as he went into the living room. He found a few more articles of clothing strewn across the floor, ashtrays bearing the remains of burned-out cigars, a partially empty whiskey bottle on the floor near an armchair, and another empty one rolled on its side in the corner. He laughed to himself when he saw a bookcase with a set of volumes whose gold-lettered spines pronounced themselves be *A Collection Of The World's Greatest Literature*. The pages looked untouched by human hands. He was equally amused to see that the piano in the window bay had a half inch of dust on the keys.

No doubt remained in his mind that the decorating and furnishings had been provided by the landlord. Even the Currier and Ives prints on the wall hardly seemed to suit the tenant's taste. The only picture that might remotely have appealed to a man like Bayne was a cheap print of Boticelli's Venus hanging on the wall by the armchair. It somehow didn't fit the rest of the room.

"Triple rats!" Freddie cursed. He had found nothing even remotely suspicious except for Bayne's penchant for collecting dirty clothing. He went back through the apartment room by room, searching every drawer, every cupboard, every nook, and every cranny. At each turn, he found objects so impersonal that they could only have come with the flat.

Freddie paced around and around the living room. He no

longer cared how much noise he was making! Damn the neighbors and damn Desmond Bayne! He rubbed his head as he paced, lost in thought.

Unfortunately, he failed to look where he was pacing and his feet became entangled in one of Bayne's discarded shirts. "Raaaaats!" Freddie flailed about, struggling to free his feet. He lost his balance and fell backward. His shoulders hit the wall with a thud as he sank to the floor, too despondent to move. He thought his misery complete until Venus, awakened by the vibration, descended from on high and clipped Freddie squarely above the right eye before rattling down onto the carpet. An agonized "Ye Gods!" and several other less appropriate words escaped the young man's lips as he kicked at the picture. Utterly defeated, he sat back to rub his head and nurse his grievances against a perverse destiny.

When at last he reopened his eyes, still cursing fate, Desmond Bayne, his dirty laundry, and his vile taste in art, something caught Freddie's attention. Venus had fallen on her face, revealing a secret. Fastened to her back was a bright metal object that gleamed in the rays of the afternoon sun.

Freddie picked up the picture. The wooden frame had a brown cardboard backing that was held in place by nails. A key had been attached to one corner of the frame with a bent nail. His excitement growing, Freddie pried the key loose. It was flat and had a code stamped into it. GNB 103. He knew what it was! He had one almost like it. It was a safety deposit box key! There was only one downtown bank with those initials--the Great Northern.

His instincts told him that this was what he had come for. This was the key that would unlock the mystery of Desmond's hold over Allworthy! He wrapped the key in his handkerchief and placed it in his coat pocket. Then he retrieved the nail that had fallen out of the plaster and rehung the picture, hoping it wouldn't look as if it had been disturbed.

Although he had no right to claim credit for his victory, since the goddess of love did all the work, he felt like a brave desperado that day. In the parlance of the brotherhood of cracksmen, of which Freddie now felt entitled to consider himself a member, he wondered whether it was not, in fact,

time to pad the hoof.[10] This he did by slipping somewhat less
noisily through the pantry window and pulling foot[11] for
home.

---

[10] Quietly leave the scene of the crime.
[11] Make a quick exit.

CHAPTER 18
Key Facts

CぉX஭

"Are you sure this will work?" Freddie asked Evangeline for the fifteenth time that morning. The two stood in front of a granite fortress on LaSalle Street which advertised itself as the Great Northern Bank.

"It will have to. We really don't have any other option, do we?" She scrutinized her companion carefully. Freddie's right arm was in a sling and his hand and forearm were encased in a mound of plaster of paris and bandages meant to approximate a cast.

"This plaster itches," he complained.

"Oh, brace up!" Evangeline's tone was unsympathetic. "If all goes well, you'll only have to wear it for another hour or so."

"An hour or so!" the young man howled. "That's easy for you to say. You aren't suffering the tortures of the damned!"

"Neither are you. Stop whining! You want to get to the bottom of this, don't you?"

The young man grudgingly replied in the affirmative.

Through narrowed eyes, Evangeline studied her friend's appearance more closely. She sighed, apparently overwhelmed by so many details not to her liking. "Why on earth are you wearing that ridiculous moustache?"

"Well, I ought to look something like him, don't you think?"

"You might have started with your height. You're a half-foot taller than he is."

The young man gave his reply through clenched teeth. "If anyone asks, I'll say I'm wearing lifts in my shoes."

"I suppose you dyed your hair black as well?" She tried to peer under his hat brim for a glimpse of his formerly auburn locks.

"It was the only way."

"I hope for your sake the dye rinses out." She smiled angelically. "I don't fancy you as a brunette."

The comment frightened the young man half out of his wits, since he had never considered the possibility that the dye was permanent. "Engie, stop it! I'm nervous enough already!"

The lady dusted off the shoulder of his coat. "You'll do. Just swagger in as if you owned the place, and no one will question who you are."

"You're not coming in?" Freddie quavered.

"No, I think it would be better if I'm not seen inside in your company. Someone might recognize me and start wondering who my escort is. I'll just take a few turns around the block and meet you here."

She patted her friend encouragingly on the back and pushed him toward the door of the bank. "Break a leg." She turned north up the block.

"You'd think an arm would have been enough for her," the young man grumbled under his breath as he passed through the entrance.

⫷⫸

Freddie looked nervously around the lobby until he spied a stairwell that must lead to the vault. Without making eye contact with any of the tellers, he steered a course directly for the stairs. When he descended, he found that he had guessed correctly. Below ground and just to the right, he saw the vault with its monstrous door gaping open like some leviathan of the deep waiting to swallow whatever hapless creature swam too near its jaws. A wooden railing with a gate and a marble counter were all that stood between him and the beast. Freddie drew in a deep breath, threw back his shoulders, and advanced toward the clerk whose job it was to guard the entrance to the subterranean depths.

When the vaultkeeper looked up at him and said a pleasant, "Good day, sir," Freddie quailed. In that split second he made a fateful decision. The disguise wasn't enough. He needed to sound the part as well. He improvised.

"Top o' the marnin' to ye, me lod." Unfortunately, the accent wasn't quite all he had hoped.

The clerk looked at him strangely. "What part of the world might you be from, sir?"

"Gosh and begorrah, it's from the emerald isle that I coom." Freddie had begun to sweat. The vault was stuffy. He prayed his hair dye wouldn't begin to run.

"From Ireland?" The clerk's voice held a slight note of disbelief. "What part?"

"Faith, have ye heerd of Belfost, boyo?"

"Yes, sir, of course I have."

"Well, I'm not from thar." Freddie had to think quickly. "I'm from the sooth of Ireland which ye may heer a bit in me speekin'. And sure it is I've traveled a wee bit. Even spent some time amoong the Hottentots. Here and thar. Hither and yon, as the sayin' is."

"I see." The clerk seemed skeptical. "How may I help you?"

Freddie reached into his coat pocket and produced the safety deposit box key. "Well, lod, you'd be doin' me a great sarvice, that ye would, if ye'd be showin' me the way to me box."

"Of course sir." The clerk took the key and checked the number. He then went to his file and drew out the corresponding signature card. "Mr. Bayne, is it?"

"Aye, lod. Thet's right. I be Desmond Bayne, himself. Withoot a doot."

"If you'd just sign the signature card, Mr. Bayne, I'll let you in." The clerk pushed an index card and a fountain pen across the counter at him. Freddie noted from the first entry that the box had been issued about two months prior to the present date. Calculating backwards, he realized that the date of issue corresponded roughly to the time Desmond appeared as a guest at the Allworthy dinner party. The last

signature was dated a week ago. He prayed that the clerk on
duty wouldn't remember Bayne on sight. The young man
took a deep breath and, with his left hand, scribbled out a
signature and a date that he hoped would approximate
Bayne's own scrawl.

The clerk compared Freddie's illegible marks to the
previous signature. He looked up in consternation. "Sir, the
signatures don't appear to correspond."

"Aye, there's the rub, lod, there's the rub. I've broke me
right hond that I use to write with. Ye see?" Freddie waggled
the stubs of his fingers that protruded through the cast. "A
wee fallin' oot with a companion aboot a week ago. Had to
deefend me honor, as the sayin' is, gosh and begorrah!"

"How unfortunate." A note of resistance in the clerk's
voice warned Freddie of trouble. "Well, sir, I'm sorry to say it
isn't our policy to admit anyone if the signatures don't
correspond."

Freddie tried to take a conciliatory approach. "Faith, it's
rother a sad way to treet a customer. Ain't it?" He waggled
his fingers again pathetically. "Boyo, I'm stuck in this plaister
for a good six moonths. It would be a hard thing if I couldn't
secure me valoobles for the nonce, don't ye see?"

"Well, I suppose that's true." The clerk relented slightly.
He tapped the counter in a fit of indecision.

"Here, I knooow," Freddie volunteered. "Pose me a
queestion and if I con't answer ready enough, why then ye
can just shoo me the way oot. How's that for fair? Boyo, I'm
appealin' to ye as a Christian. Faith, sure an' 'tis, I'm at yer
marcy." He smiled in what he hoped was a plaintive manner.

The clerk softened a bit further. "Yes, I suppose that
might work." He flipped the signature card over without
allowing Freddie to see what was written there. Cupping the
card in his hand, he asked, "Mr. Bayne, what is your
address?"

Freddie sighed to himself in relief. He rattled off .the
cursed address of the cursed apartment building with ease.

The clerk nodded. "One more question, sir. Where is your
place of business?"

Freddie's confidence began to grow by leaps and bounds.
He puffed out his chest and answered readily. "Sure tis the
grondest place of business on arth! Tis the Hyperion

Electroplate Company on the noorth side of this fair city where I'm emplooyed as Vice President." Growing reckless in his confidence, the young man gestured to the telephone on the wall. "I invite ye to call the company and ask if a Desmond Bayne woorks thar, ef ye still don't beleeve me."

The clerk paused to think the idea over. Freddie wanted to bite his tongue off for having made the suggestion. It only belatedly occurred to him that Bayne might actually have returned from the Allworthy villa and gone to work that day. It would be an unpleasant surprise if the blackguard came to the phone himself. Freddie could feel the sweat running off of his scalp, seeping through his hat band and running down the back of his neck. He prayed his shirt collar wasn't stained black with hair dye or the clerk would have even more reason to think he was odd.

The man behind the counter tapped the signature card hesitantly for a moment longer. Then he snapped it up and returned it to the filing cabinet. "No, sir, ringing the company won't be necessary. You may step this way." He held open the wooden gate to allow Freddie to pass through.

The young man wanted to break into a jig to celebrate his cleverness, but he settled for a sedate pace instead as he passed into the belly of the beast. He watched in breathless anticipation as the clerk fitted Desmond's key and the bank's key into the lock. Turning them simultaneously, the clerk swung open the flap and pulled out the safety deposit box. Handing it to Freddie, he said, "If you'd like some privacy, sir, there are rooms just outside the vault and to the right where you can go through your papers."

Cradling the box in his putatively useless arm, Freddie tried to maintain an even tone "Thank ye, lod." His heart raced as he strolled off to one of the private booths.

Once the door was securely shut behind him, he opened the lockbox with the same awe and anticipation as he might have reserved for the ark of the covenant. Encumbered by the cast, he could only work with one arm, but he managed to make a quick job of his search all the same. First he found greenbacks, quite a number of them. Approximately ten thousand dollars worth in hundred dollar bills, as nearly as he could tell. Next he found municipal bonds and stock certificates. The earliest issue date of the bonds corresponded to the date Bayne had first entered the vault. Subsequent dates indicated he had been adding to his collection of securities every few days or so. Impatiently, Freddie rifled through the rest of the stock certificates, looking for a note, a letter, a scrap of clothing that might have been used to blackmail Martin.

At the very bottom of the lockbox, hidden under the papers and money, he found what he was looking for. He bit his lip to keep from whistling through his teeth in amazement.

Freddie quickly pocketed the object and stashed the other items haphazardly in the box. Trying to rein in his excitement, he walked back to the counter and stood patiently through the ceremony of returning the safety deposit box to its home in the vault.

"Your key, Mr. Bayne." The clerk returned the bright metal object to him. Freddie put it in his pocket alongside the other bright metal object that now rested there.

"Gosh and begorrah, much obleeged to ye, lod." Freddie strolled up the stairs to the lobby and out to LaSalle Street with great dignity.

He looked around hastily in both directions for his friend. Evangeline was coming toward him but she was still about a block away. Freddie gestured to her impatiently with his good arm. When she saw him, she quickened her pace.

"Well?" she asked breathlessly, when she was within earshot. "Did you find anything?"

The young man's eyes were twinkling with self-congratulation as he produced his find.

Evangeline took the object and examined it closely. It was a miniature photograph in a gilt metal frame. The glass had been slightly cracked as if someone had thrown or dropped the picture and it had struck a hard surface. Despite the cracks in the glass, the image beneath was still clear. "Is this what she looked like?" Evangeline asked her friend.

"Well, when you see someone who's been floating in the river overnight, her features are a bit distorted, but I'd say it's Nora Johnson."

"She was very pretty," Evangeline said softly and a bit sadly as she studied the image--a solemn-eyed young woman with the hint of a smile on her lips stared back at her. An inscription had been written in a corner of the photograph. In a small, neat hand, the lettering read, "To my dearest Allworthy, remember me always. Nora." The inscription was dated April 23, 1894. Evangeline looked up at her friend. "Isn't that the date"--

Freddie completed the thought. "Yes, that was the night she died. Her body was found on the twenty-fourth."

"Hmmm." Evangeline began thinking out loud. "The date on the picture and the inscription would suggest Nora was on good terms with her murderer. Right up to the day she died. It seems to me that the drowning wasn't premeditated. She must have said something to anger him, and he pushed her in." Evangeline traced the cracks in the glass surface. "That would also explain the damage. Somebody didn't want this picture anywhere near him. It's hard enough to forget a person you've just drowned without the additional injunction to 'Remember me always.' He must have flung it away from him as soon as possible."

"It might also explain how Bayne got possession of it in the first place."

"Yes, Desmond must have been there to witness the entire scene. When the murderer fled, Bayne probably followed him and found the picture lying on the ground along the way." Evangeline frowned.

"What is it, old girl?"

She shook her head in exasperation. "Why couldn't she have used a Christian name instead of a surname! We still can't prove conclusively that it was Roland she met that night!"

"Ah, that would have been too easy." Freddie laughed ruefully. "Technically, since we still have two Allworthy suspects, what do you suggest for our next move? That is, right after we find a hammer and smash this deuced cast!" Freddie scratched at the plaster in a pointless attempt to ease his suffering.

Evangeline ignored the young man's misery. "I think the next step would best be performed by me."

"Do tell," Freddie drawled. "You mean you're actually prepared to get your gloves dirty?" He tried pounding his arm against the granite facade of the bank in the hope that he could shake the plaster away from his skin enough to alleviate the itching.

"Stop that, Freddie. You look ridiculous!" Evangeline took her friend by the arm and started to lead him up the street. Standing too long in front of the bank with a man beating his arm against the wall might draw attention. The lady regarded the young man coolly. "The next bit of detecting requires a feminine touch."

Freddie sensed a veiled insult. "Why? Don't you think I can handle it?"

"I'm sure you could, if you put your mind to it." Evangeline smiled sweetly. "I just thought that the idea of flirting with Roland might be distasteful to you."

At the mental image of making up to Roland, Freddie lost all impulse to scratch. He grimaced in distaste. "You actually think you'll get him to admit anything?"

Evangeline shrugged noncommittally. "My money is still on Roland as the killer. I don't know that he'll blurt out a confession, but being a ladies' man, his greatest weakness is that he likes to cut a dashing figure in front of an admiring female."

"Bear in mind that you'll be flirting with a murderer, Engie." A note of worry crept into the young man's voice.

"He may be a murderer, Freddie, but I'd be willing to bet he wouldn't try to strangle me in broad daylight with witnesses around. And I certainly don't intend to lead him to a secluded rendezvous."

"Well, I suppose it's worth a try. What do you expect him to say anyway?"

"I'm not sure. Some hint, some clue that he drops unawares. All I have to do is get him to start talking."

With a shudder, Freddie thought back to the infamous dinner party, when he was closeted with Bayne and Roland over cigars and brandy. "Get him to talk, by all means, just don't ask him to sing!"

CHAPTER 19
Chanson De Roland

ꙮ

"Mr. Waxman, are you in?" a young man standing in the open doorway inquired.

"Hmmm? What's that, Perkins?" The old tycoon with the white muttonchop whiskers looked up from his paperwork.

"I asked if you were in, sir. There's a lady who wishes to speak to you."

"A lady?" Waxman asked absent-mindedly. "Is it my wife?"

"No, sir." The secretary stepped forward and handed his employer a calling card. "The lady wished me to give you this."

Waxman adjusted his spectacles to read the card. "Miss Evangeline LeClair. But I don't recall...Oh, wait a minute. Yes, I do. Send her in, Perkins. Send her in."

"At once, Mr. Waxman."

The door closed briefly and then reopened to admit the lady herself. A confection in pink silk with a frilled parasol, she stepped forward into the paper-cluttered inner sanctum of the man of affairs. She held out a dainty gloved hand in greeting. "So good of you to see me without prior notice, Mr. Waxman."

"Yes, Miss LeClair, to be sure, to be sure. Very pleased to see you again!" The old man walked around his desk and solicitously helped her to a chair, afraid to tax so rare and delicate a creature with the effort of seating herself.

When he saw her comfortably settled, he resumed his place. "But seeing you again, Miss LeClair, puts me in mind of a far happier occasion before tragedy struck."

Evangeline sighed. "Then you've heard the news about Mrs. Allworthy?"

"Couldn't help but hear about it. Poisoned, eh?"

"Yes." Evangeline averted her eyes.

"I heard they arrested that medium." Waxman shook his head in puzzlement. "Just can't make sense of it. Miss Serafina seemed a nice enough young woman when we met. Soft-spoken and ladylike. Well, I guess you can't judge a book by its cover. It's a sad day for all of us when you can't even trust your houseguests not to do you in unawares! I tried to call Martin to offer my condolences, but his office said he's still up in Shore Cliff."

"Yes, I imagine he'll be staying there until the funeral arrangements are made. Did you send Roland back up to join him?"

"The very minute I heard the news." Waxman hoped Evangeline wouldn't infer that his haste in offering to dispatch Roland was prompted more by self-interest than by friendly concern.

"So he's gone to be with his uncle?"

Waxman shook his head. "Martin wouldn't hear of it. Said the boy was better off here, minding the store so to speak." The businessman tried mightily to suppress a note of regret in his voice.

"Well, that's good to know..."

"Miss?" Waxman looked at her uncomprehendingly.

"Oh, nothing." Evangeline struck off in a new conversational direction. "Just listen to me, wasting your valuable time and not telling you the purpose of my visit. You see, I'm in a quandary, Mr. Waxman, and I hoped that you might be able to help me."

Waxman's chivalrous instincts came to the fore. "Yes. I'd be happy to help, if I can. What is the nature of the problem?"

Evangeline looked as if the weight of the world rested on her shoulders. "Excess capital, sir, that's what's the problem."

"Well, well. In all my life, I've never heard it described as a problem before." The tycoon's interest was piqued.

Evangeline laughed airily. "Oh, but it is, Mr. Waxman. It is! You see, I have unfortunately inherited sacks and sacks of money and have no idea what to do with it all." She looked utterly helpless and appealing. "I really do need some guidance to invest it wisely."

Waxman gestured toward the windows behind his desk, which looked out on the bustling activity of State Street. "Perhaps some real estate?"

Evangeline flashed a winning smile. "Why, sir, you are a quick study! That's exactly the reason I'm here. I'm interested in acquiring some additional property in the city that I might rent out, and I hoped your firm could assist me. I thought Lincoln Park might be an up and coming area. You do have a few buildings there, don't you?"

"Only too glad, Miss LeClair, only too glad to help." The old man leaped at the opportunity. "I'm sure I can arrange to have one of the fellows take you around this afternoon and show you a few places." He rose and was about to go to the front office in search of a salesman when Evangeline stopped him.

"Here's an idea!" she cried. "I wonder if it would be possible for Roland to show me the properties you have for sale?"

The businessman froze in mid-stride. He turned incredulously to look at his visitor. He adjusted his spectacles to get a better look at her face since he couldn't quite believe his ears. "I'm sorry, but I thought I heard you say Roland."

"Yes, that's right." Evangeline smiled serenely. "Is he available?"

Waxman scratched his head in perplexity. He stammered, "Are...are you sure? Roland? You do mean Roland Allworthy?"

The lady nodded her head.

Waxman's bafflement was of such magnitude that it temporarily deprived him of the power of speech. When he did speak, all he could manage was a plaintive "But why?"

Evangeline laughed. "Oh, surely, Mr. Waxman, it's no mystery. I know Roland. I've met him on more than one occasion. Overwhelmed as I am when confronted by matters of business, I'd just feel more comfortable in the company of a person I already know."

Waxman stood immobilized a moment longer, impaled on the horns of a dilemma. He wanted to show his properties to their best advantage, which, as a matter of course, meant *sans* Roland, but he did not want to offend a potential customer. He heaved an immense sigh and walked out the door, feeling a fat commission slipping through his fingers as he did so. "I'll just see if I can scare him up, Miss LeClair," he said half-heartedly.

"Oh, that would be lovely," the lady enthused.

֍

Later that afternoon, after looking at several townhouses which she rejected as being too big, too small, too dark, too light, too noisy, too quiet, too cheap or too expensive, Evangeline had exhausted Roland's inventory and his lackadaisical interest in making a sale. She finally had him where she wanted him.

"Why don't we just take a stroll in the park?" she suggested. " I think I'm too done in to make a decision just now anyway."

The young man's bored demeanor immediately transformed itself into a smile of genuine pleasure. He offered his arm to escort Evangeline away from the raucous commercial streets. "At your service, Miss LeClair, to the ends of the earth, if necessary."

Smiling invitingly, the lady took the proffered arm, and the couple strolled toward the Lincoln Park Zoological Garden. "Oh, aren't the flowers lovely." She pointed to the rows of summer blooms that lined the walks. The conservatory, which housed a collection of exotic plants, stood to their left. Evangeline led in that direction with Roland, enthusiastically, in tow.

As they stepped into the humid, tropical air of the conservatory's fernery, Evangeline pretended to notice for the first time the black armband that Roland wore over his coat sleeve as a grim reminder of his aunt's death. It seemed entirely out of keeping with the rest of the apparel he had chosen--a light linen suit and a straw boater. The suit was expensive and carefully tailored. The shirt was raw silk and the sleeves studded with gold cufflinks. Evangeline speculated that if Roland had shown the same meticulous devotion to matters of business that he displayed in matters sartorial, he would be have been a millionaire in no time.

Indicating the armband, she said quietly, "I'm sorry about your aunt. Mr. Waxman said that Martin didn't want you with him up in Shore Cliff."

"Uncle didn't seem to feel the need to have me nearby to console him in his time of sorrow." There was a slight hint of sardonic humor in the youth's voice. "He said he wanted me to keep an eye on the townhouse while he's away. That's just fine with me."

"Aren't you sorry your aunt is dead?" Evangeline deliberately kept her tone of voice casual.

Roland shrugged. "I'm sorry it was Miss Serafina who did her in. I heard she was arrested. Much too pretty to be a murderer." He shook his head with regret. "Then again, auntie was all right, and it's too bad that she's the one who's the dearly departed. It's uncle I don't much care for. He's always going on about the family honor until I feel as if my head is going to explode. He's a crashing bore." Roland yawned languidly, no doubt remembering his last lecture from Martin on the subject. "I don't want to talk about him."

"What do you want to talk about?"

"Let's talk about you." Roland roguishly tilted his head to get a better look under Evangeline's hat brim.

As she returned his gaze, Evangeline noticed an unruly lock of hair had escaped the confines of his boater and flopped over his right eyebrow. He looked all of eighteen. Summoning up whatever faint enthusiasm she could muster, Evangeline smiled. "And what could you possibly want to know about me?"

"What's a lovely lady like you doing unattached? You know you could have your pick of any fellow in this city."

"That's very flattering, Roland, but just because I might have my pick, doesn't mean I'm in any hurry to make a choice."

"So much the better for me." The youth smiled in self-satisfaction. "I'm still in the running."

Evangeline decided not to set him straight on the matter of just how far out of the running he actually was. Instead, she maintained a tactful silence as they wandered through the ferns and palms and examined the celebrated fiddle-leaf rubber tree. Eventually, they found themselves at the entrance to the summer flower exhibit. The blooms were dazzling--a living rainbow of color. Red roses, shocking pink geraniums, and yellow marigolds all clamored greedily for the attention of the eye.

As they stepped through the door of the exhibit room, Roland paused and, without warning, snapped a sprig from a crimson hibiscus plant. Smiling jauntily, he handed it to Evangeline. "Allow me to present this as a tribute to your beauty."

The lady looked at him reproachfully. "It hardly seems fitting to ruin one form of beauty to honor another, Roland." She took the flower and placed the broken blossom back gently in the pot where it came from. "Besides, the gift wasn't in your power to bestow, was it?"

Unfazed by the rebuke, Roland shrugged. "I guess I'll just have to find some other way to catch your fancy."

Evangeline's gaze swept appraisingly over her companion. "Serafina was certainly right about you. You like the ladies, don't you?"

Roland threw back his head and laughed. "Like isn't the right word, Miss LeClair." He lowered his voice to a whisper. "Or may I call you Engie, the way Freddie does?"

Evangeline bit back the retort she would have preferred to make and responded evenly. "Of course you may call me Engie, if you like."

Encouraged, Roland stepped closer and folded her arm under his to escort her forward. "Oh, I do like..." He squeezed her hand ever so slightly. "...Engie."

Evangeline, incensed at his audacity, decided it was time to go in for the kill. "Did you also like Nora Johnson?"

Her words caught the youth off-guard. He stopped dead in his tracks, at a loss. "Nora? My God, I haven't thought about her in weeks. Poor Nora."

Evangeline simply stared at him. "You didn't answer my question."

For the first time, Roland seemed flustered. He looked at

the ground. "Sure, I liked Nora just fine. Liked her so much, I think that's why uncle fired me."

"What?" Evangeline was taken by surprise. They resumed their walk through the flower exhibit. An artificial waterfall trickled somewhere in the distance. The scent of lilies hung heavily in the air.

"I told you how he was forever harping on about the family honor." The youth rolled his eyes. "Anyway, I got a proper lecture about, how did he put it, 'forming an attachment beneath my station in life.' Yes, those were his words. The pompous windbag!" Roland muttered the last sentence under his breath. "Well, I wasn't about to give up the game just because uncle didn't like my choice of lady friends, so I kept on seeing her until..."

"Until he fired you?"

The youth grinned ruefully. "That's about the size of it, though he'd never admit that's what he did or why he did it. He just found me a job with Waxman because he said he thought I could utilize my talents better elsewhere!"

"Did you continue to see Nora after you left Hyperion?"

At her question, Roland's jaw became set. When he turned to stare directly at her, Evangeline thought she saw a dangerous challenge in his eyes. "Let me tell you something, Engie. I don't like having my fun spoiled by anyone, especially not by him! I decide when it's over, and it's never over until I say so!" His eyes bored into her face with a ferocity that shocked Evangeline. The intensity lasted only a moment and then Roland caught himself. He shrugged and attempted a casual smile. "Besides, I couldn't resist the urge to tweak the old goat's whiskers!"

"What do you mean?"

Roland chuckled, apparently quite pleased with himself. "I mean that I kept on seeing her on the sly after I got my walking papers. She liked it at first, but then she started acting cold toward me. She said it would be better if we didn't see each other anymore. She told me that just a few days before she had her...accident."

He enunciated the last word with such pointed emphasis and precision that it startled Evangeline. The two had paused in the center of the summer exhibit, sunlight streaming down through the glass ceiling panels and intensifying the kaleidoscope of colors that surrounded them. The scene stood in jarring contrast to their conversation. Everywhere around them, flowers dazzled the eye with exuberant life, while she and Roland spoke of nothing but blighted hopes and death.

"Did you love her, Roland?"

The youth stretched lazily in the afternoon rays. "I'm always in love, Engie. I might even be falling in love right now."

"I was asking about Nora." Evangeline refused to be dissuaded from the topic.

"Ah yes, Nora. Poor little Nora. Not good enough for uncle. I'll tell you one thing I know for sure. Nothing fuels a romance like somebody trying to keep you away from a girl! Even when Nora said goodbye, I wasn't ready to end it. Just on principle." He added angrily, half to himself, "I couldn't let him win!"

Evangeline said nothing as the two resumed their promenade through the last of the floral exhibit.

"And here's another thing," Roland said, "if I didn't know his veins were filled with ice, I'd almost think the old man wanted to keep her for himself."

"What? You actually think Martin might have had designs on Nora?" Given the elder Allworthy's horror of impropriety, Evangeline could scarcely credit the possibility.

Roland shrugged his shoulders. "He'd never admit it to me even if it was true. I'm not sure he could even admit it to himself. If auntie ever caught him mixed up with another woman, you can guess what would have happened!"

Emboldened by Roland's apparent candor, Evangeline ventured into deeper waters. "Do you think Nora was murdered?"

The youth turned to stare directly at her. "Well now, there's an interesting idea. It never crossed my mind before. Let's see. Here, I've got it! Maybe uncle was so mad when he couldn't stop me from seeing Nora that one night he just heaved her into the river. Do you suppose that's how it went?" Roland's eyes were a mask of calculated innocence as he posed the question.

Evangeline returned his gaze evenly. "Where were you the night she died, Roland?"

A sly expression distorted the youth's features. He put a finger to his lips. "Shhhh, it's a secret! Not supposed to tell."

Evangeline hoped that baiting him might draw out the truth. "Perhaps it's because you were the one who killed her."

Roland snickered. "That's a good one!" He seemed delighted at the thought. He leaned toward her and murmured in a low voice, "Would you like me better, Engie, if you thought I was dangerous?"

Evangeline made no response. She had begun to tap her foot impatiently.

Seeing that his question was not about to receive the favor of a reply, Roland relented. "Well, just so you won't think the worst of me, I'll give you a hint." He leaned in even closer and whispered in her ear. "I was in a place no respectable lady should ever know about."

Realizing how much amusement he was deriving from playing cat-and-mouse with her, Evangeline gave him a pained look and began to walk toward the exit of the conservatory. The humid air inside the greenhouse was oppressive. The moisture seemed to stick to her skin and weigh her down. It had become as cloying to her as Roland's company. She stepped outdoors and drew in a deep breath of cool, dry air. The youth followed close behind. They made their way silently up the path that led from the park to Clark Street.

Seemingly apropos of nothing, Roland finally said, "You know, there's a very clever fellow who set the poems of Edgar Allan Poe to music. One of them keeps running through my head right now. Let's see if I remember it." He hummed a few notes off-key until he could find his pitch. "That's it." He began to sing a dirgelike tune:

"Ah, distinctly I remember it was in the bleak December
    (or was it April?),
And each separate dying ember wrought its ghost upon
    the floor. Eagerly I wished the morrow; vainly I had
    sought to borrow,
From my cards surcease of sorrow--sorrow for the lost
    Lenora.
For the rare and radiant maiden whom the angels named
    Lenora. Nameless here for evermore."

He stopped and looked at her to gauge the effect. "What do you think of that? Catchy, isn't it?"

"Quite." Evangeline was completely out of patience. By this time they were standing by the curb at Clark Street, and she was attempting to hail a cab to take her back home. His song had belatedly reminded her that she had a literature class to teach that evening at Mast House. Despite her investigation, she was trying to maintain her regular classes, but very little time remained to get to the townhouse, change clothes, and have Jack drive her to Polk Street.

Roland whistled sharply as a hack came into view. He handed her into the carriage and leaned in to say, "Good-bye, Engie. I'll be seeing you again soon." With a last rakish smile as he closed the carriage door, he whispered, "Quoth the raven evermore."

ؘ؛

Evangeline raced up the stairs to the second floor of the Mast mansion where the classrooms were located. She had wasted so much time with that idiot Roland that she was nearly late for her literature class. By the time she arrived breathless at the door of the classroom, several of her students were already seated and waiting for her. A chorus of greetings in Italian, Greek, Polish, Irish, and German began the minute she entered. She waved distractedly as she rushed to the chalk board to write her somewhat disjointed lecture outline and tried to regain her composure.

The class consisted of twenty students--boys and girls, men and women ranging in age from fifteen to sixty. Some had finished their grammar school education and were taking the class to learn more about literature. A few were still struggling with the basics of English and hoped that reading poetry and prose in their adopted language would improve their vocabulary. Most lived in the neighborhood surrounding Mast House, and all worked in the factories and slaughterhouses on the west and south sides of the city. The one trait they all shared was an intellectual tenacity that matched their physical stamina. Evangeline wondered if she would have had the energy to work a ten-hour shift in a factory and then travel on foot to attend an evening class in literature.

Breathing calmly at last, she turned away from the board to face her students. After taking a quick count of attendance, she consulted the clock on the wall, and launched into her lecture.

"Good evening, everyone."

"Good evening, Meees LeClayer," they all replied with enthusiasm. The pronunciation of her name suffered a variety of deformities in the process.

She opened a large volume on the desk before her. "As I mentioned last week, we're going to begin a new phase of study with a literary form called the short story. The author I've chosen to illustrate this form is Mr. Edgar Allan Poe. He is credited with writing one of the first detective stories, and his lead was admirably followed by Mr. Wilkie Collins in England."

Many of her students looked at her blankly. Realizing she was moving beyond their depth, she smiled and retraced her steps to a more literal, if not literary, level. "We're going to start with the story I assigned you to read this week. It is called 'The Purloined Letter,' in which Mr. Poe introduces a very clever man who solves a mystery. For those of you who have read the story, can anyone tell me the name of the detective?" Several hands shot up in the air.

"Mr. Rosetti, would you like to try?" Evangeline pointed to an older man seated in the back row who deemed it appropriate to rise before answering.

"Yes, *Signora*. I know this name. It is C. Augustus..., C. Augustus...*Il mio dio! Un momento*..." Mr. Rosetti began to mumble to himself, apparently running through an extensive catalog of alternatives before selecting one.

"*Un momento, Signora! Conosco questa parola.* I know this name. It sound like a beega feesh."

"A what?" Evangeline had lost whatever phonetic association Mr. Rosetti was trying to make.

"*Si, si.* Now I remember. It sound like a...a...*come dite*! How you say...like a dolphin. The name, it is C. Augustus Dolphin."

Evangeline smiled. "Oh, I see, Mr. Rosetti. Even though your etymological reference may not be entirely accurate, I can't help but admire your unorthodox mnemonic technique."

"*Che cosa, Signora?*" Despite reading Poe, Mr. Rosetti's English vocabulary did not extend easily to five-syllable words.

Evangeline smiled again as she explained to her bewildered pupil, "In short, sir, you've come quite close."

She wrote on the board, "C. Auguste Dupin," at the same time pronouncing the name: "See Awgoost Doopan." When she turned back round to face the class, Evangeline could see several students silently mouthing the words.

"Very good, Mr. Rosetti." The man was still standing and beaming proudly at his classmates. "You may take your seat now. Can anyone tell me what the story is about?"

Several hands shot up in response to her question. "Yes, Jan." Evangeline pointed to a Polish boy seated near the door.

"This story, it is about a letter that is stolen, yet I think it does not look stolen."

"Excellent! Exactly the point. The letter has been stolen, but concealed in a place where no one would think to look. Can anyone tell me where that is?"

"Why, miss, it's right there under their bloomin' noses," replied an Irish boy seated in the front row. At that response, the entire class laughed.

"Right again. Thank you, Sean. And what point is Mr. Poe trying to make, do you think?"

Everyone fell silent. Evangeline waited a few seconds before giving them the answer. "It's all about perception, isn't it? When you expect to see a certain thing in a certain place, you don't pay any attention to it at all, do you? It's very easy to trick the mind into thinking a thing is one way when, in fact, it's just the reverse. Do you see?" A few heads nodded slowly.

"It isn't what we know that trips us up. It's what we think we know, that isn't so. It's as if--"

Evangeline cut herself short as a new thought struck her. She furrowed her brow and began flipping through the pages of *The Collected Prose And Poetry of Edgar Allan Poe* on her desk.

"A moment, if you please," she muttered. Finally locating the page she wanted, she scanned it feverishly. "Aha!" she exclaimed in triumph, poking at the text for emphasis.

"Exactly as I thought! It's what we think we know, that isn't so."

She slammed the book shut and leaned forward over her desk to gaze out at the perplexed sea of faces before her. "Quoth the raven, indeed!"

"*Che cosa, Signora?*" Mr. Rosetti asked timidly from the back row.

CHAPTER 20
Flat Notes

⊰✠⊱

Freddie breathed a sigh of relief as he threw himself into his easy chair and loosened his collar at the end of a long day. He kicked off his shoes and was just about to nod off to sleep when he heard an insistent rap at the door.

"What the devil!" the young man exclaimed to himself. "It's nearly nine o'clock. Who would be crazy enough to call at this hour!"

He swung open the door to reveal the countenance of his friend. "Engie?" he gasped in disbelief.

"The very same, though I'd think by now you might have learned to recognize me on sight."

She swept through the door and looked around. "So this is where you skulk when you aren't bothering me in Shore Cliff."

Freddie hurriedly tried to make himself more presentable by slipping on his shoes. This required him to hop on one foot, then the other, while at the same time awkwardly fumbling with his shirt and vest buttons. Collar still askew, he scurried around the parlor, quickly picking up a pair of slippers and a crumpled newspaper from the day before.

Ignoring the stir her presence had caused, Evangeline began to inspect the premises. "Rumor has it that these newfangled elevator apartment buildings haven't yet received the blessing of the upper crust as fashionable living accommodations." She advanced from the parlor into the library alcove, which was separated from the main room by a green velvet curtain swept back by a tasseled rope. "But that's just the opinion of old money, who believe that unless you have a fountain in your atrium, you're roughing it."

She peered out of the eighth-floor windows which overlooked Lake Shore Drive. "Have you ever tried dropping a flower pot from this height?" she asked speculatively.

"No, and I'll thank you not to conduct any such experiment from these premises!" Freddie was indignant. "I really wouldn't care to be evicted on your account." With a scowl, he continued the battle with his recalcitrant collar button.

"It was just a thought." Evangeline laughed teasingly. She ran her index finger over an end table. Her white-gloved hand revealed no dust. "Hmmm, very good. Apparently, you know how to fend for yourself when Mama isn't around to look after you."

"Growing up in a house full of women, how could I have turned out any other way?" Freddie's tone was rueful.

"You might have turned out as that most loathsome of all insects, a mama's boy, who expects that every female within whining distance was created for the sole purpose of smiling indulgently and waiting on him hand and foot." The lady gave her friend a sidelong look. "I'm pleasantly surprised that you're not."

Her eyes came to rest on a large houseplant sitting on a mahogany stand at the opposite end of the parlor. "Will wonders never cease! Do my eyes deceive me, or have you become a horticulturist? With an aspidistra no less!"

Freddie rolled his eyes. "It was my mother's one and only contribution to decorating this flat. She believes that plants are a civilizing influence."

"Well, I've never been of the opinion that culture can be transmitted through chlorophyll, but it does lend a certain *quelquechose*." Evangeline circled the plant appraisingly. "You've somehow managed not to kill it. Very good indeed!"

Just beyond the aspidistra was a modest dining room holding an oak pedestal dining table and four chairs.

Evangeline did not advance farther in that direction but instead turned her attention to a room on the right set off by double doors. "The bedroom, I take it?"

Remembering an unmade bed and a pile of soiled linen heaped in the corner of his sleeping chamber, Freddie hurriedly interposed himself between his visitor and the doors. "You really don't want to go in there."

Apparently judging it wise not to inquire too closely as to the reason, Evangeline stepped back. "Is this a single bedroom flat?"

"No, there's a small bedroom off the parlor for the valet whom I expect someday to afford to hire. In the meantime, I just have to shift for myself."

"I'd think the interest from your trust fund would provide you with ample means to secure one." Evangeline turned to circle the parlor one more time.

Freddie shook his head. "I'm trying to live off of my pay as a reporter. Besides, it takes some getting used to, after growing up surrounded by female relatives--and female servants, for that matter. The idea of another fellow skulking around these narrow quarters all day, folding my pajamas and dusting my knickknacks."

Unwilling to contemplate the image further, Freddie changed the subject. "To what do I owe the pleasure of your visit at this ungodly hour?" He placed a sardonic emphasis on the word "pleasure."

"Ah, yes. Well, there is that." Evangeline abruptly flounced down on the horsehair sofa and removed her gloves. "Would it be too much of an inconvenience to ask for a cup of tea?" She eyed her friend with a reproachful expression. "I certainly wouldn't want to put you to any trouble."

Freddie, unused to the role of host, felt himself flush with embarrassment. "Oh, sorry. Of course. Won't be a minute." He scurried off to the galley-sized kitchenette at the back of the flat.

The living room echoed the sounds of slamming cupboards, clattering crockery, and finally the whistle of a boiling tea kettle.

The young man emerged shortly thereafter bearing a tray with a chipped teacup, a mismatched saucer and a large pot of tea. "There you are." He proudly put the tray on the buffet table in front of his guest.

Evangeline's amused expression suggested that the presentation left something to be desired. "I think you should seriously consider hiring a valet at the first opportunity."

Freddie resumed his seat in the easy chair and watched while she poured herself a cup.

"You know I take my tea with lemon and sugar."

At this gentle admonition he flew back into the kitchen and clattered and rattled a bit more. When he returned with the lidless sugar bowl, he apologized for the dearth of lemon or milk on the premises. After Evangeline had sweetened her tea and taken a few sips without grimacing, which Freddie deemed a favorable sign, he pursued his original question. "Why are you here?"

"Glad to see you as well." Evangeline set down the cup and saucer, folded her hands in her lap, and began. "I wanted to give you the results of my chat with Roland today."

"Ahhh!" Freddie leaned forward in his chair. "Tell me all."

"I find him to be an insufferable puppy!" His friend sounded indignant.

"Maybe so, but do you still think he's a murderer?"

Evangeline lifted her eyes to the ceiling as she contemplated the question. "Well, at the beginning of our conversation, I was fairly certain, but now, I'm not so sure." She launched into an account of her conversation with Mr. Allworthy, the younger.

"He still sounds pretty suspicious to me," Freddie commented after she finished.

"But I believe he has an alibi."

"That's ridiculous! Don't tell me you believe that nonsense about 'I was in a place no respectable lady should ever know about.' That could be anywhere."

"On the contrary, my friend, it could be only one place in this city."

He looked at her in surprise. "Engie, what are you talking about?"

The lady smiled serenely. "After I got over my irritation at what I thought was a pointless waste of time, I finally realized he was trying to be clever. He actually left me a clue as to his whereabouts that night."

"Would you care to share it, or would you rather I just bump around in the dark and stub my toes on the furniture for awhile?"

Evangeline laughed. "I doubt the furniture could take that much abuse. I will enlighten you presently." She paused to take another sip of tea. In wonderment, she added, "This actually isn't bad. Darjeeling?"

"Thank you." Freddie chose to ignore the implied insult. "You were about to say..."

"I was about to say that when Roland broke into song, it wasn't for idle reasons."

"Well, that's some comfort at least. I'd hoped there'd be some recompense to your eardrums for that sort of punishment."

"As indeed there was. It's a good thing Mr. Edgar Allan Poe came to my rescue."

"Don't you use his work in your classes?"

"Yes, but usually it's the fiction, not the poetry. As I was starting to discuss one of his short stories with my class this evening, I took a moment to scan the text of 'The Raven.' I discovered that Roland had intentionally taken liberties with the original version."

"To wit?"

"To wit he altered several words that have a bearing on the matter at hand. When he came to the line 'it was in the bleak December', he added 'or was it April.' Nora drowned at the end of April, did she not?"

"Correct." Freddie was impressed.

"After that he altered the line about sorrow. 'Vainly I had sought to borrow, from my cards surcease of sorrow.' Poe used the word 'books', not 'cards'."

"What kind of cards do you suppose he meant?"

"I'd expect playing cards. I certainly don't think he meant calling cards."

"Interesting." The young man rubbed his chin reflectively.

"Then he said 'sorrow for the lost Lenora.' He put the accent on the last syllable making the name sound like Nora, not Lenore as it is in the poem."

"Go on." Freddie's interest had been piqued even further. "Anything else?"

"Well, the most significant hint of all is the word

'Evermore.' It occurs only once in the poem. At the end of the first stanza, which was the one he sang to me. He repeated the word when he said goodbye to me. But the last line of the refrain is always 'Quoth the raven, nevermore.' His last words to me were 'Quoth the raven, evermore.'"

Freddie frowned in concentration, vainly attempting to connect the hints into a coherent clue. "And what do you make of all of that?"

"He was telling me where he was the night Nora drowned."

"He was?" Freddie stopped concentrating and looked up at his friend in amazement.

"Of course. He was playing poker at a brothel that night."

"What!" the young man gasped.

Evangeline looked pityingly at her friend. "Given your previous experience in the levee during our last case--"

"Our last what?"

"I'd think you of all people would remember the name of the most prestigious, if that's the right word, house of ill fame in the entire city."

"The Evermore Club." Freddie exhaled the words. "Why, of course!"

"I believe it's the only bordello that publishes its own brochure praising the splendor of its accoutrements, including gold-plated spittoons in every room."

"The Evermore Club." The young man repeated the phrase again in wonderment. "Why didn't I see it earlier? That's exactly the sort of place a young swell like Roland would be likely to frequent."

"Given his interest in the ladies, I don't think he makes too fine a distinction over whether their affection for him is genuine or merely rented for the night."

"The Evermore Club..."

"Freddie, stop saying that," Evangeline admonished irritably. "You sound as if you're in some sort of trance."

"But it's just so...so..."

"Yes, I know. So *je ne sais quoi*. Can we move on?"

"All right then. How do we establish his alibi?"

Since his question was met by dead silence, Freddie glanced up at his friend, who sat demurely on the couch, hands once more folded, smiling placidly in his direction.

"Do I really need to belabor the obvious point of which of us will be performing that task?"

"Why is it always this way?" he asked weakly. "Why do I never see it coming?"

"Because you have an absolute talent for wandering into quicksand, that's why. Besides," Evangeline sniffed self-righteously, "I'd think it's the least you could do after what I've been forced to endure today!"

"All right, Engie, you win." Freddie shuddered at the thought of Roland's unwanted attentions being foisted on his friend, not to mention that rasping tenor voice of his. "I withdraw the objection. I capitulate utterly. What's the plan?"

The lady beamed at him over her teacup. "You see, you can be reasonable when you put your mind to it. You'll have to pay a visit to the famous Evermore Club tomorrow, see the proprietress and find out what she knows."

"You mean proprietresses, don't you? It's owned by sisters--Ada and Minna Evermore."

"I'm not privy to the sordid details of who runs the establishment!"

"And yet you somehow managed to peruse their brochure..." Freddie trailed off impishly.

Evangeline cleared her throat. "Yes, well, never mind that. We have more important matters to discuss than my choice of reading material, such as what other fish I have to fry tomorrow."

"What will you be doing while I immerse myself in that den of iniquity?"

Evangeline tapped her chin thoughtfully. "I have to sort out how many suitors Nora had actually attracted."

"What do you mean?"

"Well, Roland may have been telling the truth when he said his uncle had his eye on her as well."

"Given how much he prizes his reputation, I just can't imagine Martin Allworthy making eyes at anybody!" Freddie registered surprise.

"Well, frankly, neither can I, but it's worth pursuing just in case. Something you told me right after Nora was drowned sticks in my mind. It was something about flowers. Something her roommate said. Do you have that infernal notebook of yours around anywhere?"

Freddie leaped to his feet triumphantly. "See, I always told you it would come in handy someday!" He dashed off to the dining room where he had unceremoniously thrown his suit jacket over the back of a chair. Diving his hand into the pocket, he withdrew his most prized possession and returned to the parlor.

By this time Evangeline had tilted her head back on the sofa and closed her eyes, steeling herself for the unendurable minutiae. "Read!" she commanded. "Read out loud to me everything you wrote down right after Nora died."

With great enthusiasm and various vocal pitches to mimic the people he had interviewed that day, Freddie read. When he got to his conversation with Sophie Simms, Evangeline sat up.

"Stop!" she ordered. "Stop right there." She passed her hand across her forehead. "So Nora had been receiving flowers from an anonymous someone who called himself her 'greatest admirer.'"

"That's what it says." Freddie pointed to his notebook as if it contained holy scripture and was, therefore, incontrovertible truth.

"Perhaps I might be able to fit a face to the man with no name. Did you write down Miss Sophie's address?"

"Of course," Freddie replied with wounded dignity. His thoroughness as a reporter had been callously impugned by the question.

"Would you be so good as to jot it down for me?" his friend inquired patiently.

Freddie scribbled out the address and handed it to her.

"And she said the flowers were always delivered from a shop around the corner?"

"Yes, but I don't have the address to that."

Evangeline shrugged. "It shouldn't be hard to find. It may even be printed on the cards. Let's hope that Miss Sophie is the sentimental type."

Freddie raised a questioning eyebrow.

"Let's hope she hasn't tossed them out. I'd like to get a look at those cards and talk to that florist."

"What do you think you'll find out?"

She tilted her head to the side, considering the question. "Perhaps something, perhaps nothing." Without warning,

Evangeline stood up to go. She slipped on her gloves and marched in the general direction of the exit with the young man rushing to catch up. "If I'm very lucky I should be able to find out whether Nora's greatest admirer had gray hair or blond."

Her friend held the door open for her.

She glanced back briefly into the apartment. "Your apartment is quite nice, Freddie. It will do very well to entertain company. Thank you for the tea." She briefly eyed the mismatched china. "Once again, let me advise you to engage a valet, dear boy." She patted him on the cheek as she left. "At the earliest possible opportunity. There really are some necessities one shouldn't live without."

CHAPTER 21
Gone For Evermore

ങ്ഷ‍ॐ‍ഋ

Freddie regarded his trip to the Evermore Club with far less trepidation than the last journey Evangeline had commanded him to make to the levee during their previous detecting adventure. Having survived Mother Connelly's shabby house of sin, he considered himself a veteran of the worst the red light district could offer. He even neglected to wear a disguise this time, so confident was he of his own investigative powers.

The Evermore Club, while still part of the first ward, refused to be classed with the ramshackle sporting houses and third-rate saloons that constituted the old levee, Little Cheyenne, which extended only as far south as Harrison Street. With genteel disdain for their downscale competition, Ada and Minna Evermore had withdrawn farther south to the new levee, or the Tenderloin as it was called, where they had leased a three-story, fifty-room mansion and decorated it with a splendor hitherto unknown in such establishments.

Freddie, through apocryphal stories told by other reporters, knew something of the history of the owners. The Evermore sisters, who had both made less than blissful marriages, had pragmatically concluded some years back that the prospect of being beaten and robbed by strangers was less of a certainty than being beaten and robbed by their own spouses. They therefore pooled their resources, abandoned said spouses to their own unnatural devices, and opened a house of prostitution in Omaha. There they met with such success that they decided they were ready for the big city, whereupon they opened the Evermore Club in Chicago. They had, of course, wisely decided not to use their actual surname in this venture. The alias was a private joke, since their grandmother had always chosen to end letters to her nearest and dearest with the words 'Evermore yours.'

While Freddie felt less dismay about this visit, he couldn't completely eliminate a certain degree of nervousness since he had never set foot in Tenderloin territory before. He decided the likelihood of running into anyone he knew was more remote if he scheduled his visit for the middle of the afternoon at which time he took a cab to the address in the 2100 block of South Dearborn. After climbing out of the hack and paying the driver, he found himself standing before a sedate and imposing edifice that looked for all the world as if it could have been the home of one of Chicago's richest business tycoons. The business which was conducted in the building would never have been guessed from the outside. Only its proximity to the exotic House of All Nations, which Freddie knew was not a foreign embassy, might lead one to guess its purpose.

He rang the doorbell and was totally unprepared for what greeted him. Instead of a blowsy woman in a kimono, the door was opened by a butler with an English accent.

"Good afternoon, sir," the butler said. "Please step in."

In awe and wonderment Freddie walked into the foyer. The floor was inlaid with glossy teakwood parquet, covered by antique oriental carpeting. A young woman in a chiffon frock descended the staircase and crossed the foyer to enter one of the closed rooms on the first floor. "Good afternoon," she said, nodding pleasantly as she walked past Freddie. He stood gawking after her. She wore her hair curled in blond ringlets and reminded him of Ophelia Cartwright, the daughter of one of his mother's oldest friends. He remembered dancing with Ophelia at a cotillion once. He also remembered imagining at the time what it would be like to--

He shook himself out of his forbidden reverie when he

noticed two other young woman walking down the front hall, whispering and giggling to one another. They smiled and greeted Freddie with great civility as they passed. Certain he had made a mistake, the young man took a slip of paper out of his pocket to check the address he'd written down. It seemed to him he had wandered into a young ladies' finishing school and not the Evermore Club.

"This...this is...the...uh...Evermore Club, isn't it?" he stammered to the butler.

"Yes sir, it is. May I show you to the wine room for some refreshment? Or perhaps you would care to view the art collection first. May I take your hat and gloves for you, sir?"

"You're sure this is the Evermore Club?" the young man persisted.

"Quite sure, sir. I have been employed here for some time." The butler's voice was grave. "There can be no mistake."

Freddie took a deep breath and collected his wits. "I'd like to see one of the Misses Evermore, if you don't mind."

"Do you have an appointment, sir?"

The young man decided that such a conversation occurring in such a place as this could be classified among the greatest oddities he had ever experienced.

"An appointment? To see a ..." He trailed off, realizing that what he almost said could be construed as offensive. "Uh, that is, I mean, do I really need an appointment?"

The butler took Freddie's hat and gloves and disposed of them in the foyer closet. He returned and straightened his jacket fastidiously. "The ladies keep a very busy schedule, sir. Miss Ada is not in the house at present, and Miss Minna is immersed in paperwork."

Freddie tried a less impertinent approach. "Could you inquire of Miss Minna if she is at liberty to speak to a visitor? I won't take much of her time. Fifteen minutes, no more."

The butler looked him over, obviously judging his rank from the cut of his suit. The verdict was that he was probably a gentleman and a potential customer whom Miss Minna would not want shown to the door too hastily.

"I'll just see, sir. Whom shall I say is calling?"

Freddie fumbled quickly for his calling card case and handed a card to the butler.

The servant glanced at it. "If you'll be good enough to wait here, Mr. Simpson."

"Of course, of course. Thank you, my good man!" Freddie felt a flood of relief.

After the butler departed, the young man's eyes wandered around the foyer. He felt like a prize yokel who had just come to the big city for the first time. He gaped up at the ceiling chandelier which contained about a thousand cut crystal prisms. Freddie then glanced off to an open parlor on his left. He couldn't help but notice the piano. It appeared to be made of gold--solid gold. The heavy draperies that graced the front windows were of gold thread. His jaw dropped open. He had originally believed the brochures to be an exaggeration but after being struck by opulence from every side, he rather thought them to be an understatement.

The butler startled him by padding up noiselessly on the plush hall carpet. "Miss Minna can spare you a few moments now if you'll step this way, sir."

Freddie gawked and gaped his way down the hall past every open parlor door. One had copper walls with brass wainscoting. Another was ornamented entirely in gold—-gold curtains, gilt furniture, gold-leaf wallpaper, and, of course, a gold spittoon in the corner.

At the very end of the hall, he was led into an office with a massively carved claw-foot walnut desk. Behind it sat a tiny woman of about forty, dressed conservatively in a striped silk shirtwaist and black skirt. Her auburn hair was pulled back in a simple pompadour which called attention to her pearl teardrop earrings. A gold pince-nez was perched on her nose as she made some notes in a ledger book before her. She looked up and removed the pince-nez when she saw her visitor had arrived. Rising, she came around the desk and extended a tiny, beringed hand in greeting. "Mr. Simpson, to what do I owe the honor of this visit?"

Freddie stepped forward, bowing slightly as he took her hand. "Ma'am, the honor is all mine." He registered a sense of the absurdity of the conversation. "First allow me to say how overwhelmed I am by the splendor of your...uh...house."

Minna Evermore resumed her seat and gestured for Freddie to take a chair in front of the desk. She smiled. "Thank you, we've tried very hard, my sister and I, to make this place a cut above the average. Might I offer you some sherry, Mr. Simpson, or perhaps--"

"No, nothing, thank you, ma'am." He cut in precipitously before she offered him something more awkward to decline. "If I might ask. I noticed a few young ladies as I came in. They were very well-dressed. They aren't...uh...that is, I mean, what do they do here?"

Miss Evermore laughed. "They are escorts for the gentlemen who come to this establishment. Some of the gentlemen find their company so captivating that they manage to while away entire evenings together."

Freddie felt his eyes grow round as saucers. "But they were so...so..."

"Ladylike?" Minna completed the thought. "I'm pleased you think so since that was our intention. All our girls take elocution and etiquette lessons. Our clientele is the *crème de la crème* of Chicago society. You understand we serve only the best people. There's no reason why someone engaged in this line of work needs to act badly or be treated badly. All our girls act like ladies, and I insist that the gentlemen who patronize this establishment treat them as such."

Evidently noticing that the look of surprise had not left Freddie's face, Miss Evermore decided to elucidate the point further. "Do you know what it costs to visit the wine room here, Mr. Simpson?"

"Why, no, I can't say that I do."

"Ten dollars. We keep a very good cellar in this house. Dinner costs about fifty dollars, as would an evening with one of the ladies."

"Fifty dollars!" Freddie gasped in wonderment. "Holy Moses!"

"A bit too rich for your blood perhaps?" Miss Evermore smiled in amusement.

"No, I didn't mean that. That isn't why I'm here anyway but...fifty dollars...holy Moses!"

"It serves a dual purpose. The rates allow us to make a comfortable living and also help thin out the riff-raff we don't wish to attract as part of our clientele."

"I see." Freddie still couldn't shake his sense of amazement. "You really must know your business, Miss Evermore, but I have to say you just don't seem the sort of woman who--"

"Who chooses not to be mistreated by a man, Mr. Simpson?" Sighing, she stood up to walk around the room as she spoke. "I don't know if you've noticed, but the world seems to be skewed to the benefit of the male sex. Small wonder that is, since the laws were made by men. Before there were laws, I expect they just bullied women into doing what they wanted. Nature seems to have given them the muscular advantage to have their way in most things." She laughed sardonically. "As far as I can determine, there's only one profession in this wide world where that balance of power seems to be reversed in favor of the ladies." She ran her hand across the back of Freddie's chair as she walked past. "When it comes to affairs of the...shall we say, heart, it's a different matter altogether."

Minna Evermore resumed her seat. "I am a social realist, Mr. Simpson. Not being the sentimental type I don't get tangled up in the Divine Destiny of True Womanhood and other such philosophical nonsense. As long as men continue to be men, we poor women must make our way in the world as best we can." She looked around the office speculatively for a moment. "Someday Ada and I will retire to a quiet little town somewhere. Two maiden ladies with a substantial fortune between them and no past to speak of. In a few years. At this point, a very, very few."

Freddie was struck by the fact that Evangeline probably shared more views in common with Minna Evermore than his friend realized. He smiled. "I have a lady friend, Miss Evermore, who really ought to meet you."

The proprietress shrugged. "Well, if she's young, attractive, and can conduct herself like a lady, she may apply for employment here."

Freddie laughed out loud at the thought. "No, that isn't exactly what I meant. She's more the suffragette type."

"Unfortunately, that attitude really isn't good for our business." Miss Evermore's face was solemn.

"No, I wouldn't expect so," Freddie murmured in agreement. "If you don't mind my saying so, Miss Evermore, you must be the J. Pierpont Morgan of your profession."

Minna Evermore smiled. "Thank you, Mr. Simpson, that's quite gratifying to hear. One should always try to do one's best." She hesitated, eyeing the ledger book in front of her. "I'm sorry to be abrupt, but as you can see I have a great deal of work left to do this afternoon. Would you be kind enough to state the nature of your business?"

With a start, Freddie realized that he'd become so distracted by everything he saw and heard that he'd completely forgotten his errand. "Oh, I am sorry. I'm here because I'd like some information."

The woman behind the desk raised one corner of her mouth in a skeptical demi-smile. "Information is a valuable commodity, Mr. Simpson, like some other commodities I have for sale in my house. It may carry a heavy price tag, depending on the nature of the question. What is it you wish to know?"

"I want to know if a certain...ahem...gentleman of my acquaintance was here on the night of April twenty third."

"We aren't in the habit of revealing the comings and goings of our guests, sir," the proprietress answered lightly.

Freddie's tone grew urgent. "You must understand. It isn't idle curiosity. If I knew he was here, it might keep him out of some serious trouble. I'm not even sure you would remember who was in the place three months ago."

"Oh, I have a very good memory, Mr. Simpson. And what I forget, my little ledgers help me remember."

"Your ledgers?" Freddie didn't comprehend.

Minna Evermore gestured to a bookcase that stood against the wall to the left of her desk. From floor to ceiling it contained bound green ledger books, each one labeled on the spine with a series of dates.

"I find it useful to keep track of all my guests just in case I ever have a falling out with city hall or the police force, though heaven knows I pay them enough to mind their own business. Still, one can't be too careful." She looked at Freddie with a calculating gleam in her eye. "What are you willing to offer in exchange for the information you need?"

Freddie thought fast. "I'm prepared to offer complete silence in exchange."

The woman behind the desk stared at him coldly. "I'm afraid I don't understand."

Freddie tried to sound inoffensive. "Well, it's just that if too much public attention were brought to bear on the activities of this house, it might be injurious to your standing in the community, not to mention your profits. I'm sure that withholding that kind of information must be worth something."

Minna Evermore regarded him in silence.

"Did I happen to mention that I'm a reporter?" Freddie tried to make himself the portrait of fresh-faced innocence.

"I see." The proprietress looked grim. "For which newspaper, if I might be so bold as to inquire?"

"The *Gazette*."

"Of course. You would work for the only newspaper in town whose publisher isn't a member of my clientele."

"Yes, I believe Mr. McGill is also a temperance advocate and a member of the Civic Federation. Last I heard, the Federation really didn't approve much of what was going on in the levee." Freddie maintained a bright tone. "I was considering doing a piece on the brochures you printed up to advertise this fine house. Some people might get stirred up over an article like that. They might even start agitating to close your operation down. Don't you think they might, Miss Evermore?"

With a set jaw, Minna Evermore rose from her desk and walked toward the bookcase. "I believe you said April twenty third, Mr. Simpson?"

"Yes, yes, that's right. The evening of April twenty third, sometime around 9 o'clock or after." Freddie sprang out of his chair. He eagerly peered over the lady's shoulder as she rested the ledger book on the side of her desk and thumbed through the pages to the appropriate date.

"What is the name of the gentleman?"

"Roland. Roland Allworthy, though for all I know he might have used an alias."

Minna Evermore's voice dripped with sarcasm. "Young gentlemen who wish to be anonymous in this place rarely remain so for long. I know your young friend well and he doesn't use an alias."

She scanned the page with her index finger and stopped midway down. "Yes, here it is. He arrived at about nine-thirty with some other young gentlemen of his acquaintance. Stayed in one of the gaming rooms until well after two before retiring with Charlotte for the night." The proprietress raised her head for a moment and stared off into space. "Yes, I actually do remember that evening. We were running a poker tournament, very high stakes, and that's why I remember. I was in the room, and Roland was one of the players, though how he managed to scrape together the money I have no idea. There were at least twenty other people besides me who would have seen him lose his shirt that night."

She slammed the book shut decisively and returned it to the bookcase. "Yes, Mr. Simpson, he was here. The game started at ten o'clock, and he was here some time before it began. He stayed all night. Never left until morning." She glanced at the young man with a pained expression. "Does that answer your question or do you wish to extort any other information while you're here?"

"No, ma'am." Freddie attempted to appear humble. "That answers it, and thank you very much for being so helpful."

Minna Evermore held out her hand. "I'll be bidding you farewell then."

Freddie took her hand solemnly. "Miss Evermore, I must say it's been a pleasure."

The proprietress smiled morosely as she rang for the butler to show Freddie out. "No, Mr. Simpson, that's where you're wrong. It's a business. It's always been a business. Good day."

CHAPTER 22
Your Latest Admirer

☙❦❧

While Freddie was busy extracting information from Miss Evermore, Evangeline was on her way to question Nora's roommate, Miss Sophie Simms. She had taken the precaution of telephoning Sophie at the boardinghouse where she lived right after she got home from Freddie's flat. Evangeline wanted to find out if the girl still possessed the cards which had been sent with each of the bouquets Nora received. Her elation at hearing Sophie's affirmative response was somewhat dampened by the fact that it was too late that evening to go to Sophie's rooms to claim the cards. The girl was working all the following day, and by the time she would arrive home, the florist shop would be closed.

Evangeline's suggestion that Sophie take the day off was met by a gasp of disbelief. The girl worked at Campion's, Chicago's premier department store. Marshall Campion had a reputation for running his store like a military training camp, and employees who wished to take an afternoon off for a reason that did not involve the death of a family member would not be employees for long. Therefore, Evangeline had agreed to meet Sophie at the store and pick the cards up there.

She made less than an auspicious start on her mission.

Having been tied up with Mast House business all morning and into the afternoon, Evangeline had to rush to reach Sophie before the day was entirely gone. When she left her townhouse, she dispensed with the idea of hailing a cab. The congestion of the traffic on the city's busiest street made it quicker to walk to the downtown business district. Making haste in Chicago's Loop at any time of day was a known absurdity. The noise, coal dust, foot traffic, delivery wagons, trolleys, paper boys, and shoppers should have warned Evangeline of the folly of it. She persisted anyway and made painfully slow progress, dodging as many obstacles as she could. She fancied that even the ubiquitous street sweepers in white uniforms and helmets seemed to be conspiring to delay her.

At the corner of State and Lake, she crossed to the east side of the street, narrowly dodging a streetcar that was bearing down on her. Evangeline tried to keep her temper by reminding herself it was only an additional block to the imposing edifice that was the Marshall Campion Department Store.

Campion's took up six stories of a full square city block. Everyone who was anyone shopped at Campion's as did many nobodies who wanted to be somebody. Ever since the World's Fair, Campion's had become a landmark that had to be seen by foreign visitors before they could consider their tour of the city complete. Unfortunately, many of these visitors had decided to congregate in front of Campion's display windows to gawk at the merchandise, so that Evangeline had to squeeze through the admiring throng to reach the entrance.

Once inside, she breathed a sigh of relief, but her trials were not yet over. She now had to navigate endless aisles of ladies' hats and jewelry looking for the glove counter where Sophie had said she worked. After several twists and turns, Evangeline was finally confronted with a curved glass case displaying row after row of handwear in every conceivable style, color and fabric. Freddie had made particular mention of Miss Simms' coiffure so Evangeline had no difficulty identifying the young woman with red hair piled up in what looked like a slightly asymmetrical beehive.

"Are you Sophie Simms?" She had very little doubt as she

approached.

"Yes, I am. How may I help madame?"

Evangeline smiled to herself at the stilted form of address. "My name is Evangeline LeClair. We spoke over the telephone yesterday."

"Oh my, yes!" Sophie's hand flew to her mouth as if she'd been accused of doing something illegal. She looked surreptitiously around to see if she were being observed by a floorwalker or her supervisor. Seeing the coast was clear, she motioned to Evangeline to step to the corner, where the counter divided.

"I have them right here." She slipped a hand into her skirt pocket and removed a stack of small notes. They were the size of calling cards, and Evangeline guessed there must have been about twenty of them.

"That's quite a collection. May I look them over?"

Sophie bit her lip and glanced around again. "Yes, if you like. Just don't spread them out on the counter, or somebody might wonder what I'm doing."

Evangeline stared in curiosity at the girl. "Are you really being watched that closely?"

Sophie nodded solemnly, her beehive hairdo bobbing in assent. "All the time."

Evangeline glanced casually around at a few of the other counters to see who might be watching. No one appeared to be paying any attention to them. It struck her that all the female clerks were dressed alike. She looked back to Sophie and scrutinized her more closely. "It's funny. In all the years I've shopped here, I never realized that you all seem to be wearing some kind of uniform."

"Well, it's not a uniform exactly." Sophie corrected her. "Just a white blouse and black skirt. We get to choose the fabric ourselves."

"But not the style, apparently."

"No, we're all told that we have to present a neat and consistent appearance to the public. The store issues the clothes to us--"

Evangeline cut in archly. "And takes the cost of your apparel out of your paycheck, I expect."

"Yes, that's right. How did you know?" Sophie seemed genuinely startled at the observation.

Evangeline shrugged. "It just seemed the sort of thing Campion's would do." She cast a swift glance at the girl's hair. "I'm surprised they didn't make you dye your hair brown so it wouldn't clash with the woodwork."

Sophie's eyes showed a trace of alarm. "Oh, but you misunderstand! This is a fine place to work! A fine place! Mr. Campion always tells us so, and he's a very great man, so surely he must know. I'm fortunate to have this job at all when so many other poor girls are working in factories." Sophie hesitated. "That's why I...I..."

"Yes, my dear. I understand the need to be discreet. I won't stay but a moment." Evangeline began to sort through the note cards. After she had flipped through half the stack, she commented, "They all read the same. 'From your greatest admirer.'"

"Except for this one." Sophie reached for the bottom card in Evangeline's hand.

"'Happy birthday from your greatest admirer!'" Evangeline squinted under the garish overhead lights to get a better look at something that had caught her attention. She looked back to the previous card and then compared it to the one Sophie had singled out. Finally, she saw it. "The handwriting appears to be different."

"Does it? I never noticed." Sophie took back the final card and the one sent before it.

"You see." Evangeline pointed to the lettering. "This one was dated a week earlier than the final card. The words 'from your greatest admirer' ought to look the same if they were written by the same hand. Do you know who wrote these cards? Was it the florist or the man who sent the bouquets?"

"I'm sorry, but I don't know." Sophie shook her head solemnly. "It was all I could do to get Nora to let me see them at all. She never told me who they were from."

"Perhaps I can find out for myself. Do you know the name of the florist?"

"Why, yes, I guess I should after all those deliveries." Sophie wrote the information on a slip of paper and handed it to Evangeline.

"May I take these with me, just in case the florist doesn't remember?"

The shop girl hesitated. "Only if you promise to bring

them back, ma'am. Nora was my friend and these were special to her."

"Of course, I promise." Evangeline smiled reassuringly. "And I am sorry about your friend."

Just at that moment a man in a black suit walked up. He did not appear to be a customer. At first he said nothing but merely stared significantly in Sophie's direction. The girl looked down and began to awkwardly rearrange the contents of a box of sale gloves on the counter in front of her.

"Are you finding everything you need, madame?" he inquired of Evangeline.

"Oh yes, everything I could possibly require." Evangeline smiled graciously at the floor manager as she slipped the stack of note cards into her pocket and prepared to leave the store. "This young woman has been most helpful."

సౌ

About an hour later, Evangeline stepped off a streetcar at the corner of Clybourn and Willow. It was already quite late, but she thought the local shops might still be open for another half hour. A few doors up from the corner, she noticed a window displaying floral arrangements. Guessing this to be her destination, she entered the premises of Witherspoon Florists, where she was greeted by an elderly gentleman behind the counter. He wore no suit jacket, merely a vest and shirt with black sleeve protectors, which seemed a practical consideration since he was in the process of cutting a bouquet of roses. He had a face like a shriveled apple with a pair of bright eyes staring out from the core.

"Good afternoon, madame, how may I serve you?" He quickly reached for a towel to wipe off his hands.

"Good afternoon. Mr. Witherspoon, I presume?" Barely waiting for an acknowledgment, she forged ahead. "I'd like to order a large floral centerpiece and a few incidental arrangements to be sent to my home. I'm planning a small dinner party for tomorrow evening."

The florist's eyes grew brighter at the prospect of a large order. "Of course, madame. Of course." He stooped under the counter for his order book and began the time-consuming process of asking what the lady's preferred colors and flowers would be. As he was completing the paperwork, Evangeline skirted closer to the real purpose for her visit.

"You know there are many florist shops closer to my townhouse than this one, but I came here because your shop was recommended to me by an acquaintance of mine. He used your services quite frequently over the past several months."

Without batting an eye, the florist replied, "Oh yes, that must have been Mr. Allworthy."

Evangeline was speechless for a moment at how easily her suspicions had been confirmed. Although she had her hand cupped around the notecards in her pocket in the event she might need to prompt the florist's memory, she released them and let them sink to the bottom of her skirt pocket. She did not have to feign surprise when she commented, "Why, Mr. Witherspoon, that's exactly right! How could you have known so quickly who I meant?"

The old florist chuckled. "Well, this neighborhood is a bit off the beaten path. I don't get many customers, and when I get one who's a regular, I tend to remember."

"I'll bet you can't remember what he looks like." Evangeline tried to make the question sound innocent. She felt her heart pound with excitement--she was on the brink of discovering which Allworthy was Nora's greatest admirer.

The old florist drew himself up importantly. "Why, I certainly can, madame. He was a middle-aged gentleman, gray-haired with a goatee."

Evangeline made her face show pleased amazement instead of the shock she felt at having secretly guessed wrong. "Your memory is quite impressive, sir, I must say! Right again!"

She decided to inch a bit farther. "I don't suppose you knew the purpose of all those bouquets?"

Mr. Witherspoon shrugged. "I know they went to a lady because of the name and address they were sent to, but I had no idea what the occasion was."

"You mean you didn't fill out the cards for my friend?"

Mr. Witherspoon looked horrified at the prospect. "No, I'm sure it was a personal matter. He always insisted on filling them out himself. He'd just write something quick and seal it up in an envelope. Then he'd hand it to me to include with the flowers. I didn't think it was any of my business to inquire."

"Quite right, Mr. Witherspoon, quite right." Evangeline displayed an air of dignified propriety before changing the topic. "I don't suppose any of my friend's other acquaintances came to patronize your shop?"

"Not that I can think of, madame. I've heard no mention of the Allworthy name since he was here last. Except for the time he sent his son, that is."

Evangeline was startled for a moment. "His son? Why, what do you mean? He has no son."

The florist seemed puzzled. He scratched his head, trying to recall the circumstances. "Well, I thought it was his son since he had the same last name and sent flowers to the same address."

"He did?" Evangeline acted all amazement though she guessed who the order might have come from. "When was this?"

"Oh, about three months back. He only came in one time."

"Why that's odd! Do you think you might take a look in your order book and check the exact date and the name of the young gentleman? I might know who it was." She smiled appealingly. "You see, I'm a close friend of the family."

The florist didn't seem to think the request was suspicious. He checked the pages of his order book until he came to the entry. "Here it is. Roland Allworthy. He came in right after the shop opened on April twenty fourth. He wanted a bouquet delivered later that same morning." The florist looked up from the book. "Do you know who he is?"

"Oh yes, of course," Evangeline waved her hand airily. "That's Mr. Allworthy's nephew. A young blond gentleman, if I'm not mistaken?"

The florist nodded. "Yes, that's what he looked like all right. When I wrote down his name and saw the address the flowers were going to, I just figured he was Mr. Allworthy's son and had been sent to take care of the order in his place. I remember telling him to give my regards to his father. No wonder he looked at me so strangely."

"Well, I'm glad I cleared up that little misunderstanding." Evangeline laughed as she turned to go.

Halfway out the door, she heard the florist ask hopefully,

"Do you know when Mr. Allworthy might be back to place another order?"

She turned and answered softly. "I don't think he will. The young lady was very ill, you see. That's why he was sending her flowers so often, and...and...well, she has since passed away."

"Oh dear!" Mr. Witherspoon exclaimed as Evangeline closed the shop door behind her.

CHAPTER 23
The Guilty Party

ᘓ H ᘔ

Freddie loped up the stairs to Evangeline's townhouse two at a time and knocked impatiently at the door. He was bursting at the seams to tell her what he'd discovered at the Evermore Club and had been unable to reach her by telephone. His impatience turned to surprise when the door was opened by Jack bearing a silver tray and, on it, a glass of Champagne.

"I'll trade you, Mr. Freddie." The major domo laughed good-humoredly. "Your hat and coat for what I've got on this here tray."

Freddie took the glass suspiciously while Jack disposed of his outerwear. "What's the occasion?"

Jack shrugged. "One of Miss Engie's fancies. She told me to open a bottle of the best we had in the cellar against your arrival. She said it was some kind of celebration on account of you two had got your quarry at bay. That's the words she used for it, anyhow."

"But she doesn't even know what I found out today!"

Jack ushered Freddie into the drawing room where Evangeline sat ensconced in front of the fireplace. "There's some things as she can guess, I suppose." He closed the double-doors behind him and retreated to another part of the house. The clock on the mantel was just chiming seven.

"Ah there you are, Freddie. Just as I expected."

"Just as you expected?" the young man echoed. "You didn't know I was coming!"

"It was elementary logic that you would, dear boy, and that when you did we would have cause for celebration." Evangeline refilled her half-empty glass and sat in amused contemplation of her friend's befuddlement.

"How do you figure that?"

"When I returned from my own inquiries, Jack said that you'd been telephoning persistently all afternoon but didn't leave any message."

Freddie carefully placed his still-full glass on the coffee table and threw himself on the sofa. "And you inferred what?"

"I inferred that you were consumed with a desire to blurt out everything you'd learned at the Evermore Club. Taken together with what I discovered at the florist, I think we can safely say who the culprit is."

"But I haven't said a blessed thing yet!"

"I will give you leave to speak presently, but first a toast." Evangeline rose from her chair, glass in hand, and strolled toward her guest.

Freddie stood and skeptically raised his glass.

"To justice triumphant," Evangeline proposed.

Freddie grinned in spite of himself. "To justice," he confirmed, clinking glasses and finally sampling the contents. "Now are you going to let me tell you what I found out?"

Evangeline resumed her chair by the fire. "In a nutshell, and much as I hate to admit it since it destroys my original theory, I'd say you found that Roland had a perfectly good alibi for the night Nora was murdered."

Freddie felt the wind go out of his sails. "Well, yes, that's the gist of it."

Apparently not wishing to disappoint her friend too severely, Evangeline sat forward in an attempt to mimic an attitude of rapt attention. "But you must tell me the details! I wait in breathless anticipation!"

"Well, you needn't lay it on that thick," Freddie grumped.

Evangeline smiled, her eyes twinkling mischievously in the

firelight, but said nothing more.

Freddie decided that he could only stand on his dignity for so long when there was a good story to be told. After one martyred sigh, he gave in and regaled Evangeline with everything he saw and heard at the Evermore *Soeurs'* house of ill repute.

"Quite a fascinating place, I must say," she commented when he had finished. "But you said the card game started at ten o'clock. What time do the police think Nora drowned?"

Freddie briefly consulted his notebook. "They thought it was sometime around midnight."

Evangeline decided to play devil's advocate. "Could they have been wrong about the time of death? If it happened earlier than midnight, couldn't Roland have had time to dispatch her and still get to the poker tournament?"

Freddie squinted in the firelight as he scanned back through his notes. "It looks as if Thaddeus Sparrow, the night watchman, made his first evening rounds outside the building at nine o'clock. He didn't see anything suspicious. Even if, for argument's sake, we say that the earliest Nora could have died was sometime between nine and nine-thirty, it would have been impossible."

"Impossible?" Evangeline echoed.

"Impossible for Roland to get from the north side of town to the Evermore Club in time. It's down at Twenty Second Street. He would have needed to sprout a pair of wings to travel that distance in under half an hour. Minna Evermore said he was already at the club by nine-thirty."

"Well, that settles it then. Much as I loathe conceding defeat, I was wrong about Roland. Especially in light of what Mr. Witherspoon told me."

"It was Martin who sent her all those flowers, wasn't it?"

"All except the last. More Champagne?" Evangeline asked sweetly as Freddie's jaw dropped.

"But who..." He trailed off in surprise as she quietly refilled his glass.

"Roland did."

"Roland! But if the last flowers were from him, that must mean he killed her! I don't understand." The young man's elation was rapidly turning to frustration.

Still unruffled, Evangeline replied, "I beg to disagree.

Those flowers are the best proof that he did not kill her."

Freddie sat dumbfounded, waiting for an explanation.

Evangeline bestowed a brief smile of pity on her friend. "April twenty fourth was her birthday."

"Oh, that's right." Freddie searched through his notebook for the passage. "Sophie mentioned something about that."

"I must say, lack of verbal originality seems to run in the family when it comes to courting females. The card from Roland read 'Happy Birthday from your greatest admirer!'"

"Which means?" The young man still was not convinced the bouquet was conclusive proof of innocence.

"There was no bouquet from Martin that day."

Freddie remained silent, uncomprehending.

Evangeline sighed and pressed on. "The only reason why Martin would have failed to send a bouquet to his mistress bright and early on her birthday, thereby risking her displeasure, would have been if he knew..."

"Knew what?"

"That she was already dead," Evangeline concluded simply.

"Oh." Freddie felt a mite sheepish for having missed something so obvious.

"Since Roland no longer worked at Hyperion by the end of April, it's unlikely he would have heard the news of Nora's death until sometime during the afternoon of the twenty fourth, long after the flowers were delivered." Evangeline rose and began to stir the fire, which was beginning to die.

"Let me get that." Freddie offered to help while the lady stood back contemplatively, watching the flames slowly spring back to life.

"Something else to consider is that Roland has a whole crowd of people who can provide him with an alibi for the night of the murder. Martin's only alibi is Desmond. I find that fact to be an even more significant indication of guilt."

Freddie nodded solemnly as he continued building up the fire. "But what was Martin's motive for killing her? He doesn't seem the violent type."

"I suspect that the picture you found in the safety deposit box may have been intended as a gift from Nora to Roland, and Martin somehow got hold of it. Maybe she brought it to work with her on April twenty third intending to present it to

Roland, and Martin found it in her desk. The idea that Nora preferred the nephew to the uncle might have infuriated him. Perhaps Martin confronted Nora about it that night. While he might not be violent under ordinary circumstances, I can certainly picture him as vindictive if his pride were wounded. Vindictive enough to kill her for her duplicity."

Freddie rose from the hearth, dusting off his hands and his trousers. He stood before the fire, looking at his friend. "What about Euphemia? Why would Martin kill her?"

Evangeline gazed at him briefly then stared off into space trying to formulate a theory. "I remember the way she looked at her husband after the scene Bayne caused the night of the séance. Coming so soon on the heels of the Hyperion strike, for which she must have held Desmond responsible, it would have been the last straw. I thought there would be hell to pay after we all left that evening. I'm sure Euphemia gave Martin an ultimatum to get rid of Bayne or else. That put him in an impossible situation. If he sent Desmond packing, then Mr. Bayne would no doubt expose Martin's whereabouts on the night of April twenty third. The cat would properly be out of the bag with respect to Martin's liaison with Nora--not to mention the possibility of a murder charge. He stood in grave danger of losing not only Euphemia's fortune, as I originally thought, but his life as well."

Freddie sat up eagerly. "So he had a perfect motive for getting rid of Euphemia."

"Quite."

Freddie pondered Evangeline's theory for a few moments. "Yes, everything fits nicely together. Now all we have to do is convince the sheriff and the Chicago police that our theory is right."

The lady sighed. "And we have to do that quickly. We're running out of time. I've been sending messages to Sheriff Weston all week to keep him up to date on our discoveries. I just don't know how long he can continue to hold Serafina in the Shore Cliff jail. In fact, he may have transferred her already to the jail in Waukegan. Then the poor thing will have to go through an arraignment hearing, and it will only get worse for her from there."

A note of concern crept into Freddie's voice. "What can we do to wrap this up posthaste?"

Evangeline shrugged matter-of-factly, as if there were only one possible strategy. "We confront Martin and offer him a choice. Either he turns himself in to the police and confesses, which will probably make things go easier for him with the law, or we will expose him ourselves."

Freddie frowned. "But, Engie, what if he doesn't go along with the idea?"

"May I remind you that we now have the blackmail evidence that Bayne was using to control Martin."

"And?"

"And, we're in a position to call the tune now. Between the picture of Nora with his surname on it and the florist who can identify him sending flowers to her, there's the suggestion that he was involved with her. We could drag Bayne in and force him to testify that he saw Martin kill Nora or be faced with a charge of accessory to murder.

"That ought to make him sing," Freddie observed.

"If we can make a convincing case that Martin killed Nora, then that means we can establish his motive for killing Euphemia in order to conceal the first murder. In light of all these facts, I doubt that he would think his best interests were being served by denying everything. There's too much circumstantial evidence against him."

"But what if he panics and runs?"

"We won't give him time to do that." Evangeline smiled cryptically as she rang the bell for Jack.

Freddie raised a quizzical eyebrow.

When the caretaker arrived, she said, "Jack, prepare yourself. We have a social call to make this evening. I've heard that Mr. Allworthy has returned to town, and I long to pay him a visit."

"Will you want me to fetch the carriage, Miss Engie?" the major domo asked.

"No, Jack, I'll want you to fetch your revolver. We can walk the distance. It's only a few blocks."

Freddie winced at the mention of firearms.

Jack flashed a pleased grin, displaying his gold front tooth in the dim parlor light. "What, just the one, Miss Engie?"

Evangeline laughed. "I hate to disappoint you, Jack, but I think the shotgun might be a bit too obvious. One weapon for you should suffice, since I'll be armed as well."

The caretaker nodded and left, humming a happy little ditty as he went off in search of his cap and pistol.

Failing to notice her friend's dismay at the turn events had taken, Evangeline began to pace and think out loud. "Now which will it be? The Colt or the Derringer? Six-shooters are such awkward weapons for a lady, really. They never fit properly in a handbag, and when I try slipping one in a skirt pocket, it invariably tears the seam. A pity you don't travel armed, Freddie. I, myself, never go anywhere unprotected. Yes, I think we can hold him at gunpoint until the police are summoned, should he prove to be uncooperative. Now where did I put my reticule? I'm sure the gun's already in it. I know I left it around here somewhere--"

She stopped her search abruptly and regarded her friend with exasperation. "Don't just stand there gaping! Fetch your hat. It's past eight o'clock and we still have a murderer to catch this evening."

CHAPTER 24
Downfall

ೞ⌘ೞ

The bell for quitting time on Friday night had long since rung at the Hyperion Electroplate Factory. Martin Allworthy knelt on the catwalk above the shop floor.

It had to end, Martin thought grimly. The man was like a cancer that had to be cut away before it destroyed him completely! Ever since he first set eyes on Desmond Bayne, his life had been blighted, his prospects sent into a downward spiral by that depraved wretch. Everything the leering devil touched had become contaminated with iniquity. He had tainted the Allworthy factory, the Allworthy home, the Allworthy name itself. And now, even the Allworthy fortune!

It was bad enough that Bayne had managed to bleed the company nearly dry. Now, with Euphemia gone, the rascal was bound to bleed away Martin's personal inheritance as well. That was ironic. For the first time in his life, Martin actually had control of millions in his own right. He could do with the money as he liked. No need to ask his wife. No need to answer to anyone--except that filthy blackguard who kept whispering threats in his ear. Kept vowing to go to the police with what he knew.

Bayne did it for pure sport. Martin realized that. Just to

get a rise out of him, to send his heart racing out of control and leave him gasping for breath at the fear of exposure. And then Bayne would laugh and pat him on the back and tell him not to worry. That old Desmond was the best friend he had in the world. But Bayne had no idea that Martin was about to terminate the friendship. It had become too much of a burden to bear. His nerves were ready to snap. He was determined to make an end of it. By God, he would make an end of it, at last!

Martin stood up decisively, a wrench still in his hand. He tested the results of his labor. The catwalk railing shuddered slightly at his touch. Very good, he thought to himself with satisfaction. Just as it should be.

He looked down at the collection of metal nuts he had removed from the underside of the catwalk. The ones that held the railing bolts fastened to the platform. He had completely removed the first four and loosened a fifth just enough to allow it to fall away should any weight be pressed against the railing. Say, for instance, the weight of a man's body.

He put the hex nuts in his coat pocket and examined his handiwork with a critical eye. The catwalk ran a length of twenty feet. It was suspended approximately fifteen feet about the factory floor. His foremen used it every day to observe the business of the factory. But Martin's business would be completed before any one of them set foot on the catwalk tomorrow morning.

He scowled in dissatisfaction. Not enough. Not enough. He'd only loosened the bolts a third of the way across the length of the catwalk. The railing might still hold. He couldn't afford to have that happen. He got down on all fours and scanned the platform, trying to locate the next bolt. Hard to see in this light. Lying flat on his stomach, he reached over the edge and began to loosen the next nut with the wrench. He had to work quickly. The night watchman was down in the guard shack and might come by to make his rounds at any moment. Martin had told the man that Bayne was expected at nine o'clock. Yes, he and Bayne were to go over some important company business. He hadn't told the guard that the business would be Bayne's demise. That would be for Martin to know and the rest of the world to figure out. A regrettable industrial accident. It happened all the time in factories when people weren't careful.

Martin cursed silently at the nut and bolt. They were fused together by rust. He could hardly get the nut to budge, and he was working from an awkward angle.

What was that? He scrambled to his feet. He thought he'd heard a noise.

He peered anxiously down at the shop floor below but nothing was stirring there. The doors were all closed. Everything was silent. The factory was dark except for the single kerosene lantern he'd brought to work by. It wouldn't do to light up the whole place like a Christmas tree while he was arranging things. Too easy for someone to see what he was about.

He reached in a pocket for a handkerchief to mop his face. His skin felt clammy. This was ridiculous. Simply his imagination. Casting one more look over his shoulder into the shadows, he bent to his work again. The nut began to move grudgingly. It was agonizingly slow going but he almost had it. And then--

"Halooo! Marty? Marty are ye in here, lad?"

Martin instantly sprang to his feet, kicking the wrench across the catwalk until it bumped into the far wall with a loud clang. "I...I'm up here on the catwalk. Y...you can take the stairs over on the side if you can find them in this light." His heart was racing. He hoped Bayne wouldn't notice anything amiss. Not enough time! Not enough time!

"What're ye doing away up there, lad? And what was that noise?"

"Oh, it was nothing. When you called out, you startled me and I...uh...just tripped over a pipe lying up here. One of the foremen will hear about it tomorrow. Careless fool!"

"Gave me a turn, that it did." Bayne heaved himself up the catwalk stairs. "Sounded for all the world like a gun going off."

He was completely out of breath by the time he reached the top. When he got within a few feet of Martin, the owner of the company could detect that his vice president had been drinking again. Bayne was unsteady on his feet. So much the better.

"What's this...all about now...Marty? Why are we...meetin'

at such an odd...hour?" Bayne gasped for air, still winded from the exertion of the climb. The kerosene lantern, resting on the floor of the catwalk, sent his shadow shooting several feet up the back wall.

Martin was grateful he had chosen to use only one lantern. Perhaps in the dim light Bayne wouldn't see the railing listing ever so slightly over the shop floor or the hex nut that had fallen out of Martin's pocket as he jumped to his feet. Perhaps he wouldn't see that his benefactor was drenched in sweat. Martin silently commanded his heart to stop thumping so hard. He didn't want to appear nervous. Easier said than done.

"Well, you see, we have to settle the subject of payment for that last little service you performed for me."

Even in the flickering light, Martin could see Bayne's eyes glint and a broad smile distort his features at the mention of cash.

"Now, that's a meetin' I'd walk many a mile to attend. That I would!"

Martin tried to circle behind Bayne to maneuver him closer to the edge of the catwalk, but the man wouldn't budge. Rather than risk suspicion, Martin retreated to his previous position. "You're sure no one saw you that night?"

Bayne sighed. "As I've been tellin' ye for the past week every time you've asked the question, Marty, the answer is no! I just let meself into the factory that night after we had our little talk about hypotheticals and such. I went into the supply room like you told me to do, and I got a little packet of that powder like you described it. I put it into a plain white wrapper so there'd be no Hyperion stamp on the packet, and I put it in me coat pocket." Bayne rolled his eyes heavenward. "Just like you told me to do. I swear it on me poor old mother's grave. Then I took the train back up to Shore Cliff where you'd already gone and slipped the wee packet under the mattress in that spare room you told me about. Nobody saw me come and go, sure enough. Faith, it was just before dawn when I got the job finished. Who'd be stirrin' then?"

"I know nobody saw you at the villa, but what about here?" Martin asked urgently. "Are you sure? Not even the night watchman?"

"Oh, him." Bayne sounded abashed.

Martin felt a sting of alarm. "What do you mean 'oh, him'?"

"Well, I'd forgot about old Mr. Sparrow and that's a fact. I did see him when I was comin' in the gate, but I just told him I'd forgot something in me office."

"Did he follow you in?"

"No, no, that he didn't. Kept on makin' his rounds and wished me a good evening was all."

Martin was slightly mollified at the reassurance. "Well, I suppose that will have to do."

"Aye, 't will. There's nothing to be done about it now, boyo. But, on my honor, old Sparrow didn't see anything he shouldn't. I was just as light and easy with him as if I'd met him at a party." Bayne slapped Martin reassuringly on the back. "Now, don't you go fretting, lad. Didn't I say I have a natural gift for puttin' things to rights? And I've made a proper job of it, too."

After a brief pause, Bayne broached the subject always uppermost in his mind. "Now, what's this you wanted to tell me about me reward, as it were?"

"Ah, yes. Your reward," Martin echoed. "Well, you see, the sum you insisted on was rather steep."

Bayne's expression was angelically mild but his voice carried a veiled threat all the same. "How can ye put a price on a human life, Marty? On your life, as it happens. I'd be thinkin', if I was you, that anything you have to pay to escape the hangman's noose would be a good bargain."

"You misunderstand me." Martin tried to keep a tremor out of his voice. "I'm not disputing the price you quoted. I merely wished to point out that I would never keep a sum that large in the house."

"Oh...oh, I see." Bayne relaxed his guard.

"I have a safe here at the factory where I keep more substantial sums and I thought the...er...exchange could best be accomplished without too many prying eyes around."

"A good idea, Marty! A smashin' good idea, that one is!" Bayne thumped him approvingly on the back again. "Always a wise thought to keep a wee bit aside to tide you over for a rainy day. Something that the little woman doesn't know about."

Bayne's face took on a cunning look as a new idea occurred to him. "But now the little woman's gone, Marty, and you've no need to fear. Since I'm the nearest friend you've got in the world, boyo, we shouldn't be keepin' secrets from each other. That safe, Marty. That nice fat safe you've got here that I didn't know about. I'm longin' for you to teach me the combination to it."

Martin, outraged at the suggestion, answered without thinking. "You go too far, Irishman!"

Bayne took exception to the note of challenge in his benefactor's voice. "Do I now? I'm the one who goes too far, is it?" He advanced a step toward Martin. His shadow looming higher up the wall. "Well, I'm not the one who goes about pushin' wee little girls to a watery death, am I? And I'm not the one who gives poison to his wife to drink, am I? And I'm not the one who cooks up a scheme to plant the poison on another poor innocent, am I?" He poked Martin in the chest for emphasis. "If I was you, Mr. High and Mighty Martin Allworthy, I'd be thinkin' about who it is that's gone too far!"

Martin, his nerves stretched to the breaking point, backed away.

Bayne continued to advance. "And another thing, Mr. Allworthy, sir! I've had a bellyful of yer prideful ways. Indeed I have! Sure an' it is, I'm doin' you a good turn by keepin' yer scrawny, worthless neck out of the hangman's noose, and ye still treat me like somethin' to wipe yer boots on!"

Martin retreated another step. Without warning, Bayne took a swing at him. Dodging away from the meaty fist, Martin lost his footing. He stumbled backward against the catwalk railing.

For one awful second he was aware of the barrier bending backward, the scraping sound of metal against metal as the bolts popped loose from the floor. As he felt himself going over the edge, he clawed for something, anything to break his fall. He found it. Part of the railing remained bolted firmly to the platform. The rest was bent above the factory floor, twisted back by the weight of his body as he clung for dear life to the slippery metal railing.

Hand over hand he struggled to climb back up to the platform from the twisted perch where he swung twelve feet in the air. Martin could barely breathe from the shock. He tried to call for help but no sound escaped his lips.

Bayne, his reaction time no doubt slowed by drink, at last began to register what had happened. "Marty?" he called tentatively as he stepped forward to peer over the edge of the platform. "Marty, are ye still alive?"

He advanced closer and leaned over the edge. Martin, clinging to the railing, saw Bayne's face a few feet above him.

"Ah, the saints be praised! Ye look to be in no immediate danger of breakin' yer neck."

Bayne appeared to be genuinely relieved, not wishing to see his cash cow slaughtered in so untimely a manner. He squatted down on the platform to get a closer look at Martin's dilemma, the tips of his boots extending just over the edge.

"Well, well. This is a familiar sight, now isn't it, Marty? Where do ye think I've seen this before?" Bayne chuckled. He swayed slightly and readjusted his stance. He seemed not quite as drunk as when he arrived, but not entirely sober either.

Martin opened his mouth to scream for assistance, but the words refused to form, the sound of his terror refused to echo.

Desmond regarded him with a twinkle of wry amusement in his eyes. "There now, laddie, don't look so stricken. Wasn't I just tellin' you not five minutes ago that I've got a natural gift for settin' things to rights? I'll come to yer aid presently like I always do, but I can't help pointin' out the humor of the situation to ye."

Martin could barely hear him. The words shrieking in his brain sounded like waves crashing against rock. Waves of panic crashing in his ears.

Bayne cocked his head to one side. "There's only one set o' words fittin' for such an occasion as this. You and me, we both know what they are. We've both heard 'em before. Sure an' it is, you can guess. Don't you want to be tellin' me something, Marty? Something along the lines of 'Help me! Oh, why won't you help me? You know I can't swim.'"

CHAPTER 25
Manufacturing Evidence

 os⌘so

"Mr. Sparrow! Mr. Sparrow, wake up. We need your help!"

"Wha...who...?" The old man snorted a few times and sat up in his chair. He squinted in the dim lantern light, trying to make out the face that had invaded his sleep and his guard shack. "Who's that? Do I know you?"

"We've met before. The name's Simpson. Freddie Simpson. I'm a reporter for the *Gazette*, and I spoke to you the day Nora Johnson was drowned. You remember me, don't you?"

The old man adjusted his spectacles and stared at Freddie for several seconds. "Oh...oh, yes. That's right. I do remember. You interrupted my nap that day."

"Yes, well..." Freddie apologized self-consciously. "I seem to be making a habit of that. Very sorry to wake you again."

"Wake me!" The old man was indignant. "I wasn't asleep. Just resting my eyes, that's all. Taking a short break before my next rounds at nine o'clock."

"It's past that, Mr. Sparrow." The young man's tone was meek. "It's around nine-fifteen."

"It is?" The watchman sprang out of his chair and grabbed his lantern. "Out of my way, boy. I've got work to do."

"Just a minute, Mr. Sparrow." Freddie clutched at his coat sleeve. "My friends and I, we need your help."

"What friends? What help?"

"Oh, sorry." Freddie stepped aside from the door of the shack to reveal two other figures standing behind him. "Let me introduce my friend, Miss Evangeline LeClair, and her servant Jack."

"Ma'am." Sparrow tipped his cap to Evangeline and nodded to the colossus standing next to her.

"We need to speak to Mr. Allworthy," Freddie explained. "We went to his home, but his butler said he'd come to the factory a few hours ago and was probably still here. It's an urgent matter."

"Urgent? I don't know what all can be so urgent after nine p.m. on a Friday night, but I'll take you to him anyhow. He should still be in the factory."

Sparrow picked up his lantern and motioned the small party to follow him. "I think he's talking to Mr. Bayne."

"Mr. Bayne's here as well?" Evangeline asked. "How convenient."

"Oh, Mr. Allworthy, sir? Are you in here?" The watchman called out tentatively as he opened the door to the factory workshop. "Can't understand why he just didn't turn on the power." He flipped the main electric switch. Every shadow retreated from the glare of the incandescent bulbs.

"What in the name of..." Sparrow trailed off in amazement at the sight that greeted them.

"Something's happened," Evangeline said tensely.

"Has it ever," Freddie added.

At the opposite end of the room the group beheld a twisted metal spiral that had pulled away from a platform some fifteen feet above them.

They advanced to the middle of the room, and their first shocking sight was quickly succeeded by another.

"Oh, Good God!" Evangeline cried. "Is he--"

Freddie and Jack rushed forward to the crumpled shape lying in a pool of blood on the shop floor, directly below the metal spiral. Jack turned the body over and tried vainly to find a pulse.

"I'm afraid he is, Miss Engie."

"Oh, dear me!" Thaddeus Sparrow exclaimed. "Oh, dear me! Another accident."

"I don't think it was any accident, Mr. Sparrow."

Evangeline studied the dead man's face. "I think you should call the police. Freddie, Jack, don't touch anything until they get here!"

"But what will Mr. Allworthy say?" the guard asked plaintively. "We should wait for Mr. Allworthy. He must still be around here somewhere."

Evangeline evidently took note of the watchman's distress. Her reply was gentle. "Mr. Allworthy may not be coming back, Mr. Sparrow. If I were you, I'd call the police right away." She glanced quickly at her servant. "Jack, I think you'd better go with him and help him make the call."

"Right, Miss Engie." Taking charge of the situation, Jack led the old man to the door. "Why don't you and me go find a telephone, Mr. Sparrow."

The night watchman nodded passively and the pair left the shop floor.

Freddie waited until they were out of earshot before giving vent to his feelings. "Well, of all the rotten luck!"

Evangeline sighed. She looked at Desmond Bayne's lifeless body lying on the floor in front of her, his features somewhat flattened by the fall.

"I think you should turn the body over as we found it, Freddie. We wouldn't want to be accused of tampering with police evidence."

The young man nodded and complied.

"I suppose it was inevitable that Martin would try to rid himself of Bayne sooner or later, but the timing couldn't have been worse. Our key witness dead, our murderer flown, and no confession likely from either one to clear Serafina." Evangeline walked over and sat down on the bottom stair that led up to the catwalk, her chin sunk in her hands. "I guess it was bad luck to celebrate too early and on Friday the thirteenth, no less!"

Freddie sat down beside her. "Not to mention the fact that I've just lost the story of the century!"

The two remained silent for several moments, sunk in gloomy contemplation.

Finally, albeit somewhat listlessly, Evangeline stood up and dusted off her skirt. "As long as we're here, we might as well see what there is to be seen before the police start tramping around." Evidently knowing the reaction she was about to evoke by her next words, she braced herself for a torrent of gloating. "If you'd be good enough to jot down some notes on whatever we discover."

To his credit, Freddie only crowed for a modest three minutes before triumphantly opening his notebook.

Ignoring his exuberant display and numerous I-told-you-so's as best she could, Evangeline forged ahead with her investigation. "I suppose we ought to begin at the beginning, that is, right where we're standing." She walked over toward Bayne's prone body, then looked up toward the catwalk and pointed. "He must have fallen through the railing right about here."

Freddie scribbled furiously.

Evangeline circled the body for a few moments. "None of his clothes seem to be torn. I doubt that there was a struggle which means Martin didn't try to pitch him over the railing."

"As if he could have managed that," Freddie snorted, still writing.

His companion advanced to the twisted railing, hanging above them. "This has certainly been bent out of shape. He must have struck it with considerable force or else..."

Freddie looked up questioningly from his notes.

"Or else he was hanging off of it before he fell. There's no other way to explain why the railing looks as it does. Bent back like the lid of a sardine tin."

Freddie made scrupulous note of the shape of the railing. When he looked up again, his friend had walked off toward the stairs that led to the catwalk. He rushed up to intercept her. "Are you sure those are safe?"

Evangeline jumped up and down on the first few stairs to test them. "It feels solid enough." She climbed to the top.

Freddie followed several steps behind, cautious not to add too much weight to the stairs, just in case.

"Well, well, what do we have here!" Evangeline advanced across the length of the catwalk. She swooped down to pick up an object which she held up proudly for Freddie's inspection.

"It's just a hex nut!" he said flatly.

"Just a hex nut," the lady echoed, the faintest tone of despair in her voice. "That isn't the point, Freddie! What's it doing here?"

The young man was taken aback by her tone. "Why, anyone could have dropped it."

Before he knew what she was up to, Evangeline had dropped down flat on the catwalk and was endeavoring to stick her head through the railing, craning her neck for a better view of the underside of the guard rail that was still bolted to the platform.

"What in God's name are you doing now?" Freddie stood aghast at her unconventional posture.

"Aha!" She pulled her head back through the railing, having a care to keep a firm grip on her hat as she did so. "Just as I thought!"

"Yes?" Freddie waited expectantly, pencil raised to record her revelations.

"The bolt I found lying on the platform is the same as the ones that secure the railing to the catwalk."

Pencil still raised, the young man did not think her comment worthy of inclusion in his narrative. "So?"

"God in heaven, Freddie! How can you be so thick?"

Offended by her tone of voice, the young man attempted to defend himself. "Well, obviously, the bolt must have popped loose when the railing pulled away."

Evangeline made a superhuman effort to control her temper. "Then why isn't it lying on the shop floor down below? It's secured from underneath the platform, not on top, and there is such a thing as gravity. Unless of course you'd care to argue that the bolt did a back flip and ricocheted off the wall before it came to rest up here."

Freddie grudgingly conceded the point, and without making further reply, recorded her observation. Evangeline whisked past him and ran down the stairs like a prize retriever on the trail of a downed pheasant.

"Just have a look at this!" She held up a tiny metal object in her hand for him to see."

"Engie, my eyes aren't that good. I can't tell from fifteen feet up in the air what you're holding. What is it?"

"It's another hex nut. I can see a few others scattered around the floor down here..." She paused, then added significantly, "Where they ought to be."

The young reporter included her latest finding without dispute or contradiction.

Carefully placing the bolt back on the floor where she'd found it, Evangeline was up the stairs again. She breezed past Freddie and began eagerly sniffing out clues at the far end of the catwalk. "Well, well! This gets better and better. Freddie, come here." She gestured excitedly for him to join her.

When he arrived, he found her staring down at a wrench lying on the floor. No other tools were in sight.

"Someone might have dropped it?" he ventured weakly.

"My foot!" she shot back contemptuously. "Martin deliberately loosened this railing to make it look like an accident. When Bayne got here, he probably pushed him against the railing. It would have taken very little to make him tumble over the edge."

"But why go to all the trouble of making it look like an accident and then leave clues scattered about that suggest it wasn't?"

Freddie braced himself in anticipation of another cutting reply. Instead, Evangeline stared at her companion with a pleased smile on her face. "Why, Frederick Ulysses Simpson, that's the first rational statement you've uttered since we got here."

"I'm sure there was more than one." Freddie felt miffed by the back-handed nature of the compliment, but he was relieved not to have been rebuked again.

"You're quite right, of course." Evangeline tapped her chin and paced about the catwalk. "Perhaps Bayne arrived sooner than Martin anticipated and he didn't have time to finish the job properly. After the deed was done, he wanted to get away from the scene of the crime as quickly as he could. I fear he's on a train out of state by now." The lady sighed.

"Well, if it's any comfort, at least he left enough evidence behind to suggest that this was no accident."

"Yes, quite true." Evangeline placed the first hex nut she'd found back in the spot where she had discovered it.

"Do you notice anything else?" Freddie asked hopefully, reviewing his notes.

Evangeline scanned the platform and the shop floor below. "No, that's all that leaps to mind. I'll have to think about this for awhile to make all the pieces fit, but at least I think we know what all the pieces are."

Freddie was reviewing his jottings one last time when they

heard the outer door to the shop scrape open and the sound of several voices invade the factory.

Thaddeus Sparrow and Jack had returned with three blue-coated policemen in tow.

"Has anything been touched?" the tallest policeman demanded of Sparrow as they entered.

"No, I don't think so. That is, I didn't..." The watchman looked hesitantly toward the platform where Evangeline and Freddie were standing.

"You there! Who are you?" the cop barked across the room at Freddie.

At the sound of his voice, Evangeline looked guilty enough to mistaken for a murderer herself.

While the cop in charge advanced in their direction, Evangeline threw a nervous glance toward Freddie. She was obviously shocked to see that her friend had actually begun to smile.

"Oh, hello, sergeant," Freddie greeted the man in blue casually. "I didn't know you worked the night shift."

"Who's that up there? Do I know you?" The officer squinted up for a better look.

Freddie flipped back to the early pages of his notes, mumbling to himself as he read over page after page. "Just a moment, I've almost got it. Yes, here it is. Your name's O'Rourke, isn't it?"

The cop advanced a few more paces for a better look. "The same. How do you know that, mister?"

Freddie leaned over the railing. "I'm Freddie Simpson. The reporter for the *Gazette*. I spoke to you the day Nora Johnson was drowned here."

Recognition slowly dawned and, as it did, the sergeant's face relaxed into a smile. "Oh, right you are. Now I remember you, lad."

"Hyperion has an unfortunate tendency to attract Chicago's finest. This makes three trips in under three months, doesn't it?"

O'Rourke chuckled appreciatively. "Aye. When the call came in to the station house tonight, I had to take a razzing about the goings-on in this place. You can be sure. Well, come on down here and let's get a statement from you and the lady."

Freddie nudged Evangeline over to the stairs and the two descended to tell Sergeant O'Rourke about their discoveries. Jack and Mr. Sparrow huddled in to listen while the other two cops poked around the catwalk for clues.

After Evangeline and Freddie had related the chain of events that evening, O'Rourke removed his helmet and scratched his head. "There's just one thing that makes no sense here. Why would Mr. Allworthy go to all this trouble to kill his right-hand man?"

"Because his right-hand man was blackmailing him about the murder of Nora Johnson, that's why," Freddie announced dramatically.

O'Rourke let out his breath in a hiss. "That's a reason all right. Do you have any proof that the other was murder?"

Evangeline stepped in smoothly. "An object came into my possession quite recently that points to a romantic connection between Mr. Allworthy and Nora Johnson. If you like, I can bring it down to the station house tomorrow for you to look at."

"I'd be greatly obliged if you would do that, ma'am. Can you give me an idea of what that object might be?"

Evangeline glanced swiftly at Sparrow who seemed to be leaning in to catch every word. "I think the topic might better be discussed at the station."

Seeming to understand the reason for her hesitation, O'Rourke grinned. "Right you are, ma'am. Tomorrow will be soon enough."

Freddie chimed in ruefully, "We can't give you as much proof as we'd hoped now that the eyewitness to that murder is lying here dead."

"Well, lad, whether there's foul play in the death of Nora Johnson or not, it looks like Mr. Allworthy will have some explaining to do about what happened here tonight. We'll have to bring him in for questioning, no matter what."

"That is, if you can ever find him." Evangeline's voice was bleak.

"Don't you worry, ma'am. We'll find him all right." The policeman sounded confident. "You can count on that."

"I certainly hope so, sergeant." The lady's tone implied that she was not convinced that his sanguine expectations were warranted.

With a sweep of his arm, O'Rourke gestured them toward the exit. "Now if you folks would be good enough to step aside, me and the boys will be about the business of cleaning up this mess."

Having thus been politely told that they were underfoot in the presence of official police business, Evangeline and Freddie withdrew.

They accompanied Thaddeus Sparrow back to his guard shack, setting him to the task of contacting the general manager of Hyperion to inform him that until Mr. Allworthy turned up, he would have the unexpected honor of running the factory.

After that, Evangeline, Freddie, and Jack tramped back to North Avenue.

"Jack, would you see if you can scare us up a cab?" Evangeline asked wearily.

"That could take a few minutes, Miss Engie. Why don't you and Mr. Freddie wait here." The caretaker walked down to the next intersection to see if there were any hacks abroad at such a late hour.

After Jack departed on his mission, Evangeline unceremoniously sat down on the curb. Her friend seated himself beside her.

Freddie could read Evangeline's gloomy thoughts. "Well, after what's just happened, Serafina's future doesn't look very bright."

"We must think of a way to free her without a confession," Evangeline insisted urgently.

"Easier said than done."

She turned on her friend in irritation. "You really aren't helping."

"Sorry, old girl, but I've just about reached the end of my intellectual rope when it comes to solving this puzzle. "Thinking out loud, Evangeline asked softly, "What are the most damaging facts against Serafina?"

Freddie pondered the question for a moment before replying. "I suppose the poison packet is the worst, and then there's the letter from Euphemia."

Half to herself, Evangeline replied, "If we can't discredit Martin's testimony against her, perhaps we can discredit his evidence."

"How do you mean?"

"By finding a flaw in it, that's how."

"And just how to you propose to go about doing that?"

Evangeline's despondence evaporated as a plan began to form. She sat up excitedly. "If the supposed letter from Euphemia says that Serafina was a fraud, maybe we can find just as much evidence to the contrary."

"How?"

"By questioning the people in Euphemia's inner circle. Asking them what she really thought of Serafina. If she'd said anything, complimentary or otherwise, about those clairvoyant powers."

Freddie nodded his approval. "That might work, but who would we start with?"

"I recall that Euphemia spoke frequently to her Cousin Bessie. You remember, the one we met at the dinner party?"

"The one with the ugly daughter?" Freddie blurted out.

"Yes, Freddie, as you so ungallantly describe her, the mother of the unfortunate Miss Minerva." Even in the dim streetlight, Freddie could see Evangeline's cross look.

"Sorry," he said sheepishly.

"And while I'm calling on Bessie, perhaps you could inquire into that other piece of evidence—-the packet found under Serafina's mattress."

"I'm no expert on poisons, Engie."

Evangeline smiled. "But you do have the good fortune to know someone who is."

This time Freddie sat forward excitedly. "Of course, Doctor Doyle!"

"He was very helpful to us last time--"

The young man completed the thought. "And he said if we ever needed his help again he'd be at our service. But who knew it would be this soon?"

Their conversation was cut short by the sound of a carriage rattling across the North Avenue bridge. When the vehicle drew closer, it became obvious that Jack had successfully commandeered them a hack. The caretaker hopped out and handed them into the cab, taking a seat himself up front beside the driver.

"Perhaps all still isn't lost." Evangeline rested her head against the leather seatback, closing her eyes.

As the couple traveled on in silence, Freddie's mind wandered back to the events of the evening. A particularly pleasing thought struck him, and he broke the silence to observe, "It was a stroke of luck that I knew the sergeant in charge of the investigation, wasn't it?"

"Mmmm hmmm," Evangeline replied sleepily through closed eyelids.

"I imagine he might have given us a tough time of it if I hadn't called him by name, don't you think?" A calculating smile formed on the young man's lips.

"Mmmm hmmm."

"I suppose you'd have to say my notebook really came in handy and saved the day for us once more. Wouldn't you?" He looked impishly at his friend, hoping to get a rise out of her.

The question was met by dead silence. She never stirred an eyelash. He knew she was feigning sleep because she didn't want to give him the satisfaction of any more gloating so late in the evening.

CHAPTER 26
Poison Her Name

ෆ⌘ഓ

Late the following morning, Evangeline stood on the front porch of Cousin Bessie's Prairie Avenue residence and knocked energetically at the door. A maid answered.

"Yes, madame?"

"I'm here to see Mrs. Stilton." Evangeline handed the maid her calling card. "I telephoned earlier, and she said I might drop by anytime today to see her."

"Right this way, Miss LeClair." The servant showed her into the front parlor to wait. "I'll tell madame you've arrived."

Evangeline took a seat on the sofa. By Prairie Avenue standards the house was a modest one, containing no more than about twenty rooms, but the location alone suggested that money was not in short supply for the Stilton family. The parlor in which Evangeline found herself seemed cozy if a bit overstuffed with bric-a-brac. As she looked about her, she noticed a cage suspended near the window and in it, a canary doing its best to drown out the sound of a less than melodious piano coming from the drawing room across the hall. The bird trilled and chirped its heart out, but Evangeline was hard pressed to decide if it sang for joy or as an attempt to distract itself from the sound of "My Love's An Arbutus" being played badly and sung off-key. Evangeline could hardly believe that Bessie Stilton was capable of this auditory assault and its concomitant cruelty to a feathered friend.

As the lady of the house entered shortly thereafter with a cheery "Good day" on her lips, Evangeline told herself that she now had one more reason to pity the unfortunate Miss Minerva.

"Good day, Mrs. Stilton--"

"Please, you must call me Bessie. After making your acquaintance at Euphemia's house, I don't think we need to stand on ceremony."

"Thank you, Bessie." Evangeline tried to be tactful. "As I came in, I couldn't help but hear. Is that your daughter playing and singing in the next room?"

Bessie beamed with an appalling, and entirely unjustified, amount of pride. "Yes, that's Minerva. Quite musical, isn't she?"

"One can't help but be struck by the sound."

"It's quite true that the Lord never closes one door, but He opens another. She may not be a great beauty, but she has other gifts to compensate for that. I have always told her she has real musical talent. Even little Fortinbras thinks so. Don't you, Fortinbras?"

Bessie had walked over to address the canary. He ruffled his feathers and screeched a protest, which his owner took as a sign of enthusiastic assent. Having satisfied herself that all the world acknowledged her daughter as a prodigy, Bessie took a seat on the couch beside Evangeline.

"May I offer you some refreshment?"

"No, thank you. I just breakfasted before coming here and I'm afraid I'm rather pressed for time." Evangeline doubted her eardrums could stand the siege for more than half an hour. Minerva had now moved on to a halting rendition of "Drink To Me Only With Thine Eyes."

Bessie apologized. "Oh, I'm sorry. How rude of me to make small talk when you have important matters to discuss."

Evangeline's attention shifted back to the principal reason for her visit. She hesitated slightly before broaching such a painful subject. "I was hoping you could help me solve a little mystery relating to Euphemia's death."

A look of gloom crossed Bessie's mild face at the mention

of her dead cousin. "Oh, that terrible, terrible tragedy! I'm going to miss her so."

"As will we all," Evangeline added with heartfelt sympathy.

"I can't understand why Serafina would have done such a thing!"

"Ah, that's the purpose of my visit. I don't believe she was responsible."

"You don't?" Bessie's eyes grew round with surprise.

"No, I believe the evidence against her may have been falsified, and I'd like your help to determine if that's the case."

"Why, of course, my dear. Anything I can do."

"A letter was produced, written by Euphemia supposedly on the day of her death that denounces Serafina as a confidence trickster. I was wondering if Euphemia ever mentioned any of those doubts about Serafina to you?"

Bessie seemed quite distressed at Evangeline's words. She stood and fretted a full minute while considering the question. "But that makes no sense." She paced about the parlor. "The day of her death, you say? The very same day?"

"Why, yes." Evangeline was taken aback by the agitation she had created.

"That simply can't be. Please wait here. I won't be a moment." With that, Bessie abruptly left the room.

Thankfully, the din in the drawing room had ceased. The canary began to preen his feathers, a happy chirp now and then interrupting his ablutions.

When Bessie returned, she held a piece of paper in her hand. "Here, you shall see for yourself." She sat down again beside Evangeline and gave the scented stationery to her guest to examine.

The paper stock and the color of the ink were similar to the letters Evangeline had seen at the sheriff's office. She looked questioningly at Bessie for an explanation.

"Well, you see, it's just that this letter is from Euphemia, asking me to use my influence with Mrs. Campion on Serafina's behalf."

"Mrs. Delia Campion?" Evangeline echoed in surprise, naming the wife of the department store owner.

"Yes, the Campions live just down the block from here.

We're neighbors in fact. I am on much closer terms with them than Euphemia was, and my cousin hoped that I might convince Mrs. Campion to hold a reception in Serafina's honor. She was determined that Serafina should be invited into all the best homes and be noticed by all the best people in the city. Well, I suppose you can read it there for yourself."

Evangeline scanned the letter, reading aloud a few sentences of particular interest. "'I have grown ambitious on my young friend's behalf, Bessie. And I am determined that when she finishes her speaking tour of the country, she shall say that she was better received in Chicago than in any other great city in the land. I must enlist your support for this. Please prevail upon Delia to help.'"

Bessie leaned over her shoulder as Evangeline read. "You can see how it's dated." She pointed to the upper corner of the first page.

Evangeline looked up from the letter at her hostess. "Why, you're right. This makes no sense at all. It's dated the same day Euphemia was killed."

"Who showed you the other letter you mentioned?" Bessie asked hesitantly. "The one that said Serafina was a fraud. The one that was supposed to have been written by Euphemia."

Evangeline did not wish to divulge too many details of the investigation, but she felt the disclosure to be unavoidable. "It was Martin who brought the letter to the sheriff's attention."

"Oh dear!" Bessie exclaimed. "Oh dear, oh dear!"

"What is it?"

Bessie shot a guilty look toward her guest. "I don't suppose I ought to be telling you this, but..."

"Yes?"

"Euphemia often joked to me that she would have to keep a closer watch over her financial affairs, because Martin could sign her name as well as he could sign his own."

"I see." Evangeline's voice was terse. "That would go a long way toward explaining things." She paused. "Are you quite certain you never heard Euphemia say anything derogatory about Serafina's abilities?"

Bessie shook her head emphatically. "Far from it. I can name five ladies right off who received a recommendation from Euphemia about Serafina."

"Might it be possible for me to keep this letter awhile? It may help to clear Serafina."

"Oh by all means! Take it with you, my dear." She pressed the letter into Evangeline's hand.

"Bessie, I can't thank you enough. You've been of tremendous help." Evangeline's voice was nearly drowned out by the melodious emanations that had begun to proceed once more from the drawing room. Apparently Minerva, after resting her vocal chords for a suitable interval, now felt confident enough to attack Messrs. Gilbert and Sullivan's "Three Little Maids From School."

Fortinbras screeched his opinion of the racket by staging a frenzied concert of his own.

Evangeline hastily tried to think of an excuse to take her leave.

Bessie had once more become entranced by the sound of her daughter's recital. "Such a lovely voice," she enthused. "It's a shame she hasn't met any nice young man who could truly appreciate her." The doting mother sighed wistfully.

Evangeline was speechless. After several moments, she recovered herself enough to say, "Oh, I'm sure there must be someone out there who is blind, dumb, and deaf to superficial beauty."

Bessie was lost in thought. "That young man at the dinner party seemed rather nice."

"Roland?" Evangeline exhaled the name in a shocked tone.

"Good heavens, no!" Bessie frowned. "She's known Roland for years, but every time she sees him, he frightens the poor child half to death. She kept to her room with the vapors for a week after that last encounter! No, I meant that other young man. The one who escorted you. I remember he came from a good family. His name was Simp...Simp...something."

"Simpson," Evangeline corrected. "Freddie Simpson, and yes, he is a very nice young man from a prominent Shore Cliff family."

"Is he attached?" Bessie asked pointedly.

Knowing full well the extent of Freddie's attachment to her, Evangeline equivocated. "Well, he's not engaged." She dreaded the direction in which the conversation was heading.

"It would be a wonderful opportunity if Minerva might be thrown together with a young man like that at a social gathering some time or other. Then he might get the chance to talk to her and discover all her wonderful hidden qualities." Bessie sighed again. "She gets so few opportunities to make the acquaintance of nice young men." The mother hesitated. "I wouldn't presume to ask, but I thought, perhaps, since you know him so well, you might arrange..."

Evangeline weighed the options before her: the loss of Bessie's valuable testimony versus the possibility that Freddie might not speak to her for a week.

Minerva reached a crescendo in her performance, expanding the word "maids" to five syllables with twenty vowels, all at high C. Evangeline winced. Still, the silent treatment from Freddie was a small price to pay in exchange for Serafina's freedom. "Bessie, perhaps I might contrive a small dinner party to encourage the acquaintance. Would you approve of such an arrangement?"

"Approve?" Bessie echoed the word, her eyes glowing with gratitude. "I would be forever in your debt."

"I can promise nothing, you understand," Evangeline cautioned. She smiled grimly, contemplating Freddie's wrath when he realized he'd been handed over, trussed up like a Christmas goose, by his closest friend. "We would simply have to let nature take its course."

"To be sure. But I'm certain that once your friend has the opportunity to really get to know Minerva..."

"Good, then it's settled," Evangeline said decisively. "You may expect an invitation in a few weeks." She rose to leave before Minerva advanced on *The Pirates of Penzance.* Evangeline doubted her ears could survive the trills in "Poor Wandering One." She seriously doubted that Fortinbras could survive them either. "I really must be going now, Bessie. Thank you so much for your help."

The grateful mother accompanied her to the door. Once Evangeline had reached the relative tranquility of the sidewalk, she noticed that all the neighborhood pigeons had roosted in the elm trees across the street. Thinking of the plight of poor Fortinbras, she made a mental note to contact the Animal Welfare League at the earliest possible opportunity. Another thought struck her: if similarity of vocal talent were any basis for a match, then Minerva and Roland were meant for each other.

CHAPTER 27
Name Her Poison

☙ ❦ ❧

"Hello, *Chicago Gazette*. Frederick Simpson speaking."

"Ah, good, it's you Mr. Simpson. Archibald Doyle here. I have that information you requested."

"You do?" Freddie felt a tremendous flood of relief. He had fretted and chafed all through the weekend waiting for Doctor Doyle's findings about the poison.

"Why don't you drop by my office this morning and we can discuss it."

"I'll be right over, doctor. Don't go anywhere. I'm on my way now!" Freddie tried holding the telephone in one hand and slipping on his coat with the other.

Doyle, apparently sensing his impatience, chuckled on the other end of the line. "I'll be here. Take your time, Mr. Simpson."

The minute Freddie hung up the phone, he flew down the stairs and up the street. Doyle's office was located in a fashionable neighborhood about a mile and a half north of the Loop. Freddie jumped in the first cab he could find and told the driver not to spare the horse.

He arrived in front of the physician's discreet-looking graystone in record time. The only evidence that this was a doctor's office and not a private residence was the brass plaque beside the front door announcing the business conducted therein.

While Freddie stood at the curb paying the driver, he noticed a well-dressed woman who descended from a private coach and preempted him up the stairs. He followed directly behind her and waited while she rang the doorbell. She was about forty and looked well maintained. Freddie recalled that Doyle treated an inordinate number of wealthy, middle-aged women whose only malady consisted of something nebulously referred to as a nervous disorder. The woman who now stood before him acknowledged the young man's presence by a brief nod. Freddie tipped his hat to her but decided not to dip a toe into conversational waters.

After a few moments, the door was opened by Doctor Doyle's assistant, the same young man with the pencil-thin moustache and the patent leather hair whom Freddie had encountered on his previous visit. The attendant turned his attention to the lady first. "Why, Mrs. Fitzhugh, we weren't expecting you today."

The lady brushed past Freddie and the startled attendant. She seated herself without ceremony in the waiting room. "I was out on a round of calls and decided to drop in for some more of that special tonic Doctor Doyle concocts. It seems to have done wonders. I'll take another bottle."

"But...but...madame," the attendant stammered. "I'm sure the doctor will want to examine you to make sure there are no ill effects from the tonic. No rapid heartbeat, no increase in your blood pressure--"

The lady cut in impatiently. "Is all that really necessary?"

"I'm afraid so, madame. Doctor Doyle's tonics are strong medicine and nothing to be trifled with."

Mrs. Fitzhugh sighed in resignation. "Very well, I'll wait."

"I'm afraid it will be a few minutes, madame." The attendant was unctuously apologetic. "Doctor Doyle has an appointment with this gentleman." He indicated Freddie, who was still standing in the doorway, not sure whether to walk in or not.

Mrs. Fitzhugh crossly looked Freddie up and down. "Well, I'm sure he doesn't need the tonic as much as I do."

Freddie was about to make an impolite observation about the need for a tonic to cure rudeness, but bit back the retort.

He reminded himself of his errand.

The attendant glanced at him in mute appeal not to make the situation more unpleasant than it already was. "If you'll follow me, Mr. Simpson, the doctor is expecting you." He ushered Freddie into Doyle's laboratory at the back of the building.

Freddie noted with satisfaction that the attendant was somewhat more polite on this occasion than on his first visit. Then again, this time the young reporter wasn't soaked to the skin and looking like a street arab when he arrived.

Doyle greeted him jovially. "Mr. Simpson, good to see you!"

The attendant whispered, "Mrs. Fitzhugh is here again, doctor."

"Is she indeed?" Doyle frowned briefly. "Well, have her wait. I'll see her presently."

"Yes, sir." The attendant bowed his way out of the room and went back to deal with the ill-humored Mrs. Fitzhugh.

"Have a seat, Mr. Simpson, I'm just finishing up an experiment here." The doctor, who had been impeccably dressed during their last encounter, was without his frock coat and was in the process of rolling down his shirt sleeve. As Freddie sat down, his eyes wandered to the hypodermic needle lying on Doyle's desk.

Noticing the direction of his gaze, Doyle explained. "Just testing one of my new concoctions."

Freddie was surprised. "Wouldn't you ordinarily use mice for something like that?"

Doyle slipped on his coat and adjusted his tie before taking his own chair. "There are some formulas too good to be wasted on mice, Mr. Simpson." The physician smiled archly. "This happens to be one of them."

"Oh, I see." Freddie decided that there were many things about Doctor Doyle that were a mystery and probably better allowed to remain so. He changed the topic. "You said you had some information for me?"

"Yes, I was able to review the results of Mrs. Allworthy's autopsy as well as the analysis of the poisons found in the sherry glass and the powder packet."

"You were able to get all that information so quickly?" Freddie was amazed. "You ought to have been a reporter."

Doyle chuckled. "I think I've found my true calling in life dabbling with my little experiments, Mr. Simpson, but I thank you for the compliment just the same. And as for the speed with which I acquired certain documents, let's just say I called in a few favors."

"All the way from Shore Cliff?"

"The brotherhood of physicians in the Chicago area is a tight-knit community. One hand washes the other, so to speak."

"I'll say." Freddie took out his notebook. "What did you find out?"

Doyle sat back in his chair. "Mrs. Allworthy's body was examined for the presence of cyanide. The sherry glass from which she drank was tested for cyanide as was the packet of powder found in your friend's room."

"And?" Freddie waited breathlessly.

"Cyanide was found in all three instances."

"Oh!" The young man put down his pencil in disappointment.

Doyle studied the young man's reaction in amused silence.

"So that means the evidence against Serafina still looks fairly bad. That she's still the most likely suspect." Freddie's tone was dispirited.

"Not necessarily." Doyle's eyes held a twinkle of mischief.

Freddie sat up straighter. "What do you mean, Doctor? How's that possible?"

Doyle studied the ceiling contemplatively before speaking. "Mr. Simpson, I am very fond of driving up Michigan Boulevard in my carriage on a fine Sunday afternoon. It's drawn by a well-matched pair of bays." The physician paused.

Freddie looked at him blankly.

"A horse, Mr. Simpson, might be described in scientific terms as belonging to the family *equidae, genus equus, species caballus.* Now let's suppose I took a fancy to change one of my coach horses for a zebra."

"A zebra, sir?" Freddie was sure his ears were playing tricks on him.

"Yes, that's right, a zebra. After all, it is a four-hoofed herbivore bearing a striking resemblance to a horse, is it not?

I'm sure it could be trained to pull a carriage just as well. It even shares a common ancestor with the horse. It comes from the family *equidae, genus equus, species burchelli.* Yes, a zebra might do very well as a coach horse, although it might get a few odd looks from pedestrians as I drove it down the street."

Freddie was giving the doctor an odd look of his own. He wondered if whatever Doyle had injected into his system with the syringe was affecting his brain. He didn't wish to appear rude but he was beginning to question the point of the conversation.

The doctor's amusement seemed to grow with the young man's puzzlement. "You look confused, Mr. Simpson."

"Frankly, sir, I am. What has the zebra pulling your carriage got to do with cyanide?"

"Cyanide is like my zebra, Mr. Simpson." The doctor waited a full minute for that sentence to sink in.

Freddie finally decided to display his ignorance. "All right, doctor, I give up. In what way?"

"Because, even though I own two creatures that are remarkably alike in some ways, they are different in others. One is a bay horse of the species *caballus* while the other is a striped zebra of the species *burchelli.* Cyanide is like that. Did you know that there's more than one form of the poison? They're all equally nasty in their effect but they have different chemical structures."

"In plain English, what are you saying, sir?" Freddie had picked up his pencil and started to write. He sensed that what he was about to hear would prove to be crucially important.

"I'm saying that while the sherry glass and the poison packet both contained cyanide, they were not the same form of the poison."

"What?" Freddie practically leaped out of his chair with excitement.

Doyle laughed outright at the reaction he had caused. "The sherry glass from which Mrs. Allworthy drank contained potassium cyanide. We may safely assume this is the substance which killed her. The poison packet contained sodium cyanide. So you see, we're dealing with horses of different colors. Of a different stripe, as it were."

"But...but..." Freddie was still grappling to contain his excitement. "But why hasn't the sheriff released Serafina if he knows the poisons are different?"

"Because he doesn't know," Doyle replied evenly. "The laboratory reports weren't specific as to the form of cyanide. They just said 'cyanide.' The sheriff in Shore Cliff, no matter how skillful in the apprehension of criminals, isn't a chemist, Mr. Simpson. He would never have known enough to ask the question. What compounded the problem was that the same individual didn't perform the tests on both the sherry glass and the poison packet. No one bothered to compare the test results for consistency."

"But you did." Freddie was clearly impressed.

Doyle shrugged matter-of-factly. "I merely asked the right questions of the right people, that's all."

"You shouldn't make light of it, Doctor. You may have just saved a young woman's life."

The doctor smiled. "I'm in the business of saving lives, Mr. Simpson, though generally not as easily or as pleasantly as this." He handed Freddie an unmarked envelope. "Here. I've taken the liberty of jotting down my findings in the event that your local constabulary requires a written document of my conclusions."

Freddie took the envelope with a smile of relief. "You thought of everything, Doctor Doyle." Then his smile faded as a puzzling thought struck him. "But how did he get hold of it?"

"I beg your pardon?" The doctor seemed perplexed.

Freddie realized his progression of thought had been less than obvious. "How did Allworthy get hold of even one form of cyanide, not to mention two?"

"Oh, that." The doctor pondered the question, rubbing his chin reflectively. "It's been my experience that a person wishing to poison somebody else will generally make use of what's ready to hand."

Freddie looked at the doctor blankly.

"Tell me about this Allworthy."

"Sir?"

"Tell me about his personal habits."

"He doesn't have any habits. He owns a factory."

"A factory, you say?" Doyle's face took on a look of keen

interest. "What type of factory."

"Well, it's called the Hyperion Electroplate Company. They make--"

Doyle cut in. "There you have it!"

"What do you mean?" Freddie was mystified.

"Cyanide has many industrial uses in our modern age. If I'm not mistaken, it's used extensively in the electroplating process."

"That's right," Freddie murmured to himself. "Now I remember. Orlando said something about that." He flipped rapidly through the pages of his notebook, searching for the notes he'd made of his interviews on the day Nora Johnson's body was discovered. "He said the factory used poison and acids to make brass carriage fittings."

Doyle laughed ruefully. "Your friend Allworthy probably has a large enough supply of cyanide to poison half the city if he'd a mind to. I think you ought to check the factory storeroom, Mr. Simpson. You're bound to find what you're looking for there, but I would caution you to be careful in handling the substance. Cyanide is toxic if it is inhaled or if it comes into contact with the skin. Not the sort of thing you can afford to be careless with."

"But which form is used in electroplating--potassium cyanide or sodium cyanide?"

"It is my understanding that both forms are used."

Freddie wrote furiously. When he had finished transcribing the conversation, he unceremoniously leaped out of his chair and stuffed Doyle's envelope into his pocket. "I have to go! This can't wait. I have to tell Engie about this right away!"

The doctor chuckled at the young man's haste. "Give my regards to Miss LeClair. I urge you both to bring these little puzzles to my attention as they arise. I find solving them to be quite diverting."

Freddie shook the doctor's hand energetically. "We both owe you a debt of gratitude for this. Thank you again, Doctor Doyle. Good-bye."

"Good-bye Mr. Simpson." For a few moments after Freddie's rapid departure the doctor sat grinning to himself at the stir he had created. Then, coming back to the matter at hand, he sighed stoically and rang for his assistant. "You may tell Mrs. Fitzhugh that I'll see her now."

CHAPTER 28
The Antidote

❧❦❧

Freddie lost no time in racing from Doctor Doyle's office to his friend's townhouse to tell her the good news. Once having heard it, Evangeline lost no time in dragging Freddie to the commuter railroad station to catch the next train for Shore Cliff. It was mid-afternoon when they disembarked and made straight for the sheriff's office.

Opening the door precipitously, Evangeline rushed in and went directly to the jail cell where Serafina sat reading. A curtain was half-drawn across the bars to allow some measure of privacy to the inmate. "Great news, my dear! Wonderful news!"

Serafina stood up and came to the bars. "Yes? You have come to set me free. Is it not so?"

The sheriff looked up from his desk in mild surprise at the invasion. He stared at Freddie and Evangeline blankly.

The young man took it upon himself to explain. "We have evidence, sheriff. Evidence that will clear Miss Serafina."

Weston continued to stare at Freddie. He had seen the tall young man in the village on any number of occasions, but had never been introduced to him. "Are you with Miss Evangeline here?"

"Oh, yes indeed. Simpson's the name. Freddie Simpson.

You may know my mother and sisters. They live in town."

Recognition dawned. "Oh, is your mother the Mrs. Simpson over on Genesee Avenue? She called me in one time when she thought she heard a noise."

"She's always hearing noises." Freddie's tone was cynical.

"She was willing to swear it was an intruder come to rob her."

Freddie sighed. "Sheriff, you're still new to Shore Cliff, but you'll discover from sad experience, as I have, that my mother makes a hobby of collecting unexplained noises. That's the principal reason I moved to Chicago. I simply couldn't stand the legion of imaginary sounds in the basement and the attic she demanded that I investigate on a daily basis."

"Well, one time she just might be right."

Muttering darkly, Freddie retorted, "You'll see."

At that moment, the conversation was interrupted by Evangeline jangling the key ring to Serafina's cell. It had been hung on a hook outside the grate. "We have to get you out of there." The lady lifted the keys and began to unlock the cage.

"Hold on there, Miss Evangeline, or I'll have to arrest you for committing a jail break right under the nose of an officer of the law."

"Oh, sheriff, don't be silly." Evangeline turned around to regard Weston in surprise. "I've merely deputized myself to perform this task while you were engaged in other matters."

"Deputized, is it?" The sheriff grinned. "Now what makes you so sure I'd agree that it's time to let a dangerous criminal like Miss Serafina loose on the honest citizens of Shore Cliff?"

Evangeline stood watching the sheriff's grin widen. "Well, now you really are being silly. The idea of Serafina--" She stopped abruptly. "Freddie, show him the evidence."

The young man readily produced Doyle's statement regarding the poison packet as well as Cousin Bessie's letter from Euphemia.

The sheriff sat down and took his reading glasses out of his desk. "I'd be obliged, Miss Evangeline, if you'd step away from the bars and put the keys down until I review this here new evidence. We have to do things proper and in order."

"Very well, sheriff, if you insist." Evangeline seated herself before Weston's desk and dutifully placed the keys in front of him.

"That's better." The sheriff adjusted his spectacles. "Now let's see what we've got here."

Freddie and Evangeline waited silently, albeit restlessly, while Weston reviewed their documentation.

Still looking at the pages before him, he addressed the couple. "I received notice from the Chicago Police Department that a Mr. Martin Allworthy is wanted for questioning in connection with the death of a Mr. Desmond Bayne. Have you all heard that news, too?"

"Yes, sheriff." The two detectives spoke in unison and then both of them began to talk at once, explaining the circumstances of Bayne's death and how it was related to Euphemia's.

"Whoa! The pair of you!" The sheriff put up a cautionary hand. "I think I've heard enough. Especially after that last telegram Miss Evangeline sent me on Saturday explaining how things stood." He looked from one to the other and chuckled. "Miss Evangeline, I hereby deputize you to take that set of keys and release the prisoner."

Evangeline sprang out of her chair, snatched up the keys and freed Serafina in the time it took Sheriff Weston to blink twice.

The medium hugged her rescuer. "You see, it is as I told you before. You would find a way out."

Evangeline laughed. "There were moments when I wasn't sure this story was going to have a happy ending. Believe me!"

The two ladies walked back toward the sheriff's desk.

"I'm so relieved we didn't have to go to Waukegan to fetch her back from the county jail."

Weston's eyes held a twinkle of mischief. "Well, ma'am, only suspects who've been officially charged go to county jail for an arraignment hearing."

"But...what..." Evangeline stammered in shock. "Sheriff, you mean to tell me you held her here for a week without charging her with anything?"

Weston looked innocently at the ceiling. "I had to wait for the official lab report on that poison packet, ma'am. You know a judge would want to see that evidence."

"But...but...Doctor Doyle was able to tell Freddie what the results were. The report must have been finished sometime last week. How is it that you didn't know?"

Weston ignored Evangeline's shocked reaction. "Funny thing about that report. It kept getting lost in the mail. Kept getting sent back to the lab marked 'Return to Sender. Address Unknown.' Makes a body have some second thoughts about the United States Post Office, I can tell you."

Evangeline caught the gleam in the sheriff's eye and answered it with a smile of her own. "Why, sheriff, you amaze me!"

"Ma'am?" Weston asked innocently. "Afraid I don't know what you mean. Just doing my job. Like I told you before, a body doesn't live as long as I've done without learning something about human nature along the way. Though I will say I was starting to sweat bullets right around the end of the week. Wasn't sure how much longer I could hold Miss Serafina here without doing some serious explaining to the mayor. Lucky for me you sent that telegram telling me what you found out."

"And lucky for all of us Mr. Allworthy so obligingly pushed Mr. Bayne off that catwalk."

"Well, I have to say, that was the icing on the cake, in a manner of speaking."

"Since there's no release paperwork to fill out for a prisoner who was never charged with anything in the first place, I suppose Serafina's free to go. Is that right, sheriff?"

Weston nodded in agreement.

Evangeline turned to Freddie. "Will you please escort Serafina back to my house? I'll be along in a minute."

"But, Engie," Freddie whispered, "Delphine will be there."

"And?" his friend asked dispassionately.

"What if she won't let me in?"

"Freddie, don't be ridiculous. Serafina will be with you. Delphine would never assault you in front of a witness. Besides, you can tell her that I'm on my way. She'll have to let you in then."

"Maybe, maybe not." The young man's tone was grim as he went off to help the medium collect her things and carry them out the door.

When the two had left, Evangeline leaned back against the

door jamb, arms crossed and regarded the sheriff silently for several moments.

"Ma'am? Is there something else I can help you with?"

Evangeline tapped her chin. "Sheriff, I was just thinking. Your methods of performing your duties might be considered somewhat irregular by the sort of people who like to go by the book. Not that I'm complaining, you understand. Far from it. I'm very grateful. But, by taking it upon yourself to slow the wheels of due process, some people in this town might accuse you of...of...How should I put this? I suppose the vulgar might call it dispensing vigilante justice."

Sheriff Weston sat back in his chair, lacing his fingers behind his head. He looked at his visitor for a moment, gathering his thoughts before speaking. "Well, ma'am, I suppose there's some truth in that. There's folks in this town that might make that accusation if the facts of this case ever came to their notice. But I don't think anybody who was here today would be likely to tell them, do you?"

"No, sheriff, I don't." Evangeline stood with her hand on the doorknob, ready to depart.

"And another thing, Miss Evangeline." The sheriff smiled broadly. "If there's such a thing as vigilante justice going on in this town, and I don't say there is, mind you, but if there was, I can think of at least one other person who might be dishing it out right alongside me. Don't it seem that way to you, ma'am?"

Evangeline opened the door to let herself out. Affecting a slight drawl, she said over her shoulder, "Yes, sheriff, I reckon so."

❦❧

When Evangeline got back home, she found Serafina seated in the front parlor with Delphine hovering over her, a cup of tea in hand. Freddie was still standing in the foyer doing a slow burn.

"She won't let me go in there." He spoke through gritted teeth. "She said I might upset the young lady. Engie, one of these days, I swear..."

Evangeline patted him on the shoulder. "Don't fret. I'll protect you."

The lady of the house walked over to the open door of the parlor. "Delphine, you must let *Monsieur* Freddie in here. He is my guest."

The housekeeper looked up from her ministrations in disgust. "What stories has *le jeune monsieur* been telling you? He may go where he likes. *Ca ne me fait rien!* As you can see, I have other concerns."

Evangeline shot a significant look in Freddie's direction and gestured him toward the parlor. "It's safe now. You may enter."

Freddie sniffed once in irritation and proceeded to throw himself on the loveseat, glaring wordlessly at Delphine while she fussed over Serafina.

Evangeline was about to follow him into the room when an orange ball of fur came hurtling down the stairs and did its best to attach itself to Evangeline's ankle. "Ah, *Monsieur Beauvoir! Mon petit cher!*" she cried, scooping up the cat. "How I have missed you!"

Her tone of voice when addressing the cat never failed to disgust Freddie. "I've never seen you fuss over a human the way you do over that beast! I can be gone for two months and the only greeting I'll get from you on my return is 'Oh, there you are Freddie.'"

"It's because he doesn't have a talent for making irritating observations, as you so often do." She seated herself in an armchair, the cat purring contentedly in her lap.

Delphine turned to regard the tabby a moment. "*Voila*, now he comes to life. When you are gone, *cherie*, all he will do is sleep."

"*Mais, il mange aussi, n'est-ce pas?*" Evangeline sounded alarmed.

"*Oui, il mange bien.* That he does also. Eat and sleep. Sleep and eat. That is all. I tell him to run and go catch the fat little mice in the basement. He looks at me. *C'est tout!* He goes back to sleep."

Addressing the cat, Evangeline was all seriousness. "I won't be gone much longer. Just be patient. I'll be coming home very soon now." The cat meowed a soft acknowledgement, then transferred his attention to Serafina.

"Ah, he remembers me." The medium laughed as the cat walked over to stand by her chair, inviting her to stroke his head.

"But of course," Evangeline assented. "They never forget."

"Just like elephants," Freddie observed.

Evangeline gave him a pained look and turned back to Serafina. "My dear, you really do need to get some rest. I'd like to stay and see you comfortably settled, but I'm afraid I have to go back to the city. There are still matters I need to wrap up there."

Serafina continued to stroke the cat's fur. "I would also like to go back to the city."

"You would?" Freddie sounded shocked. "After what you've been through?"

"It is better if I do not stay in Shore Cliff." She took a small sip of tea. "There are too many bad things here to remember. And my guides, they will not return until I am far from here."

"Of course, my dear, of course." Evangeline hastened to reassure her. "Whatever you wish. My carriage is at your disposal. Where would you like us to take you?"

"I think perhaps I will go to the Templar House."

"You'd really rather stay at a hotel at a time like this?" Freddie asked in surprise.

"*Si*, it is better for me. I can be alone to think and to rest."

"I quite agree with her, Freddie." Evangeline turned to face her friend. "Sometimes the anonymity of a hotel is just the thing. All that hustle and bustle but none of it having to do with you. It's really the best place to be alone." She transferred her attention back to Serafina. "Would you like to stay the night here or collect your things and move on?"

The medium hesitated for a moment. "If it does not cause a great difficulty for you, today would be better."

"Certainly. Just as you wish." Evangeline began to organize the expedition. She turned to Delphine, who was still in the room. "Is Serafina's maid still here?"

"Fannie? *Oui*, she has been helping *chez nous*. She is upstairs, I think."

"Please tell her to pack Miss Serafina's clothes at once."

"*Bien sur, cherie*." Delphine departed, choosing to step over Freddie's outstretched leg as if he didn't exist.

Thinking aloud, Evangeline continued making plans. "Oh, and I suppose Fannie will have to go round to the Allworthy villa and collect whatever was left there. We'll need the carriage for that. Freddie?"

"What!" the young man snapped peevishly, still glaring at Delphine's departing back.

"Could you please go find the gardener and arrange for him to hitch up the horses. You'll have to do the honors of driving, I'm afraid, since Jack is in town today. He can bring the barouche back here tomorrow."

Shaking himself out of his dark mood now that he had some employment, Freddie nodded and went to arrange transportation for the small party.

Evangeline and Serafina were alone in the parlor, with the exception of Beau, who decided to stay as long as he had two doting subjects who were willing to lavish attention on him.

"Well, it's over at last," Evangeline observed.

"Yes," Serafina said quietly. "Almost."

"It's as good as over. Martin is long gone by now."

The medium contradicted her in a soft voice. "No, he is not."

"You know where he is?" Evangeline sat forward excitedly.

Serafina shook her head. "No, I still cannot see many things clearly as I used to. All I feel is that he is near. Somewhere very close. And he is afraid."

"He ought to be! He's being hunted by the police."

Serafina knit her brows in concentration as a new thought struck her. "Not only that. I feel something else. It is like he is grieving for something."

"For the inheritance he's going to lose, I suppose."

"No, it is not a feeling like that. It is more like..." She paused, trying to focus on the emotion. "Like...I think the word is regret. For something he should have done that he did not do."

"I suppose he regrets that he got caught red-handed when he shouldn't have been."

The medium's eyes were serious. "There is a heaviness in his heart for another person."

"Euphemia?" Evangeline was incredulous.

"I cannot be sure, but I do not think so. I feel it is another person for whom he is sad."

"It's hard to imagine he feels any regret for murdering Nora, but I suppose only time will tell. You're really convinced he's still somewhere in the area?"

"Of that much, I am sure. As I am also sure he feels two things very strongly--fear and regret." Serafina finished her cup of tea and bent down to stroke the cat who had curled up at her feet.

At that moment Freddie poked his head into the parlor. "Ladies, your chariot awaits."

CHAPTER 29
Dearest Nemesis

☙❦❧

Evangeline sighed as she sank into her favorite chair by the window. "It's been quite a day, hasn't it."

"Certainly has." Freddie yawned in agreement, settling himself on the drawing room couch.

The two had just returned to Evangeline's brownstone in Chicago after depositing Serafina comfortably in a room at the Templar House Hotel.

"Well, we did it. She's been freed at last," the young man observed. "Though I still think it's odd that she didn't want to stay at your house in Shore Cliff for a few days to rest."

Evangeline smiled regretfully. "If I were her, I wouldn't have wanted to stay there either. Too many unpleasant associations with death. No, on the whole, I think she made a wise decision to check into a hotel. What she needs now is peace and quiet to restore her spirit without too many people bothering her. As she would say, to bring her guides back. I'll send a message to Theophilus asking him to look in on her to make sure she's all right. I also intend to drop by to see her over the course of the next few days."

"It was a lucky break for us that Martin couldn't tell his poisons apart. If the packet had contained potassium cyanide instead of the other kind, we'd have had a rough go trying to get Serafina released, even with Allworthy being hunted for another crime."

Evangeline sounded contemplative. "Yes, I've been pondering that little mix-up for awhile. I don't think Martin was responsible for the mistake."

"Then who was?"

"Bayne."

Freddie nodded in agreement. "I suppose that would make sense."

Evangeline rubbed her head wearily as she thought through the probable chain of events. "We could verify this with Mr. Sparrow, but I suspect that Bayne went back to Hyperion the night after Euphemia died. He was acting on Martin's instructions. It was most likely he who took the poison out of the supply room and planted it in Serafina's chamber. It would have been far too risky for Martin to attempt that since he knew he was already a suspect in his wife's murder. Luckily, Bayne must have taken such a lackadaisical interest in the workings of the factory that he wouldn't have known what was kept in the storeroom and consequently got the packages confused. It's unlikely that Martin would have made that same mistake."

Freddie laughed derisively. "So Bayne ended up getting even with Martin for murdering him after all. His error made it easier to discredit Martin's accusation. Too bad he never lived to see his revenge."

"If he hadn't been killed, Serafina would still be the principal suspect in Euphemia's murder."

The young man's smile broadened. "That's two good turns he did us without even realizing his contribution. And, with Serafina free, that's one problem solved and one to go." He lightly made a show of dusting off his hands.

Evangeline frowned. "The knottier problem, to be sure."

"Have the police come up with anything about Martin yet?"

"Not so far. I checked with Sergeant O'Rourke yesterday when I dropped off the miniature portrait of Nora for him to keep as evidence. They haven't been able to turn up any trace of Allworthy since Bayne was killed."

"Not too surprising, considering the situation."

At that moment, Jack quietly opened the drawing room

doors. "Will you or Mr. Freddie be wanting anything to eat, Miss Engie?"

Evangeline looked questioningly toward her companion. He shook his head in the negative. "Just a cup of tea for me, Jack. That's all."

The caretaker nodded and went off to the kitchen to tell the cook.

Evangeline resumed the conversation. "Well, at least the Chicago police seem fairly convinced that Martin is responsible for the deaths of Nora, Euphemia and Bayne. It didn't require much argument on my part to bring them around to that conclusion."

"What do you suppose the family will do about Euphemia's funeral now?" Freddie rested his head against the back of the sofa.

"Martin's disappearance has made things rather awkward. The wake was supposed to be held over the weekend, but no one's stepped forward to take charge of the situation."

"That raises another interesting question. Who gets everything now that Martin is unlikely to surface to claim his inheritance?"

"I don't know for sure, but it's very likely to be Bessie."

"Cousin Bessie?" Freddie cried in disbelief. "The one with the ugly--"

Evangeline interrupted irritably. "Oh, Freddie, don't say it! May I point out that since Cousin Bessie is a widow, her less-than-lovely offspring is very likely to inherit a great fortune, making her instantly attractive to any number of men whose object in matrimony is the acquisition of a mint instead of a mate."

"Maybe so," the young man grumbled, "but it's hard to believe that anybody could be that hard up for cash!"

"Frederick Simpson! You are a beast!" Evangeline would have continued to upbraid her friend, but she was interrupted by the return of one of the maids bearing a tea tray.

The girl set it down on the table by her mistress.

"Thank you, Daisy. Would you call Jack in to start a fire? It's gotten surprisingly chilly in here for midsummer."

The maid was about to go in search of the caretaker when Freddie, as a gesture of repentance for his callousness, interposed. "I'll take care of it." He stood up and walked over to the grate.

"Thank you, Daisy. That's all. You may go." Evangeline dismissed the maid who let herself silently out of the drawing room.

As he began the task of stacking logs in the cold fireplace, Freddie spoke over his shoulder. "Well, somebody's going to have to make a decision soon about when to bury Euphemia. I hate to be blunt, but it's not the sort of thing that can be put off much longer, especially at this time of year."

"I agree." Evangeline lifted her teacup to her lips. "I'll telephone Bessie in the morning to find out if a date has been set." She frowned as a new thought struck her. "This is extremely unsatisfying."

"What is, old girl?" Freddie sat back on his heels to study the fitful flames beginning to rise. "Your tea?"

"No, not my tea, Freddie. The fact that three people are dead and the murderer still has his liberty."

The young man stood up, dusted off his jacket and returned to the sofa. "The police might catch him yet."

"If they don't, I'll have to pick up the trail myself, I suppose."

"And do what? Race cross-country to ferret him out?"

"If necessary." The lady took another sip of tea.

At that moment, Jack re-entered the room.

"It's all right, Jack. We don't need you to build the fire..." The puzzled look on the caretaker's face stopped Evangeline in mid-sentence.

He stepped into the center of the room and handed her an envelope. "There was a boy just now at the door, Miss Engie. He said a man paid him a dollar to deliver this letter to you."

Evangeline sat up in her chair, all vestiges of drowsiness gone.

Freddie walked over to see the note. "What is it?" He leaned over her chair in curiosity as she opened the envelope. Checking the signature first, she gasped, and then began to read aloud.

"'My Dear Miss LeClair,

I can imagine your surprise as you read this letter. I am bound to be the last person on earth from whom you expected to receive correspondence. Suffice it to say that this note is a sort of insurance policy which I have taken out against my longevity.

A man may trust the enmity of his foes to outlast his friends' affection. Under the best of circumstances, you and I have maintained a barely civil relationship. I assume that your dislike of me has deepened into a stronger emotion now that you have exposed certain events in my past which, I feel obligated to point out, were none of your business in the first place. Not content to wreck my home and business, you have also utterly destroyed my reputation--that which I valued above all else and which is now beyond redemption. I am convinced that the malice you bear toward me will cause you to pursue me relentlessly until even my life has been ignominiously forfeited to the hangman's noose. I depend upon the tenacity of your ill-will to accomplish that at last.

For all your pretensions to be viewed as a great intellect, you have made one grave mistake in your reasoning. You have given me too much credit for courage in the follow-through over the course of the past three months.

I expect you to utter a cry of disbelief when I tell you that I am innocent of the crime of murder. But I shall yet make you believe me. 'They say the tongues of dying men enforce attention like deep harmony!' Before I am finished, you shall believe me. I will follow through this one time.

Farewell,

Martin Allworthy'

"Good Lord!" Evangeline dropped the letter into her lap. Her face had grown ashen.

Freddie snatched up the note, feverishly scanning it for some clue to its deeper meaning. "I can't make heads or tails of this!" he finally cried in irritation. "What's he talking about? What's that gibberish about the 'tongues of dying men'?"

Evangeline gave her friend a stricken look. Almost mechanically, she replied. "It's Shakespeare. From Richard the Second." She completed the quotation:

"'O, but they say the tongues of dying men,
Enforce attention like deep harmony:
Where words are scarce, they are seldom spent in vain,
For they breathe truth that breathe their words in pain.'"

"It still makes no sense to me! And how can he have the gall to say he never killed anyone? Does he really think he can save his reputation now?"

"I once made the mistake of not believing a man who uttered those very words under similar circumstances. I refuse to make the same mistake twice."

"What are you saying?" Freddie asked in disbelief.

"That I must take him at his word. I don't know how it's possible but I must at least be willing to entertain the idea that he didn't murder anyone. Until now." Her expression grew tense. "Jack, how long ago did that boy bring the note to the door?"

The major domo calculated backward. "About fifteen minutes ago, I'd say."

"And the man who gave him the note?" Her voice took on an urgent tone. "Did he say how long it was between the time he received it and the time he delivered it?"

Jack shrugged. "I think he said the man had just given him the note and walked away. That was right before the boy came knocking on the door."

Evangeline stood up with a determined look in her eye. "Then we don't have a moment to lose! Jack, hail us a cab. We don't have enough time to wait for you to get the carriage ready."

Turning to Freddie, she commanded, "Get your coat. We may still be able to stop him."

"Stop him?" The young man had lost her train of thought. "Stop him from doing what?"

Evangeline flew toward the door. "Don't you understand? He means to kill himself tonight!"

CHAPTER 30
The Tide In Men's Affairs

03 ❀ 80

"Where to, Miss Engie?" Jack asked before closing the cab door.

"To Hyperion, and tell him to hurry!"

Jack shouted her instructions to the driver and the cab took off with a jolt.

"Hyperion?" Freddie asked in surprise. "You really think Martin will go there."

"I'm not sure, but something Serafina said keeps sticking with me."

"Oh, here we go again. More spectral evidence!"

Evangeline tapped her foot impatiently. "Do you have a better straw to grasp at?"

"Well, not at the moment, no." The young man cleared his throat self-consciously. "But what could she possibly have told you that would make you think he'd go there?"

Evangeline furrowed her brow with the effort of recalling the exact details. "I remember her telling me about a dream she had. She saw us standing in the middle of an island. The water around the island ran in a circle. Something like a moat around a castle."

"I suppose there might be a connection," Freddie grudgingly admitted. "The Hyperion factory is on the banks of the river."

"No, it isn't that. It's the way the water ran round and round in a circle. I distinctly remember her words. She said, 'Where it started, it also ended.'"

"The water?"

"Perhaps the water, but she might also have been referring to this dismal chain of events without realizing, quite literally, how apt her choice of words happened to be."

Freddie reasoned aloud. "Yes, I see. Nora drowned in the river right beside the factory. It's plausible that her death set this chain of events, as you call it, in motion."

"Precisely, and if that was the episode that began Martin's descent, then he will choose to finish things where they began."

"I guess there's only one way to find out." Freddie turned to face Evangeline as the carriage bounced along. "But why do you think he would kill himself at all? He could run away, start a new life. Take a new name."

Evangeline smiled bitterly. "I thought so too at first. Serafina insisted I was wrong, and the more I thought about it, the more I realized that starting over was the one thing Martin would never do. His family name mattered more than anything else to him. To lose that name would be the same as losing his life."

She stopped and pondered for a moment before continuing. "Besides, if his letter is to be believed, then he hopes to prove to me that he is innocent of murder. 'The tongues of dying men' as he put it. He is actually trying to redeem his reputation by killing himself."

The cab rattled along at a breakneck pace. The two occupants of the carriage could feel the vehicle slope upward on an incline and then begin to descend.

Evangeline glanced out the window. "We're crossing the North Avenue bridge. It's so dark. I can barely see anything. I hope all this clatter doesn't alarm him, if he's out there at all." She shifted to the opposite side of the carriage and tapped on the roof to get the driver's attention. "Stop here!" she commanded. He reined in the horse abruptly and the two passengers alighted. They were still a block away from the factory.

"Perhaps, if he's out there, we can approach without

attracting his notice." Evangeline's tone became urgent. "Hurry, Freddie! He only had a twenty-minute headstart on us, and he may have been travelling on foot." Without waiting for her companion, who was still engaged in paying the driver, Evangeline hastily crossed the street and ducked into the shadows looming across the front entrance of the factory. She inched her way along the wall of the building until she reached the corner that fronted the river.

Freddie ran to catch up with her. "Do you see anybody out there?" he asked breathlessly.

"Shhhhhh! Keep your voice down."

"Engie, maybe we'd better go and find Mr. Sparrow." Freddie peered anxiously through the gloom. All he could see were ripples dancing off the river, reflecting the moon and the gas street lamps along the bridge.

"No, Freddie. If we go off looking for him, we might startle Martin. Give him a chance to run or to..." She trailed off, gathering her thoughts. "Our best vantage point is along the building down this way. Do you remember how to get to the place where the guard rail was cracked? The place where Nora drowned."

Freddie thought a moment. "Yes, I suppose I could find it again. It's pretty hard to see anything, but I remember it was directly in line with the loading dock. You see." He pointed about fifty feet down the wall of the building. "Down there." Putting a finger to his lips, he motioned for Evangeline to follow him.

They had gone no more than ten feet when a dark shape sprang off the loading dock and began running toward the river. Freddie could barely register what was happening but he could feel Evangeline's fingers digging into his arm.

"Martin, no!" she shouted. "Don't--"

Before she could finish the sentence, the dark shape had pressed a revolver to its temple and fired.

Freddie and Evangeline broke into a run and came upon the body of Martin Allworthy, slumped halfway over the guard rail suspended above the river. His hands now hung uselessly over the other side of the railing: the gun had fallen from his hand onto the embankment. This time the railing did not give way but held him suspended above the river like a grotesque marionette whose strings had just been cut.

"What was that noise? Who's out here?" A voice echoed from the other corner of the building.

Freddie instantly recognized the tone. "Mr. Sparrow, we're over here, by the river. Come quickly and bring a lantern! Mr. Allworthy has shot himself."

"Oh, my Lord!" The watchman hobbled as quickly as he could to the place were his employer's body hung suspended.

As he shone the lantern full in Allworthy's face, the trio could clearly see the gunshot wound to the temple surrounded by a charred circle of powder. A small trickle of blood had begun to ooze from the bullet hole. Freddie touched Allworthy's neck, trying to find a pulse.

He looked at the other two and shook his head. "It's too late. There's nothing we can do. He's dead."

"Oh my Lord!" Sparrow repeated. He was too shocked by the sight to move.

Evangeline took the night watchman's arm. "Mr. Sparrow, you'll have to call the police."

The watchman mumbled to himself, repeating the words a few times until they began to make sense. "Mr. Allworthy's dead...Mr. Allworthy's shot himself. I have to call...to call..."

"The police!" Evangeline insisted. "You'll have to call them now, Mr. Sparrow."

"Yes...yes...I'll..."

"Sparrow, are you out here? What was that noise? It sounded like a gunshot." Another voice came around the corner of the building. A shadow loomed up and came into the lantern glow.

"Oh, Mr. Tinker, it's--"

Evangeline cut in. "Mr. Allworthy's shot himself."

"What?" the newcomer cried in disbelief.

"Well, you can see for yourself." Freddie stepped out of the way and let the man inspect the grisly scene.

"Mr. Tinker is the...uh... the...uh... general manager." Sparrow managed to stammer an introduction. "Mr. Tinker, this is Mr. Simpson and Miss LeClair. They were ...uh...friends of Mr...Mr. Allworthy."

A man as round as a barrel stepped forward to inspect the remains. "Oh this is terrible! Terrible!" He found himself unable to look away from the spectacle. "Sparrow, call the police at once!"

The authoritative tone of voice seemed to snap the night watchman out of his paralysis. "Right away, sir." He came to attention and scurried back to the factory.

Tinker stood shaking his head and staring at the remains of Allworthy. "Shouldn't we...uh..." He made a move toward the corpse.

Freddie intervened. "It would be better if we left everything just as it is until the police get here."

"But it seems so...so...unseemly to leave him hanging there that way."

Evangeline concurred with Freddie. "I really think it's best. The police will need to collect evidence, and our interference will only make matters worse."

Tinker took out a handkerchief and mopped his brow despite the chilly night air. Apparently, he couldn't believe the scene before him. "You're sure he shot himself?"

"Quite sure," Evangeline replied. "The gun fell out of his hand. You can see it just on the other side of the railing."

Tinker craned his neck over the other side. Since Sparrow had taken the lantern with him, the only clue to the existence of the gun was the shiny reflection of metal against the moonlight. The manager sighed. "I suppose he took it all to heart and blamed himself. He shouldn't have blamed himself though. If anybody's to blame, it's me."

The two detectives found their attention riveted to the portly man.

"What was that again?" Freddie asked cautiously.

The manager glanced from one to the other, evidently not sure how much information he ought to reveal.

"You were friends of Mr. Allworthy's?"

"We knew him far better than most people did." Evangeline's reply was smooth as glass. Freddie looked at her askance. "Please tell us what you mean."

"Well, it's just that I think he blamed himself for what happened to Nora Johnson awhile back. Why else would he choose this particular spot to do away with himself?" He looked at the couple standing before him in mute appeal.

Freddie and Evangeline looked at each other and then back at Tinker. "Maybe you can tell us," Freddie prompted.

Tinker looked troubled. "Mr. Allworthy was a very particular man, and he took his responsibilities very seriously. Everything that touched the factory became a personal reflection on him, you see. Everything good and..." The manager paused. "Everything bad."

"But it seems a bit extreme to commit suicide because somebody drowned at his factory," Evangeline objected.

"Yes, yes, I suppose so, and if anybody should have taken her death personally, it's me. He couldn't have known."

"Known what?" Evangeline asked in amazement.

Freddie was trying mightily to forestall an urge to take out his notebook and attempt to write in the dark. He sensed something significant was about to emerge.

"Well, it's just that the railing was faulty."

"What!" The couple cried in unison.

Surprised by the vehemence of their response, Tinker backed away a few paces. In a mild tone, he repeated, "The railing was old, and the wood was cracked in places. It needed to be repaired."

"And Mr. Allworthy didn't know that?"

"No, he had asked me to make an inspection of the exterior of the factory just a week before Nora died. But, you see, I had a family emergency. I had just completed my inspection and written some notes that needed to be typed up when I had to board a train and get to Memphis. I was gone for two weeks and didn't hear about the accident until I returned." The manager rubbed his forehead distractedly. "But the worst part about it was the report."

"Yes?" Evangeline prompted.

"You see Nora was a good typist, and she prepared all the reports for the company. I had just dropped my notes on her desk and had to leave to catch my train."

"Did she know what was in the report?" Freddie's hand was itching to scribble in his notebook.

Tinker shook his head sadly. "No, I'm sure she didn't. It was just another piece of paper to her. When I got back from my trip, I discovered she'd already drowned in the river and no one had stepped in to do her job. I went to her desk and shuffled through the stack of papers." He sighed. "I found my notes at the bottom of the pile. If only she'd read it, then maybe..."

"Did you tell Mr. Allworthy about the defective railing afterward?"

Tinker sighed even more ponderously. "I tried more than once, but could never work up the courage to tell him that Nora was dead because of negligence."

"So he never knew about the faulty railing at all?" Evangeline asked.

Tinker shook his head. "I'm sure of it. He never knew."

Freddie looked at his friend. She was staring off into space, tapping her chin thoughtfully. He could tell the wheels had begun to turn again but her considered response to this new fact was only a simple "Hmmm."

The little group stood in silence a few moments longer. Their stillness interrupted only by the choppy river current lapping against the retaining wall. Freddie was about to make a suggestion that they should all return to the factory when he heard a familiar voice emerge from around the corner of the factory.

"Hello, is there anybody still out here?"

"Hello again, Sergeant O'Rourke," Freddie called out. "It's Simpson with the *Gazette*. Welcome back."

The sergeant drew nearer, lantern in hand, to study the remains. He groaned in disgust before turning to Freddie. "This call makes four. Just between you and me, if there's a fifth I'll be putting in for a transfer!"

CHAPTER 31
In The Wake Of Disaster

It was a fair morning in July, two days after Martin Allworthy's suicide. The birds sang and the flowers bloomed as Freddie and Evangeline walked into the funeral parlor where Euphemia Allworthy's body was being waked.

"Why didn't they just hold the funeral in Shore Cliff," Freddie grumbled. "It would have been more convenient."

"For whom?" Evangeline asked, under her breath. "All Euphemia's friends and family are in Chicago. Not to mention that her burial plot was already purchased in Gracehill Cemetery."

"And what about Martin?"

Evangeline kept her voice to a whisper. "It was the general view that the less attention given to that matter, the better. He's being buried later privately."

The couple walked into the room where Euphemia's casket lay. At least fifty people had preceded them to pay their respects and were waiting for the funeral procession to the cemetery to form. Evangeline searched for a familiar face and saw Euphemia's cousin in the front row. She advanced to offer her condolences.

"Very sorry to see you again under such sad circumstances, Bessie."

Cousin Bessie looked up mournfully and pressed Evangeline's hand. "Thank you for coming, and for everything you did to try and make sense of this terrible tragedy."

Freddie walked up silently behind Evangeline. At the sight of him, Bessie's lugubrious expression changed to a smile. "Oh, hello, Mr. Simpson, so good of you to come." She held out her hand.

Freddie took it awkwardly, surprised at the warm greeting.

"And here, right beside me, is my dear child Minerva. Who is also very grateful, I'm sure, that you have come to pay your respects."

Freddie's confusion increased as he noticed a blush begin to suffuse Minerva's face. She smiled sheepishly, but the young man interpreted the smile as a grimace of pain. "Are you all right?" he asked the girl with some concern. "You look as if you're about to be sick."

Evangeline, rapidly preempting the social encounter about to unfold, grabbed Freddie by the arm and steered him toward the coffin. "Perhaps we ought to say our last farewell to the deceased."

Freddie, with a backward look in Minerva's direction, complied. "What a strange girl," he said under his breath to Evangeline.

"You really have no idea!" she countered as the two came to stand before Euphemia's coffin. Evangeline was struck by the composed look on Euphemia's face. She looked very much at peace. Not at all as she must have appeared just prior to her death. Evangeline said a brief prayer on Euphemia's behalf to the universal deity she favored. She glanced briefly at Freddie who appeared to be praying as well. No doubt to some Presbyterian Jehovah with a full white beard and lightning bolts, she thought to herself.

As Evangeline turned away from the casket, her attention was caught by a couple advancing up the aisle in their direction. It was Serafina, accompanied by Theophilus Creech. The latter gave more the impression of gliding up the aisle rather than walking. Freddie had just turned away from the coffin when he was confronted by the wraithlike manifestation of Mr. Creech standing directly in front of him.

He gave an involuntary yip of fright when he saw the small egg-shaped man who seemed to have emerged out of nowhere.

"Hello, Mr. Simpson." Theophilus shook hands with great civility and only a slightly amused smile. "I hope you've been well since our last meeting."

"Y...y...yes." Freddie managed to stammer a reply. "Very well, thank you."

Evangeline noticed several pairs of eyes in the crowd narrow as Serafina walked up to the next of kin. A rumbling whisper had gone up in the background as gossips told their neighbors of the medium's involvement in the demise of the dearly departed. To her credit, Bessie stood up to greet Serafina cordially, thereby silencing any speculation about how to treat the medium in future.

Serafina took Bessie's hands in both her own. "I am most sorry for your loss, madame."

"No, my dear. It is I who should be sorry for the disgraceful way you have been treated by certain members of the Allworthy family." She made the statement loudly enough to be heard in the back row.

Theophilus took Serafina's arm and escorted her to the casket to say her farewells. Evangeline nodded briefly in greeting and made way for the couple. She and Freddie took seats at the back of the funeral parlor and shortly after they were seated, a minister entered to begin prayers for the deceased. After the brief service, everyone in the room queued up to return to their carriages for the trip to the cemetery.

Blinking in the sunlight as she emerged from the building, Evangeline scanned the line of waiting carriages for Jack. She finally located him sitting patiently in the barouche, halfway down the block in the place assigned by the funeral director. He had taken the precaution of putting the top down since the day promised to be a warm one. The couple walked up to their vehicle, and Freddie helped his friend climb in. They waited what seemed an eternity for the procession to start moving.

"Did you notice that strange girl, Engie?" Freddie seemed bemused.

"What strange girl, Freddie?"

"The ugly one."

To this comment, Evangeline made an eloquent rebuke of silence.

Freddie caught himself. "Oh sorry. Minerva, I mean. She kept turning around and batting her eyes at me all through prayers."

"Maybe she had a cinder in her eye." Evangeline attempted to maintain a tone of innocence.

"Cinder, nothing. She was making eyes at me. Look, there she is. She's just coming out of the funeral home. And look what she's doing now. She's staring right at me and smiling! Why on earth do you suppose she'd do a thing like that?"

Evangeline knew full well the reason for Minerva's enthusiasm, but she didn't wish to apprise Freddie of the fact that he was going to be the main course at her next dinner party. "Freddie, you fancy every woman under the age of sixty is in love with you."

"I certainly do not!"

"Well, whatever the case, you appear to be saved." Evangeline gestured toward the lead carriage, where she could see Roland helping his cousin-by-marriage into the vehicle and kissing her hand as he took a seat beside her. Minerva recoiled nervously at his touch.

"Roland!" Freddie spat out the word. "Where did he come from? I didn't see him inside."

"I saw him arrive just as prayers ended. Today you can regard him as prayers answered. He's bound to keep Minerva's attentions all to himself, now that she promises to be worth a great fortune."

"If that's the case, I pity him." Freddie's voice held a note of heartfelt sincerity.

With a jolt the carriage began moving. Since speed was not a desirable goal in most processions, and in funeral processions in particular, the couple could anticipate a lengthy ride before arriving at the cemetery, a mere eight blocks away.

"Freddie, I've been thinking..."

"About what, old girl?"

"I had it all wrong."

"What do you mean?"

"Martin didn't actually kill anyone." She sighed.

Freddie laughed. "Don't tell me you believed his farewell note."

"It wasn't the note that convinced me. It was all the little details that could be interpreted quite differently in light of what Martin said about himself. He said I gave him too much credit for courage in the follow-through. What if, all along, his principle crime was that he failed to follow through?"

"I'd say three dead bodies, four counting himself, is a pretty impressive record for somebody who never followed through."

Evangeline barely heard him. She continued to think aloud. "All along I was searching for a remorseless villain when I should have been searching for a coward instead."

Freddie glanced at the trees along the sidewalk as the carriage inched past them at a snail's pace. "Well, I've got nothing but time on my hands. A captive audience, so to speak. Enlighten me!"

Evangeline nodded and commenced. "First, there's the problem of Nora's death. I was convinced that Martin had pushed her over the guard rail in a fit of spite because the portrait was meant as a gift for Roland. But there might be another way to look at things. Perhaps Nora and Martin were on good terms. The date on picture indicates it was a gift. What if it was meant for Martin, not Roland? An attempt to reassure the uncle of her affection in spite of the nephew. We can be fairly certain that Martin never knew about the faulty railing. Neither did Nora. As fate would have it, they chose the most dangerous place possible for their tryst. They must have been leaning against the railing when it gave way and Nora fell into the river."

"With Martin standing above, watching her splash about helplessly. That must have placed him on the horns of a dilemma," Freddie observed.

"Exactly," his friend concurred. "Martin had always been concerned about his reputation above all else. He couldn't afford to be discovered with Nora under questionable circumstances. Euphemia controlled the family fortune. If she found out that he went about rescuing damsels in distress in the late hours of the evening, she might ask certain questions that would expose the true nature of his relationship with Nora."

Freddie whistled through his teeth. "She could have divorced him and left him penniless."

Evangeline continued. "When the critical moment arrived, I believe Martin weighed his wealth and reputation against Nora's life and found her coming up short in the balance. He hesitated at the wrong moment. He didn't follow through, so to speak, in saving Nora but let her drown instead. Remorse must have afflicted him almost immediately afterward because he threw away her picture. If he was already haunted by guilt at his own weakness, he certainly didn't want to be reproached by her image or the words 'remember me always.'"

Freddie added to the theory. "And I suppose that's where Bayne came in. He must have been somewhere nearby. Seen it happen and followed Martin home, picking up the picture along the way."

Evangeline inclined her head solemnly. "And since Bayne had possession of the picture and could easily say that Martin pushed Nora in, whether that was true or not, Martin had no choice but to accept his terms."

The funeral procession came to a stop at a busy intersection until cross-traffic could be forced to a halt out of temporary respect for the dead.

Freddie groaned at the delay. "Next, I suppose Martin had to try to kill Euphemia in order to keep her from asking questions about Bayne's presence. The fact that he was out of the house when it actually happened must be his lack of follow-through."

"No, I don't think so."

"You don't?" The young man stared at his friend in surprise.

"I don't believe Euphemia was the intended victim that day."

"Then who?"

"Bayne was."

"Bayne! I never even considered that possibility!" Freddie exclaimed.

"He had to be. The pieces of the puzzle don't make sense any other way."

Freddie turned sideways to face his companion. His attention completely captured for the moment.

"If Martin was planning to kill Euphemia, why on earth would he leave the house and go for a walk? It was hardly a convincing alibi, especially since he wasn't seen by anyone along the way. More importantly, it was far too chancy to leave a poisoned glass sitting on the sideboard in the dining room hoping his wife would wander in and drink it. Serafina told me Euphemia didn't serve cordials at teatime. It was simply an accident that Roland saw the glass sitting there and got the idea of bringing the sherry in as a gesture to appease his aunt. This made the situation even more complex after Roland poured the second glass. Martin would have had to be a better clairvoyant than Serafina to predict which glass his wife would drink from. Serafina might as easily have been the victim if the poisoned glass had been handed to her instead of Euphemia--"

Freddie cut in. "But you're forgetting about the other possibility."

"What might that be?"

"That Roland actually killed his aunt. He wasn't in her good graces, after all. He was in the perfect position to know who would drink the poison since he handed the glass to Euphemia."

Evangeline stopped to ponder the suggestion a moment. "No, I don't think so. His motive wasn't strong enough. He had an alibi for the night of Nora's death. If he didn't kill Nora, then he had nothing to fear from his aunt and no real reason to kill her."

"Oh, I suppose not," Freddie admitted grudgingly, "but I'd still like to see him hang for something!"

"Well, another crime perhaps."

"Then what's your theory about what really happened the day Euphemia died?" Freddie continued to monitor their progress. The entire procession had dragged its way across the intersection at last. Four more blocks to go.

Evangeline opened her parasol. The day was becoming increasingly warm and black was hardly the best color to wear. She continued her narrative. "I'm convinced Martin intended to poison Bayne. He invited him out to the country villa on the pretext of a friendly visit. He had already reassured Euphemia that he was going to get rid of his new vice president. Little did she suspect the measures he was prepared to take to accomplish that. He could easily have poisoned Bayne while the two sat talking in the library. Martin would have been the only witness to Bayne's convulsions and could have rinsed out the poisoned glass before calling for help. He might have explained Bayne's collapse as due to natural causes without any mention of poison at all. Martin could say that Bayne had been complaining of poor health. There was no medical history on Bayne that could contradict Martin's claim. It would have been unlikely for a doctor to test for poison as a cause of death unless poison was suspected in the first place."

Freddie raised a quizzical eyebrow. "I suppose you're going to tell me that Martin failed to follow through again?"

Evangeline's attention was temporarily diverted by a butterfly that fluttered through the carriage in search of hollyhocks. "Quite. Martin failed to follow through. Apparently, after he filled the sherry glass with poison, he lost his nerve and ran out of the house in a panic. The maid said he looked ill when he left. He may have intended to go for a walk to get a grip on himself, but by the time he returned to finish the job, Euphemia was already dead. I kept asking myself why he bungled the poison evidence so badly. There's only one explanation. He never anticipated the event that actually transpired. He had already thought through an explanation for the circumstances of Bayne's death. He was completely unprepared to explain Euphemia's. Since I had hinted at his motive for killing his wife in front of the sheriff, thereby making him a suspect, Martin would have needed an accomplice to point the finger at someone else."

"What a perfect irony." Freddie laughed sardonically. "He makes his intended victim the accomplice in the murder of his wife!"

"Yes. But he could hardly tell Bayne what really happened, so the ultimate irony was that he had to say he'd planned to kill his wife all along to prevent Bayne from becoming suspicious."

"And that, in turn, would have given Bayne more reason to blackmail him."

"Exactly. He was just digging a deeper grave for himself. Martin forged the letter from Euphemia himself, but he had to rely on Bayne to get the additional cyanide from the company supply. It was too risky for him to go back to the factory and get it himself. But he didn't count on Bayne's mistake. It was the luckiest stroke for us."

Freddie eyed the head of the procession. The trees at the cemetery gate loomed into view off in the distance. "Which brings us to death number three. I think it's going to be pretty hard for you to claim that he didn't follow through on that one."

"Ah, but I can." Evangeline smiled.

With an amused look, Freddie tilted his head to the side. "I'm listening."

"In elucidating this mystery, I must give credit where it's due."

"Since when?" Freddie countered impishly.

Giving her friend a look of long-suffering forbearance, Evangeline pressed onward. "You said something the night of Bayne's death that started me thinking. Why would Martin go to all the trouble to stage a murder to look like an accident and then disappear, leaving it to look like murder? I concluded that something must have gone wrong along the way. I'm convinced that Martin planned to murder Bayne but couldn't finish loosening the railing in time. Bayne must have arrived before he was expected and Martin probably panicked. Bayne may have said something to upset him further, and he must have backed into the railing and went over the side himself."

"Now just wait a minute. It was Bayne's body that was found on the shop floor, not Martin's."

"Yes, and if you allow me to continue, I'll tell you why."

The young man rolled his eyes and remained still.

"It was the position of the body that aroused my suspicions. As we both noticed, the railing was bent back as if someone had been clinging to it before falling. If that someone had fallen from that position, he would have landed on his back, not on his face."

Freddie's face registered amazement. "Ye gods! Engie, you're right. I never thought of that."

Evangeline nodded. "What must have happened is that Martin went over the railing and somehow managed to keep hold of it. The railing bent backward and he still clung to it. Bayne crouched down to help him up, but he must not have seen that Martin had loosened the railing on purpose or he wouldn't have assisted him. It's also unlikely that Martin had tried to push Bayne and missed, because Bayne wouldn't have come to his rescue in that case either."

Freddie sat forward excitedly. "Of course! That makes perfect sense! Bayne thought Martin's fall was an accident. He didn't want to lose the source of his ill-gotten gains so he probably reached over to offer Martin a hand."

Evangeline adjusted her parasol to shield her eyes as the sun grew more intense. She picked up the thread of Freddie's narration. "Martin may have panicked and clung to Bayne, throwing him off balance. If Bayne had been drinking before he arrived, as is most likely, he probably lost his balance and went over the side, landing as we found him, on his face. Martin was able to climb to safety, in the meantime."

Freddie shook his head in disbelief. "Well, what do you know. Martin ended up killing Bayne accidentally."

"Yes, I think so. If he had wanted to kill him with certainty, since Bayne outweighed him, he would have gripped Bayne's hand with both of his own and let go of the railing. But he couldn't do that, as they would both have died. Instead Martin saw Bayne fall and, as he always did at any critical moment, he panicked and ran. Once again he didn't follow through. Though by the bye, his assertion that he never murdered anyone is making too fine a point of it. He certainly tried a number of times. He just never actually succeeded."

The carriage came to a halt, waiting its turn while the procession filed slowly through the cemetery gate.

Evangeline looked off into the distance contemplatively. "I overestimated Martin all along. His principal crime was that, in critical moments, he always lost his nerve and did nothing at all. By his own admission, he didn't follow through." She laughed mirthlessly. "You know, I gave him far too much credit. Credit for guile in plotting crimes which he never committed. And credit for the nerve to carry them out which he never possessed."

"Well, he succeeded in blowing his brains out, at least." The young man's tone was cut-and-dried.

"But even in that case, he sent a letter to me as insurance that he would follow through. He was convinced I would hound him to the ends of the earth. The letter baited me to find him. He was counting on the fact that we would trail him to Hyperion. He had effectively cut off all avenues of escape for himself. It was probably the only reason he could work up the nerve to take action that one last time."

Freddie scouted the landscape for their final destination: a gravesite at the far end of the cemetery. "Don't you think he loved Nora Johnson, at least a little? He certainly seemed to feel guilty about her death."

Evangeline pondered the question. "Serafina hinted that he felt both fear and regret just before he died. Regret for something he had left undone. Regret, perhaps for a person he had failed to save." She sighed expressively. "I suppose he loved her as much as a gray little man with a gray little soul can ever love--timidly and with one eye always toward his own self-interest. In the end, he was willing to trade her life for a scrap of propriety."

The carriage came to a stop in line behind the ten that preceded it. Everywhere, mourners were climbing out of their vehicles and walking slowly up the hill toward Euphemia Allworthy's gravesite. Freddie jumped out of the carriage and held his hand out to help Evangeline.

She stepped down to join him. "This whole miserable chain of events strikes me as being a paradox. Bayne could never have blackmailed Martin at all if he had tried to save Nora in the first place. Instead, he sacrificed her to preserve his wealth and reputation. He ended up losing both, along with his life."

"What doth it profit a man," Freddie intoned.

"What, indeed."

The couple walked up the hill to see Euphemia Allworthy laid to rest. Evangeline doubted that her husband's spirit would find anything like everlasting peace.

ഗജ‍ഉ

Author's Note

 こ₩ぬ

In the aftermath of the ARU boycott, George Pullman's fall from grace was swift. The U.S. Strike Commission held hearings in Chicago during August of 1894 and concluded that Pullman had created unnecessary hardship for his workers by refusing to arbitrate and by failing to reduce the rents in his town.

As a consequence of the investigation, the Illinois State Supreme Court ordered the Pullman Palace Car Company to divest itself of its non-manufacturing real estate. The town of Pullman, no longer privately owned, was absorbed into the city of Chicago.

There is speculation that Pullman's public disgrace took a toll on his health. He died of a heart attack three years later in October, 1897. Because his family feared that Pullman's body might be desecrated by his former employees, he was buried at night in a lead-lined casket placed in an eight foot pit with walls, floor, and ceiling of steel-reinforced concrete. The corinthian column which caps Pullman's grave in Graceland Cemetery was designed by Solon Beman, the architect of the town of Pullman.